South-Asian Fiction in English

Alex Tickell

South-Asian Fiction in English

Contemporary Transformations

Alex Tickell
The Open University,
Milton Keynes, Buckinghamshire,
United Kingdom

ISBN 978-1-137-40353-7   ISBN 978-1-137-40354-4 (eBook)
DOI 10.1057/978-1-137-40354-4

Library of Congress Control Number: 2016933997

© The Editor(s) (if applicable) and The Author(s) 2016
The author(s) has/have asserted their right(s) to be identified as the author(s) of this work in accordance with the Copyright, Design and Patents Act 1988.
This work is subject to copyright. All rights are solely and exclusively licensed by the Publisher, whether the whole or part of the material is concerned, specifically the rights of translation, reprinting, reuse of illustrations, recitation, broadcasting, reproduction on microfilms or in any other physical way, and transmission or information storage and retrieval, electronic adaptation, computer software, or by similar or dissimilar methodology now known or hereafter developed.
The use of general descriptive names, registered names, trademarks, service marks, etc. in this publication does not imply, even in the absence of a specific statement, that such names are exempt from the relevant protective laws and regulations and therefore free for general use.
The publisher, the authors and the editors are safe to assume that the advice and information in this book are believed to be true and accurate at the date of publication. Neither the publisher nor the authors or the editors give a warranty, express or implied, with respect to the material contained herein or for any errors or omissions that may have been made.

Printed on acid-free paper

This Palgrave Macmillan imprint is published by SpringerNature
The registered company is Macmillan Publishers Ltd. London.

For Nathaniel

Acknowledgements

This volume developed out of a seminar series and symposium organized by the Open University's Postcolonial Literatures Research Group. The symposium, on Contemporary South-Asian Fiction, was hosted by the Institute of English Studies at Senate House, University of London on 3 November 2012. I am grateful to Jon Millington at the IES for his help in organizing both the seminar series and the concluding symposium. I would also like to express my thanks to the Modern Humanities Research Association for a Conference Grant, which covered organizational costs for the symposium.

Special thanks are due to my colleagues in the English Department at the Open University, David Johnson, Susheila Nasta and Suman Gupta, and to Pooja Sinha, E. Dawson Varughese and Ole Birk Laursen, all of whom supported the event.

At Palgrave Macmillan I would like to thank Ben Doyle and Tomas René for their encouragement and assistance, and to the anonymous reader who provided perceptive feedback on the initial proposal. I am most grateful, as always, to Rachel Goodyear for her advice and editorial work on this project.

* * *

Suman Gupta's chapter **Contemporary Indian Commercial Fiction in English** is reprinted from Gupta, S. (2015) *Consumable texts in contemporary India: Uncultured books and bibliographical sociology* with the permission of the author. An earlier version appeared in *Economic and Political Weekly* Feb 4, 2012, vol. 47 no. 5, pp. 46–53.

Contents

Acknowledgements	vii
Notes on Contributors	xi
Introduction *Alex Tickell*	1

Part I   Regional Formations — 19

Of Capitalism and Critique: 'Af-Pak' Fiction in the Wake of 9/11 *Priyamvada Gopal*	21
'An Idea Whose Time Has Come': Indian Fiction in English After 1991 *Alex Tickell*	37
English-Language Fiction of Bangladesh *Cara Cilano*	59
Sri Lankan Fiction in English 1994–2014 *Ruvani Ranasinha*	79

Part II Contemporary Transformations 101

Writing the Margins (in English): Notes from
Some South-Asian Cities 103
Stuti Khanna

Occupying Literary and Urban Space: Adiga,
Authenticity and the Politics of Socio-economic Critique 119
Dominic Davies

Contemporary Indian Commercial Fiction in English 139
Suman Gupta

Genre Fiction of New India: Post-millennial
Configurations of Crick Lit, Chick Lit and Crime Writing 163
E. Dawson Varughese

Vignettes of Change: A Discussion of Two
Indian Graphic Novels 181
Pooja Sinha

The New Pastoral: Environmentalism and Conflict in
Contemporary Writing from Kashmir 199
Ananya Jahanara Kabir

Solidarity, Suffering and 'Divine Violence':
Fictions of the Naxalite Insurgency 217
Pavan Kumar Malreddy

Writing South-Asian Diasporic Identity Anew 235
Maya Parmar

Minor Literature and the South-Asian Short Story 253
Neelam Srivastava

Index 273

NOTES ON CONTRIBUTORS

Cara Cilano is Professor of English at the University of North Carolina, Wilmington, in the US. She is author of *Post-9/11 Espionage Fiction in the US and Pakistan: Spies and 'Terrorists'* (2014), *Contemporary Pakistani Fiction in English: Idea, Nation, State* (2013) and *National Identities in Pakistan: The 1971 War in Contemporary Pakistani Fiction* (2011).

Dominic Davies completed his D.Phil. at the University of Oxford in 2015. His thesis focused on the way in which colonial literature written at the height of the British Empire configured the relationship between imperial infrastructure and various forms of anti-imperial resistance. He is the Facilitator of the Leverhulme-funded Network, 'Planned Violence: Post/colonial Urban Infrastructures and Literature' (2014–2016), and is currently a British Academy Postdoctoral Fellow at the University of Oxford researching graphic narrative representations of post/colonial urban infrastructures. He has published articles in a number of academic and online journals, including the *Journal of Commonwealth Literature*, *Journal of Postcolonial Writing*, *Kipling Society Journal* and *Études Littéraires Africaines*.

E. Dawson Varughese is a global cultural studies scholar who specializes in India. She is the author of *Beyond The Postcolonial* (Palgrave Macmillan, 2012) and *Reading New India* (2013). She has recently co-authored a book entitled *Indian Writing in English and Issues of Visual Representation* (Palgrave Macmillan, 2015) and is currently preparing a manuscript entitled *Genre Fiction of New India: Post-millennial Receptions of 'Weird' Narratives*. She works on Indian genre fiction, graphic novels, visual cultures and style in Indian fiction in English. She is published in *South Asian Popular Culture* and *Contemporary South Asia*.

Priyamvada Gopal is Reader in anglophone and Related Literatures at the Faculty of English, University of Cambridge, and a Fellow of Churchill College.

She is the author of *Literary Radicalism in India: Gender, Nation and the Transition to Independence* (2005) and *The Indian Novel in English: Nation, History and Narration* (2009).

Suman Gupta is Professor of Literature and Cultural History at the Open University. In 2011–2014 he coordinated, with Richard Allen, a collaborative project on 'Prospects for anglophone Studies in Indian Higher Education'. Recent books include *Globalization and Literature* (2009), *Imagining Iraq* (2011), *Consumable Texts in Contemporary India* (2015), *Philology and Global English Studies* (2015) and co-authored (with Allen, Chattarji and Chaudhuri) the volume *Reconsidering English Studies in Indian Higher Education* (2015).

Ananya Jahanara Kabir, Professor of English Literature at King's College London, is a literary and cultural historian who works at the intersection of memory, embodiment, pleasure and post-trauma in the global South. Previously, she taught at the universities of Cambridge, Berkeley and Leeds. She is the recipient of a number of fellowships, including those from the British Academy, the Wissenschaftkolleg zu Berlin and the AHRC; as one of the AHRC's earliest 'Knowledge Transfer Fellows' she co-organized, in 2011, 'Between Kismet and Karma', a programme of events and exhibitions across the UK involving female visual artists from South Asia working on conflict. She is the author of, most recently, *Partition's Post-Amnesias: 1947, 1971 and Modern South Asia* (2013), and the director of 'Modern Moves', a 5-year research project funded by a European Research Council Advanced Grant, which investigates the transnational history and popularity of Afro-diasporic music and dance forms.

Stuti Khanna teaches Literature at the Department of Humanities and Social Sciences, IIT, Delhi. She obtained her MA degree at Delhi University and her D.Phil. at Oxford University. Her doctoral research was a comparative project on the city in the fiction of James Joyce and Salman Rushdie. She has published extensively on Rushdie, in journals such as *Ariel*, the *Journal of Commonwealth Literature* and the *Journal of Postcolonial Writing*, among others. She is also the author of the monograph *The Contemporary Novel and the City: Re-conceiving National and Narrative Form* (Palgrave Macmillan, 2013). Her current research focuses on the ways in which postcolonial urbanity in South Asia inflects and shapes twentieth-century narrative in a crucial, fundamental and formative way, and uses the city of Delhi as the central site of this investigation.

Pavan Kumar Malreddy is Researcher in English Literature at Goethe University Frankfurt. He has previously taught at Chemnitz University of Technology, Germany, York University, Toronto, the University of Saskatchewan, Saskatoon, and has worked with various research organizations (Canadian Council on Learning, Ottawa; Aboriginal Education Research Center, Saskatoon) as a commissioned writer and editor. He is the author of *Orientalism, Terrorism, Indigenism:*

South Asian Readings in Postcolonialism (2015) and co-editor of *Reworking Postcolonialism: Globalization, Labour and Rights* (Palgrave Macmillan, 2015). He has published over twenty academic essays and chapters on terrorism, race and postcolonial theory in journals such as *The European Legacy*, *Third World Quarterly*, the *Journal of Postcolonial Writing* and *Intertexts*, among others. He is currently working on a book-length project titled 'Towards Post-Terrorism: Insurgency, Ecology and Cultures of Violence in Postcolonial Literature'.

Maya Parmar is a Postdoctoral Research Associate in English Literature at The Open University, across two projects: 'Beyond the Frame: Indian British Connections' and 'Reading Communities: Connecting the Past and the Present'. Her research explores strategies of cultural representation, memory making and the politics of belonging amongst the South-Asian diaspora. Her research interests also include Indian East African twice migration, the networked space of the Indian Ocean and new media as a mode of archiving and online memorialization. She has published her research in the journals *Interventions* (2015), *South Asian Popular Culture* (2014) and *Atlantis* (2013), and has guest co-edited the special issue 'Re-evaluating the Postcolonial City: Production, Reconstruction, Representation' for *Interventions* (2015). Additionally, Maya has an interest in working with audiences beyond the academy, and has received funding for her public engagement project 'Expulsion: 40 years On' from the Arts Council England and the University of Leeds (2012).

Ruvani Ranasinha is Senior Lecturer in Postcolonial Literatures at the Department of English, King's College, London. Her most recent monograph is *Contemporary South Asian Women's Fiction: Gender, Narration and Globalisation* (2016), published by Palgrave. Other publications include *Hanif Kureishi* (2002), *South Asian Writers in Twentieth-Century Britain: Culture in Translation* (2007) and she is the lead editor *of South Asians and the Shaping of Britain, 1870–1950: A Sourcebook* (MUP, 2012). She is a part of the Leverhulme-funded International Network on Planned Violence (2014–2016).

Pooja Sinha is an independent researcher, having obtained a Ph.D. from the Open University (UK) in 2014. She studied contemporary Indian popular fiction for her doctorate, exploring the topic with market categories such as detective fiction and the graphic novel. Her research interests include popular fiction in India and developments in the Indian entertainment and publishing industries, with a special focus on social and cultural shifts in post-liberalization India.

Neelam Srivastava is Senior Lecturer in Postcolonial Literature at Newcastle University, UK. Her research interests include South-Asian literature in English, Italian postcolonial theories and Italian colonialism. Her most recent publication is a special issue of *Interventions: International Journal of Postcolonial Studies* on 'Frantz Fanon in Italy.' She is co-editor with Baidik Bhattacharya of *The Postcolonial*

Gramsci (2012) and the author of *Secularism in the Postcolonial Indian Novel: National and Cosmopolitan Narratives in English* (2008). She is currently completing a book entitled *Decolonizing Europe: Italian Colonialism and Resistances to Empire*, to be published by Palgrave. She is also co-editing with Rossella Ciocca a collection of essays on contemporary Indian literature, entitled *Indian Literature and the World: Multi-lingualism, Translation, and the Public Sphere*, also to be published by Palgrave.

Alex Tickell is Senior Lecturer in English at the Open University, UK. His research field includes colonial and postcolonial writing and South-Asian literary history. In 2005, Tickell rediscovered and published the first fiction in English by an Indian author, Kylas Chunder Dutt, in *Selections from 'Bengaliana'*. He is the author of *Terrorism, Insurgency and Indian-English Fiction, 1830–1947* (2012) and has researched terror and insurgency in colonial fiction and published on Indian terrorist groups in Edwardian London. Tickell also writes on contemporary South-Asian fiction and is the author of a reader's guide to Arundhati Roy's *The God of Small Things* (2007), and is working on a monograph titled *Civic Fiction: Citizenship and the Novel in the New India*. He is editor of Volume 10 of *The Oxford History of the Novel in English*, which covers the novel in South and South-East Asia since 1945.

Introduction

Alex Tickell

The Indian author Anita Desai clearly had contemporary literary history in mind when, in the closing days of the year 2000, she reviewed the first novel by a then barely-known Pakistani writer, Mohsin Hamid. The novel was *Moth Smoke* (2000), completed by Hamid during occasional breaks from his job at a New York management consultancy firm, and for Desai it was a debut that signalled a new era in the fictional representation of the subcontinent. In her review, she used the Urdu term *zamana*, meaning 'the times, the age', to express the sense of an era as a shared temporality specific to the Urdu and Hindi-speaking cultures of north India and Pakistan: 'trying to explain "our *zamana*"', she stated, 'is to hear a world of comment on our day, our history, the passage of years and of human experience'. Desai went on to contrast the slower, more contained human environments documented by an earlier generation of South-Asian authors with the edgy, urbane, drug-dealing netherworld of the Lahore elite represented in *Moth Smoke*:

> One could not really continue to write, or read about, the slow seasonal changes, the rural backwaters, gossipy courtyards, and traditional families in a

---

A. Tickell
Department of English, The Open University,
Milton Keynes, UK

world taken over by gun-running, drug-trafficking, large-scale industrialism, commercial entrepreneurship, tourism, new money, nightclubs, boutiques, politicians and civil servants noted for greed and corruption, and the constant threat of an explosion—of population, of crime, of the nuclear bomb, some kind of terrible explosion. Where was the Huxley, the Orwell, the Scott Fitzgerald, or even the Tom Wolfe, Jay McInerney, or Brett Easton Ellis [sic] to record this new world? Mohsin Hamid's novel *Moth Smoke*, set in Lahore, is one of the first pictures we have of that world and one of the first from Pakistan. (Desai 2000)

Ironically, a 'terrible explosion', which would have lasting consequences for Pakistan, happened elsewhere, outside South Asia, 9 months later, and subsequently provided the backdrop of Hamid's more successful second novel, *The Reluctant Fundamentalist* (2007). However, Desai's review of Hamid's debut work is still prescient. Although she could have named any of a number of fictions from the late 1990s to the turn of the millennium as representative of a shift, her point was that a new kind of social experience, born out of South Asia's accelerated economic and demographic growth, its global reach and its complex internal and regional politics, now demanded fictional representation, and in Hamid's novel, this new world resolved, sharply and shockingly, into focus.

South-Asian Fiction in English: Contemporary Transformations brings together original critical readings that all respond, in different ways, to recent South-Asian anglophone fictions in English that reflect on, react to or are materially implicated in this new era. My title premise—that recent South-Asian literature deserves special critical attention—demands some elaboration, however, before we can proceed. Apart from the problem of how change or transformation might be tracked in the present, the word 'contemporary' itself connotes a chronological uncertainty in its medieval Latin roots of *con*, 'together with' and *tempus/or*, meaning 'time'. As anyone who tries to write precisely about historical events or periods soon realizes, the first, chronological definition of contemporary, given by the *OED* as 'living, occurring or originating at the same time' is easily confused with the second 'presentist' definition of 'belonging or occurring in the present' or 'modern in style or design'. Books date quickly, but the contemporary always has a claim on us as an ongoing aspect of the present, which means that any critical study that employs the term without historical qualification starts off by referring to the second meaning of the contemporary, and then resolves gradually into a sometimes idiosyncratic account of the first.

There are other good reasons to be cautious when describing recent South-Asian anglophone fiction in this way. When discussing cultural and political change, argues the historian Dipesh Chakrabarty, the use of the word 'contemporary' says something particular about 'historical perceptions of the consciousness of modernity'. For Chakrabarty, the term 'speaks a double-gesture' and incorporates senses of both inclusion and exclusion (1997, pp. 49–50). This inclusionary-exclusionary aspect is manifested in the way everything is encompassed 'together' by the contemporary, but also by the fact that the term denotes a *particular* thing (the dynamic element of the contemporary) moving progressively towards the future (ibid., p. 50). Thus, in parts of the world such as South Asia, where a teleological narrative of progress and development has presented local societies as adjuncts to a more dynamic colonial history, the concept of the contemporary involves a bias towards modernity and is set against the richness of multiple, co-existent times. It is no coincidence, then, that in his counterfactual vision of South-Asian historical consciousness, *Time Warps*, Ashis Nandy calls conventional historiography a 'structure of denial' and warns that concepts associated with the contemporary, such as development, progress and historical linearity, risk a narrowing of conceptions of history (2002, p. 5).

In the face of these arguments, the use of 'contemporary transformations' in the title of this volume is something of a compromise and reflects my view that the post-Cold War period from the early 1990s to the present will be identified, within the progressive logic described above, as one of particularly radical historical and cultural change in South Asia. In Pakistan, a history of military rule and the global ramifications of the 'war on terror'—alongside wider economic and religio-political shifts over the past 25 years—have reshaped fictional imaginaries. Conversely, in India, the dominating presence in the region, sustained economic growth and rapid urban-societal developments from the early 2000s have generated a sense of possibility reminiscent of the transformative changes ascribed to certain threshold moments in European modernism (Dasgupta 2014, p. 39). In the shadow of a public narrative of growth and 'awakening', ideas about citizenship have been revised in the anti-corruption movement and the response to the 2012 Delhi Rape case. Elsewhere across the region, equally momentous transformations have taken place: in Sri Lanka, both the long running, collectively traumatizing civil conflict, which ended in 2009, and the natural disaster of the 2004 tsunami have generated extended literary reflection, and in Bangladesh, the region's youngest nation, authors have tackled globalization, accelerating urban growth and the shared subjective legacies of the 1971 liberation war in their writing. Worldwide, South-Asian diaspora communities have become integral to the knowledge economies of the global North, and the spread of forms of business process outsourcing, subcontracting and migrant labour have tied the countries of the region more tightly to the global economy.

The material contexts of South-Asian literature in English have also been transformed in the last 25 years as the internet, the digital revolution and developments in publishing technology have all altered the production and consumption of fiction. Its readership has changed too, and, as several contributors to this volume note, older patterns of consumption, in which the literary South-Asian novel in English originally catered to a 'double audience' at home and abroad (Innes 2007, p. 201), have been supplemented by the emergence, in India particularly, of a new readership for popular English fiction published specifically for the Indian market. Recent literacy statistics for South-Asian countries show that in Pakistan and Bangladesh, just over half the adult population, 56% in each case, is literate, compared with 63% in India and 91% in Sri Lanka (UNESCO and UNICEF 2012, p. 10). These figures refer to 'indigenous' languages; English literacy rates are much smaller. Hence, even with gradual changes in middle-class reading patterns, buying and reading fiction in English is still very much the preserve of an elite. Nevertheless, the size of India's population alone means that it is now home to the third largest number of English speakers, globally, outside the US and UK (British Library n.d.). Increasingly, the expanding readership represented by this group, and the authors who cater to it, will further redefine English fiction according to local tastes and linguistic particularities. Commercially, too, South-Asian anglophone fiction has boosted its profile both regionally and globally, with the spread of specialist literary festivals and new online literary journals, and through lucrative signings and continued endorsement from international literary prizes (Viswamohan 2013).

A further critical consideration is that anglophone 'South-Asian' fiction is not always published by authors who are resident in the subcontinent (a legacy, again, of its double audience) and for some regions, such as Bangladesh, the majority of successful anglophone writers live overseas. The editorial rationale of this collection has been to allow individual contributors the freedom to select resident or 'migrant' authors, as writers *of* a particular region, without being prescriptive about the residency status of individual authors. We must remain aware, however, of the often fraught politics of authenticity that attends the authorial choice of whether to live and write in South Asia (and thus retain a 'contemporary' representational claim to a country of origin, albeit in English), or to live peripatetically between different locations, usually in North America, Europe and South Asia, and assume a more 'cosmopolitan' literary persona. Although it is a generalization, one of the contextual features of the contemporary fiction discussed here is, arguably, the greater number of internationally recognized authors who now live in, or have returned to, South Asia—a trend exemplified by Arundhati Roy's continued, principled residency in India after the success of her debut novel in 1997. In order to provide more detailed commentary on the issue of authorial location across the collection, a chapter has been included in the second section on literature by writers of the South-Asian diaspora, dealing specifically with the experiences of migrants and diaspora communities, as opposed to works by non-resident authors writing back to a real or imaginary homeland.

The growth in the international profile and commercial potential of the anglophone fictions of South Asia in the 1980s and into the '90s was facilitated by its increasing visibility in university English Literature curricula in North America, Europe and Australia. (While literature in English was just one of a number of literary traditions taught in South-Asian universities, in the global North, for obvious linguistic reasons, it became disproportionately representative.) More or less simultaneously, a new critical discipline, Postcolonial Studies, superseded older 'Commonwealth Literature' approaches (see Quayson 2012; Boehmer and Tickell 2015), and fostered a body of critical theory and a conceptual vocabulary that was newly responsive to the history and politics of writing in formerly colonized societies. Postcolonial studies has been immensely influential in shaping *how* South-Asian fiction in English is read and taught and, perhaps inevitably, it has privileged certain styles and forms of literature such as the novel (Chaudhuri 2001), and shaped the way South-Asian authors represent the region to an international readership (Huggan 2001; Lau and Mendes 2011). In turn, South-Asian writers and critics have often seen 'postcolonial' as a problematic, reductive term, and it has been the subject of substantive critique (see Ahmad 1994; Mukherjee and Trivedi 1996).

Recently, critics in the global North have explored alternatives to the category of Postcolonial Literature, as exemplified in the resurgence of concepts such as 'World Literature' (Damrosch 2003; D'haen et al. 2012). Paradigms like World Literature, which can be traced partly to Rabindranath Tagore's concept of *vishwasahitya* ('world literature') first formulated in 1907 (see Dharwadker 2012), have the benefit of freeing the study of South-Asian fiction from a deterministic attention to theme and engaging with aesthetic criteria. However, they also tend to lack the contextual political acuity of the postcolonial (see Young 2012, pp. 217–21). This is not the place to provide a comprehensive account of these literary critical debates, except to say that the chapters presented in this volume all build on the legacy of postcolonial studies in their attention to situated political and historical aspects of South-Asian fiction, although a number also seek to question established approaches. As well as being attuned to neo-colonial forms of 'imperial' political engagement (associated, for instance, with the politics of terror and counter-insurgency), the critics presented below draw on publishing history, genre studies, research on memory and trauma, cultural theory and the sociology of the book in their readings. As a collective report on the literary-history of the present, their interpretative range and diversity testify to the dynamism, creativity and innovation of contemporary South-Asian writing.

*

This collection approaches contemporary South-Asian fiction in English in two ways. The first section, 'Regional Formations,' uses a spatial logic to examine what could be loosely termed 'national' anglophone fictional traditions and deals with writings from Pakistan, India, Bangladesh and Sri Lanka. Here again, however, geopolitical ruptures and underlying cultural interconnections within the region mean that in some cases, such as Priyamvada Gopal's chapter on Afghanistan and Pakistan, or Cara Cilano's concentration on literary legacies of the 1971 Bangladesh independence war, the boundaries between neighbouring nations are traversed and questioned. In other ways, the regional organization of these sections highlights recent historical developments that have been specific to the fiction of particular nation states. These include India's economic and social changes since 1991, detailed in my chapter, and Sri Lanka's traumatizing civil war, covered in Ruvani Ranasinha's reading of Sri Lankan fiction published after 1994.

The second section, 'Contemporary Transformations', deals with formal, generic and contextual developments in South-Asian fiction in English and is designed not only to provide a relatively quick survey of current literary transformations but also to explore key modes and areas, some of them transnational, in which these developments have been particularly marked. These include, as mentioned earlier, issues of form and the emergence of an urban aesthetic, developments in publishing history, new genres such as chick lit, crime writing and the graphic novel, the depiction of border areas and 'minority' forms like the short story. Taken as a whole, the combined regional and formal approach is intended to offer a sense of the multi-stranded complexity of South-Asian fiction, and to show how a distinctive feature of literary contemporaneity is a proliferation of forms and genres, which increasingly challenges the older dominance of an Indian-English canon. Inevitably, this approach risks some asymmetry in its coverage of issues and themes and in a longer collection, the lasting contribution of South-Asian women writers to a literature about women's experiences could have been more comprehensively surveyed. Other issues that can only receive cursory treatment in a collection of this kind are the self-translating linguistic complexities of anglophone South-Asian fiction and the involved transactions between journalism, memoir and fiction that have enlivened contemporary Indian-English literature in the recent past.

Regional Formations examines South-Asian fiction in terms of setting and geopolitical context. It opens with Priyamvada Gopal's chapter 'Of Capitalism and Critique: "Af-Pak" Fiction in the Wake of 9/11,' which deals with novels of Afghanistan and Pakistan written by authors with Pakistani backgrounds (who live, or have lived, in the global North and write for a transnational audience), and thus questions as much as it confirms national traditions of writing. Gopal's detailed discussion of two works, Nadeem Aslam's *The Wasted Vigil* (2008) and Mohsin Hamid's *The Reluctant Fundamentalist* (2007), notes the politicization of their settings in the contemporary period. After the attacks on the US Pentagon and World Trade Center on 11th September 2001, the wars prosecuted by the USA and its allies in Afghanistan and Iraq brought about a regional compression, and implicated Pakistan in a neighbouring conflict. As Gopal argues, the events of 9/11 also fostered attitudes to Islam, and to Muslim societies in Afghanistan and Pakistan, that were both reified and challenged by her chosen novelists. Within the nexus of political, economic and cultural ideas about how politics in these regions has played out, and following successive devastating neo-colonial incursions in Afghanistan by Soviet, US and ex-colonial powers, the representational stakes are considerable, and in a volume which seeks to account for the fiction of a whole region, Gopal's chapter introduces a cautionary note in re-emphasizing literature's ambiguous involvement in new 'orientalizing' imaginaries.

My chapter, '"An Idea Whose Time Has Come": Indian Fiction in English after 1991', covers a period during which Indian novelists have achieved international literary status and shaped the course of contemporary fiction. I discuss how selected novels of the 1990s and 2000s, including Arundhati Roy's *The God of Small Things* (1997), Aravind Adiga's *The White Tiger* (2008) and Manju Kapur's *Custody* (2011), have represented India's globalizing economic transformation and I trace their negotiation of the growing power of India's middle classes after economic liberalization in 1991–1992 (see Sen and Roy 2013). As part of this analysis, I examine the (sometimes highly ironic) literary renegotiation of a realist aesthetic as a response to India's societal transformation. My chapter also traces the effect of a new 'local' market for genre fiction on the formal scope of the Indian-English novel, and concludes by examining an author who has become synonymous with a highly popular, commercial form of contemporary literature in India, Chetan Bhagat. I discuss two of Bhagat's works which could be termed, broadly, 'campus fictions'—his debut novel *Five Point Someone* (2004) and his more recent novel *Half Girlfriend* (2014)—and my analysis reflects on assessments that see Bhagat as both the favoured author of, and the self-styled spokesman for, a new, youthful, and aspirational middle class. I go on to read his latest novel as a reflexive engagement with the cultural politics of more literary traditions of Indian-English fiction.

Cara Cilano's chapter on 'English-Language Fiction of Bangladesh' concentrates on the retrospective narrative evaluation of the 1971 Bangladesh liberation war, and shows how contemporary authors use tropes of memory and the form of historical fiction to balance the persisting trauma of the conflict with newer impulses towards reconciliation. For Cilano, the lack of a publishing infrastructure and audience for English fiction in Bangladesh, until fairly recently, is redeemed by a much longer Bengali tradition of writing in English that began in the nineteenth century, and in her view the distinctively 'fluid' geography of the country presages a symbolic openness to change and hopeful resilience in its contemporary literary production. Covering short story collections such as K. Anis Ahmed's *Good Night, Mr Kissinger and Other Stories* (2012) and Niaz Zaman and Asif Farrukhi's *Fault Lines: Stories of 1971* (2008) alongside more well-known novels by Tahmima Anam, including *A Golden Age* (2007) and *The Good Muslim* (2011), Cilano examines the ways these texts tackle difficult issues of complicity and guilt in the generations shaped by the events of 1971.

The final chapter of the first section, by Ruvani Ranasinha, on 'Sri Lankan Fiction in English 1994–2014', covers two decades that saw the launch of new Sri Lankan publishing ventures and witnessed the national-official recognition of its English-language novelists by the Gratiaen Prize (1993). If recent writings about Bangladesh return ambivalently to the 1971 liberation war, Sri Lankan fiction, argues Ranasinha, is also dominated by memories of conflict and 'appears to be haunted by the "ghosts" of its warring pasts'. The uneasy legacy of the conflict between the Sri Lankan state and the LTTE (Liberation Tigers of Tamil Eelam), which lasted from 1983 to 2009, has prompted formal interrogations of collective memory in novels such as A. Sivanandan's *When Memory Dies* (1997), and excavations of colonial history as the conflict's origins, in works like Shyam Selvadurai's *Cinnamon Gardens* (1998), alongside a more playful fictional reading of history in Shehan Karunatilaka's *Chinaman: The Legend of Pradeep Mathew* (2011). Ranasinha follows the theme of conflict in novels like Nihal De Silva's *The Road from Elephant Pass* (2003) and uncovers its wider, transnational dimension in V. V. Ganeshananthan's *Love Marriage* (2008) (see also Salgado 2007). Complementing the chapter on the South-Asian short story later in this volume, her study also takes in short fiction authors like Jean Arasanayagam and Pradeep Jeganathan, and goes on to reflect on fictional and non-fiction accounts of the devastating 2004 Indian Ocean tsunami.

The *Contemporary Transformations* section, from which the collection take its title, addresses formal, generic, commercial and contextual changes that have occurred within individual regions and across South Asia. Perhaps the most common factor to shape the imaginative topography of the contemporary novel in English is the growth of South Asia's urban centres: Dhaka, Mumbai, Delhi, Kolkata and Karachi are now all mega-cities and, in the past decade, three of these conurbations, Dhaka, Mumbai and Delhi, have all exceeded population levels of 22 million. New enterprise zones, shopping malls and exclusive residential enclaves, and an associated increase in 'informal' residential (slum) areas, environmental degradation and infrastructural pressures, have profoundly changed the texture of life in these cities. Urban existence in South Asia is now more fast-paced and competitive, more globalized and resource-hungry, more technologically networked and socially fragmented than ever before, and these transformations have proved productive for novelists, fostering urban popular genres such as crime writing and inspiring new, increasingly inventive literary expositions of citizenship and civic identity.

Stuti Khanna explores novels that take an urban underclass as their subject in her chapter 'Writing the Margins (in English): Notes from Some South-Asian Cities.' Dealing with works about smaller centres like India's Amritsar alongside larger city fictions, Khanna's analysis sees a new subaltern focus in novels such as Rupa Bajwa's *The Sari Shop* (2004), and traces its re-presentation of the contemporary city as an increasingly socially polarized space. Khanna's chapter also evaluates representations of the city as a site of jeopardy and partial citizenship in Indra Sinha's *Animal's People* (2007)—a bleak reflection on the human costs of the terrifying industrial accident at the Union Carbide chemical plant in Bhopal, where a poison gas leak killed over 3500 people in December 1984. In Sinha's novel, the magical realism conventionally associated with authors such as Salman Rushdie becomes literalized and hallucinatory as it figures the effects of neurological damage suffered by the victims of the poison gas leak. Khanna goes on to address gendered experiences of cities like Karachi in Mohammed Hanif's *Our Lady of Alice Bhatti* (2011), and reflects on the generic mega-city setting of Mohsin Hamid's third novel, *How to Get Filthy Rich in Rising Asia* (2013). (Like Adiga's *The White Tiger*, this fiction mines a rich vein of satire by using the entrepreneurial business self-help book as a formal template.) These works, argues Khanna, test new kinds of urban consciousness and imagine new subjects of the city.

Dominic Davies's chapter, 'Occupying Literary and Urban Space: Adiga, Authenticity and the Politics of Socio-economic Critique', addresses the ruthless transformative dynamic of Indian city life, and its implications for ideas of community, collective memory and civic identity, in Aravind Adiga's novels: *The White Tiger* (2008) and, more significantly, a work that has been billed as his last fictional socio-economic critique, *Last Man in Tower* (2011). Responding to a number of more negative evaluations of Adiga's writing, Davies identifies a reflexive commentary on authenticity in Adiga's fiction, and relates this to the contemporary proliferation and prominence of journalistic accounts offering an 'insider view' of the New India. Davies goes on to chart the symbolic occupancy of urban space in the residential Mumbai 'society' featured in Adiga's *Last Man in Tower* as an act of principled resistance to the neoliberal co-option of the urban commons. For Davies, Adiga thus incorporates themes of space and occupancy into a meditation on civic consciousness, and develops a critique of neoliberal changes in residential rights that have displaced an older Nehruvian civic ideal in India's cities.

The next chapter in this section, Suman Gupta's 'Contemporary Indian Commercial Fiction in English', uses a book history approach to survey recent landmark shifts in publishing in India. Covering popular commercial fiction with an emphasis on the post-2000 period, Gupta reflects on how a new generation of authors now produce commercially profitable anglophone fiction for the internal market in India. This means that patterns of production and consumption of English fiction have become increasingly involved, split between internationally recognized literary fiction, which bridges the global and the local and which culturally 'represents' India at home and abroad, and new Indian commercial fiction in English, which is marketed and consumed within India and has started to localize the English novel in India. Gupta maps a 'commercial' field that is becoming dominated by best-selling authors such as Chetan Bhagat, and takes account of the contemporary boom in genre fiction which has been linked to a younger, globally aware middle-class generation reacting to an implicit 'de-familiarization' in 'literary' English fiction. Gupta also suggests that commercial fiction may operate to 'brand' India for an internal market and touches on the class assumptions and potentially subversive messages of these works.

Developing on the commercial publishing changes elucidated by Gupta, the next two chapters look at distinct, emerging hybrid forms of fiction. The new market for commercial fiction has triggered a proliferation of Indianized genre fiction traditions including chick lit, crime writing, pulp fiction and works that fictionalize popular sports like cricket. At the same time, entirely new forms such as the graphic novel have also been pioneered in India, and take an increasingly political view of public and popular culture. In most cases, the implicit compact between author and reader in these texts assumes a cultural familiarity that was always more cautiously anticipated in 'literary' works with potentially much wider international and trans-cultural audiences.

E. Dawson Varughese's chapter, 'Genre Fiction of New India: Post-millennial Configurations of Crick Lit, Chick Lit and Crime Writing', uses a sociology of literature approach to analyse new genre fiction and makes a case for the significance of popular genre-hybrids such as 'Crick Lit', a combination of sports novels and romantic fiction. Accordingly, Dawson Varughese analyses several contemporary texts that reflect Indian's cultural and commercial investment in what has been described as the 'post-westernization' of cricket, notably Anuja Chauhan's *The Zoya Factor* (2008) and Geeta Sundar's 'crick lit crime fiction,' *The Premier Murder League* (2010). One of the major social issues shaping citizenship and middle-class aspiration in the so-called New India is corruption, and in 'Crick Lit' thematic combinations of crime and cricket speak symbolically to an increasing intolerance of institutional corruption, evidenced by the Anna Hazare protests and the passing of the Jan Lokpal Bill in 2011. Dawson Varughese concludes by considering how popular genre fiction in English symbolically figures the possibility of a personal remaking in relation to the world, and might generate a sense of 'utopian' potential on the part of its readers.

Another significant aspect of contemporary popular South-Asian book culture, the development of the graphic novel, is addressed by Pooja Sinha in her chapter, 'Vignettes of Change: A Discussion of Two Indian Graphic Novels', which analyses Sarnath Banerjee's sharp modern social commentaries, *Corridor: A Graphic Novel* (2004) and *The Harappa Files* (2011). Alongside other Indian graphic novelists like Vishwajyoti Ghosh—author of *Delhi Calm* (2010)—and contemporaries such as the Kashmiri artist and cartoonist Malik Sajad (whose work is discussed by Ananya Kabir), Sarnath Banerjee's *oeuvre* represents a sophisticated recombination of South-Asian traditions of graphic art and political illustration with the longer format of the graphic novel. Sinha argues that the form is ideally placed to provide a commentary on the social and political changes set in motion by India's economic liberalization, and suggests that these graphic texts coin a new urban 'visual lexicon'. In Banerjee's work, we also encounter a wry, satirical engagement with some of the same issues of cultural identity and middle-class aspiration that feature in Chetan Bhagat's fictions. The combination of text and image in these works allows the graphic novel form to express contradiction and disjuncture at a structural level and, for Sinha, presents its practitioners with a unique medium for social comment.

Kashmir, a contested South-Asian region that has witnessed a tragic contemporary political transformation in increasing tensions between India and Pakistan, and thus represents a latter-day continuation of Partition's geopolitical scission, is the subject of the writings covered in the next chapter. In 1949, Kashmir was divided by a Line of Control marking the ceasefire line of the Indo-Pakistani war fought there shortly after independence, and since then, the people of the region have endured decades of violence. The situation escalated in 1965 and again in 1989, when the uneasy status quo in Kashmir ended and fighting broke out between pro-independence guerrillas (the Jammu and Kashmir Liberation Front) and Indian army forces. The year 1990 is remembered as the point of intensification of an internal insurgency in Kashmir, and the year India implemented its repressive Armed Forces Special Powers Act in the region; tensions increased again in 1998–1999 when Indian and Pakistani troops exchanged artillery fire and fought a high altitude battle across the Line of Control in Kargil. Since then, calls for Kashmir's freedom have grown stronger, and in 2010, mass protests erupted against the government in Indian-administered Kashmir.

Ananya Jahanara Kabir's chapter, 'The New Pastoral: Environmentalism and Conflict in Contemporary Writing from Kashmir', addresses Kashmir's troubled history in relation to discourses of the pastoral and tropes of nostalgia and desire (particularly in an Indian national imaginary), and traces these figures in the history of representations of Kashmir's natural landscape. In showing how environmentalism intersects with forms of political resistance in the local articulation of the Kashmir conflict, Kabir concentrates on Mirza Waheed's novel, *The Collaborator* (2012), as a lament for a loss of connection with the land, and notes its presentation of *gujjar* characters as symbolic of a new 'pastoralist reclamation of Kashmir'. Kabir supports her discussion of literary-environmental inflections of the political in Kashmir with reference to the work of the graphic novelist Malik Sajad, in which the 'new pastoral' is amalgamated radically with the political through Sajad's use of figures who combine human and animal form. In a wider Himalayan area with a tradition of radical environmental protest, such as the Uttarakhand Chipko movement, Kabir's chapter highlights how the pastoral is incorporated into dynamic new forms of political resistance against national interests in the region.

In contrast to the Himalayan border-spaces and pastoral representations discussed by Kabir, Pavan Kumar Malreddy's chapter, 'Solidarity, Suffering and "Divine" Violence: Fictions of the Naxalite Insurgency,' reflects on the writings of an insurgency which threatens the Indian state internally. The present 'Naxalite' Maoist uprising in India, described by the former Prime Minister Manmohan Singh as India's greatest internal security threat, can be traced to the late 1960s but saw a resurgence in 2004, after the formation of the CPI-Maoist group, and now occupies a 'red corridor' in central Indian states that include Jharkhand, Chhattisgarh, Madhya Pradesh and Andhra Pradesh. Examining works of reportage and semi-fiction like Satnam's *Jangalnama: Travels in a Maoist Guerrilla*

Zone (2010) and Gautam Navlakha's 'Days and Night in the Heartland of Rebellion' (2010), as well as fictions such as Diti Sen's *Red Skies and Falling Stars* (2012) and Jhumpa Lahiri's *The Lowland* (2013), Malreddy deploys Slavoj Žižek's philosophical differentiation of 'subjective' and 'objective' violence in conjunction with Emmanuel Levinas's formulation of 'useless suffering' to interrogate a public discourse of insurgency as 'terrorism.' He goes on to question the ethics of solidarity in the idea of a liberal authorial 'intellectual enchantment' with insurgency and shows, through this, how South-Asian fiction often fails to take account of the Naxalite uprising's inherent variability and internal disunity.

The last two chapters of this volume address what could be termed 'minority' identities and forms in South-Asian fiction in English. Maya Parmar's chapter, 'Writing South-Asian Diasporic Identity Anew,' supplements the 'situated' regional focus of the first section of this book by analysing fictions that depict the global South-Asian diaspora or focus on the subjective legacies of migration and travel. (These works often deal with immigrant minorities, but their themes are usually well represented in a postcolonial literary aesthetics.) Exploring 're-orientations' of diaspora experience in Nadeem Aslam's *Maps for Lost Lovers* (2004), Gautam Malkani's *Londonstani* (2006) and M.G. Vassanji's *The Assassin's Song* (2008), Parmar finds a tension in these texts between the pull of lost origins and the push towards newer hybrid possibilities. Situating her reading in relation to the critical paradigm of diaspora studies, she asks how familiar concepts such as homeland, belonging and memory are rendered fluid as a 'space of interpretation' in the onward trajectories and narratives of the diaspora. Parmar's discussion centres predominantly on fictions of the South-Asian diaspora in Britain, and her reading of Malkani's youth novel plots partisan lines of solidarity amongst second-generation immigrants and traces further geographical, communal and caste differentiations in British-Asian identities. She concludes by discussing the work of a migrant writer, M.G. Vassanji, whose writing spans multiple continents and disrupts established centre–periphery models of postcolonial migrant identity.

In the final chapter of the collection, 'Minor Literature and the South-Asian Short Story,' Neelam Srivastava evaluates a fictional form that has tended to be displaced by the hegemony of the South-Asian novel—and particularly the 'Great Indian Novel'—the short story. As well as challenging the novel's ascendancy, Srivastava contends that short stories in translation—in this case, Mahasweta Devi's 'Shishu'—form part of a viable anglophone tradition within the canonizing dynamics of the anthology.

Srivastava sees the relation of the short story to the novel in terms of Deleuze and Guattari's concept of major and minor literature, and foregrounds the short story's affinity with minority 'discourses,' highlighting the way it has been facilitated by marginal periodical and small press publications such as the Indian *Civil Lines*. For Srivastava, contemporary collections such Daniyal Mueenuddin's *In Other Rooms, Other Wonders* (2009) re-anchor the short story in issues of subalternity through the figure of the servant, and reveal aspects of Pakistani culture that have not been represented in anglophone literature. By contrast, in Jhumpa Lahiri's first collection, *Interpreter of Maladies* (2000), Srivastava picks up some of the concerns already broached in Parmar's chapter and examines the short story 'When Mr Pirzada Came to Dine' as a meditation on diasporic citizenship, and the dislocations of collective memory and public identity. Srivastava's discussion reminds us that, in the short story collection and cycle, South-Asian authors have shown how sequential narrative arrangements can achieve the scale of the novel, while putting the reader in the recognizably 'migrant' position of connecting, and holding together, dispersed and disparate narrative experiences.

There are many important contemporary South-Asian texts that have not been discussed in this volume, and as a survey it is necessarily selective. However, if it introduces readers to an emerging fictional area or genre, provides a starting point for further study or just re-emphasizes the energy and technical innovation of South-Asian writing, it will have achieved some of its editorial aims. This introduction started with a review of a contemporary novel of Pakistan by an Indian author, and it seems fitting, therefore, to end with reference to a short story cycle by a Sri Lankan-British writer Romesh Gunesekera. In *Noontide Toll* (2014), Gunesekera's narrator, Vasantha, is that ancient figure in literature (and one familiar to readers of fiction by the Indian author R.K. Narayan), the guide. Ferrying tourists and visitors across Sri Lanka's scarred post-civil war landscape in his Toyota van (a narrative omnibus), his journeying is also a 'travelling' collation of stories about the difficulty of reconciling oneself to radical social and political transformation, especially if this involves the trace of terror and violence. 'You could say we have all been a little damaged by the last few decades,' Vasantha reflects early in the narrative (2014, p. 3). His use of understatement hints at the hidden costs of the Sri Lankan conflict, but it also resonates with a wider sense of the speed of contemporary change across South Asia and finally opens out into a more positive sense of journeying: 'If you are on the move' he says, 'there is always hope' (p. 5).

WORKS CITED

Ahmad, A. (1994). *In theory: Classes, nations, literatures*. Delhi: Oxford University Press.
Boehmer, E., & Tickell, A. (2015). The 1990s: An increasingly postcolonial decade. *Journal of Commonwealth Literature, 50*(3), 315–352.
British Library. (n.d.). *Sounds familiar?: Asian English* [Online]. Available from http://www.bl.uk/learning/langlit/sounds/case-studies/minority-ethnic/asian/. Accessed 29 May 2015.
Chakrabarty, D. (1997). The time of history and the times of the gods. In L. Lowe & D. Lloyd (Eds.), *The politics of culture in the shadow of capital* (pp. 35–60). Durham: Duke University Press.
Chaudhuri, A. (Ed.). (2001). *The picador book of modern Indian literature*. Basingstoke: Picador.
D'haen, T., Damrosch, D., & Kadir, D. (Eds.). (2012). *The Routledge companion to world literature*. Abingdon: Routledge.
Damrosch, D. (2003). *What is world literature?* Princeton: Princeton University Press.
Dasgupta, R. (2014). *Capital: A portrait of twenty-first century Delhi*. London: Canongate.
Desai, A. (2000, December 21). Passion in Lahore. *New York Review of Books, 47*(20), 72–74.
Dharwadker, V. (2012). Constructions of world literature in colonial and postcolonial India. In T. D'haen, D. Damrosch, & D. Kadir (Eds.), *The Routledge companion to world literature* (pp. 476–486). Abingdon: Routledge.
Gunesekera, R. (2014). *Noontide toll*. London: Granta.
Huggan, G. (2001). *The postcolonial exotic: Marketing the margins*. London: Routledge.
Innes, C. L. (2007). *The Cambridge introduction to postcolonial literatures in English*. Cambridge: Cambridge University Press.
Lau, L., & Mendes, A. (Eds.). (2011). *Re-orientalism and South Asian identity politics: The oriental other within*. London: Routledge.
Mukherjee, M., & Trivedi, H. (Eds.). (1996). *Interrogating post-colonialism: Theory, text, context*. Shimla: Indian Institute of Advanced Study.
Nandy, A. (2002). *Time warps: Silent and evasive pasts in Indian politics and religion*. London: Hurst and Co.
Quayson, A. (2012). *The Cambridge history of postcolonial literature*. Cambridge: Cambridge University Press.
Salgado, M. (2007). *Writing Sri Lanka: Literature, resistance and the politics of place*. London/New York: Routledge.
Sen, K., & Roy, R. (Eds.). (2013). *Writing India anew: Indian English fiction 2000–2010*. Amsterdam: Amsterdam University Press.

UNESCO and UNICEF. (2012). *Asia-Pacific end of decade notes on education for all: EFA goal 4, youth and adult literacy* [Online]. Available from http://unesdoc.unesco.org/images/0021/002184/218428E.pdf. Accessed 29 May 2015.

Viswamohan, A. I. (Ed.). (2013). *Postliberalization Indian novels in English: Politics of global reception and awards.* London: Anthem Press.

Young, R. J. C. (2012). World literature and postcolonialism. In T. D'haen, D. Damrosch, & D. Kadir (Eds.), *The Routledge companion to world literature* (pp. 213–222). Abingdon: Routledge.

PART I

Regional Formations

Of Capitalism and Critique: 'Af-Pak' Fiction in the Wake of 9/11

Priyamvada Gopal

At the risk of stating the obvious, I begin by noting that Pakistani anglophone fiction rose to prominence on the global literary map after 11 September 2001, bringing greater international attention to writers of Pakistani origin like Mohammed Hanif, Mohsin Hamid, Daniyal Mueenuddin and H.M. Naqvi, as well as figures such as Aamer Hussein, Nadeem Aslam and Kamila Shamsie who have been around somewhat longer.[1] To suggest that this increased visibility is not coincidental but connected to renewed public interest in the region that, in the jargon of international relations, came to be known as 'Af-Pak' in the wake of the 2001 invasion of Afghanistan is also unlikely to be controversial. Noting that a 2010 special issue of *Granta* magazine on Pakistan focuses almost entirely on the 'War on Terror years, the political upheaval, the instability, the danger and death', the Pakistani writer Bina Shah finds herself

---

[1] 'Booms' in literature are notoriously unwieldy notions. 'How many books does a boom make', asks Bina Shah, noting that the Pakistan anglophone boom might be said to include works by all the writers mentioned above as well as shorter fiction by Aamer Hussein whose *Another Gulmohar Tree* was nominated for the regional Commonwealth Book Prize in 2010. Naqvi's *Home Boy* acquired a huge India readership after winning the DSC Prize for South Asian Literature (Shah 2012, p. 143).

P. Gopal
Faculty of English, University of Cambridge,
Cambridge, UK

© The Editor(s) (if applicable) and The Author(s) 2016
A. Tickell (ed.), *South-Asian Fiction in English*,
DOI 10.1057/978-1-137-40354-4_2

wondering whether violence and 'terror' have become 'sexy to Western readers' implicating some writers in a 'cold-blooded consideration of market trends' (2012, p. 152). In an essay which is justifiably sceptical of this phenomenon, Shah ends up conceding, however, that events pursuant to 11 September 2001 'have been so overwhelming and all-surrounding' that they cannot be evaded as creative concerns by writers from the region (p. 151). The 'most dangerous country on earth,' she notes wryly, 'is a pretty exciting place in which to be a writer' (p. 153).

Whatever the relationship between individual authorial choices and the global publishing zeitgeist, the address of anglophone literature from predominantly non-anglophone contexts is often necessarily transnational, and at least partially directed at an English-speaking readership located elsewhere. The present prominence of Pakistani anglophone fiction invites us to think about the ways in which that transnational address shapes commercially and critically successful literary representations of Pakistan-in-the-world after 9/11. The relevance of this now canonized date is not that of a moment of self-evident global significance whereby a national tragedy automatically becomes a universal one. It is, rather, a historical conjuncture at which certain geopolitical contradictions— including the USA's financing of Islamist militants as a bulwark against communism during the Cold War—came to a head, spelling a long period of crisis for Pakistan as a nation-state. With the retaliatory invasion of Afghanistan that swiftly followed the al-Qaeda attacks on the World Trade Center in New York, Pakistan would become both an ally and a target of a military campaign, its sovereignty repeatedly undermined by the US military action, which has included ongoing illegal drone strikes on its north-western frontiers and, indeed, further inland. It is this conflicted and wounded relationship with the USA in the context of an ongoing military conflict and the rise of anti-Muslim racism globally that emerges as the most noticeable, though not sole, preoccupation of recent anglophone fiction from and about Pakistan. This concern renders both the content and the address of much of this fiction distinct from anglophone Indian fiction, especially given the ways in which the latter—due, in part, to the emergence of a very substantial domestic market—has started to turn away from its familiar transnational address. Relatedly, where much of the Indian anglophone tradition has been in thrall, both admiringly and subversively, to the English literary heritage, an explicit engagement with American letters often emerges in the work of recent Pakistani anglophone writers.

One of the pitfalls of focusing on this particular trajectory in Pakistani fiction is that it risks consolidating a much-used optic, familiar to us from journalistic and political discourse, which reduces contemporary Pakistan to the USA-sponsored 'War on Terror' and its pervasively deleterious consequences. In fact, what we learn from some of this fiction is that this is a war better understood as and termed a War *of* Terror with more than one party, including NATO and the USA, deploying indefensible violence against civilians. At the same time, writers such as Mohsin Hamid and Mohammed Hanif have sought explicitly to interrogate regnant political and cultural representations of Pakistan in the West. With the caveat that Pakistan with its myriad regions, denizens, languages and communities is not contained by these events, for all that they figure larger than life in international representations, I examine two critically-acclaimed anglophone texts which are clearly shaped by the moment and afterlife of the 2001 al-Qaeda attack on New York's twin towers and the subsequent US military presence in (indeed, construction of) the 'Af-Pak' region. Tracing how both novels explicate the region's complicated relationship with the USA and the geopolitical West more broadly, this chapter traces the emergence and limits of a literary critique of this relationship. The question of responsibility for rendering this region vulnerable to multiple depredations—and the subsequent effect of this condition on relations between this part of Asia and the geopolitical West—is posed by both texts, but in markedly different ways. *The Wasted Vigil*, an acclaimed novel by British-Pakistani author Nadeem Aslam, is not set directly or exclusively in Pakistan, but in neighbouring Afghanistan, mainly in the border and trading town of Jalalabad. It draws most directly on familiar Anglo-American perspectives on the region.

Adapted into a 2014 Hollywood film by the director Mira Nair, Mohsin Hamid's hugely successful tragic love story, *The Reluctant Fundamentalist*, charts the emergence of ambiguity towards and dissent from these perspectives.

Poetic Affect and Ideological Effect: *The Wasted Vigil*

Aslam's *The Wasted Vigil* (2008) came out to wide critical acclaim in Britain and the USA, the third novel of an author already well-known for his prize-winning *Maps for Lost Lovers* (2004) and the less successful *Season of Rainbirds* (1993). The generally laudatory reception accorded to this novel is not hard to understand. On the face of it, since it brings together characters representing different parties to the conflict in Afghanistan, to a crumbling and beautiful old house in the town of Usha, the narrative aim might be encapsulated in the worthy observation made by the saintly Marcus, an ageing Englishman who has dedicated his life to the country: 'here everyone is human and must try to understand each other's mystery. Each other's pain' (2008, p. 198). In Marcus's old house, a destroyed perfumery, where he is the custodian of a giant ancient Buddha statue which has withstood an attack by the Taliban, an all but allegorical cast of characters come together: 'Look at the three of us here! Like a William Blake prophecy! America, Europe and Asia!' (p. 183). Along with Marcus—who has converted to Islam but who has had his hands cut off by his late wife Qatrina (declared an adulteress) under orders from the Taliban—there are the Russian, Lara, looking for her brother Benedikt, a soldier who defected from the Soviet Army while it was in Afghanistan; David, an American who has lost his brother in Vietnam and whose fiercely anti-communist CIA connections are kept from the reader until a quantum of reader sympathy towards him has been accrued; Casa, an orphaned boy soldier with the Taliban, and, in a cameo, Dunia, a young Afghan schoolteacher who notionally represents the ordinary person's version of Islam in Afghanistan and the aspirations of Afghan women to education and selfhood. The dead Qatrina herself haunts the edges of the narrative, staunchly, if privately, atheist and a feisty critic not only of the Taliban but Islam itself. The stage in the theatre of war that is Afghanistan is set for the emergence of insight and understanding in the face of unspeakable violence and the brutal exigencies of realpolitik.

While mildly deprecating *Vigil's* 'operatic effusions', a fairly representative review by Lorraine Adams in *The New York Times* avers that in *Vigil*, the novelist demonstrated that he was 'unafraid of political complexity' while 'unflinching in his examination of depravity'. Adams's approving list of the novel's iteration of 'the documented savagery of Afghanistan', however, invokes a cornucopia of cliches:

> land mines (especially those that look like toys, designed to lure children); inventively vicious rapes (of girls, of a main character, of a historical figure); rough public justice, including a stoning and the amputation; warlords and their intractable feuds; misguided Americans and their obstinate meddling; abominable methods of torture, inflicted by both warlords and Americans. (2008, para. 7)

This is not, unfortunately, an unjust adumbration. The undoubtedly opulent rhetorical style of this novel, something of a literary trademark for Aslam, the son of a poet, ends up not so much articulating complexity as standing in for it, displacing its possibility. The novel is dotted with long passages where linguistic flourishes and internal monologues in italicized print (mostly in Casa's head) conceal generalizations of somewhat startling crudity and questionable historical insight in relation to Afghanistan, Afghans and Islam: 'a woman seen is a Western idea' (Aslam 2008, p. 185); '*If you do not fight He will punish you severely and put others in your place*, said the Koran'(p. 187); '*A tribe's greatness is known by how mighty its enemy is*, the clerics at the madrassas would say' (p. 210). There is an unmistakeable elision of lines between what could be construed as the brainwashed thoughts of a single character and what could represent Afghanistan or Islam more widely. Indeed, even when a character like Marcus is made to suggest in passing that 'the West was involved in the ruining of this place', we are invited to read the comment as evidence of his characteristic liberal generosity rather than truthful historical insight (p. 74). Qatrina, we are immediately informed, would not have agreed and hers, of course, is implicitly the more grounded view of native informant: 'The cause of the destruction of Afghanistan, she said to me toward the end of her life, is the character and society of the Afghans, of Islam' (p. 77). In many ways, with its relentless emphasis on the crude savageries of the Taliban as both *Islamist* and *Islamic*, this is the novel's view too: 'One can only wonder, Qatrina would say, at what these lands could have been had they not been set back by the arrival of Islam' (p. 220). The only comparable savagery in the novel is that of communism which, like Islamism, articulates a thoroughgoing critique of the (capitalist) West. To this effect, the characters too are etched with quite different sets of brushes and colours. Casa ('Home/House') and Dunia ('World'), the two living Afghan characters, are the supporting cast with the text insistently and alternately foregrounding the three white non-Afghan protagonists, Lara, Marcus and David, a narrative choice with determinate ideological consequences. Even as the omniscient narrator switches perspectives frequently, the narrative consciousness suffusing the telling of the tale overlaps significantly with that of the three white non-Afghans.

The real ideological sleight of hand, however, has to do with how the narrative understands and explicates the notion of ideology itself. Aslam puts in place an operational distinction between characters whose motive force is ideological and conceptual in the first instance—that is, every thought and feeling is crudely referred back to an authoritative set of external precepts—and those who are to be read through their affective and psychic existence, an organic concatenation of feeling, thought, ideas, reflection and engagement. Within this frame, Islamism and communism are understood to be ideological: coherent, if delusional, bodies of thought whose adherents, occasional doubts notwithstanding, are incapable of either critical reflection or breaking free. Their every action and thought is determined by this ideological or textual force-field although they can elicit our sympathy as victims of brainwashing who have been made to believe in the most ludicrous scenarios, 'seed sprouted from the blood-soaked soil of Muslim countries' (Aslam 2008, p. 13). Casa, the main living Afghan character, belongs to the tribe of the ineluctably tunnel-visioned, referring every idea and action back to the Koran or to the teachings of madrassa preachers, brainwashed and pathologically unable to imagine alternatives. In contrast, David, Lara and Marcus enjoy rich and 'complex' affective lives; they may be complicit in the occasional ideological manoeuvre but they are 'in touch' with their feelings, endowed with empathic self-reflection, able to rue mistakes and criticize themselves. They are, in short, capable of transformation. David may be a former CIA agent with a murky past of his own, but it is as a mourning lover of Zameen, Marcus's and Qatrina's daughter, that we come to know and empathize with him; Lara is Benedikt's grieving sister who has long repudiated any Soviet connection; the long-suffering Marcus transcends all ideology, 'one of those few humans who lent dignity to everything their gaze landed on. Like a saint entering your life through a dream' (p. 33). His life is imbricated with the liberal largesse of the British empire as one who thinks 'too lovingly of the other races and civilisations of the world, who left his own country in the West to set up home among them in the East, and was ruined as a result' (p. 74). He—and thereby we—know that the 'entire world…had made mistakes in this country' but it is unclear 'who to blame for those consequences' even as it is conceded that left to itself, the country might have done well (p. 34).

Fredric Jameson has written, in the context of his reading of Joseph Conrad, about the ways in which *Lord Jim*'s 'unconscious denunciation of ideology' is 'no less dependent for its realization on a rather different level of ideological production, namely that of the aesthetic' (1982, p. 211). Aslam's intricately poetic language also shores up an ultimately crude opposition between ideology and aesthetics. If Casa and a good number of other Afghans and Pakistanis who constitute peripheral characters are to be distinguished by the manner and extent to which they have committed to the totalizing ideological—they have pathologies rather than psyches—the three white outsiders share a profound sense of beauty and pleasure which constantly reshapes their political leanings and habits of thought, enabling them to espouse an open-endedness which is conspicuously absent in those around them. Indeed, Marcus and other Westerners must take on the role of custodians of Afghanistan's own aesthetic heritage. By extension, then, the ideological reasons for the West's presence in the region, like those of David, the CIA man, are 'good' and 'genuine', if prone to occasional mistakes.

A sense of itself as post-ideological is, of course, fundamental to capitalism's self-understanding and self-representation. In the novel's delineation of the making of contemporary Afghanistan, we are made aware of a conflict between communism and Islamism, on the one hand, and between the communist Soviet Union and the anti-communist USA on the other. *Vigil* thus rehearses capitalism's great vanishing trick, rendering itself simultaneously invisible and all-pervasive: it is not an ideology but natural, like the air we breathe. Read through this lens, the situation in Afghanistan has no material underpinnings: it is, in every direction, ideational, a war of ideas. Beauty, humanity, freedom and open-endedness stand defensive guard against the totalizing brutality of the 'isms' propagated by those who have religious and/or political claims to make. There are occasional concessions to 'mistakes' made by the West in the decimation of Afghanistan itself, drawing on an opposition between contingent flaws and wrong turns, on the one hand (the West) and constitutive evil (communism and Islamism), on the other. So, for instance, we are invited to think about David's clubbing to death of a hapless coyote after hearing of his brother's disappearance in Vietnam in terms of a single, ultimately understandable, human crisis of ethics and emotion; Casa, on the other hand, participates in the routine killing of young animals not because the Taliban must learn to kill without emotion but because 'no true Muslim should shrink from killing in cold blood' (Aslam 2008, p. 104).

For all that he is explicit about devoting his life to fighting communism (not distinguished here from the Soviet Union) and doing everything he 'can to fuck up the Reds', David is presented less as an ideological warrior than thoughtful dissenter, one himself who admires the optimism of his left-wing relatives but knows what is good for

Afghanistan: 'People like these had to be told that communism wasn't the only way to end inequality...Revolutions that eventually devoured their children and turned half the planet into a prison' (Aslam 2008, p. 128, pp. 142–3). He symbolically replaces an unnamed Afghan communist as Zameen's lover and his own political commitments to an invisible ideology—and nation—are, once again, figured as affective in the first instance: 'As he spoke, had she detected something like satisfaction in him? A contentment at how his family had been given the chances to improve themselves over the decades and generations, slowly and patiently encouraged to thrive by America in American sunlight' (p. 99). In contrast, when it comes to the Taliban as ideological warriors whose 'cruelty and degradation' we need not equivocate about, the novel indulges in something very close to a pornography of violence while the death and destruction inflicted by, for instance, American drone-bombing is alluded to at best in notional ways. Indeed, such a critique would fall clearly into the category of texts 'which teach them nothing except how to invent grievances' feeding 'an addiction to brooding on ancient wounds'(p. 278).

Driven by this imperative to not reflect on wounds, in the end, *The Wasted Vigil* does not embrace difficulty or complexity, the elaborate textual apparatus of nuance and poetic insight notwithstanding. Yet, the mantra of 'complexity' is iterated all through the critical reception of *Vigil*, gesturing towards what is clearly much-needed and hard to come by in engagements with contemporary Afghanistan and Pakistan, fictional and otherwise. It is neither easy nor expedient to articulate a position which can pronounce a plague on the cruelties and the willed retrogression of formations like the Taliban while at the same time and with equal force repudiating the murderous and amnesiac militarized racism of British and American imperialisms under whose auspices the former came into being and flourished. In reality, 'complex' voices, when they do emerge, suffer both suppression and silencing as in the case of the doughty Revolutionary Association of the Women of Afghanistan (RAWA), who have consistently stood up to the Taliban while firmly repudiating attempts by Western powers—whom they denounce as imperialist occupiers—to appropriate the cause of Afghan women. Where Af-Pak is concerned, *Vigil* does little, ultimately, to rectify this existing problem of representation. We are finally left with one message, through Dunia, that is as much about capitalism as country: 'The USA is loved by its people so it can't be destroyed' (Aslam 2008, p. 269).

Terms of Disengagement: *The Reluctant Fundamentalist*

In contrast, the USA, the West, capitalism and ideology are very much linked and at the forefront of Mohsin Hamid's acclaimed novel, *The Reluctant Fundamentalist* (2007). The novel's undoubted literary merits include a tightly controlled narrative structure and a delicate but compelling evocation of the atmosphere of menace and wariness between the first-person narrator and his unnamed, silent American interlocutor who might or might not be a potential assassin or, conversely, a potential target. At its best, the novel is deftly allusive, evoking modern American fiction, most explicitly F. Scott Fitzgerald's *The Great Gatsby*, as well as popular culture, mainly Hollywood cinema. As in *Vigil*, however, there is fairly heavy-handed allegory with, for instance, the beautiful blonde Erica standing in for the libidinal pull of Am/Erica itself, her dead boyfriend representing America's Chris/tian traditionalism from which Am/Erica cannot fully disengage and the corporate power that is Underwood Samson (initials, U.S.) whose ultimate reluctant janissary Changez (the name evoking an Asian emperor, Genghis Khan) becomes. Allegory, of course, has its uses, and like some of the texts Jameson discusses in his notorious essay, *Third World Literature in the Era of Multinational Capitalism*, Hamid's is a narrative of coming to national consciousness, and even, as Changez suggests at one point, something like a Third World sensibility. *The Reluctant Fundamentalist* tells the story of a young Pakistani man enamoured by the promise of America and the undoing which is also a political awakening that takes place for him after 11 September 2001. In what Hamid describes as an inversion of the traditional immigrant story, a transformed Changez returns to Pakistan cherishing a new-found geopolitical clarity and new political commitments. While advocating Pakistani disengagement from America, he is quick to announce in the opening pages: 'Do not be frightened by my beard: I am a lover of America' (Hamid 2008, p. 1).

What are these commitments and how do they sit alongside this insistence on a continued affection for a country on which the narrator has so determinedly turned his back? The narrative documents Changez's increasing resentment of the always racialized terms of engagement in multicultural America, which evolve into flagrant racism in the wake of 9/11. Gradually, his increasing unease with Underwood Samson's corporate practices comes to a crisis during a brief, rather schematic, pedagogical encounter with the Chilean leftist bibliophile, Juan-Bautista.

Consequently, Changez decides to embrace what he regards as his difference from his corporate colleagues and from Americans more generally, despite his intense love for the cool blonde, Erica, who cannot return his feelings. The titular reluctance would refer, it would seem, both to Changez's incremental discomfort with corporate practice (Underwood Samson's motto is 'Focus on the Fundamentals') and to his final disengagement from America. His conversion into an anti-USA campaigner when he returns to Pakistan would, of course, be indistinguishable from religious fundamentalism in American public discourse, generating a set of expectations that Hamid plays with in the course of the narrative: 'Perhaps you have drawn certain conclusions from my appearance, my lustrous beard' (p. 87). As Tariq Ali puts it, the single optic through which the West views Pakistan has been 'bearded fanatics skulking in the Hindu Kush' (2007, p. 4). But we are given no reason to believe that Changez, in his 'fundamentalist' avatar, embraces religion in any explicit sense: we know only that he returns to Lahore and teaches finance while advocating Pakistani disengagement from America.

If Changez is indeed no fundamentalist in the more familiar religious-political sense, then the burden of the titular reluctance falls as much on his growing unease with his status as a janissary for American capitalist imperialism as on his transformation into an anti-Americanist of sorts. It is suggested that even as he throws himself enthusiastically into his job as a capitalist functionary, the seeds of reluctance are already to be found in his sense of being something of a cultural misfit (which his boss Jim (mis)-reads as the same class unease that he, with his working-class origins, has also had to contend with). The reluctance of the fundamentalist is, in that sense, as much that of someone who is unsure of his commitment to the basic tenets of a faith, in this case, to corporatism—'my days of focusing on the fundamentals were done'—as it is of someone who embraces a new ideology, anti-Americanism, that doesn't quite fit him, especially given his lingering and still powerful affections for the object of disengagement. At the same time, while the critique of American imperialism in the novel is represented as congruent with a rejection of capitalism, the connections are sketchily made. At the outset, for instance, Changez's nascent resentment of the USA is described primarily in cultural and civilizational terms rather than through a grasp of political economy. Standing in the magnificent lobby of Underwood Samson for the first time, Changez's meditation on the USA as 'the most technologically advanced species known to man' elicits an anguished sense of civilizational reversal:

> Four thousand years ago, we, the people of the Indus River basin, had cities that were laid out on grids and boasted underground sewers, while the ancestors of those who would invade and colonize America were illiterate barbarians. Now our cities were largely unplanned, unsanitary affairs, and America had universities with individual endowments greater than our national budget for education. To be reminded of this vast disparity was, for me, to be ashamed. (Hamid 2008, p. 38)

Changez's later damning assessment of himself as an imperial janissary nonetheless retains an admiring sense of the world-altering possibilities of high finance for those like him who are chosen to be its functionaries. Those who, 'shorn of hair and dressed in battle fatigues...would have been virtually indistinguishable' (p. 43). He is quite clear about what an induction into these ranks entails for him, and moreover, his diminished family prestige: the recovery of a lost class *and* imperial civilizational power. His nostalgia, like Pakistan's, is a longing 'not for what my family had never had, but for what we had had and lost' (p. 81).

Changez is described throughout the narrative as an exceptionally high performer, a kind of capitalist ingénue. Why then and when does his Damascene moment take place? What occasions the broadening smile when, to his own surprise, he is 'remarkably pleased' to watch the towers falling in a Manila hotel room? It is a moment which Changez, still somewhat taken aback by his own reaction, describes in terms of 'America brought to her knees', a not insignificant inversion given his own prior feminized sense of himself as a 'perfect breast' for corporate purposes. The reasons for his unexpected response are opaque to Changez himself: 'So why did part of me desire to see America harmed? I did not know, then; I knew merely that my feelings would be unacceptable to my colleagues'(p. 84). What follows in the second half of the narrative is a retrospective accounting for these feelings as they consolidate in Changez's mind. The latent unexpected resentment underlying his smile of pleasure is, unsurprisingly, only exacerbated by the xenophobia and racism that awaits him upon his return to the USA from Manila, commencing at the airport immigration desk. These hostilities function, within the narrative, as a kind of clarifying optic: Changez starts to look at America differently through his own 'othering'. Earlier, he had believed his foreignness helped him. Now he starts to identify all the ways in which he is repudiated culturally and racially. His discomfort with corporate practice is markedly slower to intensify. Indeed, as the 'mighty host...was duly raised and dispatched—but homeward, towards my family in Pakistan', Changez describes himself as 'cavorting' with Erica and 'clad in my armor of denial', continuing to excel at his job 'with continuing and noteworthy success' (p. 108).

The point beyond which Changez can no longer practise 'so thorough a self-deception' (p. 114) takes place when he finds himself making a critical connection between 'the mismatch between the American bombers with their twenty-first-century weaponry and the ill-equipped and ill-fed Afghan tribesmen below' and the older workers at a New Jersey company whom the mighty Underwood Samson will help make redundant through his own 'single-minded attention to financial detail' (pp. 112–13). As he watches television images of American soldiers equipped with night-vision goggles commence the invasion of Afghan territory, he is again surprised by his own reaction but starts to join the dots: 'Afghanistan was Pakistan's neighbor, our friend, and a fellow Muslim nation besides.' Already uncomfortable with Jim's description of their origins in a working-class industrial town and Pakistan respectively as places 'condemned to atrophy', Changez finally finds himself questioning his own commitment to the 'fundamentals' of corporate practice, including Jim's asseveration that theirs is a 'field of endeavour that would be of ever-greater importance to humanity and would be likely, therefore, to provide [... him] with ever-increasing returns' (p. 111). Like Aslam, Hamid rarely uses the word 'capitalism' but it is clear that Underwood Samson (US) represents the capitalist mantra that resistance is futile—'misguided' or 'at least myopic' (p. 111).

The moment of connection between peoples variously exploited by the rapacity of corporate practice and the aggressive American nationalism that sustains it is, however, short-lived. Following this moment of connection between political economy and nationalist ideology, Changez's critical reflections return to the civilizational inversions that have troubled him earlier:

> For we were not always burdened by debt, dependent on foreign aid and handouts; in the stories we tell of ourselves we were not the crazed and destitute radicals you see on your television channels but rather saints and poets and—yes—conquering kings. *We* built the Royal Mosque and the Shalimar Gardens in this city, and *we* built the Lahore Fort with its mighty walls and wide ramp for our battle-elephants. And we did these things when your

country was still a collection of thirteen small colonies, gnawing away at the edge of a continent.' (p. 115-6)

As he bemoans both Erica's and America's retreat, exacerbated by the New York attacks, into 'a powerful *nostalgia*', Changez also confronts what he calls 'the growing importance of *tribe*' when he is racially abused as a 'fucking Arab' (p. 129, pp. 133–4; original emphases). His retaliatory response is initially restricted to the defiant beard, 'a form of protest on my part, a symbol of my identity...I know only that I did not wish to blend in with the army of clean-shaven youngsters who were my co-workers, and that inside me, for multiple reasons, I was deeply angry' (p. 148). His own personal process of disengaging with America involves unlearning his own 'entitled and unsympathetic' Americanized habits of gaze and thought and reconnecting with his Pakistani side during a brief return home: 'It was far from impoverished; indeed, it was rich with history' (p. 142). At Underwood Samson, by contrast, 'we went about the task of shaping the future with little regard for the past' (p. 132). To be Pakistani, then, is to appreciate history, symbolized here by Changez's dilapidated family home with its 'enduring grandeur, its unmistakable personality and idiosyncratic charm' (p. 142).

The shift to the language of civilizational grandeur which undergirds Changez's retaliatory critical nationalism is worth pausing on. Changez tells us that he now becomes obsessed with reading about the 'ongoing deterioration of affairs between India and Pakistan' and 'the negative impact the standoff was already beginning to have on the economies of both nations' (p. 149). US nationalism, he deduces, supports Indian aggression by legitimizing 'the invasion of weaker states by more powerful ones'. The nationalist solidarity he experiences upon his return home entails 'unanimity in the belief that India would do all it could to harm us, and that despite the assistance we have given American in Afghanistan, American would not fight at our side'. It is this that renders him 'a kind of coward in my own eyes, a traitor' for returning to the USA and 'abandon[ing] his people in such circumstances' (p. 145). It is in this resentful frame of mind that Changez arrives at his third and final learning moment in Valparaiso, Chile, where he encounters the truculent leftist, Juan-Bautista, something of a caricature with his thick glasses, unfiltered cigarettes and aphoristic observations on the value of books and the humanities. This encounter in Neruda-land is integral to Changez's 'blinders' coming off as he is 'dazzled and rendered immobile by the sudden broadening of my arc of vision...now I saw that in this constant striving to realize a financial future, no thought was given to the critical personal and political issues that affect one's emotional present' (p. 165). As his 'inflective journey' gathers momentum, Changez's response amounts to action short of a strike; first a slowdown and then a withdrawal of labour altogether in a final powerful gesture of repudiation and refusal. The face-off between him and his immediate boss is presented as one between the imperatives of finance and the claims of poetry—and it is now that Changez must and does make his choice, while Juan-Bautista cannily appeals to his familial connection to Punjabi poetry: 'I had thrown in my lot with the men of Underwood Samson, with the officers of the empire, when all along I was predisposed to feel compassion for those, like Juan-Bautista, whose lives the empire thought nothing of overturning for its own gain' (p. 173). As a Pakistani he knows from 'alternating periods of American aid and sanctions—that finance was a primary means by which the American empire exercised its power' (p. 177).

The anti-imperial sentiments Changez is now able to collate into his more clearly defined politics are, nonetheless, articulated in the language of lost imperial glory, of sadly superseded empires which have given way to the new aggressor. Through this lens, Lahore and Valparaiso share not so much the 'Third World sensibility' Changez alludes to in Manila, but a type of late post-imperial melancholia: 'In this—Valparaiso's former aspirations to grandeur—I was reminded of Lahore and of that saying, so evocative in our language: *the ruins proclaim the building was beautiful* (p. 163). When he duly returns to Pakistan wielding, on the one hand, his 'ex-janissary's skills' as a college teacher of finance and on the other, the critical acumen of his new-found anti-imperialism, Changez becomes an iconic campus figure whose mission is 'to advocate a disengagement of your country by mine'. This is not, in the Pakistani context, a position that can simply be conflated with religious fundamentalism, speaking as it does to a wide cross-section of the citizenry, 'communists, capitalists, feminists, religious literalists' (p. 204). Changez's own 'anti-American' polemics are figured, on the one hand, as intrinsic to his anti-imperialism and on the other, as a *cri de cœur* to the beloved, Am/Erica herself. In his mind, he is calling on America to 'reflect on the shared pain that united you with those who attacked you' as well as expressing an insurmountable longing which continues his 'inhabitation' of that country.

How do we read this critical defiance in the face of a continued psychic inhabitation of the USA? The narrative draws to a close, deliberately so, without giving us any clearer a sense of where Changez's 'inflective journey' takes him, or how we might situate him within a diverse Pakistani political spectrum. What we cannot really know is whether Changez's critique of high finance as a weapon of American domination can broaden into a more developed critique of capitalism that is also cogizant of conflicts and trajectories of exploitation within the Pakistani plural pronoun 'we' than is indicated by Changez's use of it in relation to both the USA and India. Or is this a critique specifically and only of American high finance and capitalist practice as Changez grooms a generation of politicized young people with 'an aptitude for cash flow statements' into a variety of neoliberal nationalism widely pervasive across the border in discourses of Indian economic power, discourses which can sit very comfortably alongside identitarian and statist politics? With the novel ultimately silent on it, the question remains unanswered: are the terms of disengagement always laid down by America in advance, or has the pursuit of capitalist fundamentals been abandoned in a more thoroughgoing sense?

Conclusion: Reframing 'Af-Pak'

In his thoughtful editorial introduction to an excellent special issue of *Critical Muslim*, Ziauddin Sardar asks on the topic of Pakistan: 'Can a nation exist as a surrogate of an imperial power or can it determine its own destiny?' (2012, p. 15). Aslam and Hamid appear to provide very different responses to this question. For Aslam, a turn away from the ideological—in his case, Islamism (which, in his rendering, is not entirely distinguishable from Islam itself) and communism—provides the only hope in a landscape that he renders in bleakly hopeless terms. For Hamid, a turn to the cultural and civilizational offers the resources for resistance. In Aslam's case, the Western-as-capitalist remains ineffable and somehow outside ideology, providing a horizon of transcendence; for Hamid, a former financier, like Changez, America-as-capitalism is profoundly ideological, exercises material violence and has to be resisted. But it remains unclear whether this is done by separating 'America' from 'capitalism' or whether Pakistan has to turn away from both elements. As Sardar notes, a turn to the language of culture and religion does not necessarily spell resistance to the depredations of capitalism or, indeed, the 'self-reliance' and 'self-assertion' that he, like Hamid, sees as vital for Pakistan's future. In this instance, Islam as faith has to be separated from Islamism as ideology which provides 'a sense of moral superiority' to the hopeless but, in fact, 'is no friend to the poor and the marginalised...an aggressively capitalist and ugly enterprise, a natural ally for the conservative middle class by which it is eagerly embraced' (pp. 6–7). Nonetheless, where Aslam's novel ends up reifying the ossified assumptions that underlie ideologies of 'civilizational clash', Hamid's tightly-controlled narrative poses questions that need to be asked. What remains as yet unanswered is this: when the dispossessed and violated of this region do find a vehicle of representation, who will be listening?

WORKS CITED

Adams, L. (2008, October 11). Torch song for Afghanistan. *New York Times*. [Online]. Available from http://www.nytimes.com/2008/10/12/books/review/Adams-t.html?_r=0

Ali, T. (2007). Pakistan at sixty. *The London Review of Books* [Online], 29(19), 12–15. Available from http://www.lrb.co.uk/v29/n19/tariq-ali/pakistan-at-sixty

Aslam, N. (2008). *The wasted vigil*. London: Faber and Faber.

Hamid, M. (2008). *The reluctant fundamentalist*. London: Penguin [First published 2007].

Jameson, F. (1982). *The political unconscious: Narrative as a socially symbolic act*. Ithaca: Cornell University Press [First published 1981].

Sardar, Z. (2012). Introduction: *That* question mark. *Critical Muslim* (4, October–December), 19–44.

Shah, B. (2012). Paperback writers. *Critical Muslim* (4, October–December), 143–154.

'An Idea Whose Time Has Come': Indian Fiction in English After 1991

Alex Tickell

The famous 'Tryst with Destiny' speech delivered by Jawaharlal Nehru to the Constituent Assembly at midnight, 14 August 1947, on the eve of India's independence, is remarkable not just as the defining statement of India's postcolonial nationhood but also as a piece of political discourse that has since become sutured into the fabric of Indian-English literary history. Nehru's salute to the awakening nation, with its epochal rhetoric and its pledge to raise a mansion of free India for 'all her children' provided both metaphor and structure for Salman Rushdie's now canonical novel, *Midnight's Children* (1981), and even though Rushdie's fictional reflection on the moment of independence was an ironic one and involved a metahistorical questioning of the new nation, the speech itself was untouched by this irony. Its literary credentials were reinforced by Rushdie on the 50th anniversary of India's freedom when it was included as the first text in his controversial *Vintage Book of Indian Writing 1947–1997* (1997), co-edited with Elizabeth West. Since then, Nehru's unique contribution to the development of English literary prose in India has been further recognized (Khilnani 2003, p. 156) and the elision of a 'messianic' awakening to national and literary legitimacy has

A. Tickell
Department of English, The Open University,
Milton Keynes, UK

shaped subsequent literary-historical surveys (see, for instance, Mee 1998; Naik and Narayan 2004; Sunder Rajan 2011).

Finding an analogous rhetorical threshold-moment for the generation of authors associated with the era of India's economic liberalization is a little more difficult, but a strong contender might be Manmohan Singh's budget speech for 1991–1992. Singh later became Prime Minister, but at the time he was Finance Minister in P. V. Narasimha Rao's Congress government, and his speech, introducing his New Economic Policy, marked a turning point in the country's economic history. In response to a crisis in its balance of foreign payments, the Indian state had avoided payment default by taking on large structural readjustment loans from the IMF and the World Bank. These loans were secured on the promise that India would adopt a raft of neoliberal measures, opening up the country to foreign investment, restricting trade licences and reducing the public sector (see Ahmed 2011, p. 45). The reforms targeted the corruption of the old, protectionist business licence system (designed to shelter India from neo-colonial exploitation), and privileged the Indian consumer, whose interests had allegedly been neglected by the command-economy (Singh 1991, p. 3).

Manmohan Singh's speech, which runs to over 150 paragraphs and includes the usual taxation and budget figures, has little of the concision or rhetorical balance of Nehru's midnight address. It also reveals the Finance Minister's awareness that the new measures might be seen as a betrayal of the economic principles of the Nehru era. Singh thus presents the New Economic Policy as a continuation and development of the political trajectories of the past, rather than a break from these traditions. Hoping to temper the potentially damaging social impact of the free market, he warns his audience against the 'mindless and heartless consumerism we have borrowed from the affluent societies of the West' (ibid., p. 8) and recommends austerity and faith in M. K. Gandhi's concept of trusteeship as a social counterbalance. In his closing sentences, he returns to the rhetoric of Nehru's 'Tryst with Destiny' speech as if to co-opt its resonant moral authority:

> I do not minimise the difficulties that lie ahead on the long and arduous journey on which we have embarked. But as Victor Hugo once said, 'no power on earth can stop an idea whose time has come.' I suggest to this august House that the emergence of India as a major economic power in the world happens to be one such idea. Let the whole world hear it loud and clear. India is now wide awake. We shall prevail. We shall overcome. (1991, p. 31)

As Rana Dasgupta has noted in his perceptive reading of this speech, the closing reference to India being 'wide awake' extends the metaphors of Nehru's address confusingly, so as to suggest that the nation's awakening at independence was a precursor to its more energetic neoliberal 'awakening' (2014, p. 58). Yet the new awakening was also a kind of loss: a relinquishing of the grander social and political principles of the past in favour of a narrower, albeit more economically lucrative, vision of India's future (ibid., p. 59).

While the architects of India's liberalization reprised the rhetoric of the freedom struggle and the Nehru era to make their reforms acceptable, the first major Indian novel in English of the post-liberalization era, Vikram Seth's 1500-page epic *A Suitable Boy* (1993), also revisited the immediate post-independence period. Alongside its range and its narrative co-option of the techniques of nineteenth-century realism, Seth's novel presents a meticulous retrospective investment in the cultural and constitutional experience of the 1950s middle class—something Priyamvada Gopal describes as a 'a project in self-fashioning that had ramifications not only in the social and political spheres but also for familial structures, interpersonal relations, and structures of feeling and being in the world' (2009, p. 108). The novel's overarching plot-concern, the search by the genteel Mrs Rupa Mehra for a suitable husband for her daughter Lata, captures the contemporary expression of a middle-class identity as the culmination of nineteenth-century concepts of modernization balanced against other status-markers like caste and family. *A Suitable Boy* gains significance as an early example of 'post-liberalization' fiction when we read its retrospective appraisal of middle-class Indian mores, at a particular postcolonial moment, against the transformative contemporary context of economic reform in which it was written. Whether or not the figuration of history in Seth's novel is interpreted as postcolonial nostalgia (see Walder 2011), as a tragic pre-scripted belatedness (Mee 2004) or as an interrogation of the end of a secular consensus in India (Srivastava 2004), the fact that it revisits 1950s Indian middle-class culture at the cusp of its impending 'neoliberal' transformation (and deploys a reassuring 'readerly' prose as the historical antithesis of the unpredictable energies unleashed by globalization) says much about the uncertainties of the new economic dispensation.

To develop this reading of contemporary anglophone Indian fiction, it is necessary to review the social affiliations of the novel in greater detail. The origins of the modern novel are conventionally associated with the rise of the European middle class in the eighteenth and nineteenth centuries, mainly because of the form's affinity for modes of spiritual-economic accounting, mercantile individualism (Watt 1963) and a 'disenchanted' realism (Eagleton 2005). However, as a global postcolonial form, the novel has long since exceeded these narrow historical associations (see Moretti 2007), and the novel's literary-cultural field, as Pierre Bourdieu defines it, has taken on a complexity and autonomy that means it cannot be reduced to the direct 'reflective' expression of a particular social group (Bourdieu 1993). Yet in the case of the Indian novel in English, there is some justification for identifying the form as distinctively middle-class; certainly, the association of a group of key Indian novelists[1] of the 1980s and early '90s with elite institutions such as New Delhi's St Stephen's College (Bhattacharjea and Chatterji 2000) invites claims that, in its recent history, the Indian-English novel has tended to refract an upper caste, liberal-cosmopolitan sensibility[2] (even as the form has fostered sophisticated forms of auto-critique). Moreover, the mere fact that the novels discussed here are written in English (a middle-class *lingua franca* and the more exclusive of the Republic's two 'official' languages) means that their consumption has always been restricted to a small proportion of the Indian population (current figures put the percentage of fluent English speakers at around 100 million, or 10 % of the population), and a relatively expensive pricing policy has also limited their mass appeal.

For many commentators, the internationally marketed Indian-English novel, which became really successful in the 1980s, is inextricably linked not only to Indian readership but to the literary tastes and critical-theoretical priorities of readers in the global North, with whom cosmopolitan Indian authors have entered into a sophisticated cultural dialogue (see Huggan 2001). The success of diaspora writers in purveying an image of India *globally*, and the process by which these images constitute a reflexive 're-orientalizing' of India (Lau and Mendes 2011), which resonates with pre-existing discourses about the subcontinent, have further complicated the representational politics of the contemporary novel in English. Against this history of transnational endorsement and local expansion, fierce debates

---

[1] This group included, among others, Rukun Advani, Upamanyu Chatterjee, Amitav Ghosh, Mukul Kesavan, Anurag Mathur, Makarand Paranjape, I. Allan Sealy and Shashi Tharoor.

[2] Leela Gandhi suggests that 'most "Stephanian" novels are boringly—if skilfully—indicative of the sensibility through which the newly élite Indian middle-classes recognize their community in the nation. Very few challenge the limits of this sensibility—fewer still refuse the postcolonial middle classes the narcissistic pleasure of self-recognition' ('Some Notes on the Rise of the Stephanian Novel' in Bhattacharjea and Chatterji 2000, p. 157).

continue over the significance of literature in India's other scheduled languages, and by extension, over the relative rewards and recognitions open to Indian novelists writing from marginal regional, economic and linguistic contexts (see Sadana 2012). I will not rehearse these debates further here. Rather, in this chapter I want to approach the Indian–English novel after 1991 as an evolving literary mode, as a reflexive type of symbolic capital, and as a literary form operating in, or in relation to, India's 'structurally adjusted' fields of economic and political power.

The questions India's new economic order poses for literary critics are insistent, but they have not yet been comprehensively addressed: in post-liberalization fictions, how have the middle-class associations and institutional contexts of the novel been challenged? Does the contemporary Indian-English novel still envisage its implied reader, and its wider audiences, in the same ways? And if 'international' anglophone Indian fiction established its cosmopolitan aesthetics and many of its formal conventions before 1991, has the economic transformation of India necessitated new formal and representational techniques—in kinds of realism, for instance? In view of the cross-fertilizations of political rhetoric and literary allusion noted above, a final question (one which a lasting critical interest in nationhood and identity politics has occluded) centres on how the post-liberalization Indian-English novel presents and re-narrates middle-class concerns as the collective embodiment of 'an idea whose time has come.'

The first three texts discussed here all achieved international critical recognition and cultural prestige as 'literary' fiction: Arundhati Roy's *The God of Small Things* (1997), Aravind Adiga's *The White Tiger* (2008) and Manju Kapur's *Custody* (2011). In the pages below, I will argue that the formal developments discernible in these works encode larger, more complex changes in the contours of middle-class identity albeit from within the particular caste/class genealogies of their authors (and in relation to the exigencies of 'the literary field'). However, as noted above, any account of contemporary Indian-English fiction must acknowledge the recent robust growth in the domestic Indian publishing market for anglophone genre fiction. The second part of this chapter will concentrate, therefore, on two popular novels by the best-selling author Chetan Bhagat: *Five Point Someone* (2004) and *Half Girlfriend* (2014). My analysis thus ranges between the 'literary' and popular while acknowledging the constructed (and increasingly blurred) nature of these markers of taste. Not only are these distinctions important for how we approach contemporary fiction as a type of cultural capital; the rise of popular genre fiction alongside literary novels also poses pressing questions about the former's political-discursive potential. Stuart Hall's work on popular culture offers a critical frame here in its insistence that popular literary forms like genre-fiction are rarely simply 'escapist' or hegemonic. For Hall, the popular is, rather, an agonistic entity: 'popular culture is one of the sites where [… a] struggle for and against a culture of the powerful is engaged: it is also the stake to be won or lost in that struggle. It is the arena of consent and resistance' (1994, p. 466).

*

Before we further investigate the fictions cited above, the sweeping impact of the New Economic Policy on India's middle class must be assessed. The assumption that a homogenized, expanding middle class has been the privileged beneficiary of economic liberalization in India since 1991 has become something of an article of faith amongst journalists and political analysts. However, a more considered assessment reveals that across a spectrum of educated, managerial, professional and white-collar workers in India, the forces of liberalization and globalization have been experienced variously: as the private sector has grown, there has been both a widening of opportunities and the generation of wealth, but also an increased competition for jobs and housing as older public sector-occupations and career-paths become less certain (Ganguly-Scrase and Scrase 2009, p. 3). These changes have not only led to new internal differentiations and fractures within the middle class, but have also arguably brought about a greater circulation of different forms of economic, symbolic and cultural capital. Changes in the middle class have been shaped, too, by more gradual shifts in the citizenship status of diaspora communities, and a greater mobility between middle-class families resident in India and overseas (Brosius 2010, p. 28).

There is a strong sense among cultural commentators that liberalization has, at the very least, fostered new middle-class alignments. The emergence of a dynamic private sector in India, employing skilled white-collar professionals, has added new strata to India's middle class. Alongside an 'old middle class' of secular professionals who dominate administration and education, and tend to see themselves as the keepers and arbiters of Indian cultural values against public, globalized culture, a 'new middle class' that is likely to work in emergent sectors such as the media, technology and commerce. This 'new middle class', which can be further differentiated between the elite of a transnational knowledge economy and those working in business processing outsourcing jobs (see Radhakrishnan 2011, p. 43), increasingly generates and consumes India's public culture, and is often seen as the driving power behind India's economic growth. We must also note, with Radhakrishnan, that 'older' and 'newer' middle classes are not always as distinct as this model suggests, and 'most of those who make up what has been dubbed India's "new" middle class had parents who were part of the "old" one' (2011, p. 42). A third layer within the middle class is a large aspirational *petit bourgeoisie*, which has an appreciably smaller 'provincial' stock of educational, economic and cultural capital, but nevertheless aspires to the rewards of liberalization through a combination of ambition, hard work, education (including a proficiency in English) and an identification with the values of the neoliberal project.[3]

While I want to keep this schema in mind, the process of categorizing class in this way is rarely comprehensive or exact, and involves the consideration of a combination of factors including occupation, education and income, as well as, in India, caste and ethnicity (see Béteille 2001, p. 77–83). Indeed, it may be more appropriate to think of 'middle-classness' in contemporary India as a self-defining process rather than as a social category (Liechty 2003, p. 20), an approach that allows for a sense of the performativity of social identity and conveys the experience of being middle class as 'an aspirational way of being' (Donner 2011: 13). This dynamic model of class is adopted by social commentators like Leela Fernandes, who notes that India's new middle class is not simply a *product* of liberalization, although it is undoubtedly shaped by contemporary economic factors. Instead, she suggests that it is the *mutually constitutive* connection between liberalization and India's middle class that is new, so that being middle-class in present-day India involves the continuous production of 'a distinctive social and political identity that represents and lays claim to the benefits of liberalisation' (Fernandes 2006, p. xviii).

Fernandes's key point is that India's 'new' middle class now represents citizenship in ways that it never could before. Instead of the hydro-electric schemes and tractors that figured national progress in the Nehru era, the contemporary symbols of progress are consumer goods such as TVs and cellphones (2006, p. xv). Similarly, 'While earlier state socialist ideologies tended to depict workers or rural villagers as the archetypal objects

---

[3] For a full discussion of the different strata of the middle class discussed here, see Dwyer 2000, p. 91.

of development, such ideologies now compete with mainstream national political discourses that increasingly portray urban middle class consumers as the representative citizens of liberalizing India'(p. xv). As others have noticed, 'more than ever before, Indian society looks at itself as middle class-centred' (Jaffrelot and van der Veer 2008, p. 19)—the operative verb is apt here as an increased access to television now literally enables Indian society to 'look' at itself, aspire to (and question) a globalized version of consumer-affluence (Derné 2008, p. 32; Rajagopal 2001).

The new currency of middle-class values, anticipated so ambivalently in Manmohan Singh's warning against heartless consumerism, finds a fictional expression in the pro-liberalization perspective of another novel about the search for a 'suitable' marriage partner, Swati Kaushal's *Piece of Cake* (2004). Published a decade after Seth's *A Suitable Boy*, Kaushal's novel offers an intriguing comparison with the latter work: written by an Indian author based in the global North, *Piece of Cake* is similarly invested in India's middle class, but in a contemporary rather than a historical setting. (Seth's long-awaited sequel to *A Suitable Boy* promises a similar historical update.) However, Kaushal's work is also profoundly different from Seth's: as a version of popular chick lit, her novel claims none of the cultural status of Seth's writing, and while the plot of *A Suitable Boy* involves a heroine whose (potential) husband's career in manufacturing must be reconciled with white-collar middle-class identity, in Kaushal's narrative the heroine, Minal, is directly involved in business herself, and works for a multinational food company marketing western-style cakes in India. In place of Lata's courtship in Seth's fiction, *Piece of Cake* delivers a fast-paced narrative in Minal's confidently acquisitive American English.

> Sorry Mom, no deal. Sure I want to get married but … I think I'll find my own man, thank you … Someone who'll bring me flowers and buy me diamonds and laugh and flirt and throw parties and take happy pictures on our overseas vacations with a six-mega-pixel digital camera. No postcolonial hangover, no quixotic desire to reform the world, just a healthy wholesome twenty-first century pursuit of wealth and prosperity. And a really classy car. (p. 6)

Like other variants of the chick lit genre, Kaushal's novel resists any overt political or social commentary through a continuous confessional self-parody, and here consumer capitalism appears not as an economic apparatus but as a 'healthy wholesome' need. Minal's dismissal of an outdated 'postcolonial hangover' thus chimes with Pavan Varma's insight that, with liberalization, 'material wants were […] suddenly severed from any notion of guilt' (Varma 2006, p. 82), and hints at how the contemporary audience for Indian-English fiction has diversified and changed as well as revealing how neoliberalism has become embedded in India's public discourses (see Chowdury 2011). Admittedly, global commerce also shapes local middle-class identity in *A Suitable Boy*, but in Seth's work it is the more utilitarian shoe industry, 'Praha' (modelled on the worker-orientated Czech multinational, Bata), not cakes and cookies, that enshrines a kind of modernity in Haresh's challenge to the low-caste associations of shoe-making. In contrast, the politics of Kaushal's novel is subsumed in the ultimate consumer product—confectionery—and figured in its protagonist: a career businesswoman, who, at the same time as she claims a space for women in the Indian corporate workplace, shrugs off the obligations of any wider postcolonial political responsibility.

Literary Fiction Post-Liberalization

The macro-economic changes put in motion by the Narasimha Rao government did not become strongly evident in India until the millennium (Corbridge et al. 2013, p. 129). Yet even if we take a relatively early post-liberalization work such as Arundhati Roy's *The God of Small Things* (1997) as a case in point, the impact of economic reform is already apparent. In the publicity surrounding Roy's Booker Prize win, and the subsequent critical readings of her work (see Tickell 2007), an often overlooked detail was Roy's careful gauging of the impact of global corporate forces on her rural South Indian setting. This social critique is a correlative of the novel's chronological structure, which alternates between the late 1960s and the early 1990s, and thus presents a 'before-and-after' account of the arrival of satellite television and package tourism in the Kerala backwaters. One of Roy's characters, Baby Kochamma, a spinster aunt disappointed in love, embodies these infrastructural changes when she abandons her 'fierce, bitter' garden, and becomes a recluse, addicted to watching the newly available television channels: 'She presided over the World in her drawing room on satellite TV … in Ayemenem, where once the loudest sound had been a musical bus horn, now whole wars, famines, picturesque massacres and Bill Clinton could be summoned up like servants' (Roy 1997, p. 27). When read against the novel's figurative emphasis on the blindness of caste-prejudice, references to television's blinkering effect look forward to a selectivity in India's broadcasting, which now disproportionately features middle-class lifestyles (Drèze and Sen 2014, p. 266).

As the imaginative lives of the inhabitants of Ayemenem suddenly turn inwards, towards the images channelled into their TV sets from orbiting satellites, their local economy also changes with increasing tourism in the region (which refashions local culture as commodity), and in the short-term profits generated by Indian migrant labour in the Persian Gulf states. *The God of Small Things* registers these and other changes—such as the environmental degradation of Kerala's rivers (see Mukherjee 2010)—as subtle negative adjustments in the temper of the local space of the narrative in a way that recalls Arjun Appadurai's account of the social constitution of the neighbourhood. In Appadurai's view, a considerable work of narrativization, associational recognition and a shared history is required in 'the production of locality' (Appadurai 1996, p. 188). And in globalizing settings like 1990s Kerala, the necessary production and reproduction of the neighbourhood is hampered by the inherent instability of the social relationships generated there. In these places, Roy's response to liberalization thus involves a careful critical tracking of the sometimes uncanny effects of multinational capital incursion as the locality of her setting becomes a *translocality*, reshaped by its economic value for the state and its position at a confluence of global capital flows.

On a formal level, Roy similarly reduces the scale of the 'national epic' and subtly recalibrates an influential magical realist style (Rushdie's literary-aesthetic hallmark), compressing it into a form of psychological realism that conveys the linguistically playful perspectives of her child-protagonists (formal developments which have been matched by Roy's personal statements, in which she distances herself from the preceding generation of 'St Stephen's writers'; Bhattacharjea and Chatterji 2000, p. xvii). If we think of *The God of Small Things* not as Roy's only novel to date, but as part of the continuum of her fictional and non-fiction writing, then its most telling feature, alongside its local environmental concerns, is its critique of caste- and gender inequalities in the fated, caste-challenging love affair between Ammu, a Syrian-Christian divorcee, and Velutha, an 'untouchable' carpenter. As other chapters in this volume show, the slow-burning Maoist insurgency supported by *adivasi* and *dalit* groups in central India, detailed in Roy's recent journalism, is perhaps the most troubling political counterpart to India's economic rise, and throws a long shadow over the visible affluence of the middle class. In *The God of Small Things*, the origins of this insurgency are registered in Velutha's possible Naxalite sympathies, and traces of gender- and caste violence persist in the mute psychological injuries which scar the adult protagonists, and which are unresolved by the bigger economic changes occurring around them.

While Roy's novel could be said to mount an early critique of liberalization's local effects, Aravind Adiga's *The White Tiger* (2008), also a Man Booker Prize winner, goes much further in interrogating India's new economic order. The novel is narrated as a series of emails written to the Chinese premier by Balram Halwai, the son of a rickshaw operator and inheritor of all the poverty and stifled opportunity conventionally associated with rural Bihar (the state is depicted as a Conradian 'darkness'— a rejoinder to the 'India Shining' rhetoric of the early 2000s). Through a combination of luck and cunning, Balram becomes a servant for one of the landowner families of his village and eventually lands a job in New Delhi as driver-factotum for the landlord's son, Mr Ashok. After narrowly escaping being framed for a car accident caused by his employer's wife, Balram murders Mr Ashok and steals his money and identity, escaping to start a new life as an entrepreneur in the tech-hub of Bangalore. Adiga's novel thus presents a harshly disillusioning insider-view of India's new middle class, narrated with all the satire of Swift's 'Directions for Servants'. As Adiga's anti-hero models his highly unreliable narrative on the pirated business self-help books pedalled at traffic intersections in India's cities, his story morphs into a nightmarish version of this new entrepreneurial market logic.

In the New India, Adiga's caricaturing prose-style implies, social and political realities are so extreme that only a sustained form of 'ironic' or exaggerated realism can represent them. The objectivity implied by realism is also challenged by Balram's narrative opinion that the state's public discourses are inverted: 'you can take almost anything you hear about the country from the prime minister and turn it upside down and then you will have the truth about that thing' (Adiga 2008, p. 15). A conventional effect of realism is that it suppresses or effaces its own ideological function (Barthes 1989) and therefore invites the reader to ascribe a specious authenticity to it. Thus, for some reviewers, it is exactly Adiga's manipulation of the real that stands out as a mode of social critique: 'It is precisely because Adiga's is a strange, often disorientating mess of a book that it gives the most penetrating insight into a certain aspect of postliberalization India that, for good or bad, throws notions of the "authentic" or real into disarray' (Masterson 2012, p. 59). Part of this disruption of the real in *The White Tiger* involves a fabular inflection of the 'disenchanted' realist mode of the novel. To manipulate literary realism is not only to question the 'given-ness' of the world, it is also a challenge to assumptions about objectivity, rationality, empirical truth and the paternalistic engagements of older forms of social realism that structure that world view (see Mohapatra 2014). The predatory society presented through Adiga's 'tigerish' beast-fable can thus be interpreted as an expressive formal response to the war-like commercial drive which some commentators have attributed to India's new urban elites (Deb 2011, p. 56).

Here, as in Roy's novel, the violence of social inequality is shadowed by the possibility of 'Naxalite' violence, when Balram encounters a pavement bookseller who warns him that India is on the verge of revolution. I have argued elsewhere that Balram's violence against his employer can be seen as analogous to a revolutionary levelling impulse, but articulated, ironically, as the logic of entrepreneurial competition and self-fashioning (see Tickell 2015a). For Megha Anwer, the ironic undermining of every ideological position in the novel achieves a curiously depoliticized effect, which can be read as 'classic middle class anti-politicism' (Anwer 2014, p. 312). Yet the class-satire of Adiga's novel begs further consideration when we realize that the targets for Adiga's socio-economic critique are the old *zamindar*-class and its local government allies, and the so-called new middle class, presented as the metropolitan scions of landed money. A question that remains is whether Adiga's depiction of the 'vulgar' lack of cultural capital shown by Mr Ashok and his wife (who decorate their apartment in 'Buckingham Towers' with giant portraits of their Pomeranian dogs) effectively co-opts the reader in a condemnation of both the new middle class and its aspiring hangers-on, like Balram, while effacing the complicity of the 'St Stephanian' elite (which appears nowhere in the novel) in India's present power structures.

For other contemporary authors, such as Manju Kapur, India's economic ascent has not so much challenged the representational capacity of the realist novel, as it has resulted in a greater proliferation of narrative options and possibilities for Indian authors (Tickell 2015b). Some of these are explored in *Custody* (2011), her fifth novel, which returns to Kapur's favoured terrain of the micro-dynamics of marriage and family relationships, but does so to reflect on the scramble for India by foreign multinationals after 1991. As Kapur suggests in an interview: 'At the risk of sounding like a political scientist, *Custody* was inspired by globalisation and economic liberalisation. Who owns you? As far as most Indian women and children are concerned, a man does. But that's changing' (Kidd 2011). In *Custody*, the motif of the socially unacceptable romance, which Kapur uses elsewhere to explore forms of gendered self-realization, counterpoints the operation of global capital when the marriage of a naïve young business executive, Raman, is threatened by the arrival in India of his new boss, Ashok Khanna, who immediately starts to make advances towards Raman's beautiful but vapid wife, Shagun. In Ashok and Shagun's ensuing affair, and the exhausting, protracted divorce case and custody battle for Raman and Shagun's children that follows, the question of 'who owns you?' is posed repeatedly, redefining subtle familial identities and relationships and brokering them, increasingly, as possessions.

In her depiction of Ashok as a ruthlessly adapted corporate animal, Kapur's prose edges close to political satire. Ashok is motivated by a near-evangelical adherence to 'The Brand', the globally marketed soft drink he promotes in India. His adulterous conquest of Shagun, the reader suspects, involves a similar commodity fetishism. While in Adiga's novel, entrepreneurial individualism is presented as a homicidal force which can be directed back against the middle class as terrible violence, in *Custody* its destructive effects are primarily emotional. And at the same time as the middle-class family seems to implode or fragment through its encounter with global capital in these texts, the state or para-state institutions that operate as a correlative of family life, schools and nurseries, are similarly infiltrated, and subtly changed, by market forces.

In Kapur's novel, as in the preceding texts discussed here, the Indian experience of globalization cannot be mapped onto simple, increasingly dated binaries like tradition and modernity, although a manipulation of such concepts is implicit in liberalization's cultural politics. As Rachel Dwyer argues, 'new middle class modernity is not just about consumerism but is complicated and ambivalent, seeking to view religion and morality as part of tradition, whereas they are often part of this very modernity' (Dwyer 2011, p. 188). What makes *Custody* effective as a literary treatment of India's economic contemporaneity, and lends it an intriguingly postcolonial angle, is its attention to the lingering historical continuities between the imperial custodial ownership of India and the claims of business. These continuities are apparent in the networked power that allows Ashok, as an old boy, to secure a place for Shagun's son in an elite public school. India's long postcolonial trajectory is displaced by the distinctly colonial rituals of the school, and in his guise as corporate trouble-shooter, Kapur figures Ashok as a latter-day incarnation of Edmund Burke's colonial 'birds of [prey and] passage', whose interventions in Indian civil society are acquisitive and partisan rather than responsive to the structures he encounters. More broadly, the novel tests the resilience of certain aspects of Indian middle-class culture and its values in the face of the more visible profit-motives of the post-liberalization era.

POPULAR FICTION AND THE NEW INDIA

The author Chetan Bhagat has been so commercially successful in India (sales of his first six novels have reached seven million copies) that his first novel, *Five Point Someone* (2004), is now regarded as a turning point for the domestic publishing industry.[4] Although there has long been a readership for anglophone popular fiction in India, Bhagat's 2004 debut revealed new commercial possibilities for cheap mass-produced fiction in English, and introduced a novelist who seemed able to tap directly into the concerns and cultural expectations of a post-liberalization generation. However, Bhagat's success has also generated criticism from more 'literary' writers, who self-identify through an artistic ambivalence towards the marketplace (see Gelder 2004, p. 26), and represent what Bourdieu calls the inverted relation of cultural and economic value operating in the 'field of restricted production' (Bourdieu 1993, p. 119). In my view, this opposition overlies deeper differences of taste between a cosmopolitan, transnational middle class, for whom liberalization has brought benefits and opportunities, and more modest sections of the middle class who are still 'mostly at the receiving end of globalisation' (Derné 2008, p. 128).

Bhagat's impact is due, in no small part, to his ability to open up the anglophone novel to new audiences *within* India. A considerable number of younger, less linguistically confident English language readers (identified disingenuously as 'the CB family' on his website) consume his work—readers who would not normally buy highbrow Indian-English fiction (see Dhaliwal 2014). His novels are routinely adapted for Bollywood and, as Bhagat himself alleges, literary competitors are not as important for him as the various media formats (blockbuster films, TV shows, apps and video games) with which his high-grossing crossover novels contend. In response to his detractors, Bhagat has repeatedly claimed that his fiction is not meant to be 'literary' and, as Priya Joshi has suggested, he contests a literary 'economy of prestige', in which the highbrow prevails over the popular,

---

[4] For further details, see Suman Gupta's chapter "Contemporary Indian Commercial Fiction in English" in this volume.

by claiming that in spite of its lack of cultural capital, his fiction endures in his reader's love rather than their critical admiration (Joshi 2015, p. 316).

Bhagat's early novels can be described as a kind of 'situation fiction' since they incorporate the same fast-paced, self-conscious dialogue, laconic irony, light romance plotting, observational humour and adolescent fear of social embarrassment that have made sitcoms like *Friends* such an international export. (Bollywood buddy films like *Dil Chahta Hai* (2001) also provide an important template.) The 'situations' of Bhagat's novels are recognizably the aspirational spaces of India's middle class: the elite IIT colleges (Indian Institute(s) of Technology), call-centres and tech outsourcing operations that gained such notoriety in the early 2000s as the front line of India's global marketization.[5] In subsequent works, Bhagat has tackled social issues such as inter-regional marriage (*2 States*) and communal conflict (*The Three Mistakes of My Life*); as a columnist in English and Hindi newspapers, he presents himself as a vocal spokesperson for a somewhat younger post-liberalization generation, and espouses a faith in Indian national culture that his more urbane literary counterparts have long since disparaged.

Five Point Someone (2004), Bhagat's first novel, is a comic exposé of the fierce competitiveness of the Indian IIT college network and features three undergraduate protagonists, Hari, Ryan and Alok, whose prospects are seemingly blighted because of their low 'five point something' grade point average. In a foreshadowing of the reflexive transaction with non-fiction genres we encountered earlier in the management-guide idiom of *The White Tiger*, Bhagat's IIT campus novel presents itself, initially, as the antithesis to educational self-help guides in its defiant subtitle: 'what not to do at IIT!' Yet the novel is far from a comprehensive subversion of the high-pressure educational cultures it depicts. The three friends of *Five Point Someone* rebel against the soulless competition for grades at their IIT college by devising a radical solution: to duplicate their assignments and 'co-operate 2 dominate', but their collectivizing strategy is ultimately shown to be unfulfilling and becomes a statement of their shared humanity rather than a challenge to the system. In fact, the novel's less confrontational message (one that Bhagat echoes journalistically) is that India would be better served by the IITs through a cultivation of students' originality and creativity rather than a slavish 'mugging' for grades.

---

[5] The settings of Bhagat's novels, and the metanarrative of youthful ambition they embody, can be tellingly contrasted with the claustrophobic pre-liberalization vision of bureaucratic careers in works such as *English, August* (1988) by the St Stephen's alumnus, Upamanyu Chatterjee (see Dalmia and Sadana 2012, p. 140).

The novel's politics is thus subtly balanced: Bhagat maintains enough critical and comic distance from the competitive culture of IIT to question, very gently, the middle-class equation of academic success with fulfilment, yet he also contains this criticism and provides an unthreatening aspirational endorsement of IIT's professionalism for more conventional readers. As my earlier reference to Stuart Hall's work suggests, *Five Point Someone* can thus be located as operating within the social fractures of post-liberalization: at one level the novel encodes a comic 'resistant' subversion of hierarchy and an attack on a culture of entitlement; on another, his fiction eagerly reproduces the corporatist ethos of Bhagat's own career-background in multinational finance, and embraces a populist, progressive outlook. The notable discursive effect of this balancing in *Five Point Someone* is its avoidance of politics. In contrast to the engaged political cultures on other Indian university campuses, Bhagat's fictional students are strangely unconcerned about events such as the first Gulf War, and initially 'cheer on America' because 'most of our foreign aid came from rich American firms and quite a large percentage of our alumni went on scholarship there and for jobs' (Bhagat 2004, p. 52). In the end, Bhagat's student narrator concludes passively that 'it was impossible to take sides … and it was all pointless for us anyway' (ibid.).

Bhagat revisits the campus setting in *Half Girlfriend* (2014), and here again Hall's insight into the double movement of containment and resistance offered by popular culture is pertinent. *Half Girlfriend*'s protagonist, Madhav Jha, who hails from small-town Bihar, has managed to get into Delhi's elite St Stephen's College on the strength of his ability as a basketball player, but constantly struggles against the stigma of his provincial origins. He falls in love with a fellow student, the wealthy and effortlessly beautiful Riya, and as the novel's romance plot unfolds it becomes apparent that here the campus setting is being used to figure the exclusion of the new middle class from the entitled position afforded by fluency in English. Madhav enjoys Bhojpuri films and Hindi music, but nervously conceals these markers of lower-class taste from other St Stephen's students, and when he tries to talk to Riya's sophisticated friends his spoken English is met with incredulous hilarity:

> 'Would you like to order anything?' I said. The three girls froze and then began to laugh. It dawned on me that they were laughing at me. My English had sounded like this: 'Vood you laik to aarder anything?' I didn't know this was such a cardinal sin. (p. 27)

The often comic class commentary in Bhagat's novel is subtly calibrated so that Madhav and Riya's romance is not so outlandish as to be unreal. Madhav, in the tradition of the nineteenth-century English novel, is not a true subaltern and is redeemed by coming from an illustrious branch of the Bihari aristocracy fallen on hard times. (Moreover, his chosen 'foreign' sport, basketball, balances some of his parochial regionalism.) By being Bihari and bad at English, Madhav's viewpoint sensitizes the reader to issues of class mobility but he is also allowed a legitimacy through his background (again, the caste and class tensions that we might expect to have shaped Madhav's background as a Bihari landowner are notably absent).

Half Girlfriend conceals a further metanarrative in its campus setting, because of the association, noted earlier, of St Stephen's with the elitism of the anglophone Indian novel of the 1980s and 1990s. Bhagat negotiates this literary legacy, and like his deprecating comments about his own literary credentials, his novel *about* St Stephen's is evidently not a 'St Stephen's novel'; instead, it trespasses provocatively on the site of this more highbrow literary tradition. The internal mirroring effect of this tactic is complemented by the framing authorial appearances and metafictional references that Bhagat works into his writing, so that when Riya helps Madhav prepare a speech in English, she gives him a ten-point plan for fluency and recommends that he read 'simple English novels, like, the one by that writer, what's his name, Chetan Bhagat' (2014, p. 149).

The narrative moves beyond the campus and becomes another kind of novel when Madhav and Riya graduate and lose touch: Madhav returns to Bihar to help in a school his mother runs, and unexpectedly meets Riya again when she arrives in Patna to work for a confectionery multinational (the parallels between Riya and Swati Kaushal's Minal are strong here). Their relationship is rekindled and the speech she helps Madhav write becomes pivotal to the plot as it is delivered to a delegation headed by none other than Bill Gates, who is visiting India with his NGO, the Gates Foundation. By overcoming his fears about speaking in English, and successfully communicating his 'vision' for the school, Madhav wins Gates's sympathy and financial support, and eventually travels to New York on a United Nations internship in order to search for his former 'half girlfriend' who has vanished mysteriously. The novel ends cinematically, with Madhav sprinting through the snow-bound streets of Manhattan to be reunited with Riya, who has gone there to follow her own dream of becoming a singer.

It is in its latter sections that Bhagat's novel switches from the pointed social critique of his language theme to an endorsement of more conventional ideas about India's post-liberalization future. Where the representatives of the Indian state are corrupt and risk-averse, his work suggests, the only solution is to bypass government and forge partnerships between philanthropic capital (produced by IT monopolies) and local stakeholders. This familiar neoliberal strategy, David Harvey reminds us, allows a previously state-supplied public good to be neglected and its importance as a commons to be ignored (Harvey 2012, p. 80). In *Half Girlfriend* the future of Madhav's school thus depends on its remaking as a (neo-colonial) site for foreign investment, so that it eventually becomes part of a tourism initiative: 'Madhav explained how they had started rural school tours which included a stay in the *haveli*. People came from all over the world allowing the school to earn revenue in dollars' (2014, p. 258). In its trajectory of Delhi–Bihar–New York the narrative works towards similar ends, enabling the reader to imagine him/herself in the guise of the transnational middle class. Thus, in direct contrast to the native informants of earlier Indian anglophone fiction, who 'explained' India to non-Indian readers, Bhagat's writing does the opposite: introducing his implied Indian reader to international travel and the 'experience' of America as a component of middle-class cultural capital: 'It was my first trip outside India and the first thing I noticed was the colour of the sky … the second thing that hit me was the silence. The taxi sped on a road filled with traffic. However, nobody honked, not even at signals' (p. 215). Elsewhere American coffee-cup sizes and mobile phone plans are detailed with painstaking care, allowing Bhagat's readers the vicarious experience of being global consumers.

The complex political currents that flow beneath the surface of Bhagat's misleadingly shallow fictions show that a neoliberal consumer-culture is now an idea whose time has come not only in the more obvious media of television and the internet; it has also arrived and is now being tested in the previously sequestered medium of the anglophone novel. As Indian fiction in English reaches a much wider audience *in* India, the novel can no longer co-opt transnational or cosmopolitan readers (including Indian diasporic elites) in a critique of the faceless homogenization or the perceived vulgarities of post-liberalization commercialism in South Asia. As we have seen, highbrow postcolonial literary texts have carefully registered the damaging social and political effects of globalization, but contemporary anglophone fictions, such as Bhagat's, show how literary politics is diversifying and tilting away from a default critique of the Indian state's neoliberal project. Like the populist rise of forms of identity politics, which has reshaped Indian democracy so comprehensively, this diversification presents public middle-class culture with a certain 'commercial' narrowing of its possibilities. However, it also represents an exciting new stage in the history of the Indian novel—one in which the form starts to speak in new, previously ignored voices.

WORKS CITED

Adiga, A. (2008). *The white tiger*. London: Atlantic.
Ahmed, W., Kundu, A., & Peet, R. (Eds.). (2011). *India's new economic policy: A critical analysis*. New York: Routledge.
Akbar, A. (2011, March 11), *Custody* by Manju Kapur [Review]. *Independent on Sunday*.
Anwer, M. (2014). Tigers of an-other jungle: Adiga's tryst with subaltern politics. *Journal of Postcolonial Writing, 50*(3), 304–315.
Appadurai, A. (1996). *Modernity at large: Cultural dimensions of globalisation*. Minneapolis: University of Minnesota Press.
Barthes, R. (1989). The reality effect. In R. Howard (Ed.), *The rustle of language* (pp. 141–148). Berkeley: University of California Press.
Béteille, A. (2001). The social character of the Indian middle class. In I. Ahmad & H. Reifeld (Eds.), *Middle class values in India and Western Europe* (pp. 73–85). New Delhi: Social Science Press.
Bhagat, C. (2004). *Five point someone: What not to do at IIT*. New Delhi: Rupa.
Bhagat, C. (2014). *Half girlfriend*. New Delhi: Rupa.
Bhattacharjea, A., & Chatterji, L. (2000). *The fiction of St Stephen's*. Delhi: Ravi Dayal.
Bourdieu, P. (1993). *The field of cultural production: Essays on art and literature* (R. Johnson, Ed.) Cambridge: Polity.
Brosius, C. (2010). *India's middle class: New forms of urban leisure, consumption and prosperity*. New Delhi: Routledge.
Corbridge, S., Harriss, J., & Jeffrey, C. (2013). *India today: Economy, politics and society*. Cambridge: Polity.
Chowdhury, K. (2011). *The new India: Citizenship, subjectivity, and economic liberalization*. New York: Palgrave Macmillan.
Dalmia, V., & Sadana, R. (Eds.). (2012). *The Cambridge companion to modern Indian culture*. Cambridge: Cambridge University Press.
Dasgupta, R. (2014). *Capital: A portrait of twenty-first century Delhi*. Edinburgh: Canongate.

Deb, S. (2011). *The beautiful and the damned: Life in the new India*. London: Penguin Viking.
Derné, S. (2008). *Globalisation on the ground: Media and the transformation of culture, class, and gender in India*. New Delhi: Sage.
Dhaliwal, N. (2014, April 24). Chetan Bhagat: Bollywood's favourite author. *The Guardian* [Online]. Accessed 21 Jan 2015. Available from http://www.theguardian.com/books/2014/apr/24/chetan-bhagat-interview-bollywood-favourite-author-india
Donner, H. (Ed.). (2011). *Being middle-class in India: A way of life*. London: Routledge.
Drèze, J., & Sen, A. (2014). *An uncertain glory: India and its contradictions*. London: Penguin.
Dwyer, R. (2000). *All you want is money, all you need is love: Sexuality and romance in modern India*. London: Cassell.
Dwyer, R. (2011). Zara Hatke ('somewhat different'): The new middle classes and the changing forms of Hindi cinema. In H. Donner (Ed.), *Being middle-class in India: A way of life* (pp. 184–209). London: Routledge.
Eagleton, T. (2005). *The English novel: An introduction*. Oxford: Blackwell.
Fernandes, L. (2006). *India's new middle class democratic politics in an era of economic reform*. Minneapolis/London: University of Minnesota Press.
Ganguly-Scrase, R., & Scrase, T. J. (2009). *Globalisation and the middle classes in India: the social and cultural impact of neoliberal reforms*. London: Routledge.
Gelder, K. (2004). *Popular fiction: The logics and practices of a literary field*. Abingdon: Routledge.
Gopal, P. (2009). *The Indian English novel: Nation, history, and narration*. Oxford: Oxford University Press.
Hall, S. (1994). Notes on deconstructing 'the popular'. In J. Storey (Ed.), *Cultural theory and popular culture: A reader* (pp. 455–466). Hemel Hempstead: Harvester Wheatsheaf.
Harvey, D. (2012). *Rebel cities: From the right to the city to the urban revolution*. London: Verso.
Huggan, G. (2001). *The postcolonial exotic: Marketing the margins*. London: Routledge.
Jaffrelot, C., & van der Veer, P. (2008). *Patterns of middle class consumption in India and China*. New Delhi: Sage.
Joshi, P. (2015). Chetan Bhagat: Remaking the novel in India. In U. Anjaria (Ed.), *A history of the Indian novel in English* (pp. 310–323). New York: Cambridge University Press.
Kapur, M. (2011). *Custody*. London: Faber and Faber.
Kaushal, S. (2004). *Piece of cake*. New Delhi: Penguin.
Khilnani, S. (2003). Gandhi and Nehru: The uses of English. In A. K. Mehrotra (Ed.), *A history of Indian literature in English* (pp. 135–156). London: C. Hurst & Co.

Kidd, J. (2011, March 13). Manju Kapur: Pride and prejudices. *The Independent* [Online]. Accessed 25 May 2015. Available from http://www.independent.co.uk/arts-entertainment/books/features/manju-kapur-pride-and-prejudices-2240299.html

Lau, L., & Mendes, A. (Eds.). (2011). *Re-orientalism and South Asian identity politics: The oriental other within*. London: Routledge.

Liechty, M. (2003). *Suitably modern: Making middle-class culture in a new consumer society*. Princeton: Princeton University Press.

Masterson, J. (2012). Aravind Adiga: The white elephant? Postliberalization, the politics of reception and the globalization of literary prizes. In A. I. Viswamohan (Ed.), *Post-liberalization Indian novels in English: Politics of global reception and awards* (pp. 51–66). London: Anthem Press.

Mee, J. (1998). After midnight: The Indian novel in English of the 80s and 90s. *Postcolonial Studies, 1*(1), 127–141.

Mee, J. (2004). Temporality and the transition to modernity in *A suitable boy*. In G. J. V. Prasad (Ed.), *Vikram Seth: An anthology of recent criticism* (pp. 107–121). Delhi: Pencraft.

Mohapatra, H. S. (2014). Babu fiction in disguise, reading Aravind Adiga's *The white tiger*. In K. Sen & R. Roy (Eds.), *Writing India anew: Indian English fiction 2000–2010*. (pp. 129–144). Amsterdam: Amsterdam University Press.

Moretti, F. (2007). *The novel*. Princeton: Princeton University Press.

Mukherjee, U. P. (2010). *Postcolonial environments: Nature, culture and the contemporary Indian novel in English*. Basingstoke: Palgrave Macmillan.

Naik, M. K., & Narayan, S. A. (2004). *Indian English literature 1980–2000*. New Delhi: Pencraft.

Radhakrishnan, S. (2011). *Appropriately Indian: Gender and culture in a new transnational class*. Durham: Duke University Press.

Rajagopal, A. (2001). Thinking about the new Indian middle class: Gender, advertising and politics in an age of globalisation. In R. Sunder Rajan (Ed.), *Signposts: Gender issues in post-independence India* (pp. 57–99). New Brunswick: Rutgers University Press.

Roy, A. (1997). *The god of small things*. London: Harper Collins/Flamingo.

Sadana, R. (2012). *English heart, Hindi heartland: The political life of literature in India*. London: University of California Press.

Seth, V. (1993). *A suitable boy*. London: Orion.

Singh, M. (1991). Budget speech of 1991-2. Accessed 27 May 2015. Available from http://indiabudget.nic.in/bspeech/bs199192.pdf

Srivastava, N. (2004). Secularism in Vikram Seth's *A suitable boy*. In G. J. V. Prasad (Ed.), *Vikram Seth: An anthology of recent criticism* (pp. 87–106). Delhi: Pencraft.

Sunder Rajan, R. (2011). After *Midnight's children*: Some notes on the new Indian novel in English. *Social Research, 78*(1), 203–230.

Tickell, A. (2007). *Arundhati Roy's The god of small things*. London: Routledge.
Tickell, A. (2015a). Driving Pinky Madam (and Murdering Mr Ashok): Social justice and domestic service in Aravind Adiga's *The white tiger*. In P. K. Malreddy et al. (Eds.), *Reworking postcolonialism: Globalization, labour and rights* (pp. 150–164). Basingstoke: Palgrave Macmillan.
Tickell, A. (2015b). An interview with Manju Kapur. *Journal of Postcolonial Writing, 51*(3), 340–350.
Varma, P. K. (2006). *Being Indian: Inside the real India*. London: Arrow Books.
Walder, D. (2011). *Postcolonial nostalgias: Writing, representation, and memory*. Abingdon: Routledge.
Watt, I. (1963). *The rise of the novel: Studies in Defoe, Richardson and Fielding*. Harmondsworth: Penguin/Peregrine.

English-Language Fiction of Bangladesh

Cara Cilano

In an interview conducted in 1977 and published in 1998, Kaiser Haq, perhaps Bangladesh's most prominent contemporary English-language poet, asserted that no one can 'envisage an anglophone literary community evolving' in that country because '[i]ndividual Bangladeshis [are] still trying to write English work[s] in isolation' (Quayum 1998, p. 22). Nearly two decades on, Haq's prognosis for the future of English-language literary production in Bangladesh provokes several interconnected responses. By asserting the isolated nature of working in English, for instance, Haq makes a self-fulfilling prophecy of his observation about the absence of a literary community that would, presumably, nurture and expand cultural production in this area. This point about isolation/community speaks to what may have been a paucity of venues, including publishing houses, through which Bangladeshi authors using English could gain audiences for their work. However, with the 2012 entrance onto the publishing scene of *Bengal Lights*, Khademul Islam's new literary online and print magazine, the recent launch of Bengal Lights Books in 2014 (Bengal Lights 2015) and the first Dhaka Hay Festival, in 2013, which, according to author and festival organizer Tahmima Anam, hosted several major publishing houses and resulted in young writers receiving their first contracts, the problem

---

C. Cilano
University of North Carolina, Wilmington,
DE, USA

© The Editor(s) (if applicable) and The Author(s) 2016
A. Tickell (ed.), *South-Asian Fiction in English*,
DOI 10.1057/978-1-137-40354-4_4

of appropriate venues appears to be lessening (Shook 2013, p. 47). Nonetheless, the question of audience brings up some related points: the state and status of English in Bangladesh and the forms and themes found in contemporary Bangladeshi English-language literature. Moreover, Haq's use of the adverb 'still' also subtly cues a surprisingly necessary recognition: namely, that writers from across the vast expanse of the South-Asian subcontinent have long produced English-language literature—since the publication of Sake Dean Mohamed's travel writings in 1794 (Fisher 2000) and continuing through the nineteenth century with the publication of Kylas and Shoshee Chunder Dutt's work in the 1830s and 1840s (Mukherjee 2000, pp. 52–5; Tickell 2005, pp. 7–22)—a historical reality that prompts its own set of questions regarding what literary students and scholars mean when we talk about anglophone/global literary production.

With a specific emphasis on Bangladeshi English-language fiction from the first decade of the twenty-first century to the present, this chapter explores the points raised above by tracing a number of trajectories. First, I focus on how Bangladesh's historical circumstances shape English-language literary production and its audiences, and then I evaluate how recent fiction by Bangladeshi authors, including Niaz Zaman, K. Anis Ahmed and Tahmima Anam, represents the 1971 Liberation War and its legacies. Other English-language writers, such as Neeman Sobhan, Adib Khan and Khademul Islam, focus on 1971 as well. However, Bangladeshi English-language fictions take on a wide range of subjects. Farah Ghuznavi's 2012 collection, *Lifelines: New Writing from Bangladesh*, for instance, features just over a dozen short stories by women that deal largely with gender and everyday life. In addition to two novels that touch upon 1971, *Seasonal Adjustments* (1994) and *Spiral Road* (2007), Adib Khan, now a resident of Australia, has also penned fictions that can, to borrow Rajini Srikanth's (2005, p. 50) phrase, be called 'writing what you're not': Khan's 2003 *Homecoming* is about a white Australian man who fought in Vietnam and struggles to re-acclimatize to civilian life in that country; his 2000 *The Story Teller* features a story-telling dwarf who creates worlds through his fictions that compete with the realities of Delhi's slums.[1] By focusing on 1971 fictions, though, my purpose is to highlight linked themes and to suggest one approach to these literatures: namely, to consider them in relation to major historical events and as a retrospective engagement with

[1] See Rashid Askari's 'Bangladeshis Writing in English' for a longer list of poets and fiction writers.

Bangladesh's turbulent national history. And, by way of a conclusion, I consider how the specificities of this (re)vitalized field of literary production bring to the fore larger theoretical questions concerning how we imagine a field called 'anglophone' or 'global literatures in English'.

As with its larger subcontinental neighbours, Bangladesh's regional and national histories require from the start an acknowledgement of the fluidity of any boundaries marking internal from external. Before the British East India Company's settlement on the banks of the Hooghly river and the Raj's establishment of Calcutta as the seat of its colonial empire, the area that became part of Bangladesh—that is, Bengal—had already seen waves of invaders, missionaries and merchants. Watery imagery seems particularly apt in this context for, as Willem van Schendel observes, 'a multilayered culture has always been the hallmark of the Bengal delta' (2009, p. 267). Looking ahead to Bangladesh's twenty-first century future, he continues, 'The delta's history of multiple, moving frontiers has simply entered a new and exciting phase' (ibid.). Van Schendel's apparent optimism for Bangladesh's future, premised metaphorically as it is on the literal shifting sands of the region's delta geography, draws upon the positive flexibility that can accompany constant change. The likelihood of change thus emerges as a key concept in and a reality throughout historical and cultural accounts of English-language literary production in Bangladesh.

Although artificial in the light of this brief discussion of Bangladeshi geography and its metaphorical import, I want to draw a line around current discussions of the internal dynamics that writers and critics identify in their attempts to conceptualize the state and status of English-language literary production in Bangladesh. Like van Schendel, Fakrul Alam invokes a model of change in specific relation to Bangladesh's anglophone literature. While Alam concedes that, at present, Bangladesh is the 'least developed in the subcontinent in terms of its English writing resources' (2007, p. 37), he also marks the late 1980s–early 1990s as the moment of resurgence in English-language literary output across South Asia, including in Bangladesh. According to Alam, factors such as 'international mobility', education in English, audience interest at home and abroad in English-language work and, of course, the critical accolades showered upon Salman Rushdie for the 1981 publication of his *Midnight's Children* continue to influence this change in status for South-Asian and Bangladeshi English-language literature (2007, p. 43). Joining Alam in his admissions of Bangladesh's purported underdevelopment when it comes to 'BWE' or 'Bangladeshi Writing in English', Rashid Askari views this specific field as 'very feeble,' so much so that he can't yet assemble a 'chronological list' to represent any form of tradition or canon (Askari 2010). In line with the quotation cited at the beginning of this chapter, Kaiser Haq locates Bangladeshi anglophone literature 'on the fringe' of South Asia, even further out from the centre than either Pakistan's or Sri Lanka's (Quayum 1998, p. 22). And yet, even in the face of these apparent deficiencies, others identify shifting tides. According to *Bengal Lights*, 'Creative writing in English is on the verge of a real efflorescence in Bangladesh today' (Bengal Lights 2013). While the factors Alam lists are likely to be responsible for the change anticipated by Khademul Islam, the editor of *Bengal Lights*, questions remain regarding the apparently moribund state of English up until this time.

One partial answer to these questions involves the language politics within Bangladesh that affected education policy and have shaped audiences' interest in English-language literary production. Despite Bangladesh's historical inclusion in British Bengal, 'the most Westernized and cosmopolitan part of the Raj', Haq argues that, upon its independence in December 1971—and, arguably earlier, given the language politics that plagued the nascent conjoined wings of Pakistan as early as 1948—Bangladesh 'has since been transformed by lingual nationalism into a virtually monoglot state proud of the thousand year-old [Bengali] literary tradition' (Quayum 1998, p. 22). In Haq's view, the rise of East Pakistani/Bangladeshi nationalism, which necessarily focused on regional and linguistic specifics so as to distinguish itself from the dominant Pakistani nationalism promulgated by what was then West Pakistan, significantly and deliberately foregrounds Bangla and that language's centuries-old literary tradition as part of its collective identity.[2] Further, according to Alam, this linguistic nationalism, 'linked' as it is to Bangladesh's independence, resulted in English 'almost disappear[ing] from higher education; for a while not even elite schools were allowed to use English as a medium of instruction' (2007, p. 42). Farah Ghuznavi, one of the many emerging English-language fiction writers in the country, attests to the accuracy of Alam's claims. In a recent interview, Ghuznavi characterizes herself as a 'sacrificial lamb' to the ascendant political climate that prevailed immediately after independence in 1971. As a result of a 'political decision',

---

[2] Haq doesn't give a specific title to the type of nationalism he describes, but I see it as akin to the 'Bengali nationalism' that van Schendel sees developing into 'renewal nationalism' from the mid-1970s onwards (2001, p. 108).

Ghuznavi's parents, for whom English was a first language, sent her to a Bangla-medium school (Shook 2013, p. 45). Without a presence or official status in the educational system, neither writers nor audiences had easy access to English as a medium of creative output.

And yet, to chalk up the tidal ebbs and flows of Bangladeshi English-language literary production to a generically-posited idea of nationalism overlooks what critics and authors alike see as a more complex set of dynamics that continue to shape cultural output and conversations. One such conversation recognizes what contemporary Bangladeshi English-language writers see as a decline in a cosmopolitan disposition among authors over the past 40 years (Shook 2013, p. 46). At the base of these conversations is a tension between historical observations, such as those metaphorized through the region's delta environment and historiographical explanations for attitudes towards English. My use of the term 'historiographical explanations' refers to how historical discourses shape what we understand to be the circumstances surrounding literary production in the subcontinent. Speaking of South Asia generally, Alam states that,

> in the aftermath of partition [i.e. 1947] there would be a centrifugal tendency [in English-language writing] because of linguistic policy as well as the evolution of the nation-states of the region that would enervate and delay the establishment of this category of writing. (2007, p. 42)

While least apparent in India, Alam claims, this doubled process of enervation and delay did take place in Bangladesh and purportedly manifested itself in two dominant nationalistic currents.

According to van Schendel, the first type of nationalism operating in a nascent Bangladesh was Bengali nationalism, which constituted the 'first flowering of post-communalism' in the subcontinent through its focus on language and region over religion (2001, p. 108). With the rapid decline of the ideals that motivated this nationalism, however, came an effort to renew the promise that originally fuelled the drive for Bangladesh. This renewal was felt at its fullest force, van Schendel claims, around 1990, when Hussain Muhammad Ershad's dictatorship fell (2001, p. 109). Van Schendel refers to this resuscitated Bengali nationalism as 'renewal nationalism', which, like its earlier iteration, valued 'nationalism, secularism, socialism, and democracy', but with a particular edge whose design was 'to discredit the authoritarianism and injustice of the new rulers' (ibid., pp. 108–9). In effect, 'renewal nationalism' attempts to restore an 'original' idea of

Bangladesh and, in doing so, pointedly resists what such nationalists view as the false dichotomy separating Bengaliness and Bangladeshiness. If 'Bengaliness' brings together language, region and (literary) culture, then 'Bangladeshiness' rests on the conviction 'that the Bangladeshi nation was the ultimate manifestation of the delta's Muslim-Bengali identity' (quoted in Alam 2011, p. 181). In van Schendel's view, 'Bangladeshiness' finds its voice in a 'religious nationalism' that positions a Muslim-Bengali identity as 'under attack' externally from the 'tutelage and corrupting influence of the West' and internally from 'Bangladeshi secularism' (2001, p. 110). Thus, even while 'renewal nationalism' purports to resist the bifurcation of 'Bengaliness' and 'Bangladeshiness', these two concepts nonetheless provide the basis for historiographical explanations of why Bangladesh has not (yet) been flooded with English-language literary output (van Schendel 2001, p. 110). That is, in so far as these two concepts dominate the conversation, little discursive space exists for the emergence of cultural tributaries outside the frames of reference they establish.

The power of such explanations cannot be wholly deterministic, however, for as van Schendel and others observe, the cultural history of the delta region is plural and multifarious. Thus, with an acknowledgment that 'cultural space in Bangladesh is always political', van Schendel and his co-author Meghna Guhathakurta identify a 'contested terrain between [...] orthodoxy and syncretistic cultural trends' (2013, p. 367). In the midst of such tensions, acknowledging the shifting representations of Bangladeshi national belonging becomes difficult. With the goal of identifying—but not reinforcing—competing narratives of belonging to Bangladesh, Reece Jones concludes that although '[t]he two Bengals have been separate for over 60 years, there have been political efforts to differentiate the populations [in Bangladesh and India] by narrating divided histories and futures, and the border [between the two countries] is fenced and securitized [since 2002], ...a strong sense of loss regarding' the idea of an inclusive homeland remains (Jones 2011, p. 392). These discursive and political efforts illustrate the sociological costs that come with efforts to impose a rigidly national identity. To counter the force of such efforts, van Schendel proposes another paradigm based on cultural pluralism. Such an interpretation of Bangladeshi history, politics and cultures features two characteristics particularly germane to the present discussion. First, an interpretation based on cultural pluralism 'refuses to accept' that the nature of the Bangladeshi nation and its history are solely a debate 'between Bengalis, that is, members of a relatively well defined linguistic and ethnic group'.

Also and relatedly, such an interpretation 'emphasizes the unequal power relations between cultural groups in Bangladesh, and aims at exposing the political uses of ignoring this reality' (van Schendel 2001, p. 111). In effect, with these dimensions in place, cultural pluralism allows for the decoupling of collective identity and monolingualism. Further, the difficulty of this decoupling reveals the cultural forces working against and in favour of writers, readers, publishers and others who take part in English-language literary production and consumption. To expand this line of thinking outward, cultural pluralism helps us see the continuation of language, culture and their combination in literary production in a context more aligned to subcontinental realities, that is to Bangladesh's connections to the English language through the previous three centuries and more.[3]

So far, I have traced how Bangladesh's regional and national histories shape the circumstances in which we can discuss the state and status of this country's English-language literary output. I will now turn to the fictions themselves, exploring some themes that connect the works of a small selection of established and emerging writers. In order to do so, I deliberately focus on fictional treatments explicitly dealing with 1971 and its aftermath, examining how they potentially 'imagine otherwise'—that is, how they engage with historical discourses about the war and independence.[4]

In addition to being a momentous historical occasion and one with a still-unfolding legacy, the 1971 Bangladesh Liberation War occupies an inverse position in Bangladeshi and Pakistani English-language fictive traditions. Any reading of the literature from either country in this period remarks on how 'in Bangladesh, the war of liberation has exerted a greater and much more profound influence on creativity' than in Pakistan (Zaman and Farrukhi 2008, p. xix). This statement needs some qualification, however, as the flourishing of creative literary activity in Bangladesh took place largely in Bangla. And, while Asif Farrukhi contests Muhammad Umar Memon's assertion that Urdu-language literature on the war is 'surprisingly both sparse and casual' (Zaman and Farrukhi 2008, p. xix; Memon 1983, p. 107), until recently, even this literary output outpaced English-language

---

[3] Embedded in this expanded view is a line of conversation regarding what Alam wants to see as a trans-South-Asian English-language literature. I will develop this point in the chapter's final section.
[4] I mean to invoke Kandice (2003) Chuh's work (2003) in *Imagine Otherwise: On Asian American Critique* on how literary production can function as critique as much as object of study.

fiction by both Bangladeshi and Pakistani writers. According to Zaman and Farrukhi, Tahmima Anam's 2007 novel, *A Golden Age*, is the first English-language Bangladeshi novel on the war, though Adib Khan's *Seasonal Adjustments* was published 13 years earlier and his *Spiral Road* came into print the same year as Anam's first book.[5] As for short fiction in English, the texts readily available are of a recent vintage, many with twenty-first-century publication dates. The increase in Bangladeshi English-language fictions around 1971 substantiates Khademul Islam's claim that Bangladeshi English-language literary production is about to blossom into a new period of growth (Bengal Lights 2013), and it also introduces an important critical consideration (one, once again, shared by Pakistani English-language fiction on the same event): time. With nearly two generations past, contemporary Bangladeshi fictive representations of 1971 and its legacies possess the potential to reflect, to refract and/or to reinvent the frames through which Bangladeshis and other English-speaking audiences understand the war and the nation it created.

In effect, I want to consider the ways in which several Bangladeshi English-language fictions about the war and its aftermath explicitly and implicitly foreground this temporal distance and to what ends. The presence of temporal distance allows for more than just the inclusion of memory, which can serve as a barometer of trauma. Temporal distance in many Bangladeshi and Pakistani English-language fictions about the 1971 war also creates a space for critical narrative reflection on the war's legacies, including the disillusionment born of failed nationalisms and other attempts at creating inclusive claims to belonging. The temporal distance in these works is not often figured as a nostalgic return to some moment purportedly free of the troubles and inequities of the present either. Any return characters make to their 'younger' selves frequently involves a condemnation of their own naivety. These critical perspectives locate the novels' political concerns, as well. In the fictions I discuss, two distinct treatments of temporal distance emerge: the first uses the temporal distance to assess the possibilities of reconciliation and forgiveness for the war's atrocities; the second frames the legacy of independence as troubling and bleak.

[5] Both Anam and Khan now reside outside of Bangladesh, thus their works may also be considered diasporic. Anam's second novel on the subject, *The Good Muslim*, came out in 2011. According to Claire Chambers, Anam intends to publish a third novel to complete her Bengal Trilogy (2014, p. 142).

Both K. Anis Ahmed's 'Good Night, Mr. Kissinger', the titular story from his 2012 short story collection, and Niaz Zaman's 2004 short story, 'A Lucky Escape', use temporal distance to explore the possibilities of healing the wounds Bangladeshis suffered during the 1971 war. Ahmed's story adds geographical distance to the temporal kind by placing James D'Costa, the story's first person narrator, in twenty-first-century New York City. James's geographical displacement comes about through his own volition. He confesses to 'always liv[ing] in a state of seething rage' (Ahmed 2012, p. 91), a behavioural tendency that results in his being sacked from a teaching post in Dhaka. With few opportunities for employment there, James emigrates to the US and files for asylum, a status readily given because James is 'a Christian with a record of secular activism from a country growing ever more radical' (Ahmed 2012, p. 90). James's revelation that he presented himself to US immigration as an asylum seeker—and his qualifications for doing so—suggests that he felt threatened in Bangladesh because of his religious and political identities and convictions. Yet the story, again narrated by James himself, gives no real indication of discrimination or threat.

James's emigration, and his distance in miles and years from Bangladesh, helps heal his 'seething rage'. Through his first person narrative voice, which functions as a confessional of sorts, James relays his memories of the early months of the 1971 war. Pakistani soldiers approach his family's home, and James 'remember[s] most vividly' how his 'father came out to the verandah, already bent in submission, appeasement dripping from his voice. […] The image of my father on his knees, shirt open, pleading for his family' (Ahmed 2012, p. 91). As the soldiers are departing, one, whom James describes as the 'idiot soldier' because of his obvious mental deficiencies, fires his gun at the family's goat. This indiscipline enrages the major, who then orders the other soldiers to kill James's father (p. 92). Marked as the origin of James's later problems with rage, this episode stokes in him a desire for 'symbolic justice' (p. 92). But, as James grows into adulthood, he comes to understand that 'justice was the only thing my country failed to deliver' (p. 92). The way James frames his anger and its aim suggests, first, his view that the violence of the war was senseless. That one soldier's 'idiocy' and the major's order, which serves as a non sequitur to firing at the goat, condemn West Pakistan's treatment of its eastern wing. The new nation of Bangladesh does not emerge unscathed, however, as James presents his quest for even 'symbolic justice' as one that is unfulfilled. With the 'killers and collaborators [becoming] ministers' even after 'democracy was restored in the early '90s' (p. 93), James condemns his compatriots in the same way he did the West Pakistanis. And yet James does not heal just because he leaves Bangladesh. Instead, his life in the US clarifies his rage's origin story.

'Good Night, Mr. Kissinger' insists on adding another dimension to James's story: that of American involvement in the 1971 conflict. Unlike many other English-language fictions about 1971, from both Bangladesh and Pakistan, Ahmed forces an acknowledgment of a fourth player (if West Pakistan, East Pakistan and India are counted as the first three). As the story's title suggests, a fictionalized Henry Kissinger appears throughout Ahmed's story as a diner in an exclusive New York restaurant, the Solstice, at which James works as a waiter. At their first meeting, Kissinger struggles to identify the capital of Tajikistan, so, with some nerve, James 'took a chance' by providing the older man with the name (Ahmed 2012, p. 87). Kissinger's lapse or moment of ignorance highlights an irony: the former National Security Advisor and Secretary of State who exerted significant influence over the USA's Cold War activities does not know the specifics of the parts of the world that felt the effects of his actions. Within the narrative, James figures that Kissinger resents being corrected by a mere waiter—and a Bangladeshi, at that—for the former diplomat comments to James, 'I hope your country isn't still a basket-case for the sake of those who are stuck there' (p. 88). Kissinger's condescension inspires in James a rage-induced fantasy of grabbing the dessert knife so that he could 'pierce [...] Kissinger's neck [which] was soft and crumply enough' to be vulnerable even to this 'blunt instrument' (p. 88). Subsequent encounters at the restaurant—Kissinger is a frequent diner—further enrage James and, upon recognizing his obsessive murder fantasies, James makes a seismic acknowledgment: 'The more I thought about it, I also realized that no injury I could cause him [Kissinger] would get either Kissinger himself or the world to see him as I wished' (p. 98). James's perspective on Kissinger holds the latter partially responsible for the ravages of the 1971 war, as Nixon famously 'tilted' towards Pakistan under Kissinger's advisement. The futility of actually harming Kissinger prompts James to 'realize the impossibility of finding satisfaction in the event of a great wrong' (p. 99). As a result, James begins to wonder whether 'you [can] forgive those who don't even know that they need to be forgiven' (p. 99). James's reflections on his emotional state illustrate his own healing process. Notably, he does not focus on the question of forgiveness for those West Pakistani soldiers who murdered his father or the Bangladeshi politicians whose corruption sullied the dream of independence. Moreover, by locating himself in the position to forgive Henry Kissinger, James effectively redefines the power dynamics between not just these two figures but also between the two historical actors they stand for: Bangladesh and the US. That is, James's ability to forgive Kissinger, which he does (p. 100), creates a vision of the future in which Bangladesh has the power to move forwards under its own agency.

Zaman, in 'A Lucky Escape', also inserts reflection upon the past in her narrative. From the start, for instance, the reader recognizes the story's metafictional status. 'A Lucky Escape' centres on a public witnessing: the main character, an older woman who recounts her experiences in the 1971 war, relays her painful memories in front of a pan-South-Asian group in the present day. As the story calls the audience to witness, it illustrates how individuals on other sides of the conflict also suffered. For example, one of the audience members was the wife of a West Pakistani soldier who killed himself after he took part in the raid the protagonist recounts from memory. The embrace of the two women at the close of the story signals the possibility of reconciliation, long in coming. The third person narrator reveals, 'It was a story she had told many times since that April day in 1971...' (Zaman 2008, p. 38). This metafictional announcement alerts the story's audience to the narrative's constructed status. Yet, the urgency of the framed story itself is so intense that the narrator's breaking of the frame towards the story's end startles. Fully engrossing in its portrayal of the fear of a Bengali family hiding from Pakistani soldiers on the banks of a pond, the narrative abruptly, jarringly shifts:

> The noise of the [soldiers'] boots on dry leaves came closer and closer. She [the protagonist who, in the story's present, is telling the narrative of her past] kept her eyes closed. Dear God, she prayed, let it be quick, let it be quick. Let me not suffer, let the children not suffer. Ever closer came the footsteps, and, as the frail old women told her story, the people in the audience could almost hear the sound of the boots on the dry leaves. They came closer, she said, closer and closer.... (p. 43)

The insertion of the dialogue line 'she said' occurs only at this late juncture in the story, and its appearance highlights the character's/storyteller's efforts to build suspense, to signal to her audience that this moment of near-discovery represents the point of her story. The awareness of such story-telling concerns hints at a skilled and practised (fictionalized) author, one who knows the effect the retold story has.

The reflection implied by this knowingness—a reflection enabled by the story's explicit foregrounding of temporal distance—develops the power stories may have to encourage forgiveness. Both the temporal distance and the metafictional elements suggest the persistence of this character's memory and the circumstances in which she relays her tale—she does, after all, have an audience that is, pointedly, made up of 'Bangladeshis, Indians, Pakistanis' (p. 45)—further point towards a collective memory still processing the war over this character's lifespan. As the audience disperses at the conclusion of the framed story, for instance, the storyteller finds 'a tiny woman standing in front of her' (p. 45). This woman confesses her hatred for the storyteller, a revelation the storyteller does not expect, for '[s]he did not know the old woman' (p. 45). As the old woman from the audience explains herself, the storyteller realizes that she has just provided details of the other woman's own loss: her husband, a West Pakistani soldier, was one of the soldiers who were searching near the pond for the storyteller and her family. According to the old woman from the audience, her husband told her about the encounter and other instances when he had killed East Pakistanis under orders. His acts made him 'ashamed of belonging to an army that killed helpless men, women and children', according to his wife (p. 45). When the old woman receives news that her husband's gun went off unintentionally, she knows he committed suicide, and she lives her life blaming the East Pakistanis. At least, she blames them until she hears the storyteller's own account (p. 45). The story closes with a vision of reconciliation: 'The two old women held each other's withered hands as tears coursed down their cheeks' (p. 45). Woven into this possibility for healing is the explicit acknowledgment of (West) Pakistani blame and responsibility. In other words, Zaman's story allows for personal, individual healing between a Pakistani and a Bangladeshi but, notably, only after making clear that this healing depends on their mutual agreement that Pakistan is a nation at fault. Moreover, unlike Ahmed's story, 'A Lucky Escape' appears to provide closure through the image of the women's conjoined 'withered hands'. The story appears to offer an image of healing, of moving beyond a painful past. However, given the two women's ages, the story does not offer any particular promise for the future.

The ambiguity characterizing the conclusion of Zaman's story, thus, uses its temporal distance to illustrate the closing of an era through the closing of two lives, those of these two old women. With this pervasive sense of loss and grief, 'A Lucky Escape' fits more neatly into the thematic tropes Zaman and Farrukhi identify in much Bangladeshi fiction about the Liberation War. Framing this war as a 'victory at a great price', Zaman and Farrukhi argue that 'many of the Bangla stories are of failure, failure of the people, failure of the government, failure of the country to live up to the promise of the nationalistic movement' (2008, p. xviii). In Zaman's story, such failure is not rehabilitated into success but, rather, gets reworked into a tired relinquishment of decades-old hatred (p. 45). Ahmed's story offers a point of contrast, as James can recognize failure on multiple levels—even his own personal failures—but manages, nonetheless, to turn towards the future.

The last two Bangladeshi English-language fictions about 1971 that I will discuss, Tahmima Anam's novels *A Golden Age* (2007) and *The Good Muslim* (2011), both employ temporal distance and, as with these two short stories, use that remove to comment upon the possibility of the future. In doing so, neither novel offers an uncompromised vision but, rather, one combined with a bleak, troubling tone.

In content and because of their sequential nature and publication dates, Anam's two novels about the 1971 war and its legacies rely upon temporal distance. Anam's *The Good Muslim* continues the story first seeded in her 2007 *A Golden Age*, that significant English-language fiction about the 1971 war by a Bangladeshi author. In large measure, that first novel centres around Rehana Haque, a young Urdu-speaking widow who resides in East Pakistan during the 1971 war. Near to the novel's opening, Rehana manages to reclaim her children, Sohail and Maya, who have been living in West Pakistan with her dead husband's family because they did not think Rehana could raise the children on her own. By the time the war begins, Sohail and Maya are in their teens and eager to join the Bangladesh movement. Despite early fears and reservations, Rehana, too, eventually joins the resistance movement, and the family's assorted contributions help win the war. None of them return to Rehana's house in Dhaka unchanged, however. Maya stays away for years, partly out of a sense of duty to her poorer compatriots and partly out of a sense of alienation from her mother and brother. Sohail does return to his mother's house with his wife, Silvi, who bears him a son, Zaid, and dies soon after. After the war, Sohail espouses a fervent religious faith that materially alters how the house appears (Anam 2007, p. 305) even as it changes the dynamics between the family members. This story is the one Anam picks up in *The Good Muslim*, the second instalment of her planned Bengal Trilogy.

Both of Anam's novels use temporal distance within the narratives as a fulcrum to examine what Bangladesh has become after the Liberation War. Maya's long absence from her mother and brother in *A Golden Age* first introduces this critical and reflective predilection. The narrator comments, for instance, that 'somewhere along the way [Maya] had decided to become a lady doctor instead of a surgeon' (Anam 2007, p. 303). The imprecision of this temporal marking—Maya's decision occurred at some point after the end of the war—hints at significant shifts in this character's thinking, shifts perhaps prompted by other unplanned-for changes. And, indeed, Sohail's conversion to the intense Islam practised by the 'Tablighi Jamaat' suggests the nature of these other changes, both in her brother and in the country (p. 313). By raising this possibility, Anam's first novel sets out one of the central themes of her second: how can secularist nationalists, like Maya, who are akin to van Schendel's 'renewal nationalists', contend with the influx of the 'religious nationalism' embodied in Sohail's changed views? Even with this question hanging over it, *A Golden Age* appears to close on a hopeful note:

> The house was changed, but it had survived. And [Maya] had made it, two train rides and a ferry across the country, and she was laying her head on her mother's lap, and there was nothing to do now but remember all the times they had returned to this house, she and her brother, to find everything was the same and not the same, to find their mother waiting, waiting. (p. 317)

Such an ending implies a resilience and, notably, a return, which itself suggests the ability to relocate, recentre, to come back to first principles, even if 'everything was the same and not the same'. Further, this conclusion emphasizes Rehana's constancy and, more abstractly, the inviolacy of the parent–child relationship, which can be read as a positive future-orientation. Thus, while *A Golden Age* does not extend the romanticization suggested by its title to the post-independence era, it does retain a hopeful vision for the future.

Interestingly, the difference/distance between Anam's two novels significantly alters how they comment on the future in light of what Bangladesh became after independence. Maya's decision to become a 'lady doctor' as *A Golden Age* reports it, for instance, evolves partially from her sense of what her compatriots, especially her female compatriots, need (Anam 2007, p. 303). In the account of Maya's decision that *A Golden Age* provides, Maya 'didn't think of the debt she was repaying, that each of the babies she brought into the world might someday be counted against the babies that had died, by her hand, after the war' (p. 303). The purpose of and use to which Maya puts her medical training thus shifts from aborting to delivering babies. She carries out both duties, though, under the heading of 'the good of the nation' or what she thinks her compatriots need. Importantly, the narrator makes a point of Maya's lack of awareness of her debt or guilt as a motivating factor in her decision. In *The Good Muslim*, however, Maya confesses her guilt to Sohail. The story Maya recalls for Sohail is particularly poignant, because it involves a young woman, Piya, for whom Sohail had strong feelings. Maya tells Sohail that she 'knew what to do; [she] had done it all the time, persuading the girls they were doing the right thing, for their families, for the country' (Anam 2011, p. 243). And, yet, after Maya tells Sohail that Piya did not go through with the abortion, she reveals, 'You thought I was enjoying the days after liberation. But they were blood-soaked, Bhaiya, for everyone' (p. 248). Maya's reflections on the immediate post-war period and her role in sanitizing the nationalist vision for the new nation, which were not begun 'until later, much later' (p. 51), evidence her struggle with guilt and her disillusionment with what Bangladesh became.[6]

Similarly, Anam's first novel merely mentions Zaid, Sohail's son, without also characterizing him as already neglected by his parents, a key plot point in *The Good Muslim*. This plot point comes to a head when Maya pleads with Sohail to remove Zaid from the madrassa where the young boy lives apart from his family. Sohail dodges a commitment to do so, and the narrator, privileging Maya's interior perspective, articulates Maya's suspicions: '[Sohail] could not mean what he appeared to be saying. He wouldn't go, he wouldn't rescue his son from whatever hell-hole he had sent him to' (Anam 2011, p. 261). Determined to save Zaid herself, Maya travels to the madrassa and collects her nephew, all the while blaming herself: 'She feels a sharp twist of guilt now, for the chappals she never bought him, for allowing him to be caught stealing, for not treating him more like he was hers, like something of her own' (p. 275). Unlike the measured optimism that surrounds the maternal figure at the close of *A Golden Age*, *The Good Muslim* features breaches in the maternal bond, first by having Zaid's mother die and then by framing Maya as unable/unwilling to connect with her nephew in a maternal way. Within this shifted paradigm, Maya's recollection of the few moments after the rescue as 'the sweetest she has ever known, because the boy breathes beside her, the years unmarked

---

[6] Chambers reads Maya's role as abortion provider differently. Less inclined to see Maya's reflections and confession as part of a critique of the new nation and, implicitly, of Sheikh Mujib, Chambers argues that 'Anam reveals certain blind spots. For example, Mujib is only fleetingly criticised for the pressure he put on the rape victims to have abortions [...]' (2014, p. 143). While both Anam's novels incorporate real historical figures into their fictions, a move that bolsters Chambers's point about the failure of *The Good Muslim* to offer a more pointed and direct critique, I read their use of the family as an instrument through which to test and assess nationalist discourses in Bangladesh.

ahead of him' (p. 276) seems to express much the same optimism as Maya herself felt upon her return to her mother in *A Golden Age*. This sweetness proves momentary, though, for Zaid deliberately casts himself into the Jamuna river and drowns (p. 276). Both Sohail and Maya thus emerge at the novel's close as culpable for endangering Zaid's life and, in Maya's case, for aborting pregnancies in the name of nationalist convictions.[7] This doubled condemnation shapes the novel's vision of the future. In its epilogue, *The Good Muslim* jumps forward to 1992, to a scene of public and historical reckoning. Maya is now a mother, and she accompanies Piya, the girl from her own and Sohail's pasts, to this reckoning so that the latter can testify about what she suffered in the war. The narrator captures Maya's frame of mind at this event, showing that her thoughts are with her brother and nephew. While Maya 'recognizes the wound in [Sohail's] history, the irreparable wound, because she has one too' (p. 293), the novel does not offer the hope that the siblings will reach over what divides them, and certainly Maya cannot ever reconcile with Zaid. The balance, then, between Maya's own rehabilitation—she is a mother at the end of the novel, which suggests she has developed a future-orientation—and her past, which has familial and national dimensions, remains unsteady and troubled.

This brief survey of some key English-language fictions about the 1971 war highlights distinct treatments of that event and its legacy, treatments that range from forgiveness to reconciliation to acceptance of an 'irreparable wound'. A disquiet over what Bangladesh became after independence links these four fictive examples and draws an at least provisional line between the growing English-language tradition and the existing Bangla one. Indeed, this exploration of Ahmed's, Zaman's and Anam's fictions illustrates one of the critical benefits of expanding what we think of as 'Bangladeshi literature' to include English-language output: the building of a comparative framework joining Bangla- and English-language texts. Similarly, a concentration of Bangladeshi English-language fictional representations of an event such as the 1971 war encourages another type of comparison, that between Pakistani and Bangladeshi representations, of which English-language texts comprise a growing subset. This latter comparative project begins the work Fakrul Alam envisions when he identifies a 'trans-South Asian phenomenon'

---

[7] This point reinforces Chambers's claim that, in *The Good Muslim*, 'Anam suggests that the borders between religion and secularism are more porous than is often assumed and that each conceptual category contains its share of reason and illogic, moderation and extremism, ethical and unethical behaviour' (2014, p. 142).

that could result in the creation of 'South Asian Writers in English' as a label that stretches across national boundaries (2007, p. 40). In Alam's view, this label would have as '[i]ts claim to fame' the 'ability to represent the subcontinent as a whole and not any single part' (p. 40). Clearly, Alam's vision sets out a challenging critical task: that of conceptualizing and valuing the vast diversity of South-Asian voices captured by English-language literary production under the umbrella of a single term.

On a related note, Alam's interest in recognizing the distinctiveness of South-Asian English-language literary production leads to questions of influence and development, which have dogged the emergence of English-language literary traditions outside of the UK, the US and Australia for decades. K. Anis Ahmed takes up these issues in two stories from *Good Night, Mr. Kissinger*. In 'The Poetry Audition', Bahram, who revels in his autodidacticism, and Jamshed, who unexpectedly develops a voracious interest in poetry, argue over the directions in which literary influence flow. Jamshed, the neophyte, sees the influence of Bengali literature on European 'masters', while Bahram vehemently argues against influence flowing in that direction (Ahmed 2012, p. 31). Ahmed's 'Ramkamal's Gift' engages in this debate, too, by framing its titular character as impatient with others who refuse to acknowledge the flows of influence: 'There was no scope for any writer [of any nation or place] in the modern period—meaning since the invention of steamboats—to pretend that they did not know the frontiers that had been breached in world literature' (Ahmed 2012, p. 115). Ahmed's characters enact fictionally the very points young Bangladeshi authors who choose to write in English make. Both Ahmed and Mahmud Rahman identify a broader socio-historical shift in Bangladeshi literary culture that obstructed the flows of influence. In the 1960s and 1970s, Ahmed and Rahman claim, Bangladeshi authors were significantly more cosmopolitan in their reading habits, even if they struggled with languages other than Bengali (Shook 2013, p. 46). Whether due to the emergence of more rigid forms of nationalism or to the changing educational system, this literary cosmopolitanism waned, creating a more provincial literary culture that Ahmed and Rahman hope to revitalize and expand.[8]

---

[8] Significantly, Ahmed points out that the provincialism of Bangladeshi literary culture is not unique: 'The truth is, this is not something uniquely Bangla; it's not that you become a good writer once you write in English. English writers don't become good writers if they've not read something from Spanish or Russian or French, and so on with every culture' (Shook 2013, p. 46).

Moreover, the appearance of these questions about literary influence and development in Ahmed's stories points towards a broader critical discussion of how a type of literary production, like Bangladeshi or trans-South-Asian English-language literature, 'fits' into a larger arena commonly called 'anglophone' or 'global literatures in English'. Aamir Mufti takes on a version of this question in his 'Orientalism and the Institution of World Literature', claiming,

[T]he deep encounter between English and the other Western languages and the languages of the global periphery as media of literary expression did not take place for the first time in the postcolonial era, let alone in the supposedly transnational transactions of the period of high globalization but, especially, at the dawn of the modern era itself and fundamentally transformed both cultural formations involved in the encounter. (2010, p. 461)

Mufti's concern encompasses not just literary production in English by non-European, non-American writers, but his point about the historically early, transactional and transformational nature of colonial, economic and cultural encounters pertains to the smaller field of anglophone world literature, as well. When we frame Bangladeshi English-language literature as 'emerging', we need to qualify this characterization, not only in its national context but also its regional and historical ones, too.

Works Cited

Ahmed, K. A. (2012). *Good night, Mr. Kissinger and other stories*. Dhaka: The University Press Ltd.
Alam, F. (2007). Imagining South Asian writing in English from Bangladesh. *South Asian Review, 27*(1), 37–49.
Alam, F. (2011). Tagore and national identity formation in Bangladesh. *Journal of Contemporary Thought, 34*, 179–196.
Anam, T. (2007). *A golden age*. Edinburgh: Canongate.
Anam, T. (2011). *The good Muslim*. Edinburgh: Canongate.
Askari, R. (2010, August 14). Bangladeshis writing in English. *Daily Star* [Online]. Accessed 7 June 2014. Available from http://archive.thedailystar.net/newDesign/news-details.php?nid=150619
Bengal Lights. (2013). About us. *Bengal lights* [Online]. Accessed 13 Sept 2014. Available from http://www.bengallights.com/about.php
Bengal Lights. (2015). News. *Bengal lights* [Online]. Accessed 13 Jan 2015. Available from http://www.bengallights.com/news_detail.php?nid=2

Chambers, C. (2014). Tahmima Anam's *The good Muslim*: Bangladeshi Islam, secularism, and the Tablighi Jamaat. In C. Chambers & C. Herbert (Eds.), *Imagining Muslims in South Asia and the diaspora: Secularism, religion, representations* (pp. 142–154). London: Routledge.
Chuh, K. (2003). *Imagine otherwise: On Asian American critique*. Durham: Duke.
Fisher, M. (2000). *The first Indian author in English: Dean Mahomed (1759–1851)*. Delhi: Oxford University Press.
Ghuznavi, F. (Ed.). (2012). *Lifelines: New writing from Bangladesh*. New Delhi: Zubaan.
Guhathakurta, M., & van Schendel, W. (Eds.). (2013). *The Bangladesh reader: History, culture, politics*. Durham: Duke.
Jones, R. (2011). Dreaming of a golden Bengal: Discontinuities of place and identity in South Asia. *Asian Studies Review, 35*(3), 373–395.
Khan, A. (1994). *Seasonal adjustments*. St Leonards: Allen and Unwin.
Khan, A. (2003). *Homecoming*. Sydney: HarperPerennial.
Khan, A. (2007). *Spiral road*. London: Fourth Estate.
Memon, M. U. (1983). Pakistani Urdu creative writing on national disintegration: The case of Bangladesh. *The Journal of Asian Studies, 43*(1), 105–127.
Mufti, A. (2010). Orientalism and the institution of world literatures. *Critical Inquiry, 36*, 458–493.
Mukherjee, M. (2000). *The perishable empire: Essays in Indian writing in English*. Calcutta: Oxford University Press.
Quayum, M. A. (1998). Introducing an English-language writer from Bangladesh: An interview with Kaiser Haq. *The Gombak Review, 3*(1), 21–30.
Shook, D. (2013). Opening Bangladesh to the world: A conversation with four contemporary writers. *World Literature Today, 87*(3), 45–48.
Srikanth, R. (2005). *The world next door: South Asian American literature and the idea of America*. Philadelphia: Temple University Press.
Tickell, A. (2005). Introduction. In A. Tickell (Ed.), *Dutt, Shoshee Chunder. Selections from 'Bengaliana'* (pp. 7–22). Nottingham: Trent Editions.
van Schendel, W. (2001). Who speaks for the nation? Nationalist rhetoric and the challenge of cultural pluralism in Bangladesh. In W. van Schendel & E.-J. Zürcher (Eds.), *Identity politics in Central Asia and the Muslim world: Nationalism, ethnicity and labour in the twentieth century* (pp. 107–147). London: I.B. Taurus.
van Schendel, W. (2009). *A history of Bangladesh*. Cambridge: Cambridge University Press.
Zaman, N. (2008). A lucky escape. In N. Zaman & A. Farrukhi (Eds.), *Fault lines: Stories of 1971* (pp. 38–45). Dhaka: The University Press Ltd.
Zaman, N., & Farrukhi, A. (2008). Introduction. In N. Zaman & A. Farrukhi (Eds.), *Fault lines: Stories of 1971* (pp. ix–xxxii). Dhaka: The University Press Ltd.

Sri Lankan Fiction in English 1994–2014

Ruvani Ranasinha

TEXTS AND CONTEXTS

This chapter discusses recent trends in Sri Lankan anglophone fiction of the last two decades; it contextualizes and reviews the fiction of some of the best-known Sri Lankan authors, notably Shyam Selvadurai, alongside others less well-known outside the island, such as Ameena Hussein. Sri Lankan writing is especially marginalized in the canons of postcolonial and contemporary fiction and in the academic study of 'South Asia' more generally.[1] It has not reached the international visibility of 'Indian writing in English' in part because of its smaller literary output and comparatively nascent anglophone publishing culture. Thus the location and politics of publishing has had considerable impact on Sri Lankan anglophone writing, favouring authors published abroad and marginalizing the distinctive per-

---

[1] Minoli Salgado's (2007) detailed analysis of how cultural nationalism has influenced the production and reception of eight leading Sri Lankan writers provides an important intervention in this regard. See also Qadri Ismail (2005); Maryse Jayasuriya (2012) and my own discussion of Sri Lankan writers in Ranasinha (2007). More recently Shyam Selvadurai's anthology of Sri Lankan literature (poetry and prose) *Many Roads Through Paradise* (2014), structured not by language or chronology but by four interlinking themes, celebrates the diversity of modern Sri Lanka's peoples and cultures and features translations of some iconic works written in Sinhalese and Tamil.

R. Ranasinha
Department of English, King's College, London, UK

© The Editor(s) (if applicable) and The Author(s) 2016
A. Tickell (ed.), *South-Asian Fiction in English*,
DOI 10.1057/978-1-137-40354-4_5

spectives of local writers, leading to contrasting culturally *located* reader-responses. Lankan-based reviewers prove far more critical of Lankan texts than their counterparts elsewhere. However, as I've argued elsewhere, these distinct readerships have shifted within the last two decades (Ranasinha 2013). The power of the Euro-American reviewer to *confer* 'authenticity' on chosen diasporic writers is now increasingly interrogated, as are texts perceived as manufactured for easy Euro-American consumption.[2] Moreover, geopolitical shifts (the Sri Lankan polity's move away from allegiance to the former colonizing power towards the multiple centres, and economic powerhouses China and India) has rendered less significant 'the stamps of approval from the centre'.[3]

The wider range and new generation of diasporic and resident Sri Lankan writers who have emerged within the last two decades has lessened 'the burden of representation' on Sri Lanka's still best-known diasporic writers, Michael Ondaatje, Romesh Gunesekera and Selvadurai, who are based in Canada and the UK. The growth of domestic writers and readers of anglophone Sri Lankan fiction has been fuelled by two main factors: the now long-established Gratiaen Prize (founded by Ondaatje in 1993 after his novel *The English Patient*'s Booker Prize win) for the best unpublished or published work in English by a resident Sri Lankan, alongside publishing ventures such as the Perera-Hussein Publishing House founded in 2003. To differing degrees, both have provided a platform for emerging and established Sri Lankan writers. The Gratiaen's most notable success is its award in 2008 to first-time writer Shehan Karunatilaka's *Chinaman: The Legend of Pradeep Mathew* the unpublished story of modern-day Sri Lanka through its favourite sport, cricket. Self-published in 2010 with the Gratiaen Prize money, *Chinaman* (discussed further below) was subsequently picked up by Jonathan Cape in 2011 and went on to win widespread acclaim, as well as the Commonwealth Book Prize and DSC Prize for South Asian Literature in 2012. The prize and new publishing ventures, alongside reviews in locally produced journals such as *Nethra, Phoenix* and *Navasilu*, have stimulated internal assessments of Lankan fiction, and self-referential conversations between home-grown readers and writers about the historical and material conditions they inhabit: key questions have been posed about inequality, divisions of social class, the role of English and the politicization of Buddhism[4] that have little interest to

---

[2] See Vihanga Perera's criticisms of expatriate writers in *Phoenix*, 3 (2011), pp. 53–9.

[3] The approval that Thiru Kandiah (1997) called on Sri Lankan critics to resist when Romesh Gunesekera's *Reef* was published and shortlisted for the Booker Prize in 1994.

[4] Gratiaen Prize-winner Madhubashini Ratnayake's novel *There is Something I Have to Tell You* (2013) is a prime example of this kind of writing.

Euro-American readers. This increasingly challenges the construction of diasporic authors as *privileged* insiders. While the dominant status of English as the global language results in a focus on anglophone writers, overshadowing writing in vernacular languages in the global marketplace, the Gratiaen award includes the H. A. I. Goonetilleke Translation Prize, which recognizes those translators who provide English readers access to writing in Sinhala and Tamil. English is only one strand of Sri Lanka's rich literary and linguistic heritage. It is spoken as a first language by less than 1 % of the population. Although proficiency levels exceed this, access to English remains *classed*. Thus a question that haunts anglophone writing in Sri Lanka remains to what extent is it circumscribed within the interests and viewpoints of the privileged. Sri Lankan anglophone writing's recent focus on Sri Lanka's civil war (1983–2009) signals a shift from the narrower class interests of earlier writers.[5]

Twenty-six years of armed conflict have cost the small island nation 80–100,000 lives and indelibly marked its political terrain. Sri Lanka's protracted civil war, and experience of terrorism long before 9/11, received scant international attention, although the war's brutal last phase culminating in the death of thousands of civilians in May 2009 attracted much controversy and influenced Sri Lanka's international standing. (Both the Sri Lankan state and the Liberation Tigers of Tamil Eelam [LTTE] leaders who surrounded themselves with a human shield disregarded the human cost of the conflict.) Nevertheless, the war remains little understood in the West. However, this discussion focuses on fictional representations of Sri Lanka's civil war and nationalist insurgencies not to educate the Euro-American reader, but because of their immense social and political implications. The cataclysmic events of Sri Lanka's conflicts raise crucial questions of citizenship, national identity and gendered social relations that many Sri Lankan writers (in all three languages) attempt to engage with.

Recent Sri Lankan anglophone fiction appears haunted by the 'ghosts' of its warring past. A considerable part of this body of fiction is informed by the recuperation of history as a method of fictionalizing experience subject to the inevitable distortions of memory. The trope of memory operates in even broadly social realist novels (such as A. Sivanandan's *When Memory Dies* (1997)) that manifest the tensions between fiction and history by thematizing the fictionalizing of history, exceeding the recovery

[5] For a reading of this shift, see Jayasuriya (2012).

of untold stories and underscoring the fragmentary changing nature of memory. Others (like Michael Ondaatje) dislodge hegemonic representations of the nation in both form and content, in more pronounced ways: in his hybrid texts (such as *Running in the Family* and *Anil's Ghost*) that confound the generic divisions between fiction, history, autobiography, memoir, personal and national experience. V.V. Ganeshananthan's episodic figuration of her female protagonist's reflections on stories of the past in her debut novel *Love Marriage* (2008) represents an effort to make visible fragmented, nonlinear experiences that challenge and disrupt metanarratives and nationalist discourse, and question assumed understandings of this period of Sri Lankan history. Several diasporic Sri Lankan writers' interrogation of the country's fraught politics challenge insider/outsider and resident/migrant categories. Thus, without eliding the differences (of address, publishing contexts, and so on) between them, this chapter explores both resident and diasporic authors.[6] It begins with a discussion of three (one resident and two disaporic) writers who engage with Sri Lanka's turbulent past in order to understand, rather than simply rehearse and trivialize, its conflicted present.[7]

Hybrid Genealogies: Contesting the Nation: Sivanandan, Selvadurai and Muller

The outbreak of a fully-fledged civil war between the Sinhala majority-led government of Sri Lanka and the LTTE fighting for a separate Tamil state is dated to the horrific anti-Tamil violence of July 1983. However, although July 1983 marked a pivotal turning point, the ensuing eruption of civil war was a culmination of previous events; it is this formative period (of the early twentieth century) that diasporic writers Canadian-Sri Lankan Shyam Selvadurai and the radical ideologue A. Sivanandan (director of the

---

[6] Due to space constraints, I will not consider Sri Lankan authors' treatment of migrancy which remains the usual focus of the existing, limited literary discussion of Sri Lankan fiction. Migrancy has been explored by diasporic writers including Romesh Gunesekera, Roma Tearne, Yasmine Gooneratne, Chandani Lokuge and Roshi Fernando.

[7] I refer to the dehistoricized, exoticized treatment of Sri Lanka's ethno-political crises in Romesh Gunesekera's early fiction. Similarly Roma Tearne's mapping of Sri Lankan conflicts in her novels *Mosquito* (2007), *Bone China* (2008) and *Brixton Beach* (2009) is governed by an aesthetic ideology that privileges retreat from the brutal political violence through the redemptive power of art.

Institute of Race Relations in London) revisit in their historical novels published in the late 1990s.

Selvadurai's second novel, *Cinnamon Gardens* (1998), which is set in Sri Lanka in the 1920s, continues the subtle critique of gendered and sexual norms and the decoupling of the conflation of Sinhala Buddhist ethno-religious identities with the nation that he began in *Funny Boy* (1994), discussed below. At *Cinnamon Gardens*' centre is the subversion of social conventions and sexual norms by the minority anglicized, Christian upper class/caste Tamil protagonists who live in Colombo's residential area Cinnamon Gardens, at the turn of the century: Annalukshmi, who refuses to marry, and Balendran, beset by his transgressive passion for his former lover Richard Howlands. This historical novel encompasses the social concerns of caste oppression, the Women's Franchise Union's campaign for universal suffrage won in 1931, the growth of the labour movement and the economic exploitation of the colonial era during the early twentieth century. However, on publication in 1998, it spoke most powerfully to Sri Lanka's contemporary crisis by underscoring how this war has been fuelled by a right wing logic and model of nationalism: the pre-independence transfer of power and the debates over a new constitution that would reflect the island's multicultural population. The struggle over political representation is dramatized in the widening rifts between majority Sinhala and minority Tamil politicians. The former favour a territorial centralized system, while the Tamil politicians promote a federal model, fearing a Sinhala Raj will replace a British one. *Cinnamon Gardens* disrupts the dominant conflation of Sinhala Buddhist ethno-religious identities with the nation. Balendran's Sinhala best friend and fellow congress member, F.C. Wijewardena, bemoans the caste, ethnic and religious divisions 'appearing where [he] didn't even know there were any … and not a bloody bugger is thinking nationally, except us in the Congress'. His complacent concept of the nation is punctured by Tamil Balendran's understated rejoinder: 'Perhaps the Congress needs to redefine what "national" is.' Furthermore, Selvadurai's text does not simplify the conflict in terms of a Sinhala-Tamil binary (unlike other writers such as Roma Tearne). Instead it signals the competing class, caste and religious interests that complicate these broad groupings. The pompous Mudaliyar's resistance to the demands for universal suffrage unlinked to property and educational qualification appears a transparent bid to maintain his position of privilege: 'It would put the vote in the hands of the servants in our kitchen, labourers and the beggars on the street' (Selvadurai 1998, p. 64).

Like *Cinammon Gardens*, A. Sivanandan's mature, debut novel, *When Memory Dies* (1997), delineates how the fraught politics of Sri Lanka's civil war are imbricated in stories of the past. His tightly structured trigenerational account of a Jaffna Tamil family similarly decentres dominant narratives of the nation. Beginning in the 1920s, it traces a narrative different from Selvadurai's. It charts the various forms of resistance adopted by the Left, particularly the Lanka Sama Samaja Party, which, from its inception in 1935, has played a decisive role in Sri Lankan politics. It mobilized militant trade unions, strikes and anti-colonial demonstrations. It constituted the main opposition to post-independent governments initially opposing the contentious 'Sinhala only' Language Act passed by the Sinhala majoritarian government less than 10 years after independence from Britain in 1956. This made Sinhala the official state language and elevated Buddhism to a state religion. This ill-judged constitutional act was intended to placate Sinhala nationalists by redressing both the perceived over-representation of Tamils under British rule, and the balance of influence of the minute English-speaking elite who controlled much of the power. However, although perceived by some as a democratizing move because of the displacement of the English-speaking elite, it alienated and discriminated against Tamil speakers; anti-Tamil riots followed in 1958. Although Tamil remained an official language (enshrined in the Tamil Official Act 1958) and Tamil speakers continued to be able to study and work in Tamil, the Sinhala Only Act (1956) transformed Sri Lanka's sociopolitical and cultural landscape. It also prompted a questioning of the role of English, the English-educated and the English language creative writer. *When Memory Dies* dramatizes how the Left, fissured by communal interests, failed to prevent this institutionalizing of Sinhala Buddhist hegemony. It ends with the anti-Tamil riots in 1977, the draconian Prevention of Terrorism Act (1979), which enabled the army to arrest and detain Tamils with impunity, and the beginning of separatist violence in 1980s.

The novel's dialogue between the three generations signals its enterprise of historical reclamation dramatized through the contrasting perspectives of a range of characters, and lends a metaphoric density to its title. It is concerned with the re-writing of the nation's past by colonial accounts as well as Sinhala and Tamil nationalists. The novel's most powerful contribution is its emphasis on inter-ethnic friendship, class solidarity and inter-marriage, underscoring that Sri Lanka's diverse communities are not inevitably mutually incompatible, antagonistic and hostile. Rajan's reflections from exile in England on past amity stand in poignant contrast to the present violence:

I thought I lived in a world where there was no communal hatred or conflict, where we didn't kill each other just because we spoke different languages. It is not even that we had so much in common, Sinhalese and Tamils, Buddhists and Hindus, or that we derived from the same racial branch of the tree of man. We were one people. We sang each other's songs as our own, ate each other's food, talked each other's talk, worshipped each other's Gods. (Sivanandan 1997, p. 283)

This recreation of a peaceful, culturally different co-existence is an important part of the book's argument to counter representations of the civil war as an 'ethnic' or 'religious' war and challenge the culturally buttressed belief that the struggle between the ethnic groups is an ancient one. It shifts the debate from intrinsic differences to wider questions of power sharing and social relations. It further problematizes portrayals of Tamil as menacing Other in the context of the rise of terrorism in the 1990s.[8] Sivanandan's recollection of a gentler era of harmony, shared lives, spaces and the portrayal of Tamil Rajan's loving marriage to Sinhalese Lali stand in contrast to other, younger writers who appear less confident about the possibilities of coexistence and intercommunal marriage and friendship.[9]

Where Sivanandan's self-consciously collective history of Sri Lankan Tamils emphasizes coexistence, Carl Muller's rich trilogy on Sri Lanka's tiny Burgher community foregrounds the hybridized nature of the Sri Lankan nation via this 'hotch-potch' of mixed European descent 'that was for convenience classified as Burgher' (Muller 1993, p. 27). Written during a time of heightened Sinhala nationalism, Muller's novels *The Jam Fruit Tree* (1993), *Yakada Yaka* (1994) and *Once Upon a Tender Time* (1995) challenge ethnic classification and the Sinhala-Tamil binary that Sinhala and Tamil nationalism operates on with its emphasis on racial authenticity that disallows hybrid possibilities, and point to a more polyphonic reading

---

[8] For a critique, see Perera (2012), pp. 103–11.
[9] For instance, in Selvadurai's *Funny Boy*, all the transgressive pairings across ethnic divides ultimately fail. In contrast to the subversive thrust of the novel, these failures do not challenge the fixity of constructions of ethnic difference. See also Roma Tearne's portrayals of Sinhala-Tamil marriages as doomed alliances caught up in a bitter feud of prejudices and hatred and intercommunal friendships marked by mutual suspicion. Similarly, the potential for intercommunal solidarity and friendship via protagonist Krishna's involvement with a Marxist group is negated by his friend Iqbal's elitist comments in Pradeep Jeganathan's short story 'At the Water's Edge' (Jeganathan 2004, p. 100).

of national identity.[10] *The Jam Fruit Tree* (1993) celebrates cross-cultural marriages, and satirizes Burgher Cecilprins's objection to his daughter marrying a Sinhalese as irrational:

> So never mind. You thinking we are special or something? Good to go to top market buying *bombili* ... from Sinhalese man... get children's bicycle made by Sinhalese man ... eat rice and curry and *stringhoppers* like Sinhalese man.... Father telling in church love the neighbour. See, will you, who the neighbour is. Sinhalese, no? (Muller 1993, p. 43)

Subsequent writers such as Shehan Karunatilaka have commented on the inspiring influence of Muller's Lankanizing of Standard English: the way his prose mimics Sinhala rhythms by altering the syntax. At the same time, Muller's construction of the Burgher community, during the height of the civil war, as an example of a 'tiny minority who can live in absolute freedom and be accepted by the majority', defined in contrast to 'those other guys who are going around throwing bombs and demanding separate states' (p. 137) is an over-simplification of the distinct socio-political concerns facing Sri Lanka's different minorities. Similarly, the text's radical subversion of passive female stereotypes results in a gendered homogenization of 'fruitful, tough, always in bloom... full-blooded Burgher women who think long and lustily about sex' (p. 20).[11]

JULY 1983 AND ITS AFTERLIFE: SELVADURAI (1994), JEGANATHAN (2004), WIJESINGHE (2006), GANESHANANTHAN (2009)

The funeral of 13 Sinhalese soldiers ambushed and killed by the LTTE in Jaffna in July 1983 sparked off the horrific spate of state-sanctioned murder of Tamil citizens and burning of Tamil-owned homes and businesses

---

[10] Similarly, Ameena Hussein's Booker-long-listed *The Moon in the Water* (2009) foregrounds the multiplicity of Sri Lankan identity with its insights into a Sri Lankan Muslim family, which is seldom explored in Sri Lankan fiction. Although Sri Lankan Muslims comprise the island's second largest ethnic minority, they tend to be erased in nationalist essentialized binaries of Sinhala versus Tamils. Like these other authors, Hussein documents a gentle cultural hybridity. A Muslim protagonist attends a Catholic school where her best friend is a Buddhist. Arjuna, adopted by a Sinhala Buddhist family, articulates his fascination with Hindu temples, in a time when Islamic identities were less heightened, recreating the author's childhood era when Muslim girls attended school without wearing hijab.

[11] For a feminist critique of Muller's work, see Ranasinha (1994).

in the capital and elsewhere. 'Black July' marked a defining turning point in both the conflict and for Sri Lankan creative writing, searing the optimism and creative sensibilities of a generation of authors writing in its aftermath and beyond. A notable example (in the period covered here) is Selvadurai's debut novel *Funny Boy* (1994). This poignant *Bildungsroman* set in 1970s Sri Lanka masterfully unifies its twin critique of the brutalizing effects of the ethnic conflict and of sexual norms. It sensitively portrays the young, gay Tamil narrator Arjie's bewildering sexual awakening, alongside his increasing awareness of family conflicts, political realities and ethnic polarization. When these tensions erupt in the anti-Tamil violence of July 1983, Arjie's grandparents are burnt to death when their car is set alight. His family home is violated and he and his family go into hiding before migrating. Upheavals in the personal sphere merge with the wider upheaval: family, home and nation become uninhabitable by the end of the novel.

Similarly, Manuka Wijesinghe's female *Bildungsroman*, *Monsoon and Potholes* (2006), vividly recreates the Black July pogrom through the death of the narrator's long employed Tamil family retainer, Podian. The novel directly indicts the then president J. R. Jayewardena for holding a mass funeral for the Sinhalese soldiers despite 'knowing that this was the final push the magma chamber of Sinhala anger needed to explode' and moreover for allowing the killing and looting to continue unchecked for 4 days (Wijesinghe 2006, pp. 332, 357), as well as the involvement of the police in the looting. (This is the first fictional book to do so and stands in marked contrast with Edward Gunawardena *Blood and Cyanide*.) This direct comment interwoven with allegory, satire and humour reflects the intricacies of narrating politically loaded events in a climate of fear. If this emphasis on politicians and political opportunism obscures the role of the ordinary perpetrators of ethnic violence, she nevertheless charts important factors that contribute to ethnic disharmony. Moreover, like Selvadurai, Wijesinghe encompasses a critique of *both* ethno-nationalism *and* gendered and sexual norms in her irreverent coming of age novel narrated by a female protagonist who self-consciously subverts traditional gendered norms in a fusion of autobiography and history that is both hilarious and poignant.

In contrast to Selvadurai's off-stage account of the murder of Arjie's grandparents, Pradeep Jeganathan's short story 'Sri Lanka', published two decades after the event, presents a rare, explicit and graphic description of the violence inflicted on Tamil citizens in 1983: 'They bashed their heads on our wall, and then smashed their skulls with blocks on concrete …

just broke their skulls in' (Jeganathan 2004, p. 67). Jeganathan's seven interlinked stories in his collection, *At the Water's Edge*, also set in the 1970s, invite us to consider the cultural and social values that enabled mass violence. They chart the creeping militarization of society, the construction of anti-Tamil ideology embedded in the education system in 'The Front Row' alongside the unchallenged racism that becomes heightened post-1983 captured in a conversation on 'A Train from Batticaloa': '... should have finished the Tamils off in 1983. We left too many of them and see what is happening now' (p. 78). Jeganathan further critiques the role of the Tamil diaspora in the conflict: the influential Mr Sundar living in Boston speaks articulately on Tamil discrimination in Sri Lanka, but stands far removed from Tamil fighters and victims in the North in terms of his privilege, caste and class affiliation.

Like Jeganathan, V.V. Ganeshananthan—the most recent diasporic Sri Lankan writer to engage with the fall-out of 1983—also dramatizes the *transnational* dimensions of what is often misunderstood as highly localized ethnic civil war, in her debut novel *Love Marriage* (2008). This is achieved through fragmented vignettes of the heroine's globe-scattered extended Sri Lankan Tamil family, its emphasis on the role of the diasporic Tamil Tigers from the 1970s and the critique of the global network of diasporic Tiger money-laundering and drug-dealing in cities like Toronto: 'This is not a noble fight. It has nothing to do with the people dying in another country. It has to do with territory here, territory now, in this Western city... No one is selfless. People profit off this war. In Sri Lanka they do it by selling arms' (Ganeshananthan 2009, p. 254). Born in July 1983, the novel's diasporic heroine Yalini (like Saleem Sinai, enmeshed with India's post-Independent history in *Midnight's Children*) is inextricably and self-consciously linked to this watershed event in Sri Lankan history; Yalini represents a generation with no knowledge of a pre-war Sri Lanka: 'I heard stories about Tamils disappearing, Tamils tortured, Tamils killing Tamils ... I learned to believe that a government could kill its own and drive them to commit unspeakable crimes. That no-one would be right, but that some would be more wrong' (p. 255). The novel acknowledges the hollowness of LTTE's claim to be freedom fighters representing all Tamils, highlighting the ruthless eradication of anyone (even an old Tamil schoolteacher who organized a cricket match with the Sri Lankan army) who challenged its authoritarianism and cult of violence.

Like Selvadurai and Wijesinghe, Ganeshananthan encompasses a critique of ethno-nationalist and patriarchal norms with a focus on gender.

As the daughter of migrant Tamils resident in the US, Yalini remains protected from Sri Lanka's conflict until her uncle Kumaran, a former Tiger leader diagnosed with cancer, is allowed to come to Canada to die (in a fictionalized version of the fate of LTTE ideologue Anton Balasingham). Yalini's situation is counterpointed with that of her cousin, Kumaran's daughter Janani, whose role as female militant remains circumscribed within patriarchal social constructions, even after migration.[12] However, *Love Marriage*'s critical intervention is its powerful, feminist portraits of the little-known lives of previous generations of Tamil women: Yalini's aunts and great-aunts in Jaffna; the beautiful, talented Kunju badly disfigured when her sari caught fire from an oil lamp, 'her face irrevocably undone ... a burden to the men who might have married her' (Ganeshananthan 2009, p. 71); Harini's 'Marriage to the Wrong Man' ends in domestic violence. These moving accounts provide an insightful addition to Sivanandan's male-centred collective history of Tamils in Sri Lanka in *When Memory Dies* and his masculinizing of agency.[13] She continues this focus in her forthcoming novel about a Tamil female combatant.

Ganeshananthan's literary account of the conflict also helps us to rethink and delegitimize dominant narratives of global war and violence. The novel emphasizes the power of narrative, especially the 'certain set of stories' (Ganeshananthan 2009, p. 298) through which children learn about the origins and nature of the conflict from their families and underscores the extent to which the Sri Lankan conflict is marked by a level of contestation over basic facts: 'None of the stories will be absolutely complete, but their tellers will be absolutely certain. This is how we make war' (p. 120). The novel implies that if clashing versions of events create war, stories can play an equal role in unravelling these conflicts. Careful to apportion blame on both sides, critiquing LTTE violence whilst delineating legitimate grievances, Ganeshananthan does not demonize Kumaran, unlike many Lankan portraits of the LTTE. Instead, the text shows that the man who plotted countless deaths was also Yalini's mother's beloved brother 'who shared every meal with her' and charts his tipping point into 'insanity', violence and terrorism (p. 111).

---

[12] However, see V. Chandrasekeram's play *The Forbidden Area* (Gratiaen Prize-winner 1998) for a more complex, nuanced treatment of the patriarchal structures masked by the rhetoric of gender and class equality that provides an illusory appeal to the Tamil female militant protagonist.

[13] See Ranasinha (2007) for a discussion of this aspect of Sivanandan's fiction.

War, Terror and the Politicization of Violence: De Silva, Ondaatje, Thwaites, Arasanayagam, Fernandopulle

The fragmented and painful nature of individual and communal memories of civil war heightens the challenge of representing conflict, and is at odds with larger unities of the novel form. Resident writers and Gratiaen award-holders Jean Arasanayagam (1995), Jean Thwaites (1999) and Neil Fernandopulle (2000) deploy the short story form expertly to narrate the fragmented lives and disparate perspectives of a range of agents and victims of political violence in their literary representations of the 'everyday' experience of war. Thwaites's 'Nihal's War' dramatizes a visiting writer's brief encounter with young Sinhalese soldiers on the east coast of Arugam Bay during the height of the civil war. Within its few pages it powerfully captures the soldiers' physical vulnerability—'they can see for miles in every direction, which means the LTTE can see them as easily' (Thwaites 1999, p. 75); their hospitality, sharing their meagre provisions and tea 'without milk or sugar' and abstaining themselves, to share their limited provisions with their guests; their resigned acceptance of their duty with no end in sight—'not convinced there will ever be an *after the war*'; and most poignantly their youth—'When you write, write that I am very young' (p. 77). 'Rohan's War' foregrounds a Sri Lankan middle class cocooned from the war, apart from a random LTTE suicide bomber's strike in Colombo; it satirically juxtaposes Colombo society attending lectures about the war and sipping arrack cocktails with the actual fighting raging in the North and East. The dialogue hints at a key reason for the protracted nature of the war and lack of political will to find a political rather than military solution: it is not 'rich men's sons fighting this war' (p. 154). Instead, unemployed youth join the army to lift themselves and their families out of poverty and in the process become cannon-fodder. Fernandopulle's collection 'Shrapnel' dramatizes perspectives that range from a suicide bomber to a war widow in 'Left Behind'.

Jean Arasanayagam's (a long-established poet and prose writer of Dutch Burgher origin married to a Tamil painter and poet) short story collection *All is Burning* contemplates the ordinary victims 'tired ... of the horrors of this eternal war' (Arasanayagam 1995, p. 42). It traces the violation of communal space now turned into a 'territory of fear' (p. 391). Images of bodies inscribed and pitted with bullets abound.

In 'I Am an Innocent Man', narrated by a Tamil school teacher from an East coast village, the title becomes a plaintive refrain by the narrator who in fact feels 'besmirched and defiled' (p. 41) by witnessing the extra-judicial slaughter of an entire village of Tamil males above the age of 15 by government forces. That all Tamil men are considered suspects of subversive activity because separatist guerrillas move 'freely among the people and did not always wear uniforms' indicts both the security forces and the guerrillas using the civilians as a human shield (p. 26). Arasanayagam forces us to scrutinize the impact of civil war on gendered subjects at the margins of patriarchies: the heart-breaking suffering of mothers searching for their sons—they 'wait by the camps to get a glimpse of them peering through the grill or a half-shut door' when they are rounded up by the forces never to be seen again; the women act as 'death couriers' as they find bodies and carry the news back (pp. 32, 36). 'The Man Without a Mask' dramatizes the politicization of violence in an era of assassinations by shadowy groups whose alignment is not clear; the role of hired assassins and mercenaries highlights the transnational dimensions of the violence.

If Sivanandan emphasizes *past* intercommunal amity, then the late Nihal De Silva's[14] achievement in his Gratiaen and State Literary Prize winning novel, *The Road from Elephant Pass* (2003), is his delineation of the *potential* for intercommunal reconciliation in his convincing portrayal of the developing relationship between two adversaries from the opposite ends of the political spectrum. In his narrative, concentrated into a single month in 2000, a Sinhalese army officer and female LTTE cadre (supposedly turned informer) are forced to escape together through the rebel-held Jaffna peninsula and abandoned Wilpattu jungle on foot. They have to overlook their political differences to overcome the dangers facing them. Tracking their hazardous journey in a gripping plot, the novel charts their relationship as it shifts from mutual distrust and irritation, to grudging respect and eventually to love. The characterization does not escape ethnic stereotyping or patriarchal constructions: the macho, hot-headed army officer from the South is defined in contrast to the skilled female LTTE activist's calm, 'cold-blooded control' (De Silva 2003, p. 144). The narrative privileges the politics and point of view of the Sinhalese army

---

[14] The author was tragically killed in a landmine explosion in Wilpattu national park (described so lovingly in this book) in 2006.

officer-narrator. Nevertheless, the protagonists' intense debates attempt to capture perspectives from opposing sides of the conflict.[15] Their discussions prompt each to confront the prejudices and propaganda of their own organizations, as well as the wider issues that keep their estranged communities apart.

Ondaatje's novel *Anil's Ghost* (2000) engages with a critical juncture in Sri Lanka's civil war: its entanglement with the JVP Sinhalese insurgency[16] against the government in the south in the late 1980s, the state's counter-terrorism and the rise of the Sri Lankan state as violent and corrupt: 'we were caught in the middle. It was like being in a room with three suitors,[17] all of whom had blood on their hands' (Ondaatje 2000, p. 150). In contrast to war reportage and analysis, the narrative foregrounds the 'unofficial' human context and stories. It conveys the tactics of terror, the 'night visitations, kidnapping or murders in broad daylight' that created the 'unfinished ... loss' of the disappearances and 'scarring psychosis' in the 'fearful nation' (p. 52). The protagonist, Anil Tissera, a forensic expert based in the US, returns to her native Sri Lanka after 15 years as part of a Human Rights investigation into the role of the Sri Lankan government in political murders. Ondaatje deploys the fictional conventions of a detective story as Anil tries to solve the 'truth' behind the murder of an anonymous man who is now only a burnt skeleton: 'to study history as if it were a body' (p. 189). Maintaining his characteristic

[15] In contrast, see critiques of more partial one-sided Sinhala accounts, Punyakante Wijenaike's *The Enemy Within* or Shirani Rajapakse's *Breaking News*, in Perera (2012).

[16] The Janatha Vimukthi Peramuna (JVP) first came to prominence in the late 1960s with the aim of establishing a socialist state. It was founded by Rohana Wijeweera, educated at a Soviet University, who brought a rural revolutionary attitude to this antigovernment rebellion. The JVP's first period of insurrection (April–June 1971) was crushed by the then socialist government (explored in the fiction of Ediriweera Sarachchandra among others). The background to *Anil's Ghost* is the second, more brutal insurgency (mid-1980s to late 1980s) that almost brought down the UNP government; this insurgency and the government's equally vicious repression resulted in the death and 'disappearance' of an estimated 60,000 people. Minoli Salgado's novel *A Little Dust on the Eyes* (2014) explores lives 'enmeshed in this hidden war that failed to make international news ... masked by the shrieking headlines on the larger war between the government and the LTTE .. that lacked the comfortable logic of race and ethnicity, religious, cultural difference, easy distinctions favoured by those who liked to keep things simple and clean' (Salgado 2014, p. 76).

[17] The three 'suitors' are the anti-government insurgents, separatists and the government's forces against both.

fragmented narrative style, Ondaatje weaves between past and present in this collation of multiple stories, memories and vignettes. The impersonal third-person narrator shifts from one focus to another, as Anil forms an uneasy alliance with the remote Sarath, the archaeologist appointed to assist her, and his solitary brother Gamini who is scarred by the war in different ways.

Polarized critical responses to *Anil's Ghost* emerged: Sri Lankan reviewers tend to interpret the novel in terms of an attenuation of Sri Lankan history and politics. Qadri Ismail (2000, p. 25) argues that it fails to critique hegemonic Buddhist, Sinhala nationalism. Even Radhika Coomaraswamy's defence of *Anil's Ghost* expresses concern with the under-representation of Tamils: she concludes that the novel does not aim to foster a 'multi-cultural alternative' for Sri Lanka (Coomaraswamy 2000, p. 29). In contrast, Marlene Goldman (2005, p. 28) argues that, while the novel may appear to promote the idea of a sanitized Sri Lankan Buddhist faith transcending history, it actually suggests how the religion has become enmeshed with politics in Sri Lanka with the political killing of the Buddhist monk Narada by anti-government insurgents and reference to the 'fields where Buddhism and its values met the harsh political events of the twentieth century' (Ondaatje 2000, p. 300). In the context of dewhitening trauma theory, however, Heike Härting (2009, p. 240) suggests the novel presents only a limited critique of 'the discourses of global humanitarian intervention'; while for Victoria Burrows (2008, p. 177) the narrative 'exposes the way the western world *turns away* from the experience of trauma that so often blights postcolonial subjects'.

POLITICS AT AN ANGLE: SHEHAN KARUNATILAKA'S *CHINAMAN: THE LEGEND OF PRADEEP MATHEW*

In contrast to the grim depictions of war-torn Sri Lanka described above, Shehan Karunatilaka's debut novel *Chinaman* (2011) is a tumultuous, irreverent reading of the last few decades of Sri Lankan history viewed through the alcoholic haze of its unreliable narrator. W. G. Karunasena, a dying, down-and-out retired sports journalist, tracing the reasons for the mysterious disappearance of 'the greatest cricketer to ever walk the Earth': Pradeep Mathew, once famed for his signature ability to perform the particular bowling delivery referred to in the title (Karunatilaka 2011, p. 195). At first, Karunatilaka thought the hybrid genre of a cricket-mystery novel would enable him to side-step 'the big issues' of war and politics.[18] However he suggests these themes 'crept in' despite his intention to exclude them.[19] Indeed, the civil war simmers beneath the surface with people's identities polarized into a simple murderous opposition: 'men with clubs and knives stormed the bus and asked passengers to speak Sinhala, to say words that Tamils found tricky to pronounce.... An elderly gentleman ... did not [pass the test]. He was dragged out and set on fire' (p. 69). Deploying cricket as a metaphor for the malaise of Lankan politics, the novel subtly deploys match-fixing, ball-tampering and Pradeep's mixed Sinhala and Tamil heritage to probe pervasive corruption, racism, snobbery and terrorism alongside the role of rumours and the blurring and manipulation of fact and fiction in cricket-obsessed Sri Lanka. This twisting, non-linear narrative of fragments encompasses alcoholism, paedophile sex tourism, male friendships and fathers and sons. It moves effortlessly between tragedy and farce, mixing violence and humour. Multiple prize-winner, hailed as the long-awaited 'Great Sri Lankan Novel', this scathing portrait nevertheless celebrates the vitality of life in Sri Lanka.

WAVE AND OTHER STORIES

During a brief ceasefire between the Sri Lankan army and the LTTE, a second, natural catastrophe struck the region, particularly affecting the coastal communities already afflicted by the impact of chronic civil war. The 2004 Indian Ocean tsunami killed over 35,000 people in Sri Lanka alone, affected another 800,000 people in the coastal areas and devastated more than half of its coastline. Sri Lankan expatriate economist Sonali Deraniyagala's extraordinary, haunting memoir *Wave: Life and Memories after the Tsunami* (2013) describes the loss of her two young sons, her husband and her parents in the tsunami that she survived, while on holiday in Sri Lanka.

Although not a work of fiction,[20] her finely crafted memoir offers a harrowing insight into one woman's personal loss and the desolation

---

[18] Although strikingly different to *Chinaman* in other ways, Tissa Abeysekera's *Bringing Tony Home* (Gratiaen winner 1996) also explores social issues obliquely. It combines fiction, memoir and history in sensuous, detailed meditations on adolescence, memory and ageing.

[19] Shehan Karunatilaka, Sri Lankan Writers Talk, Asia House, May 2011.

[20] A number of tsunami fictions have been published by Sri Lankan writers, including Ashok Ferrey's collection of short stories *Love in the Tsunami* (2012), Minoli Salgado's *A Little Dust on the Eyes* (2014) and Simon Harris and Neluka Silva's *The Rolled Back Beach: Stories from the Tsunami* (2008).

that followed: what it is 'to be bereft in a way that cannot be imagined' (Deraniyagala 2013, p. 103). She describes how her grief changes but does not lessen: from suicidal fury, she tries to indelibly imprint '*they are dead*' on her consciousness, and to eventually come to terms with her irreplaceable loss and survivor's guilt (p. 79). Initially, she tries to resist memories, but over the ensuing years she reaches for quotidian details to memorialize her family. Slowly she allows herself to retrace the idyllic life she now mourns: from their family home in London, to the birth of her sons, to meeting her adoring English husband at Cambridge, to her privileged childhood in Colombo. In exquisite prose, she distils the process of memory: brief vignettes that emerge in non-linear ways triggered by spaces, objects, the quality of light and smells. Her treatment of memory as mourning contrasts with Sivanandan's and his nostalgia for national 'lost time'.

With unsparing candour and precision, she reveals her anger at a surviving, sobbing child: 'I didn't try to comfort him. Stop blubbing …you only survived … because you are so fucking fat … Just shut up' (Deraniyagala 2013, p.16). For Deraniyagala, her hitherto charmed, 'always safe' life makes her loss even more unbearable (p. 37); privilege shattered for the first time by this natural disaster. Despite the reader's sympathy for her unfathomable grief, the author remains remote. At the same time, an online Euro-American reviewer bluntly observed that this 'unique' memoir has resonated with so many precisely because the victim, an expatriate academic in an interracial marriage based in London, 'is us and not some unnamed villager'.[21] Thus the reception of the memoir raises interesting, potentially uncomfortable questions about empathy, as well as the lure of non-fictional accounts of disaster. As readers we are lodged claustrophobically within her consciousness. So deeply entrenched in the extremity of her situation, there is no narrative space for an allusion or image of the impact of this mass tragedy beyond the author's devastating personal loss.

Isankya Kodithuwakku's collection of short-stories *The Banana Tree Crisis* (Gratiaen Winner 2006) re-imagines the tsunami's impact on a range of coastal villagers' lives with extraordinary attention to detail, sensitivity and a special emphasis on its impact on the women. In the story 'Buffer Zone', a young mother struggles comes to terms with the loss of her baby in the wave:

---

[21] See 'Avidreader' in Community Reviews of *Wave* www.goodreads.com

How can I put it behind me? Look, look. Harriet pointed at the bodice of her dress, wet on the front.

'Milk's still coming to me, *akka*.' (Kodithuwakku 2006, p. 124)

This story engages with complexities of tsunami aid and the ensuing culture of dependence. It critiques the gendered politics of aid that 'hands the money to Harriet's husband because he was the head of the household. Harriet never saw a rupee of that money. Instead it was all spent in the *mudalali's* boutique' (p. 151). At the same time the story acknowledges the importance of the NGO's psychosocial healing to women affected 'in a country that gave no place to the needs of the mind and concentrated on the necessities of the body' (p. 154). 'Shallow Canoes' explores the impact of the tsunami on an already impoverished Muslim community displaced by the war.[22]

POST 2009

Despite the absence of armed conflict since 2009, the prospect of a just society where diversity and dissent are respected remains elusive. Sinhala nationalism has since flourished and issues of devolution for Tamil populations in the North and East remain unresolved. Journalists critical of the Rajapakse government (2005–2015) have been murdered and intimidated. The aftermath of the war has seen increasing militarization of state and society, censorship and polarization and threats to civil society and rule of law. While many Sri Lankans are relieved that the war is now over and they are free of the fear of the LTTE, some remain troubled by this aftermath and the state's triumphalism since winning the civil war. Selvadurai (who heads the *Write to Reconcile Project* designed to give voice to young authors to write about war, trauma, memory and reconciliation) expresses concern at this post-civil strife government brutality. His public question about whether Sri Lankan writers are dealing with the 'great material of Sri Lanka's past in the general atmosphere of fear and stifling dissent' (*Groundviews* 2012), relates to his own attempt to engage with the past in his recent novel *The Hungry Ghosts* (2014).

Looking beyond the trope of 'lost paradise' of his earlier fiction, Romesh Gunesekera's masterly new collection of short stories, *Noontide Toll* (2014), thematizes the central questions facing Sri Lanka today. What

[22] This theme is also explored in Ameena Hussein's novel *The Moon in the Water* (2009).

can peace mean for a country riven by almost 26 years of civil war? How do we address the past? Do we excavate it or bury it in the flurry of hotel-building and post-war reconstruction? Writing in the context of the government's attempt to erase the past by obliterating LTTE monuments, this collection underscores the importance of memory to the nature of conflict and echoes Selvadurai's emphasis on the role of fiction writers to create spaces to remember and think freely. Gunesekera's stories are narrated by the perceptive taxi-driver Vasanthan, now able to drive his 'white van' (a notorious symbol synonymous with abductions and 'disappearances') to parts of Sri Lanka previously off-limits during the war. He sees the scale of the impact of the war that many would not have seen because of managed reporting. Peopled by ambivalent émigrés, foreign investors in scrap metal left over from the fighting, this cycle of interwoven stories provides startling glimpses of a country grappling with the early stages of the 'toll' of its post-war existence.

Furthermore, post-war Sri Lanka has seen the emergence of new forms of ethno-religious violence and religious extremism. The defeat of the LTTE has neutralized the threat of a Tamil expansionist agenda heightened by Sinhala nationalists. However, this new political reality has created space for a renewal of the construction by Sinhala Buddhist[23] nationalists of Muslims as threatening cultural and economic competitors (by drawing on a discourse that dates back to the 1915 anti-Muslim riots) with the connivance of the authorities. This led to waves of assaults on Muslim-owned shops in 2013. In June 2014, a virulent, inflammatory hate speech by the leader of Bodhu Bala Sena (or Buddhist Power Front, an extreme Buddhist organization established in 2012) incited attacks on Muslims and their shops and homes in the southern coastal town of Aluthgama.

Ameena Hussein's novel *The Moon in the Water* (2009) engages with the backdrop to some of these ethno-religious tensions emerging in post-war Sri Lanka. The novel articulates an uncompromising critique of Wahhabi-funded fundamentalist organizations infiltrating poor countries with large Muslim populations like Sri Lanka through the story of Shahul

---

[23] Madhubashini Ratnayake explores the politicization of Buddhism in her novel *There is Something I Have to Tell You* (2013). Shyam Selvadurai's *The Hungry Ghosts* (2014) provides a different critique of how Buddhism is practised in Sri Lanka: how concepts of Karma are used to explain away social injustices of racism, homophobia and caste discrimination. Similarly, Minoli Salgado's *A Little Dust on the Eyes* explores how religion can obstruct justice: those traumatized by violence lived by the 'lie that there was no point in trying to enforce earthly mechanisms of justice' (Salgado 2014, p.183).

Hameed, a Sri Lankan Imam from the coastal town of Kalpitiya. The son of an impoverished Imam, Hameed is lured by the promise of education and travel to a religious madrassah in Pakistan (funded by the Wahhabis from Saudi Arabia). This school turns out to be a 'religious prison' of 'unquestioning rote, rigid hierarchy and intolerance' and indoctrination run by 'sadists' (Hussein 2009, p. 206). Hameed eventually manages to escape but his experience encourages him to 'seek out new and compassionate interpretations of the religion' and he now encourages Sri Lankan Muslim 'youth to debate and probe intricate principles' of Islam (p. 207). But he knows it is a losing battle in Sri Lanka with hundreds of villagers returning from jobs in the Middle East 'bringing with them the strict Wahhabi interpretation that in his opinion broke its spirit'. Hussein privileges a nation-centred conception of Sri Lankan Muslim identity rather than Global Ummah, and negates the identification of Sri Lankan Muslims with Arabs as misplaced. Thus Shahul observes: 'We are not Arabs. So why do we want to dress like Arabs? We belong to this country that has a proud and rich history. We must not forget our contribution to this country of ours. We have no need to look elsewhere for our heritage but take pride in being a Sri Lankan' (p. 208) However, Hussein also presciently indicates the Sinhala ethno-nationalism that discourages Sri Lankan Muslims from identifying with Sri Lanka: '"Look Imam," a few would retort lightly "this country seems to have no need for us, and we, we are descended from Arabs"' (p. 208). This is an ethno-nationalism that has increased at horrifying rate since the novel was first published in 2009.

Whether and how Sri Lankan fiction in English will engage with these renewed ethno-religious tensions, the erosion of human rights (posited as 'Western' and alien) and democracy, and the breakdown in law and order remains to be seen. The Sri Lankan state, headed by Mahinda Rajapaksa (2005–2015), needed the fear of renewed war to maintain its repressive regime, and for its authoritarian and military priorities to remain tolerated in times of peace. Thus the role that literature and literary criticism can play in bolstering or questioning hegemonic patriarchal ethno-nationalist imaginaries is clear, especially given the part it has already played in shaping perceptions of this period in Sri Lankan history and in indicting ethno-nationalist ideologies and imagining ethnic coexistence. But if it is to have a wider circulation (in terms of both class and community) and deeper impact, Sri Lankan writing in English requires a sustained programme of translation into Sinhala and Tamil (and vice versa) to enable its intersection and dialogue with Sinhala and Tamil writers and readers.

Works Cited

Arasanayagam, J. (1995). *All is burning*. Delhi: Penguin India.
Burrows, V. (2008). The heterotopic spaces of postcolonial trauma in Michael Ondaatje's *Anil's ghost*. *Studies in the Novel*, 40(1&2), 161–177.
Coomaraswamy, R. (2000). In defence of humanistic ways of knowing: A reply to Qadri Ismail. *Pravada*, 6(9/10), 29–30.
De Silva, N. (2003). *The road from Elephant Pass*. Colombo: Vijitha Yapa.
Deraniyagala, S. (2013). *Wave: A memoir of life after the tsunami*. London: Virago.
Ganeshananthan, V. V. (2009). *Love marriage*. London: Phoenix.
Goldman, M. (2005). Representations of Buddhism in Ondaatje's *Anil's ghost*. In S. Totosy de Zepetnek (Ed.), *Comparative cultural studies and Michael Ondaatje's writing* (pp. 27–38). West Lafayette: Purdue University Press.
Groundviews. (2012, December 19). Writing to reconcile in Sri Lanka. *Groundviews* [Online]. Accessed 30 Sept 2014. Available from http://groundviews.org/2012/12/19/writing-to-reconcile-in-sri-lanka/
Härting, H. (2009). From ethnic civil war to global war: (De)legitimizing narratives of global warfare and the longing for civility in Sri Lankan fiction. In S. Bernstein & W. D. Coleman (Eds.), *Unsettled legitimacy: Political community, power, and authority in a global era* (pp. 216–240). Vancouver: UBC Press.
Hussein, A. (2009). *The moon in the water*. Colombo: Perera Hussein Publishing House.
Ismail, Q. (2000). A flippant gesture towards Sri Lanka: A review of Michael Ondaatje's *Anil's ghost*. *Pravada*, 6(9/10), 24–29.
Ismail, Q. (2005). *Abiding by Sri Lanka: On peace, place and postcoloniality*. Minnesota: University of Minnesota Press.
Jayasuriya, M. (2012). *Terror and reconciliation: Sri Lankan anglophone literature 1983–2009*. Lanham: Lexington Books.
Jeganathan, P. (2004). *At the water's edge*. Boston: South Focus Press.
Karunatilaka, S. (2011). *Chinaman: The legend of Pradeep Mathew*. London: Jonathan Cape.
Kodithuwakku, I. (2006). *The banana tree crisis*. Colombo: Vijitha Yapa Publications.
Muller, C. (1993). *The jam fruit tree*. Delhi: Penguin India.
Ondaatje, M. (2000). *Anil's ghost*. Toronto: McClelland and Stewart.
Perera, V. (2012). *Dismissive necessities in post 2009 Sri Lankan English fiction*. Kandy: Creative Printers.
Ranasinha, R. (1994). *Jam fruit tree* and Carl Muller's construction of women. *Nivedini*, 2(1), 18–27.
Ranasinha, R. (2007). *South Asian writers in twentieth-century Britain: Culture in translation*. Oxford: Oxford University Press.
Ranasinha, R. (2013). Writing and reading Sri Lanka. *Journal of Commonwealth Literature*, 48(1), 27–39.

Salgado, M. (2007). *Writing Sri Lanka: Literature, resistance and the politics of place*. London: Routledge.
Salgado, M. (2014). *A little dust on the eyes*. Leeds: Peepal Tree Press.
Selvadurai, S. (1994). *Funny boy*. London: Jonathan Cape.
Selvadurai, S. (1998). *Cinnamon gardens*. Toronto: McClelland and Stewart.
Selvadurai, S. (Ed.). (2014). *Many roads through paradise: An anthology of Sri Lankan literature*. Delhi: Penguin India.
Sivanandan, A. (1997). *When memory dies*. London: Arcadia.
Thwaites, J. (1999). *It's a sunny day on the moon and other stories*. Colombo: Nikang Press.
Wijesinghe, M. (2006). *Monsoon and potholes*. Colombo: Perera Hussein Publishing House.

PART II

Contemporary Transformations

Writing the Margins (in English): Notes from Some South-Asian Cities

Stuti Khanna

This chapter examines some contemporary works of fiction that have emerged from South Asia in recent years and which, more particularly, centre the experience of their protagonists in the cities they call their homes. Owing to this fact alone, these novels are able not only to address some of the most significant social, economic and political changes that continue to convulse the region, but also to challenge and extend Anglo-American meanings of the urban, as well as to invoke newer forms of narrative that map, linguistically and stylistically, the experience of a fractured, incommensurable 'citiness'. The cities in question—Amritsar, Bhopal and Karachi—are all, regardless of their size, to a greater or lesser extent, cities in crisis, owing mainly to the staggering disparity in the ownership of resources—money, land, water, education and opportunity—exacerbated by the rapid, headlong and uneven urbanization of much of the global South in the last few decades.[1] Rupa Bajwa's Amritsar may at first glance

[1] Recent reports tell us that the seven largest megacities (defined as areas of continuous urban development of over ten million people) are located in Asia. The fastest-growing megacities over the past decade have been primarily in the developing world. Karachi, Pakistan, has led the growth charge, with a remarkable 80 % expansion in its population from

S. Khanna
Department of Humanities and Social Sciences, Indian Institute of Technology Delhi, India

© The Editor(s) (if applicable) and The Author(s) 2016
A. Tickell (ed.), *South-Asian Fiction in English*,
DOI 10.1057/978-1-137-40354-4_6

have the placid feel of a small town, but it seethes and pulsates with the powerless rage and frustration of its angst-ridden protagonist (*The Sari Shop*, 2004). Indra Sinha's Khaufpur ('Terror Town', a thinly veiled reference to Bhopal in the aftermath of the 1984 gas tragedy) is a ruined city with a devastated populace that, like its eponymous hero Animal, learns to hope and trust once again despite the corruption and callousness it encounters repeatedly at every step (*Animal's People*, 2007). The casually, gratuitously, almost absurdly violent Karachi that Mohammed Hanif's Alice belongs to (*Our Lady of Alice Bhatti*, 2011) could be straight out of a Quentin Tarantino film, except that it refers to a very real, very contemporary city that is struggling with sectarian violence, extremist groups and organized crime mafias that work more often than not in cahoots with a woefully inadequate police force. Mohsin Hamid's unnamed city in 'rising Asia' in which the (also nameless) protagonist lives out his rags to riches story has an abstract, mythic quality to it that, however, refuses to become a fairy tale by its insistence on laying bare the often unsavoury, extra-legal dealings that mark ambitious undertakings in the global South (*How to Get Filthy Rich in Rising Asia*, 2013).[2] All of these novels write into being the fractured, pullulating South-Asian city from the standpoints of characters who constitute its vast underclass and will be the focus of this chapter, raising the issues of writing and representation that this chapter is particularly interested in exploring. Precariously positioned as all these protagonists are at the outer reaches of the contentious urban terrains they inhabit, disadvantaged and disempowered by virtue of their class, caste and sometimes both, they also occupy the margins of English-language fiction in South Asia, in that they have generally not been seen to constitute worthy literary subjects. They form a direct line of descent from Mulk Raj Anand's eponymous Bakha in his 1935 novel *Untouchable*, who has tended to be replaced in the intervening decades by the genteel middle-class or upper-

---

2000 to 2010. The growth economies of China and India dominate the rest of the list of most rapidly growing megacities (Kotkin and Cox 2013). Mike Davis predicts that cities will account for '*all* future world population growth, which is expected to peak at about 10 billion in 2050.' Of this stupendous build-up of humanity, 95 % will occur in the urban areas of developing countries. In his relentless, hard-hitting essay combining prognosis, exhortation and lament, Davis warns us about the impending 'global catastrophe of urban poverty', the vast, and increasing, growth of slums on the edges of 'urban spatial explosions' that is the direct outcome of a neoliberal globalized economy. See Davis (2004, pp. 5–6, 12, 14).

[2] Although recognizably Lahore, Hamid's refusal to name the city in the book is a gesture towards its generic quality, its substitutability by any city in the global South.

class protagonists of Anita Desai or Salman Rushdie. In different ways, they all assert a relationship with the English language, the language that not only 'describes' them but is also the language of the moment, one they are keen to claim and master. Bajwa's timid sari shop assistant perhaps desires it most fiercely, tied up as it is with the new life he longs to make for himself someplace outside the narrow lanes of the city that will go on, in the course of the novel, to swallow him up entirely.

THE DOUBLESPEAK OF ENGLISH

Only thing is ... you know, I am sure you have also noticed it at times, I sometimes feel she is a little snooty, maybe because her English is so good, because the Bhandaris are certainly not very rich. (Bajwa 2004, p. 23)

Although a job selling saris to women in a midsize Punjabi city does not, strictly speaking, require great facility with the English language, Ramchand, one of the shop assistants at Sevak Sari House in Rupa Bajwa's *The Sari Shop* embarks one day on a project to teach himself English. His reasons are not entirely clear even to himself: the language carries an automatic, albeit vague, aspirational quality that brings together Ramchand's long-dead father's unfulfilled hopes of sending his son to an English-medium school with the aura cast on him by the stately home of the wealthy Kapoors where he is unexpectedly asked to take sari samples for the daughter to choose from. Rina Kapoor's wedding becomes the occasion for Ramchand to step out of his narrow, stultifying existence, split between the shop he works in all day and the bare, single, rooftop room he calls his home, into what is for him a whole new world, gleaming, graceful and elegant. As he listens to Rina chattering easily in English with her family and friends, oblivious of his presence in the room, she comes to stand for the long-lost sense of possibility that had disappeared from his life early on with his parents' untimely death. He has grown up into a mildly depressed young man who spends hours every morning staring blankly at his ceiling, able to participate only fitfully in the playful banter and rambunctious outings of his colleagues, unable to find any worthwhile meaning or purpose in the life he leads.

In a narrative that, although conventional in style, combines existential angst and social comedy, Ramchand's bungling attempts to teach himself English become a disarming vehicle of comedy and pathos; the always-already doomed nature of the project serving only to highlight how even the acquisition of tools of empowerment (in this case, the English language) is predicated upon a certain 'in-group' membership to begin with. With a sketchy formal education and no one to turn to for guidance, Ramchand hits upon a 'brilliant idea', so 'mind boggling that it took his breath away': 'If he started at the beginning of the dictionary, and learnt the meanings of each and every word, working his way from A to Z, one day he would know all English, completely and irrevocably' (Bajwa 2004, p. 85). His other pedagogical material includes volumes, procured after some hard haggling at the second-hand book stall, of *Radiant Essays— for Schoolchildren of all Ages*', '*The Complete Letter Writer*' and '*The Magic Lime Tree*', with 'words like hearth, pixie, bashful, wither, wicked and toadstool in it.' Armed with his battered Oxford dictionary, Ramchand assiduously spends hours each day poring over, among other things, correspondence between a Peggy and a Phyllis of Kent, planning out details of a 'really jolly tour through Wales' in the new car that a certain George is 'frightfully proud of' (pp. 27, 77). The complete disconnect between the world he inhabits and the worlds he reaches out to in his attempt to learn the words the inhabitants of this other world speak is as laughable as it is sad. The contradictions and anomalies that have come to be accepted as the norm in an anglophone postcolony such as India are nowhere more evident than here.

Not surprisingly, the endeavour is short-lived. Despite his best efforts to keep to himself, the broken, shattered lives of the people around him press in upon him with an immediacy and force that cannot but disrupt his perusal of the entries in *Pocket Science for Children* and letters demanding renewal of lapsed subscriptions. His colleague's wife Kamla's brutalization at the hands of patriarchal and state power and the dhaba owner Lakhan Singh's unassuaged grief at the killing of his teenage sons in the Army's attack on the Golden Temple coalesce in his mind to show up the futility and meaninglessness of his ambition to improve his lot—for how is one to aspire to a 'better' life, what, indeed, does a 'better' life even mean, when he is surrounded by so much violence, injustice and pain. The upright, dutiful policeman he reads about in his *Radiant Essays* who walks around carrying a protective baton morphs into the policeman who arrests Kamla on the flimsiest of grounds and beats and rapes her with his lathi all night; the yards of colourful fabric he rolls and unrolls each day for his customers transform into her soiled, bloodied sari, into the turban cloth with which the Army soldiers tied the hands of Lakhan Singh's sons behind their back, stood them in a line and shot them dead.³ The sordidness and brutality Ramchand sees around him render all his efforts at self-improvement, at introducing a degree of discipline and rigour into his life, irrelevant and without meaning. The only thing to do is rid yourself of both aspiration and empathy, keep your head down and survive—and after a brief breakdown, Ramchand seems to decide to do just that. In an ironic reversal of traditional symbolism, the arrival of the long-awaited monsoon rains with which the novel ends coincides not with resurgence, renewal and hope but with a disillusioned acceptance of inertness as the only effective strategy of survival.

This bleak hopelessness is focalized through the city of Amritsar, presented in the novel in terms of two stark, sharply divided spheres, those of the haves and the have-nots. As Ramchand manoeuvres his borrowed bicycle through the stray cows and piles of garbage in the narrow lanes where he lives and works to the spacious, open environs of the Kapoor house, it is as if he has crossed from one world into another. Rina Kapoor's wedding and the designer trousseau she is busy organizing for herself could not be further removed from the description of Kamla's simple wedding and the battered tin trunk with its two items of clothing that she carries with her to her husband's house. Despite these stark differences, the lives of the two sets are intertwined in complex albeit unacknowledged ways, with one group possessing the potential to cause deep and lasting harm to the other: the wretched, battered Kamla is seen to pose enough of a threat to the Kapoors for her to be beaten up, paraded naked and finally murdered by their goons. While the conversations and interactions among the city's elite constitute an excellent comedy of manners, playfully revealing the shallowness, hypocrisy, class anxieties and self-absorption that mark it, its interaction with the have-nots is casually exploitative when not actively malevolent. There is no romanticization of the city's poor either, who are self-serving, apathetic and deeply misogynist; although the comradely banter among the shop-assistants has a liveliness and charm to it that is absent from the affected, self-conscious conversations among the upper class, there is little real empathy or friendship to be seen between them.

---

³ Under Operation Blue Star, a military operation mounted in June 1984, the Indian Army stormed the Golden Temple, one of the holiest Sikh shrines, with the objective of flushing out members of the Sikh separatist group who were hiding there. Innocent devotees trapped inside during the ten-day siege had reportedly been lined up and shot outright by the Army. Four months later, Indira Gandhi, the Prime Minister who had ordered the operation, was assassinated by her own Sikh bodyguards, following which there was widespread violence against Sikhs all through the city of Delhi, with the tacit abetment of the party in power, the Congress.

The city, then, becomes the means by which the novel is able to do two very different things. While, on the one hand, it underpins the unrelievedly dark, bleak vision of the novel, on the other hand, it imparts to the narrative its sense of energy and profusion[4]. The violence embodied by both the extremist groups and the State they are up against is as much a defining feature of postcolonial urbanity as the gaping economic divides and fractured social relations across its terrain. This violence, and its attendant suffering and ugliness, pervades the world of the novel and the lives of Lakhan Singh, Kamla and of course, Ramchand, whom we leave at the end of the novel entirely solitary, disillusioned and depressed. At the same time, the minutely observed details of bazaar and shop, the sheer momentum and pace of life in the crowded streets and by-lanes of Amritsar, offer a dynamic, compelling invitation into the cityscape. We walk through a 'maze-like network of lanes', 'narrow alleys' that 'nudge aside unyielding walls and squeeze themselves painfully through' a 'jumble of old red-brick houses, aged grey concrete buildings, shops, signboards, numerous tiny temples at street corners and crowded lanes thronged with people, cows, stray dogs, and fruit and vegetable carts'. We learn to tell the difference between 'Paraag Daily Wear Saris' and 'Paraag Fancy Saris for Occasions', and the right width and length (two and a half metres) of a Sardarni' schunni. We hear Ramchand 'practice English-speaking in front of the mirror every day. At least for twenty minutes' (pp. 4, 5, 8, 9, 36). We follow the narrative as it takes us into the inner world of a semi-educated shop assistant not normally seen to possess an inner world at all, and through him, into an unspectacular urban terrain that yet inspires great pity and great terror.

THE GROTESQUE AND THE 'NORMAL'

'If you want my story, you'll have to put up with how I tell it.' (Sinha 2007, p. 2)

While mastering the English language might have been the primary concern of Ramchand, the protagonist of Indra Sinha's *Animal's People* seems insouciant about his lack of facility in English, enlisting his partial,

---

[4] The profusion being referred to is primarily a descriptive profusion, the packed paragraphs trying to keep up with, and cram in descriptions of the plethora of sights and sounds in the marketplace.

informal knowledge of a range of languages and registers as he becomes the storyteller of his city. The noxious gases that leaked from the malfunctioning pesticide plant set up in Bhopal by the multinational giant Union Carbide might have, in Sinha's novel, deformed and damaged the main protagonist Animal's spine irretrievably, but it has (luckily, for our purposes) not made the slightest of dents on his ability to tell a story. In one of the worst industrial disasters in the world, a gas cloud composed of 40 tonnes of the poison methyl isocyanate accidentally leaked from the factory in the early morning hours of 3 December 1984. In a city that had suddenly turned into a nightmare, thousands of people awoke suffocating and ran through the dark streets in panic, inhaling more of the toxic fumes in the process. Those who were not killed immediately by exposure to the toxic gas either died in the following weeks or survived but suffered severe damage to their eyes, lungs, brain and muscles as well as their gastrointestinal, neurological, reproductive and immune systems, the effects of which often manifested themselves gradually over the next few years. Large numbers of children born after the disaster to gas-exposed parents suffered birth defects and developmental disorders.[5] In the case of our narrator, the poison he inhaled as a new-born baby (which killed both his parents) took 6 years to course through his system and deform the muscles and bones of his back to the extent that they 'twisted like a hairpin', making his 'arse' the 'highest part' of him and forcing him to walk on his hands and arms like a 'jaanwar', an animal, which also becomes his name (Sinha 2007, p. 15).

While the narrative establishes its credibility and acquires a great deal of immediacy and verve by claiming to be a literal translation (from Hindi into English) and transcription of Animal's oral account recorded on tapes for a journalist (so that we hear Animal's voice directly as it were, with all its profanities, bawdiness and horseplay intact), it also, somewhat puzzlingly, calls the city it is centred in by the fictional name of Khaufpur (Terror Town) instead of its real name, Bhopal. This is accompanied by a tongue-in-cheek paratext: a website the 'editor's note' helpfully points us to (www.khaufpur.com), which humorously hosts, among other things, a Khaufpur gazette, interviews with its citizens (many of them characters

---

[5] See Narain, S. and Chandra, B. (2014). 30 Years of Bhopal Gas Tragedy: A continuing disaster. *Down to Earth*. [Online]. 12 August. Available from http://www.downtoearth.org.in/coverage/30-years-of-bhopal-gas-tragedy-a-continuing-disaster-47634

in the book), as well as sections on tourism and 'what's on' in the city.⁶ As with Bhopal, though, 'all the world knows the name of Khaufpur, but no one knows what things were before that night'; it is only the cataclysmic event of December 1984 that is the city's claim to worldwide fame. 'You have turned us Khaufpuris into story-tellers, but always of the same story. Ousraat, cette nuit, that night, always that fucking night' (pp. 14, 5). While 'Bhopal' is forever caught in a freeze-frame for the rest of the world, most of which knows it (if at all) solely in relation to the gas leak, its replacement by Khaufpur in the novel, heavily symbolic though it may be to those who understand the Urdu reference, liberates it somewhat, freeing it from the dead weight of associations carried by the original name and opening up, paradoxically, a space for acts of reading and writing that are not wholly subsumed by the one event. It also enables what we go on to recognize as a dominant narrative device in the novel: an interplay of distance and proximity that forces the reader to occupy an uneasy terrain. Khaufpur, the City of Dread, is a name that by its very formulaic symbolism, its artificiality and its parodic quality serves to create a distance from the reader, allowing us to see the terror that it stands for without being engulfed and entrapped by it.⁷ It is the place of unspeakable horrors, of healthy people who have been afflicted overnight by terrible, chronic diseases if not outright killed, of foetuses that were maimed and disfigured while in the womb and of shameless evasions by a corporate giant trying to squirm out of its responsibilities towards those it harmed so grievously. Much of the novel is about the Khaufpuris' legal battle that has been dragging on for years, demanding that the 'Kampani' pay them adequate compensation as well as clean up the toxic waste it had left behind that had leached into the groundwater, continuing to poison everyone. At the same time, Khaufpur is also the site of Animal's *Bildungsroman*; of life-affirming friendships and camaraderie; of the forging of familial bonds between two completely unrelated people such as Animal and Ma Franci; of the courage and spirit shown by Zafar and his associates who struggle, undauntedly and selflessly, for justice; of unlikely love, as that which blossoms between Ellie and Somraj; of the generosity and good humour of people like Hanif and Huriya who have nothing to call their own and yet find it in them to offer a complete stranger their warmth and hospitality.

---

⁶ This website is no longer in existence.

⁷ Other names in the novel serve the same purpose: the hopelessly corrupt 'Minister for Poison Relief' has the name Zahreel Khan, literally Poisonous Khan.

In a way that would have been hard for a city called Bhopal to effect in the novel, the Khaufpur of Animal and his people contains multitudes: it is both Dystopia and Utopia.

Writing the devastated city into existence requires a further articulation of two conflicting narrative pulls. There is, on the one hand, the robust immediacy and directness of Animal's narrative, its unmediated quality and its establishment of a clear, strong sense of factuality and reality. Alongside this, on the other hand, runs a phantasmagoria, not so much intersecting the primary narrative from time to time as forming a substratum to it. Ma Franci shares frequent and graphic descriptions of the 'Apokalis' she believes started on 'that night' in Khaufpur:

> 'I see a star fall from heaven, the abyss opens, out pours smoke like from a great furnace, the sun and the day are gone.' [...] Animal, when the time comes these little [scorpions] who live in the walls of our house, they will come creeping out and grow huge. They'll reach the size of horses. [...] They'll have faces like people and long hair like women, but their teeth will be like lions' teeth, which they'll gnash in the most horrifying way. (pp.62–63)

Animal himself is schizophrenic: 'voices' talk to him. In periodic 'roundabouts of madness', manifestations of the neurological damage caused by the poison in his system, 'the voices in [his] head start yelling, new voices come gupping all kinds of weird and fantastic things, words that make no sense, [...]' (p. 55). One of his frequent interlocutors is 'Khā [friend]-in-the-Jar', a two-headed embryo preserved in a hospital laboratory for research.[8] Towards the end of the novel is an extended, vivid, hallucinatory cannabis 'trip' experienced by Animal as he loses his way and nearly his life in the forest. Further, his everyday life is a grotesquerie, living as he does in a scorpion-infested corner of the very factory that unleashed such havoc in Khaufpur, walking about on all fours, fighting stray dogs for his share of the leftovers scavenged from rubbish bins. This hyper-real dimension of the novel is quite clearly a function of the hyper-reality of life in Khaufpur and the ways in which the grotesque and the phantasmagoric have invaded its very fabric. The normal has been subverted in a universe in which mothers assiduously squeeze out milk from their breasts only

---

[8] As the doctor tells Ma Franci, Animal's acting mother, 'Be grateful this boy's no worse, madam, that could have been him in the jar. Half of those who were expecting on that night aborted and as for the rest, well let's just say some things were seen in this town that were never seen before' (p. 58).

to spill it into the dust instead of feeding it to their hungry infants, fearful of the toxic chemicals they may be passing on to them in the process (p. 107). The skilful co-presence of the warts-and-all 'real' of Animal's narrative with the constant undercurrent of the 'extra-real', the 'sur-real', serves to elaborate the interchangeability of the two in the terror town that is Khaufpur. As Ma Franci sadly responds to Animal:

> 'C'était un film,' I tell Ma Franci when we get home. 'C'est normal'.
> Says Ma, 'Pauvre Jaanvar à quatre pattes, pour toi c'est quoi le normal?'
> Poor four-foot Animal, for you what is normal? (p. 61)

Despite a necessarily flimsy hold on a reality that blends seamlessly with the hallucinatory and nightmarish, Animal's grasp of the language he uses to convey this intermeshing is resoundingly sure-footed and confident: as the single narrator of the novel, his voice, in all its idiosyncrasy, irreverence and earthiness, comes across with clarity and force. With a shrewd awareness of the workings of language, its shape-shifting quality, and the games it can be used to play, Animal resolutely refuses to let it have power over him.

> I said, many books have been written about this place, not one has changed anything for the better, how will yours be different? [...] You'll talk of *rights, law, justice*. Those words sound the same in my mouth as in yours but they don't mean the same, Zafar says such words are like shadows the moon makes in the Kampani's factory, always changing shape. On that night it was poison, now it's words that are choking us. (p. 3)

His very adoption of the name that was used to poke fun at his deformity—Jaanvar—is precisely that: a political stance of emptying out a label of mockery and disrespect and investing it with pride and ownership, refusing to capitulate to the insult represented by the word.[9] As he puts it in his inimitable way:

> [...] if I agree to be a human being, I'll also have to agree that I'm wrong-shaped and abnormal. But let me be a quatre pattes animal, four-footed and

---

[9] Although it would be hard to overlook the oftentimes self-serving, irresponsible stance that taking on the name of 'Animal' helps him maintain; as his friend Farouq points out, 'You run wild, do crazy things and get away with it because you're always whining, I'm an animal, I'm an animal' (p. 209).

free, then I am whole, my own proper shape, just a different kind of animal from say Jara, or a cow, or a camel. (p. 208)

Animal's witty, acerbic, worldly-wise, determinedly unsentimental voice carries the main burden of the novel's narrative. He speaks with the assurance and bravado of a seasoned city dweller—though no doubt the rough-and-ready edge to his voice is also a protective front behind which he hides his fears, insecurities and hopes. Language becomes a pliable tool at his disposal as he effortlessly weaves his way through street-Hindi conjoined with smatterings of English and French, playing masterfully with all three as the occasion demands. Faced with the expectant Australian 'jarnalis' visiting Khaufpur to dig out 'the really savage things, the worst cases',

> I said, 'Don't fucking stare or I won't speak'. I said it in Hindi, I'm not supposed to let on that I know some Inglis, Chunaram gets an extra bunce for translating. You gave a thumbs-up, carried right on staring. I called you a wanker. You nodded, smiled at me. Khaamush, silent then I'm. After some time I've joined another silence to the first. (p. 4)

Animal's canny ability to milk the situation for all its financial worth coexists with a deeper discomfort at being consumed as a poster boy of the gas tragedy by the thousands of 'eyes' that stare at him through 'the holes in [the journalist's] head', potential readers (yes, us) greedily seeking to devour him and his life to satisfy their taste for the sensational. If he must tell his story, he will do it on his terms and in his way: 'Tell mister cunt big shot that this is my movie he's in and in my movie there is only one star and it's me' (pp. 7, 9). It is this voice and this spirit that stops the dark book from becoming a bleak one. The energy and joie de vivre embodied in Animal and his people draws no doubt upon the resilience and undying hope with which the people of Bhopal carry on with their struggle for justice even three decades after the event.

Upwardly mobile

> *Yes, the city remains intermittently perilous, in, for example, the slashing thrusts of its vehicles, the ferocious extremes of its temperatures, and the antibiotic resistance of its microorganisms, not to mention the forcefulness of its human predators, [...].* (Hamid 2013, p. 212)

There are two possible ways in which to write about chaos and bedlam. The first seeks to impose a pattern and order upon it and invest it with coherence of some sort. The second throws caution to the winds and joins in the whirling, giddy dance with relish. These, broadly speaking, are the contrasting narrative choices made by Mohsin Hamid and Mohammed Hanif, respectively. The embodiment of bedlam in both is the exponentially expanding, massively overcrowded, notoriously violent and yet 'rising' city in South Asia—Karachi, Lahore and Islamabad. Karachi, in particular, a trading megacity with a busy port and a very large influx of migrants from other provinces, is a hotbed of violence of all kinds: sectarian, ethnic, gangster, land related and casual, with roadside muggings in broad daylight being par for the course.[10] As the harried protagonist of Saba Imtiaz's slight but wonderfully evocative novel, *Karachi, You're Killing Me!*, relates,

> Get to the site after spending twenty minutes stuck in traffic begging the cab driver to find a shortcut out of the snarl. He asks me why I'm in such a rush, and when I tell him I'm a journalist, he tells me about his nephew who was shot in broad daylight when a thug from an anti-Pashtun political party heard the Pashto song that was his phone's ringtone. (Imtiaz 2014, p. 18)

She is accosted at a high-end party by an admirer who breathlessly tells her: 'Oh I LOVE your work. That piece you did, about the bloodstained roads and how the gangs were dragging around corpses and playing football with severed heads...' (p. 59). Similarly, casual, even light-hearted references to violence of all kinds—sexual assaults, bomb-blasts, shootings and muggings—are littered through *Our Lady of Alice Bhatti*. Hanif's unruffled narrator recounts the blackly comic chain of events triggered by Teddy Butt's distracted firing of a gun into the air, which accidentally hits a truck driver who loses control of his vehicle and collides with a rickshaw carrying schoolchildren—'Five children, all between seven and nine, in their pristine blue and white St Xavier uniforms, become a writhing mess of fractured skulls, blood, crayons and Buffy the Vampire Slayer lunchboxes'—quickly spiralling into large-scale mob frenzy, gratuitous gangster attacks and a 3-day shutdown in which 'the city stops moving', 11 more people are killed and 'three billion rupees' worth of Suzukis, Toyotas and Hinopaks are burnt' along with buses, rickshaws, ambulances, paan shops

---

[10] See S. Inskeep (2011), *Instant City: Life and Death in Karachi*.

and 'at least one KFC joint' (Hanif 2011, pp. 103–106). Alice Bhatti, Replacement Junior Nurse at the rundown Sacred Heart Hospital, has learnt to somehow navigate her way at work through groping hands and the penises thrust in her face, but there is,

> not a single day – when she didn't see a woman shot or hacked, strangled or suffocated, poisoned or burnt, hanged or buried alive. Suspicious husband, brother protecting his honour, father protecting his honour, son protecting his honour, jilted lover avenging his honour, feuding farmers settling their water disputes, moneylenders collecting their interest: most of life's arguments, it seemed, got settled by doing various things to a woman's body. (p. 142)

As a Christian woman and member of the Choohra untouchable caste in an Islamic state, she could not conceivably be lower in the social pecking order. Paradoxically, the only advantage she could hope for as an untouchable, 'that people won't touch her without her explicit permission', is also denied to her—'the same people who wouldn't drink from a tap that she has touched have no problem casually poking their elbows into her breast or contorting their own bodies to rub against her heathen bottom' (p. 140). As the novel hurtles jerkily, crazily, to its tragic close, it leaves us with an overwhelming sense of the contingent and the incidental: no necessary logic shapes the course of events, which could just as well have turned out completely differently. One would be hard put to look for a better way to produce, narratively and mimetically, the arbitrariness, the messiness and the quality of the accident that defines everyday life in the expanding South-Asian metropolis.

Albeit very different in style, offering as it does an orderly, 12-point progression from poverty to 'filthy' richness, Hamid's narrator in *How to Get Filthy Rich in Rising Asia* is—like Hanif's—a seasoned city dweller, not easily shocked or moved, dry, imperturbable and unflappable. And witty. As the unnamed protagonist—'you'—journeys through a novel masquerading as a self-help book that purportedly guarantees what everyone in 'rising Asia' aspires to, he takes all the necessary steps on the path to success: he moves from the village to the (unnamed, generic) city, gets an education, sets up a bottled-water business, befriends bureaucrats, enlists the help of gangsters and, almost magically, arrives at his promised goal about halfway through the book. 'You have thrived to the sound of the city's great whooshing thirst, unsated and growing, water incessantly being pulled out of the ground and pushed into pipes and containers. Bottled hydration has proved lucrative' (pp. 120–121).

Compromises, some of them big, have been made on the way—the 'rising' city enables, indeed encourages, the taking of shortcuts and the bypassing of procedures—but the narrative is not one to dwell on them; it has places to go and things to do. As assistant to an airgun spray painter, 'your' brother's occupation requires

> patience and the fortitude to withstand a constant sense of low-level panic, [...]. In theory it also requires protection in the form of goggles and respirators, but these are clearly optional, as your brother and his master have neither, placing thin cotton rags over their mouths and noses instead. Hence, in the near term, your brother's cough. Over the long term, consequences can be more serious. But a painter's assistant is paid, the skills he learns are valuable, and in any case over sufficiently long a term, as everyone knows, there is nothing that does not have as its consequence death. (pp. 31–32)

This even, dispassionate, borderline-ironic tone does not vary through the book, no matter what it is telling us about and sounds very similar to the narrator of *Alice Bhatti*. I have proposed that this narrative voice is the voice of the city, a city voice, one that has seen it and done it all and refuses to be roused or incensed by much. And yet, there are in both novels places where the narrative seems to pause and linger and tell us a little bit more than is really necessary. For instance, the 'boyish gunman', a hit-man hired by 'your' business rival to intimidate 'you', whom we meet getting ready for an encounter that will shortly prove fatal for him. We see him listening to 'movie songs on a promotional soda-can-shaped radio and shaving above his upper lip in the aspiration of one day provoking a mustache', smoking the single loose cigarette he has bought on the way while waiting for 'you', 'a new habit good for making him forget that he is hungry', wishing he could afford the purple T-shirt with the 'psychedelic hawk' on it which he is sure would impress the 'girl with dimples' in his neighbourhood whom he has not summoned up the courage to speak to (p. 133). None of this is, strictly speaking, information we need to have about someone who has a minuscule part in the novel; yet, the novel forces us to get to know him, his compulsions and his aspirations. In *Alice Bhatti*, we are told of Teddy's gentler side when,

> On another occasion he only pretended to take his turn with a thirty-two-year-old Bangladeshi prisoner after a small police contingent had shuffled out of the room. He just sat with her and played with her hair while she sobbed and cursed in Bengali. The only word he could understand was Allah. He had walked out adjusting his fly, pretending to be exhausted and satisfied, even joking with the policemen [...]. (pp. 96–7)

While this serves to tell us something about Teddy, it also, at the same time, pushes us to confront the wretchedness and outrage of the nameless Bangladeshi prisoner, and no doubt others like her we are sure to find (Kamla in Amritsar), were we ever to look, held indefinitely within the city police's lock-ups. It is as if the narrative, even as it mimes the hard-boiled nature of city life, seeks to compensate for it, to pause and take a careful look at the people—expendable, insignificant—that the city intent upon 'rising' at breakneck speed has no time for.

In different ways, all the novels this chapter has examined have mobilized the cities they are about, to shape and elaborate their subjects and narratives, allowing us to see perspectives and hear voices that have, more often than not, charted inventive, hitherto un-novelistic terrain. The very scope of the city, the vast range of character-actors and extras that are available so readily for its dramas, allow the narrative its expanse and contradictoriness, allowing it to gesture towards multiple, infinite possibilities. South-Asian fiction in English has seized upon these possibilities and has been doing so since, at least, the 1980s and 1990s, when Salman Rushdie famously brought Bombay—and India—on to the world literary map in novels such as *Midnight's Children* (1981), *The Satanic Verses* (1988), *The Moor's Last Sigh* (1995) and *The Ground Beneath Her Feet* (1999). The more recent works that this chapter is based upon can, however, be seen to mark a trend (the most well-known example of which is Aravind Adiga's 2008 novel, *The White Tiger*), in which the burden of the story is placed upon the shoulders of characters who have traditionally occupied small, marginal roles in fiction—servants, shop assistants, minor traders and junior nurses. This allows the narrative to embrace, in wholly plausible ways, the city in its entirety, its ugly underbelly as much as its murky nooks and corners. Where narratives have sought to do so in the past, they have had to strain and take recourse to ingenious plot turns and devices in order to justify their entry into the twilight world of poverty, dereliction, crime and violence that importantly constitutes any burgeoning city in the global South. I have argued elsewhere how Rushdie's Bombay novels are constrained by the typically sheltered lifestyles of his upper-class protagonists, who have to depend upon 'magical real' turns of the plot in order to gain entry into aspects of the city they would normally never have reason to encounter.[11] In contrast, the novels this chapter has discussed invite us to inhabit, quite 'naturally', urban minds, lives and settings we have had little occasion to meet in literature, generally speaking. Like the South-Asian

[11] See S. Khanna (2013), *The Contemporary Novel and the City*, 133–146.

city, and indeed any burgeoning city in the global South today, literature from the region continues to introduce us to new, imaginative, innovative ways of being in the world.

WORKS CITED

Bajwa, R. (2004). *The sari shop*. New Delhi: Penguin.
Davis, M. (2004). Planet of slums: Urban involution and the informal proletariat. *New Left Review, 26*, 5–34.
Hamid, M. (2013). *How to get filthy rich in rising Asia*. New Delhi: Penguin.
Hanif, M. (2011). *Our lady of Alice Bhatti*. Noida: Random House.
Imtiaz, S. (2014). *Karachi, you're killing me!* Noida: Random House.
Inskeep, S. (2011). *Instant city: Life and death in Karachi*. New Delhi: Penguin Viking.
Khanna, S. (2014). *The contemporary novel and the city: Re-conceiving national and narrative form*. Basingstoke: Palgrave Macmillan.
Kotkin, J., & Cox, W. (2013, April 8). The world's fastest-growing megacities. *Forbes* [Online]. Available from http://www.forbes.com/sites/joelkotkin/2013/04/08/the-worlds-fastest-growing-megacities/
Sinha, I. (2007). *Animal's people*. London: Simon and Schuster.

Occupying Literary and Urban Space: Adiga, Authenticity and the Politics of Socio-economic Critique

Dominic Davies

MISREADING *THE WHITE TIGER*: THE POLITICS OF AUTHENTICITY

Amitava Kumar's review of *The White Tiger* (2008) offers a provocative, if misplaced, critique of Aravind Adiga's Man Booker Prize-winning novel. He dismisses its characterization as 'utterly cartoonish, like the characters in a bad Bollywood melodrama', and finds Adiga's 'presentation of ordinary people [...] not only trite but offensive' (Kumar 2008). Kumar's objection is Adiga's apparent assumption that he can 'authentically' represent the inner thoughts of a Bihari villager called Balram, the novel's first-person narrator. However, Kumar's confession that he projects his own personal anxieties as a novelist onto *The White Tiger* may explain why he seems to misread the parodical style that informs Adiga's characterization and which, in a review of Adiga's more recent novel, *Last Man in Tower* (2011), Peter Carty has described as an aspect of the 'Dickensian breadth' of Adiga's prose (Carty 2011). It is the melodramatic tendencies of Adiga's novels—a rhetorical tactic typical of the nineteenth-century novelist and especially, as Juliet John has shown, in the portrayal of his villains (John 2003, pp. 1–2) that are here skilfully imitated to buttress the satirical edge of Adiga's social commentary through the first-person narrative of his own villain, Balram Halwai.

D. Davies
British Academy Postdoctoral Fellow, English Faculty, University of Oxford, Oxford, UK

© The Editor(s) (if applicable) and The Author(s) 2016
A. Tickell (ed.), *South-Asian Fiction in English*,
DOI 10.1057/978-1-137-40354-4_7

Kumar extrapolates his critique of Adiga's 'authenticity' to other Indian novelists writing in English, who, 'like Adiga, have taken the bus, or at least hired a taxi, to the hinterland', relying on this first-hand experience to legitimize their narrative. This 'reportage' is, however, 'only an inoculation against the charge of inauthenticity' (Kumar 2008). This critique of *The White Tiger* is especially illuminating for this chapter's study of Adiga's most recent novel, *Last Man in Tower*. Kumar understands the realist novel as a form of journalism or 'reportage' that, because of its fictional ability to inhabit the inner lives of its characters, has an ethical responsibility to represent them with heightened authenticity—an anxiety rooted, if anachronistically, in Gayatri Spivak's now well-known conclusion that 'the subaltern cannot speak' because the subaltern voice is usurped, or drowned out, by that of the writer–critic (1988, pp. 277, 308).

Looking to the many recent anglophone publications that, like Kumar's own novel *Home Products* (2007) and Adiga's *Last Man in Tower*, are set in Mumbai, it appears that this novelistic formula has been reversed to produce a genre that has subsequently circumvented this anxiety. A proliferation of journalistic texts—what William Dalrymple calls 'India's new wave of non-fiction' (Dalrymple 2012)—has blurred conventional generic boundaries between documentary writing and conventional fiction narratives, framing themselves as forms of 'reportage' whilst the reading is more like novelistic prose. Suketu Mehta's *Maximum City* (2005), Gyan Prakash's *Mumbai Fables* (2010) and Katherine Boo's *Behind the Beautiful Forevers* (2012) are just some examples.[1] They are all concerned with the lowest strata of Indian society, lacking much anxiety about the 'authenticity' of their ability to represent. A slightly broader survey of the titles of recent non-fiction books about India written in English reveals an astonishingly repetitive titular formula. Consider, for example, Sonia Faleiro's *Beautiful Thing: Inside the Secret World of Bombay's Dance Bars* (2011), Pavan Varma's *Being Indian: Inside the Real India* (2011), Anand Giridharadas's *India Calling: An Intimate Portrait of a Nation's Remaking* (2012) and Akash Kapur's *India Becoming: A Portrait of Life in Modern India* (2012). The first clause of these titles denotes each text's

---

[1] As Dalrymple points out, 'What Florence was to Italian literature in the 14th century, or Paris to the French novel in the late 19th, so Bombay/Mumbai has been to recent writing about India' (Dalrymple 2012). Nevertheless, Delhi has also been the subject of this new generic mode in works such as Aman Sethi's *A Free Man: A True Story of Life and Death in Delhi* (2012) and Rana Dasgupta's *Capital: A Portrait of Twenty-First Century Delhi* (2014).

specialist angle on India, whilst the second reaches for some 'beyond' that is often framed ('a portrait') as an attempt to grasp something of India's 'inner truth'. Importantly, this is always from a position that is *external* to the subcontinent itself. Though mostly disregarded within the texts themselves, the crisis of authentic representation continues to frame, if not underpin, anglophone writings on twenty-first-century India.

This crisis is not a recent phenomenon but rather a long-standing issue for anglophone Indian writing. Kumar's criticisms are preceded by an earlier argument between author Vikram Chandra and literary critic Meenakshi Mukherjee, who observed that 'when it comes to English fiction originating in our country, not only does the issue of Indianness become a favourite essentialising obsession in academic writings and the book review circuit, the writers themselves do not seem unaffected by it' (1993, p. 2607). The result, Mukherjee argues elsewhere, is 'a certain anxiety about constructing an India that is recognisably different from the West' through the deployment of a 'kind of exotic rhetoric' (2000, p. 55). Writing for the *Boston Review* in 2000, Chandra refuted these anxieties. He agrees that many anglophone Indian novelists tend to be 'assailed by a constant, oppressive sense of unreality', believing themselves to be 'improperly contaminated by the West' whilst 'the "Real India"' remains, 'by definition', beyond their 'grasp' (Chandra 2000). However, he continues:

> English has been spoken and written in [...] the Indian subcontinent for a few hundred years now, certainly longer than the official and literary Hindi that is our incompletely national language today. [Those] who see the anxiety of Indianness everywhere are in truth eaten at by this anxiety themselves, and the ones who battle the malign hand of the West in every action of every day are completely determined by the West. (Chandra 2000)

Nevertheless, well into the twenty-first century, anglophone Indian novelists continue to come under criticism (see Sadana 2012) for producing 'negative' representations of India for their readerships in the global North. After winning the Man Booker, Adiga's first novel was launched into the centre of this ongoing debate. However, the very first line of *The White Tiger*—'Neither you nor I can speak English, but there are some things that can be said only in English' (Adiga 2008, p. 3)— actively engages these ongoing contentions. Balram self-consciously positions his narrative as a mediation between this linguistic—and social and economic—gap, funnelling India's many other languages into a unified anglophone narrative. Ana Cristina Mendes also considers 'the capability of a highly-educated author (who studied English literature at Columbia and Oxford universities [...]) to grasp the experience of the Indian underclass' (Mendes 2010, p. 286). By analysing the novel's melodramatic mode and explicit cast of stereotypes (misread by Kumar as 'an "India for Dummies"'; 2008), Mendes argues that Adiga is 'quite explicitly mocking the longing ideal of authenticity', a tactic epitomized in his 'construction of an overtly essentialised main character' (Mendes 2010, p. 287).

Whilst Kumar finds Balram's description of rural India as 'the area that is the Darkness' to be 'unsettling', Adiga's use of the phrase is not lazily reductive or discriminatory (Adiga 2008, pp. 14–15). Through its reference to 'the map of India' and 'the black river' that runs through 'the Darkness', Balram instead invokes a hierarchical rhetoric rooted in colonial discourse—Marlow's famous words from the opening pages of Joseph Conrad's *Heart of Darkness* (1899) are clearly invoked here.[2] Balram's explicit invocation of colonial tropes draws attention to the theme of (mis)representation through the reading of maps—themselves representational technologies—that dominates these passages. As Ines Detmers argues of *The White Tiger*, Adiga's 'political agenda' is not to retrieve 'another weak life-account of an allegedly dislocated—if not un-locatable—subaltern self', but instead 'to explore the failure of such an enterprise' in the anglophone Indian novel (Detmers 2011, p. 539). Balram's position as both character *and* narrator allows Adiga to play with the anxieties around authenticity and essentialism and, in so doing, to interrogate—if not to satirize—the politics of representation.[3] These ideas, this chapter argues, are taken up and extended by *Last Man in Tower*.

However, before turning to this novel, Katherine Boo's *Behind the Beautiful Forevers* offers a useful point of comparison. Though written by an American rather than an Indian and without any of these self-reflexive

---

[2] 'It had become a place of darkness', writes Conrad. 'But there was in it one river especially, a mighty big river that you could see on the map, resembling an immense snake uncoiled, with its head in the sea, its body at rest curving afar over a vast country and its tail lost in the depths of the land' (Conrad 2006, p. 8).

[3] Despite these critical celebrations of the self-reflexivity of Adiga's novel, Toral Jatin Gajarawala has accused *The White Tiger* of eliding 'caste questions'—though acutely *class* conscious, Balram exhibits little, if any, *caste* consciousness (2012, p. 132). The result, she argues, is that the 'social hierarchy of caste' is 'forgiven or made acceptable', a tendency that is symptomatic of the Indian anglophone novel more broadly (pp.143, 151).

narrative tactics, Boo has not received these criticisms. Winner of the US National Book Award for Nonfiction in 2010, it is mostly evaluated by its reviewers as a piece of extended journalism. Vikas Swarup, the author of the novel *Q&A* (2005) on which Danny Boyle's British-made film, *Slumdog Millionaire* (2008, notably the same year as the publication of *The White Tiger*), is based, commends *Behind the Beautiful Forevers* for the way in which Boo 'overcome[s] barriers of language, culture and ethnicity to get inside the minds of her subjects to decode their innermost thoughts' (Swarup 2012).[4] Swarup's sentiment is shared by many of Boo's Indian reviewers. They note the tendencies of books written by foreigners to draw on and perpetuate the 'subcontinent's reputation for being a mass of congestion, disease, inequality and tragic deprivation' (Pal 2012), whilst arguing that Boo has in fact managed to write 'a "Big India Book" that is anything but' (Munshi 2012).

Despite being categorized as non-fiction, *Behind the Beautiful Forevers* reads astonishingly like a fictional narrative, with the only allusion to Boo's own presence as reporter concealed in an 'Author's Note' in the book's final six pages. Here, Boo attempts to authenticate her novelistic infiltration into the thoughts of her subjects in illuminating terms:

> When I describe the thoughts of individuals in the preceding pages, those thoughts have been related to me and my translators, or to others in our presence. When I sought to grasp, retrospectively, a person's thinking at a given moment, or when I had to do repeated interviews in order to understand the complexity of someone's views—very often the case—I used paraphrase. (Boo 2013, p. 250)

Despite these language barriers and her use of 'paraphrase', she readily employs characters' direct speech and includes sentences that assume, through a free indirect discourse, access to their emotional and subjective thoughts throughout. Boo herself remains an omniscient, all-seeing narrator. What is curious is that Boo—an American semi-fictionalizing the lives of Mumbai's underclass for, as the Nonfiction Award indicates,

---

[4] Interestingly, in an article for the *New Yorker* published in 2009, Boo documents the tumultuous reception of *Slumdog Millionaire* in Mumbai. Slum dwellers greeted the film's opening, she writes, 'by threatening to burn fifty-six effigies of the director, whose movie title equated human beings with dogs', whilst more 'educated, successful Indians' also disliked the film not because 'it slighted the poor', but rather because 'they thought it slighted the increasing affluence and prominence of their country' (Boo 2009).

consumption by a primarily US readership[5]—displays no sense of obligation to 'authenticate' her work. Though teeming 'with characters and situations that would seem stereotypical if they were summed up in quick phrases' (Pal 2012), Boo's lucid and sensitive storytelling style apparently justifies itself. Deepanjana Pal argues that it is the novelistic 'qualities' of Boo's narrative that shift it beyond a simple journalistic critique of policy failure, economic inequality and political corruption in order to capture the way in which, in twenty-first-century urban India, 'personal ethics are tilted on an increasingly selfish axis'. For Pal, this is the 'truly depressing reality' of the Mumbai that Boo captures (Pal 2012), a social symptom of neoliberal globalization that is, as this chapter will show, also critiqued by Adiga's *Last Man in Tower*.

This slight detour sheds light on the discrepancy between the accusations of authenticity levelled at Adiga's work and, say, that of Boo's. The difference between each author's reception appears to be rooted in their choice of genre, as Spivak's warning lingers in the minds of literary critics and reviewers of novels, but is not so rigorously applied to the recent surge in non-fictional writings. Boo's critiques of India's corrupt bureaucracy and violently unequal economy remain legitimate because she manages to sustain the 'credibility of non-fiction' through her extensive research and narrative detail (Pal 2012). Adiga, however, writing an explicitly fictional text as a self-confessed novelist, is criticized for engaging in a similar project. In response, Adiga has woven these debates around authentic representation into the political project of *Last Man in Tower*. The dexterity of Adiga's narrative in this work allows him to critique these accusations whilst *also* producing a social commentary akin to that of Boo's. In addition, the novel demonstrates how the preoccupation with authenticity can in fact detract from, or limit, a text's capacity for critical social commentary. Like both *The White Tiger* and Adiga's collection of short stories, *Between the Assassinations* (2008), *Last Man in Tower* critiques a range of socio-economic problems of twenty-first-century urban India before withdrawing, somewhat cynically, from that practice. As he claimed in an interview with Radio 4's *Front Row* shortly after the novel's publication: 'I've written three books now on present day India and each one has run

---

[5] According to the National Book Foundation website, the Awards' mission-statement is 'to celebrate the best of American literature, to expand its audience, and to enhance the cultural value of great writing in America.' See http://www.nationalbook.org/aboutus_history.html#.U-HyHOd2i4E. Accessed on 6 August 2014.

into controversy [t]here, and I sometimes do wonder if I've had enough. [...] This is the last book I intend to write about socio-economic change in India' (*Front Row* 2011).

LAST MAN IN TOWER: OCCUPYING LITERARY AND URBAN SPACE

The remainder of this chapter revolves around two distinct, though interrelated, arguments that demonstrate how *Last Man in Tower* initiates a socio-economic critique whilst also developing a literary response to issues of authenticity. These are approached through a distinction between 'literary' and 'urban' spaces, before then demonstrating that an allegorical relationship maps them back onto one another throughout the novel. *Last Man in Tower*, on one level, self-reflexively tackles critiques such as Kumar's, subtextually condemning them for their obscuration of the broader political work of socio-economic satire. The recurring concern around the 'politics of authenticity' and the problems of reportage, Adiga suggests, stifles the novel as a potential space of dissent. The Indian novel in English still occupies, to use Pablo Mukherjee's words, 'a privileged cultural position in the globalised market regime of neo-colonialism' and is thus, to some extent, complicit with the 'extension and regulation of this regime'. However, as Mukherjee goes on to argue of other Indian-English novelists, Adiga's narrative self-consciously registers 'an artistic critique of [his] own sociological position', deconstructing the politics of privilege and authorial representation within the text itself (Mukherjee 2010, p. 8). This chapter shows that Adiga's self-reflexive tactic in *Last Man in Tower*, enabled by its literary rather than journalistic or non-fictional discourse, engages with these debates as an integral aspect of its socio-economic critique.

Building on this assertion, I argue that *Last Man in Tower* moves beyond idiosyncratic concerns around issues of authenticity, thereby operating as a discursive space of dissent in opposition to the economic inequalities and pervasive corruption of the socio-political context in which it is set. The narrative throws the wider political and socio-economic effects of neoliberalism into relief as they manifest primarily in the policies of urban land redevelopment that are symptomatic of Mumbai's contentious history around property and land rights. As Suketu Mehta argues, the Bombay Rent Act of 1979 'removed the right to property as a "fundamental right" from the constitution along with the right to be compensated when the state expropriates property', resulting in ongoing insecurity for both owners and tenants alike: the former are placed in a 'situation of continuous doubt' whilst the latter are kept constantly 'on the move' (Mehta 2005, pp. 128–129).[6] However, whilst interrogating this specific sociopolitical issue through its plot, the novel also uses it as a lens with which to shed light on the corruption and profit-oriented complicity of various national and state institutions that have, in twenty-first-century Mumbai, become the servants of capital.

Adiga's self-reflexive writing and the novel's discursive socio-economic critique are, in fact, allegories of one another. Adiga's resistant and self-labelled 'last man' of his 'tower', Masterji, becomes determined to 'occupy'—a loaded term within the contemporary context of urban anti-neoliberal resistance (see Chomsky 2012)—the space of his flat and thus prevent the redevelopment of the surrounding slum. The slum's inhabitants, who inhabit the novel's marginal spaces, eventually inform and politicize Masterji's self-sacrificial act with which the novel climaxes. However, the novel also invites the reader to build an analysis of Adiga's self-reflexive positionality out of the motions of its plot so that this, too, on a meta-textual level, becomes a political act defined by the occupation of a space of dissent. Just as Masterji's political act occurs within the text through his occupation of urban space, Adiga himself critiques the political complicity of several institutional frameworks—including journalism—with an increasingly neoliberal society through his occupation of the discursive space of the narrative. In this way, *Last Man in Tower* frames the novel, as a form, as one of the few remaining locales from which to initiate a comprehensive socio-economic critique of twenty-first-century Mumbai.

Nevertheless, the novel still registers the limitations, if not implicit failure, of such a stance, a trajectory that also reinforces the allegorical relationship between Masterji and Adiga himself, and their respective occupations of urban and literary spaces. Though Masterji makes his political stand, he becomes alienated from the social group or 'society' of which he is a part and, in the final instance, is murdered by its members. Adiga's decision to stop writing novels that comment upon contemporary India's socioeconomic development—made in direct reaction to the criticisms his work has received (and that, significantly in the case of Kumar's critique,

---

[6] See also Minar Pimple and Lysa John's chapter, 'Security of Tenure: Mumbai's Experience', for a concise historical overview of the various Bombay Rent Acts since independence, as well as a thorough breakdown of the city's demographic spread more generally (Durand-Lasserve and Royston 2002, pp. 75–85).

are from other Indian novelists writing in English)—frames *Last Man in Tower* as an allegorical narration, through its central protagonist, of Adiga's own authorial withdrawal from the literary space of dissent that this novel, at least, has sought to generate and occupy.[7]

Writing 'Slumbai': The Politics of Land Redevelopment

The urban setting of *Last Man in Tower* is central to the novel's politics. As David Harvey argues in his recent study, *Rebel Cities* (2012), within the context of neoliberal globalization, urban environments are increasingly becoming the site of different forms of political, social and economic contestation. Cities across the world, from Santiago to Johannesburg to Mumbai, have witnessed huge building booms for the wealthy, an astonishingly swift process of gentrification matched only by the increasing influx of impoverished migrants and rural peasantries dispossessed through 'the industrialization and commercialization of agriculture' (Harvey 2012, p. 12). The resulting juxtaposition of dramatically polarized class and economic populations is, as Harvey demonstrates, 'indelibly etched into the spatial forms of our cities'. This phenomenon is epitomized in what he describes as 'creative destruction': urban restructuring that dispossesses the poor, underprivileged and marginal inhabitants of the urban landscape in order to make way for privatized, profitable land redevelopment and the creation of homes for the wealthy, be they corporate businesses or individuals (Harvey 2012, pp. 14–15). Harvey takes Mumbai as a case study for these processes: as this Indian city is transformed into a global financial centre, the land that is currently occupied by some six million 'official' slum dwellers, sometimes without legal title, becomes increasingly valuable. Dharavi, one of Mumbai's most prominent slums, was valued at $2 billion in 2012, and those that live there must resort to their own informal lobby groups and the support of local NGOs to protect themselves from dispossession and their land from privatization and redevelopment. The democratic voice of these marginal

---

[7] It should be noted that *The White Tiger*'s protagonist/narrator, Balram, likewise operates at this allegorical level, as his racism, individualist worldview and morally questionable actions—'the sorrowful tale of how I was corrupted from a sweet, innocent village fool into a citified fellow full of debauchery, depravity, and wickedness'—actually work to repudiate the ethical imperative of authenticity that Kumar propagates (Adiga 2008, p. 197).

populations is often pushed aside as the state backs large financial powers which, in turn, lobby 'for forcible slum clearance', dispossessing inhabitants who have been living on the land for over a generation (Harvey 2012, p. 18).

These slums and their inhabitants haunt the marginal spaces of *Last Man in Tower*, as it tells the story of a cut-throat entrepreneur, Shah, who 'entered the business of "redeveloping" chawls and slums—buying out the tenants of ageing structures so that skyscrapers and shopping malls could take their place; a task requiring brutality and charm in equal measure' (Adiga 2011, p. 88). The novel includes a frontispiece map of Mumbai, with Vakola, the area Shah is determined to purchase and redevelop, at its centre. The map depicts a peninsula gridded with arterial transport routes connecting the city's ports—both air and sea—to the subcontinent's interior, reflecting the economic drivers of the city's infrastructural development and implicitly gesturing to the international nature of capital circulation. By contrast, the surrounding slums are represented as nothing more than blank space, despite the fact that, as the novel's second paragraph tells us, 'one-fourth of the city's slums are here' (Adiga 2011, p. 3). Lacking legal title, secure architectures and formal infrastructures, and echoing Balram's invocation of Marlow's blank map of the Congo, the slums are discursively rendered as empty landscapes, waiting to be accumulated by an expanding capitalist economy. It is in the 'heart' of the blank space of Vakola and at the centre of Shah's redevelopment project that the main action of the novel is set: Vishram Society, 'a building' that is, 'like the people living in it', 'middle class to its core' (Adiga 2011, p. 9).

Adiga's description of the building as middle class *itself* is historically informed. As Florian Urban documents, Mumbai's mass housing programme has its roots in the 1900s when, as the city became a central hub of international trade under British rule, 'two types of collective dwellings were built that can be deemed the predecessors of modernist mass housing: the Western-style upscale apartment block and the chawl, a cheap form of dwelling for industrial workers' (Urban 2012, p. 141). The post-independence ramifications of this colonial architecture has been 'an acceptance of multistorey buildings among Mumbai's privileged classes that is unmatched in most Western cities' (p. 142). What were originally intended to be 'egalitarian tower blocks' continue 'to clash with the country's extreme social inequality, converting them into a symbol of wealth rather than marginalisation' (p. 148). This unequal urban geography is written into the novel's cityscape, as Adiga describes the surrounding slums that,

> branching out from [Vishram], encroached on to public land belonging to the Airport Authority of India, and expanded like pincers to the very edge of the runway, so that the first sight of a visitor arriving in Mumbai might well be of a boy from one of these shanties, flying a kite or hitting a cricket ball tossed by his friends. (Adiga 2011, p. 35)

In this opening passage, the narrative registers the likelihood that the reader, like the visitor arriving at the international airport, observes from abroad—be it from a cultural, socio-economic or geographical distance. Adiga writes the distance between that which he represents and the audience to which it is represented into the novel's opening descriptions of the city's spatial organization, echoing an observation made more explicitly by Boo in her non-fictional work, as she writes of the 'international businessmen descending into the Mumbai airport' whose responses to the slums vary from 'disgust' to 'pity' (Boo 2013, p. 42).[8]

It is necessary to give a brief outline of the novel's plot so as to understand how the narrative cumulatively builds its socio-economic critique. In his determination to purchase and demolish the middle-class tower block of Vishram Society and redevelop both that land and the surrounding slum, Shah offers each of its residents 250 % of their flat's market value. The only condition is that all the tower block inhabitants must accept this offer by his given deadline, some 6 months away, thereby setting the time frame for the novel. In a short epigraph, entitled 'A Note on Money', Adiga points out that Shah's offer is around £210,000 for each flat owner at a time when the average per capita annual income in India was around £500. It is enough for the residents to live on for the remainder of their, and possibly their children's, lives, and opens up, quite literally, worlds of opportunity to them. Each resident speculates about how they would invest their new capital. Mr and Mrs Pinto of Flat 2A would send large chunks of the money to support their children living in the USA; Mrs Puri of Flat 3C would use it to employ a carer for her son Ramesh, who has Down's syndrome. The other inhabitants of the tower block are driven to accept the

---

[8] Mehta, too, begins with a portrait of Mumbai from an aerial perspective: 'From the air, you get a sense of its possibilities', he writes. 'On the ground it's different' (Mehta 2005, p. 15).

offer throughout the course of the novel by the incremental infiltration of a set of money-centred values that pervades both the novel and the city it represents. The narrative is littered with comments claiming that 'every man has his price'; that 'a man must want *something*'; that the only thing money cannot buy in Mumbai is 'clean air' (Adiga 2011, pp. 244, 231). Only one character, Yogesh Murthy (or Masterji), resident of Flat 3A, a retired but respected school teacher whose wife has recently passed away, continues to refuse the offer. As the novel hurtles towards Shah's deadline, Masterji is at first ostracized, threatened and, eventually, in the novel's closing pages, murdered, not by the land-hungry capitalist—and here is one of Adiga's more sinister political points—but by his fellow residents.

This series of events can be mapped onto broader socio-economic patterns and trends, an allegorical reading justified textually by a close reading of the novel and one that illuminates its politics of resistance. The novel narrates, quite explicitly, the conflict between a 'neoliberal ethic of intense possessive individualism', as Harvey would describe it (Harvey 2012, p. 14), and a set of communitarian or socialist ideological values that are reminiscent of Nehru's founding vision of post-independence India. Influenced by the Fabian society and his time travelling in Soviet Russia, Nehru attempted to shelter India from the vicissitudes of multinational capital in the early years of independence. He practised a political policy of Cold War non-alignment and focused on the subcontinent's internal development by implementing a series of Five Year Plans. Rana Dasgupta's recent study, *Capital: A Portrait of Twenty-First Century Delhi* (2014), charts the disintegration of Nehru's vision. Prior to 1991, Dasgupta argues, 'any politician who came out and said that the so-called "Socialist" system did not work implied, thereby, that he or she was disloyal to the sacred legacy of the nation's founding father, Jawaharlal Nehru' (Dasgupta 2014, p. 50). However, with the fall of the Berlin Wall and the break-up of the Soviet Union in the late 1980s and early 1990s, India entered into 'the global system' with a jolt. Dasgupta exhibits a distinct nostalgia for the old socialist policies which, as shall be seen in a moment, also permeates Adiga's novel. For Dasgupta, the (re-)opening up of the subcontinent to the tentacles of global capital—a cross-border economic internationalism alluded to by *Last Man in Tower*'s frontispiece map—'was in many respects a humiliating defeat for everything on which the country's greatness stood' (p. 59).

Turning back to *Last Man in Tower*, these processes are encoded at the levels of character and community. In its opening pages, Vishram Society is described as a 'Registered Co-operative Society' that, as a lawyer tells Masterji before he is later paid off by Shah, 'neither you nor any member of any registered co-operative housing society anywhere in this state is the proprietor, strictly speaking, of his or her flat. Your Society is the sovereign of your flat' (Adiga 2011, pp. 282–3). As residents decide to accept the offer, those who refuse are repeatedly ostracized and dismissed as 'Communists'. Mrs Pinto, prior to her acceptance of the offer, argues that '"This is a democracy [...]. No one will silence me. Not you, not all the builders in the world"', only to be told by her interlocutor that '"even a Communist must understand that when someone comes and offers us Rs 20,000 a square foot we should say yes"' (pp. 96, 157, 180). The novel inscribes these ideological values into the tower block at the centrepiece of this economic contention, whilst also allegorizing Masterji as a representative of its Nehruvian argument:

> In old buildings truth is a communal thing, a consensus of opinion. Vishram Society had retained mementoes, over forty-eight years, of all those who had lived in it [...] Now Masterji felt the opinion of him that was engraved into the building—in its peeling paint and 48-year-old brickwork—shift. As it moved, so did something within his body. (p. 216)

Both the building and Masterji himself, each here configured as representative of an old socialist Indian ideal, have their architectural foundations shaken by the infiltration of neoliberal values into Vishram's previously co-operative, if not communistic society. The narrative allegorizes Dasgupta's non-fictional narration of the same process at a micro-social, rather than national or governmental scale.

However, the novel departs from a semi-nostalgic narration of the death of a Nehruvian India modelled on collectivism to interrogate the new neoliberal social realities that the twenty-first century has thrown up. A new political dimension to these contestations is instigated by the class divide that pervades the novel's descriptions of the spatial organization of Mumbai, with the slum dwellers and their informal habitations remaining peripheral features of its landscape. This much broader conflict, though marginalized at first, is eventually written back into the architectural space of Masterji's flat. In the last quarter of the novel, he begins to identify with the slum dwellers and labourers who have thus far remained silent and unrepresented by Adiga's novel. Walking through Mumbai, Masterji eventually

> sensed that he was fighting *for* someone. In the dark dirty valley under the concrete overpass half-naked labourers pushed and slogged, with such little hope that things might improve for them. Yet they pushed: they fought.

[People] across Vakola were fighting to keep their huts. [...] for now their common duty was to fight. (pp. 301–302)[9]

Opposed to this sense of commonality is the competitive individualism of Masterji's fellow tower block residents that culminates in their conscious decision to murder him. Lena Khor, in her reading of *The White Tiger*, argues that Balram is driven to murdering his employer by the logic of an underdevelopment–modernization binary in which the 'neoliberal globalisation paradigm is the inescapable hegemon that rules the world' (Khor 2012, p. 42). This naturalization of a neoliberal logic likewise provides the backdrop to Masterji's murder and is again the subject of *Last Man in Tower*'s critique. The novel presents a developing, Indian, urban middle-class society writ small into the allegorical and architectural space of Vishram Society, as each of its middle-class inhabitants accepts significant financial advancement and, in the process, disregards the population of slum dwellers that their actions will dispossess. What Adiga records so cogently is the process whereby self-interested individualism, as a hegemonic norm underpinning neoliberal globalization, creeps slowly but steadily into the daily lives of his characters. Pal's observation that Boo's *Beautiful Forevers* narrates the way in which the 'personal ethics' of Mumbai's inhabitants 'are tilted on an increasingly selfish axis' is equally true of Adiga's novel (Pal 2012).

Resisting Neoliberalism: The Novel as Space of Dissent

In *Globalization and Postcolonialism* (2009), Sankaran Krishna argues that whilst cultures of neoliberal globalization have the effect of

> naturalising and depoliticising the logic of the market, or logic of the economy, postcolonialism is the effort to politicise and denaturalise that logic and demonstrate the choices and agency in our own lives. (Krishna 2009, p. 2)

---

[9] In *The White Tiger*, Balram experiences a similar kind of identification with Delhi's dispossessed, marginal figures, as drives he through the city at night: 'if something is burning inside me as I drive, the city will know about it—she will burn with the same thing. [...] *if there is blood on the streets*—I asked the city—*do you promise that he'll be the first to go—that man with the fat folds under his neck?*/ A beggar sitting by the side of the road, a nearly naked man coated with grime, and with wild unkempt hair in long coils like snakes, looked into my eyes:/ *Promise*' (Adiga 2008, pp. 220–221).

Krishna's twenty-first-century definition of postcolonialism (which, as he specifies, though bearing some similarities to 'postcolonial theory' is, nevertheless, distinct from it; p. 4) helps us to understand Masterji's actions as a form of political resistance to the naturalization of a neoliberal ideological framework. Masterji's ongoing refusal to accept Shah's monetarily profitable offer as a 'natural' next step and, furthermore, to find reasons that are distinctly political in order to justify this decision, are configured, within Krishna's terminology, as a 'postcolonial' act. Masterji's flat becomes a space of resistance written physically into the city of Mumbai. Adiga's protagonist demonstrates that the claims of the novel's neoliberal advocates—that 'the logic of the markets' is 'something above politics' (p. 4)—is itself a quintessentially political claim. By adamantly adhering to his Nehruvian societal values in direct contrast to an expanding free market, Masterji de-naturalizes this neoliberal logic and exposes the historical contingency of its hegemonic framework. The dark irony underpinning Adiga's novel is that, although Masterji is condemned and socially ostracized for his 'insane' behaviour, it is in fact the other characters who, to return to Harvey's terminology, have enacted the 'neoliberal ethic of intense possessive individualism' to the point of 'human personality socialisation'. They exhibit what he would call 'increasing individualistic isolation, anxiety, and neurosis', all of which drives them to commit an act of fatal violence (Harvey 2012, p. 14). Though members of the society are united in their final murderous act, they remain isolated from, and suspicious of, one another, disregarding the less fortunate urban inhabitants of Mumbai and leaving them exposed to the violence of Shah's redevelopment plans.

If Masterji's dissent is both framed and enabled by his occupation of the architectural space of his property and, in turn, the wider space of the urban slum he thereby prevents Shah from redeveloping, the literary space of this novel is, through the allegorical patterns it has put in place, the vehicle for Adiga's own dissent. Adiga creates an implied reader that is, in fact, not a Western reader but rather a member of the growing Indian middle class: as he himself commented, 'this book shows very solid middle class people changing, and I thought that would be the real challenge, to [...] write a book about [...] the people who will be buying the book in India, middle class people, and show them changing' (*Front Row* 2011). He reorients his cultural location so that rather than occupying a geographically peripheral position on the Western market, he is instead situated as a peripheral Indian writer. In this reading, the novel's opening arrival from abroad signifies not only a geographically and socially distant reader, but also the novel's, and even Adiga's, own arrival in Mumbai as an outsider. Mumbai, and the co-operative society owned by an assortment of Indian middle-class characters, are placed at the novel's centre: the journalistic or 'tour-guide' narrative-style positions Adiga on the outside looking into the society that he represents. He positions himself in a peripheral social space in relation to the centricity of the India that the novel explores.

Last Man in Tower's multiple references to newspapers—indeed, one particular newspaper, the *Times of India*, is a device used repeatedly throughout the novel to indicate the middle-class status of its characters—also suggest that this novel is intended not so much for his Western readership but, perhaps, for an English-speaking Indian middle class. This might be the same Indian, if not global, middle class that would have comprised the readership of his journalism—prior to becoming a novelist, Adiga wrote for both *Financial Times* and *Time Magazine*. Within the novel's narrative, and after both state and law have failed him, Masterji makes a final turn to the media in an attempt to gain wider public support for his cause. This last ditch attempt to resist the redevelopment of his tower block takes on a physical and architectural dimension as he makes his way to the *Times of India* building, which speaks to him in a peculiarly italicized narrative moment: '*The heart of Bombay—if there is one—it is me, it is me!*' (Adiga 2011, p. 294). However, Masterji's contact at the *Times* fails him, refusing through lack of response to give him the public profile he needs to save his own life. Leaving this symbolic home of journalism which, in turn, is located at the symbolically spatial *heart* of the city, a disappointed Masterji enters instead that other renowned institution, McDonald's, with all the connotations of corporate globalization and neoliberal values that the golden arches signify.

Masterji's movement through the city suggests that, as the media becomes complicit with, and an advocate of, a neoliberalist logic of progressive individualism and economic growth as the sole measure of development, it is only the peripheral social space of Adiga's own socio-economic critique—found not in journalism proper, but instead in his own satirical and journalistic fiction—that is capable of creating space for voices of dissent to inhabit. Masterji's misguided faith in the social justice that, Adiga implies, should be the responsibility of press investigation, is simultaneously used as a meta-textual device to speak back to the politics of authenticity raised earlier. The novel qualifies its own political assertion by framing authenticity as in fact stifling the anglophone Indian novel's potentially political capacity. This might be read as a direct response to critics such as Kumar, who draw attention away from this important political work as it was undertaken in Adiga's first novel, *The White Tiger*. Reading texts such as Boo's in the light of this commentary, *Last Man in Tower* functions as both a critique of journalism's complicity with an increasingly pervasive neoliberal ethic whilst also highlighting the capacity of the *literary* as an emergent site of socio-political resistance.

This is, again, inscribed into the novel's plot. The list of institutions to which Masterji can turn for support diminishes as his peers slowly conspire against and eventually murder him. The novel offers no redemptive solution as, after his death, Masterji's sanity is questioned and, in the final pages, his cause quickly forgotten:

> For two months after his death, Masterji was a residue of dark glamour on the Vakola market, a layer of ash over the produce. Then other scandals and other mysteries came. The vendors forgot him. (pp. 400–401)

Journalism's short-termism inhibits its capacity to demand socio-political justice when state institutions fail, a malaise enacted symbolically here by the vendors. The only document that remains as a testimony to Masterji's spatio-temporal act of resistance is Adiga's novel itself—a fictional narrative, certainly, but based on a true story that Adiga had read about in a newspaper (*Front Row* 2011). It is here that the allegorical relationship between the occupation of literary and urban spaces crystallizes most clearly. Just as Adiga has claimed that this will be his last socio-economically oriented novel, with his career as dissident and social commentator coming to an end, Masterji—the master, the author of Vishram Society as indicated by the 'Minutes' of a special 'Co-operative meeting' offered to the reader in the novel's opening pages (p. 8)—himself comes to his fictional, but nevertheless fatal conclusion. Adiga writes his own career as social dissident allegorically into what he has proclaimed will be his last socio-economic novel. As Mukherjee observes, 'despite their obvious commodification as cultural objects in the contemporary global market, [...] the irreducible literariness of the [Indian English] novel—the way in which it performs its story—introduces a series of disturbances into the everyday lives of [its] audience, which disrupts the cultural and ideological status quo' (Mukherjee 2010, pp. 10–11). Though Adiga appears to have killed off his literary career along with his resistant protagonist,

Last Man in Tower still posits the idea that it is only the novel—regardless of whether it is written in English or not—that has the capacity to go on weaving threads of dissent into India's densely knotted social fabric.

Conclusion: Allegories of Occupation

Since the publication of Adiga's *Last Man in Tower*, cities have continued to become increasingly crucial sites for political action and revolt against various socio-economic conditions—from austerities to inequalities—that are symptoms of neoliberal globalization. In 2012, less than a year after the publication of Adiga's novel, Al Jazeera's programme *Activate* reported on new, democratically coordinated efforts of slum dwellers in Mumbai to resist the demolition of their homes (Khan 2012). The Occupy movement that has spread from New York City to different parts of the world, converting public spaces into 'political commons', and the centrality of physical spaces such as Gezi Park in Turkey and Tahrir Square in Egypt, suggest, as does Adiga's novel, that urban space is now central to the contestation of global inequalities (Harvey 2012, p. 161). Like Adiga's novel, the ambiguity of the alternative political vision that these movements represent—and for which they have been criticized—in fact gains its power simply because it is just that: the ability to 'demonstrate the choices and agency in our own lives' as a political end in itself (Krishna 2009, p. 2). By allegorizing this process, *Last Man in Tower* suggests that as the urban space is reclaimed as a site in which to express political agency, so also is the literary.

Works Cited

Adiga, A. (2008). *The white tiger*. London: Atlantic Books.
Adiga, A. (2011). *Last man in tower*. London: Atlantic Books.
Boo, K. (2009, February 23). Opening night: The scene from the airport slums [Online]. *The New Yorker*. Available from http://www.newyorker.com/magazine/2009/02/23/opening-night-3
Boo, K. (2013). *Behind the beautiful forevers: Life, death and hope in a Mumbai slum*. London: Portobello Books.
Carty, P. (2011, June 12). Last man in tower, by Aravind Adiga [Online]. *The Independent*. Available from http://www.independent.co.uk/arts-entertainment/books/reviews/last-man-in-tower-by-aravind-adiga-2296318.html
Chandra, V. (2000, February 1). The cult of authenticity. [Online]. *Boston Review*. Available from http://www.bostonreview.net/vikram-chandra-the-cult-of-authenticity

Chomsky, N. (2012). *Occupy*. New York: Zuccottie Park Press.
Conrad, J. (2006). *Heart of darkness*. London: Norton & Company.
Dalrymple, W. (2012, June 22). Behind the beautiful forevers: Life, death and hope in a Mumbai slum by Katherine Boo – Review [Online]. *The Guardian*. Available from http://www.theguardian.com/books/2012/jun/22/beautiful-forevers-katherine-boo-review
Dasgupta, R. (2014). *Capital: A portrait of twenty-first century Delhi*. Edinburgh: Canongate Books Ltd.
Detmers, I. (2011). A new India? New metropolis? Reading Aravind Adiga's *The white tiger* as a 'condition-of-India novel'. *Journal of Postcolonial Writing*, 47(5), 535–545.
Durand-Lasserve, A., & Royston, L. (Eds.). (2002). *Holding their ground: Secure land tenure for the urban poor in developing countries*. Sterling: Earthscan Publications.
Front Row. (2011, June 30). *BBC Radio 4*, 19:15. Available from http://www.bbc.co.uk/programmes/b0124pxj
Gajarawala, T. J. (2012). *Untouchable fictions: Literary realism and the crisis of caste*. New York: Fordham University Press.
Harvey, D. (2012). *Rebel cities: From the right to the city to the urban revolution*. London: Verso.
John, J. (2003). *Dickens's villains: Melodrama, character, popular culture*. Oxford: Oxford University Press.
Khan, F. A. (2012, October 24). Activate – Mumbai land grab. Al Jazeera. Available from http://www.aljazeera.com/programmes/activate/2012/10/2012101411374674215l.html
Khor, L. (2012). Can the subaltern right wrongs? Human rights and development in Aravind Adiga's *The white tiger*. *South Central Review*, 29(1&2), 41–67.
Krishna, S. (2009). *Globalization and postcolonialism: Hegemony and resistance in the twenty-first century*. Plymouth: Rowman & Littlefield.
Kumar, A. (2008). Viewpoint: On Adiga's *The white tiger* [Online]. *The Hindu*. 2 November. Availabe from http://www.thehindu.com/thehindu/lr/2008/11/02/stories/2008110250010100.html
Mehta, S. (2005). *Maximum city: Bombay lost and found*. London: Headline Book Publishing.
Mendes, A. C. (2010). Exciting tales of exotic dark India: Aravind Adiga's *The white tiger*. *Journal of Commonwealth Literature*, 45, 275–293.
Mukherjee, M. (1993). The anxiety of Indianness: Our novels in English. *Economic and Political Weekly*, 28(48), 2607–2611.
Mukherjee, M. (2000). The local and the global: Literary implications in India. *English Studies in Africa*, 43(2), 47–56.
Mukherjee, U. P. (2010). *Postcolonial environments: Nature, culture and the contemporary Indian novel in English*. New York: Palgrave Macmillan.

Munshi, N. (2012, March 30). beyondbrics review: *Behind the beautiful forevers*, by Katherine Boo. [Online]. *Financial Times*. Available from http://blogs.ft.com/beyond-brics/2012/03/30/bb-review-behind-the-beautiful-forevers-by-katherine-boo

Pal, D. (2012, February 15). The dangers of novelising non-fiction [Online]. *Mumbai boss: Making sense of the city*. Available from http://mumbaiboss.com/2012/02/15/the-dangers-of-novelising-non-fiction/

Prakash, G. (2010). *Mumbai fables*. Princeton: Princeton University Press.

Sadana, R. (2012). *English heart, Hindi heartland: The political life of literature in India*. London: University of California Press.

Spivak, G. (1988). Can the subaltern speak? In C. Nelson & L. Grossberg (Eds.), *Marxism and the interpretation of culture* (pp. 271–313). Urbana: University of Illinois Press.

Swarup, V. (2012, May 12). Life on the edge: Review of Katherine Boo's *Behind the beautiful forevers* [Online]. *Financial Times*. Available from http://www.ft.com/cms/s/2/5ac61e16-99c9-11e1-8fce-00144feabdc0.html#axzz39baDvpdJ

Urban, F. (2012). Mumbai's suburban mass housing. *Urban History, 39*(1), 128–148.

Contemporary Indian Commercial Fiction in English

Suman Gupta

The means of production for literature in English have seen significant changes in India since the late 1980s. A remarkable proliferation of both independent and international publishers with 'Indian-English literature'—particularly fiction—has taken place. In this regard the current phase of development can be traced back to the independent publisher Ravi Dayal's (established 1988) success with Amitav Ghosh's *The Shadow Lines* (1988) and to the setting up of Penguin India in 1985. A corresponding diversification in categories and genres of such literature has evidently occurred. Within the Indian market, Indian 'commercial fiction' in English has unquestionably been the principal area of diversification, while 'literary fiction' in English—as much a market category as 'commercial fiction'—and translations from Indian vernaculars have become more varied and numerous too.

This chapter is addressed to Indian commercial fiction in English since the 1980s, with a particular emphasis on the post-2000 period. It offers some more or less speculative observations on Indian fiction in English, which is produced with the expectation that it will enjoy a profitable career *within* the Indian market. Though this kind of fiction has a significant presence in India, it is little known and only perfunctorily registered

---

S. Gupta
Department of English, The Open University, Milton Keynes, UK

elsewhere. For the purposes of this chapter, 'commercial fiction' is characterized more emphatically by market performance than the intrinsic features of texts, that is, than the putative generic features, themes and stylistic devices that can be discerned in specific texts. Here I offer neither readings of particular texts nor a survey of these and their authors. Nor do I examine the material forms in which commercial fiction circulates in the market, appearing as tangible books. The observations here approach commercial fiction tangentially, in terms of some available evidence of production, circulation and reception, and consider the inferences that follow with Indian social circumstances in view. These could be regarded as observations which might usefully precede a critical engagement with commercial fiction texts and their material forms, and which are predominantly concerned with the social context which construes such books and is construed by such books.

COMMERCIAL AND LITERARY

The Indian 'commercial fiction' in English which circulates predominantly within the country can be regarded as reasonably distinct from the 'literary fiction' in English which has a larger-than-Indian presence. Neither are mutually impervious or exclusive areas. Despite numerous efforts to describe these terms according to content—as if texts have immanent qualities of commercialness and literariness—both are plausibly understood as market-led categories (on this point, see Gupta 2009, Chap. 6). Both make pre-eminent sense in terms of appealing to and anticipating specific sorts of readership, and being designed, publicized, circulated and discussed or disregarded accordingly.

In a general way, 'literary fiction' evidently has greater international visibility and is occasionally regarded as coeval with 'Indian-English literature' per se. This is so especially outside India, but sometimes within India too, in academic circles and establishment cultural discourses (to do with prizes, reviewing, literary festivals and events, etc.). Naturally, this does not mean that *all* Indian literary fiction has international visibility; much that is published as such, even recipients of Sahitya Akademi Awards, do not go far in the Indian market and travel indifferently abroad. But success in literary fiction is measured by texts which have circulated well in a wider Anglo American market and have enjoyed concordant critical attention and cultural currency. What is produced and consumed as Indian commercial fiction in English is generally regarded as a matter of internal or domestic interest. It is consumed primarily within India, seen to display a kind of 'Indianness' that Indians appreciate and is not meant to be taken 'seriously' or regarded as 'literary'. Literary fiction is the respectable public face of Indian literature in English at home and abroad, while commercial fiction is the gossipy café of Indian writing in English at home.

Numerous academic surveys and commentaries on Indian fiction in English dwell exclusively on literary fiction and establish a canon which functions as both a repository and confirmation of literariness. The contemporary literary canon consists of a roll call, such as Salman Rushdie, Amitav Ghosh, Vikram Seth, Arundhati Roy, Amit Chaudhuri, Rohinton Mistry, Anita Desai, Shashi Tharoor, Allan Sealy, Anita Nair, Vikram Chandra, Kiran Desai, Mukul Keshavan, Rupa Bajwa, Aravind Adiga, Rana Dasgupta and so on. Most are mentioned in no particular order, but the progenitor at the top of the list is usually Rushdie and the novel that sets this phase rolling is *Midnight's Children* (1981). Rushdie is (slightly ironically) the 'messiah' of the Indian-English literary 'renaissance' from the 1980s in John Mee's survey of novels in the 1980s and 1990s (2003, p. 318); and, similarly, the most highly regarded novels over the same period are '*Midnight's Children*'s Children' in Naik and Narayan's (2004, Chap. 3) survey covering 1980–2000. As the next decade progresses, we find Chaudhuri (2008, pp. 113–121) concerned about the superlative significance given to Rushdie's work; Gopal (2009) tracing 'Midnight's Legacies' as a consistent thread while working her way towards the 'contemporary scene' of the Indian-English novel; and Rajan (2011) still charting new developments in Indian novels from 'After *Midnight's Children*'. None of these dwell on Indian commercial fiction in English: the heritage from Rushdie seems to have a particular investment in 'literariness', with normative connotations intact. As this is written (in 2014) the early glimmerings of academic exploration of Indian commercial fiction in English as a separate and unrelated line to the literary canon—as a kind of alternative canon or counter-canon—are becoming available. A couple of extended surveys of different genres of Indian commercial publishing have been undertaken in that vein (for example, Dawson Varughese 2013; Sinha 2014). These look to specific commercial fiction texts in terms of their distinctive use of generic conventions to tease out how contemporary 'Indianness' is articulated. They draw upon a fairly recent (primarily 1970s and onwards) critical tradition of understanding popular/pulp/mass-market fiction in a general way (Sutherland 1981; Birch 1987; Bennett 1990; Nash 1990; and onwards). The latter is strongly associated with the theory-led shift from literature to cultural studies; that is, from a normatively underpinned notion of literariness to a relatively inclusive grasp of cultural production and sociological exegesis in engaging books. Naturally, insofar as that meant analysing the popular with academic 'seriousness', this tradition began somewhat defensively in anticipation of dismissive literary critical appraisal (and was strategically celebratory about commercial fiction at times) and construed its interest as counter-canonical. The nascent move to analyse Indian commercial fiction in English is now similarly defensive about and separated from literariness, and celebratory about the 'Indianness' of commercial fiction texts. No doubt more academic research work along these lines will continue to appear.

However, it is primarily in a non-academic register that the burgeoning Indian commercial fiction has been registered so far: in claims made by publishers and other professionals and authors in the mass media (particularly newspapers and magazines). Such claims come with not only an alternative-to-academic authority but also as a matter of expertise, but hands-on expertise in production processes and reading markets rather than in studied critical understanding. Publishing professionals are apt to be cited as experts here: At different stages in their careers, Thomas Abraham of Hachette India, Chiki Sarkar of Random House India, Ravi Singh of Penguin India, V.K. Karthika of HarperCollins India, Kapish Mehra of Rupa, Nilanjana Roy of EastWest and Westland Books, Nandita Bhardwaj of Roli Books and so on. The lines of expertise between academic and publishing professional discourses are generally fairly clearly drawn. The former are predominantly ensconced in scholarly forums and confined mainly to literary fiction; the latter in mass media forums and devoted to both Indian literary *and* commercial fiction in English. While the former attend predominantly to the nuances of postcoloniality and (literary/cultural) history, the latter gesture towards globalization and the transcendence of the present. When the former pronounce on the quality of literary fiction, the latter agree and offer disclaimers about the literariness of commercial fiction and point to their market penetration.

There is an air of heroism about the authority of the publishing professional apropos of Indian fiction in English. They appear at the cutting edge of literary production, while academic criticism appears after the fact. Especially in relation to commercial fiction, publishing professionals increasingly partake of a sort of greater authorship: they seem to speak as authors of a commercial field of literary production and reception in which the immediate authors—the functional writers of commercial fiction—contribute in a subsidiary way. Publishing professionals are allocated their own record and narrative as super-authorial figures through interviews and addresses (some collected, for instance, by Ghai 2008a, b) and embody a much-discussed growth industry (much as call-centre workers did for the Indian outsourcing industry recently). Publishers sometimes speak candidly of their stronger sense of authorship in India than their counterparts may feel elsewhere. After moving from Bloomsbury, UK, to Random House, India, publisher Chiki Sarkar (2009) found that she was having 'so much fun' because she could decide what sorts of books she wanted to publish and then find authors for them and suitable media coverage. By way of repartee, Aditya Sudarshan (2010) observed that 'Indian publishing needs to get less fun' because 'kitsch' (read 'commercial fiction') was beginning to dominate Indian-English fiction lists—not because readers or writers necessarily want it, but 'because our editors felt like it'. Sudarshan's complaint about the editors' super-authorship is evidently not because that complicates notions of authorship but because he found the products wanting qualitatively; in a way, this was a complaint about commercial fiction itself.

At any rate, while the academic expert places Rushdie as progenitor of contemporary Indian 'literary fiction' in English, the publishing expert appoints Chetan Bhagat the same for 'commercial fiction'. So, a 2007 report in *Hindustan Times* observed: 'Why did we stop looking down on commercial writing? The answer, say publishers, can be found in two words: Chetan Bhagat' (Gulab 2007). And, similarly, an article from *The Telegraph* (Kolkata) opined: 'It's not as if Indian writers never penned commercial fiction before. [...] But this never developed into a body of work. That has changed ever since bestselling author Chetan Bhagat hit the scene' (Dua 2009). Bhagat's role in the relatively recent great leap forward of Indian commercial fiction in English is widely acknowledged. Irrespective of the aptness of Bhagat's progenitor status (his *Five Point Someone* was published in 2004, while Shobhaa De's *Socialite Nights*, 1989, and Anurag Mathur's *The Inscrutable Americans*, 1991, have strong pioneering claims for the contemporary commercial fiction field), the career of his novels does typify the kind of production and circulation that this chapter is concerned with.

It is often noted that sales figures set Bhagat's novels apart from contenders, and these put the scope and scale of the Indian market for commercial fiction into perspective. By 2008, *Five Point Someone* (2004) had reportedly sold 700,000 copies in India, and Bhagat's more recent novel then (*The 3 Mistakes of My Life*, 2008) had a first print run of 200,000 (Mahapatra 2008). Within India, for English-language fictional works, this is equalled only by phenomenally successful international bestsellers: for instance, in 2005, J.K. Rowling's *Harry Potter and the Half-Blood Prince* reportedly sold over 100,000 copies on the first day (Ahmad 2005), and in 2007 around 240,000 copies of *Harry Potter and the Deathly Hallows* were pre-ordered in India before release (Raja 2007). Rowling's novels were, of course, considerably more expensive; at under INR 100 Bhagat's novels were produced to be affordable. According to Bhagat's publishers Rupa, their other successful books generally sold 40–50,000 copies (Fernandes 2010, p. 21). The sales figures of Bhagat's novels (six by 2014) have been tracked with admiration and envy in the news media periodically ever since. However, this success in the domestic market is not reflected in the international passages of Bhagat's novels. *Five Point Someone* (2004) did not find a co-publication deal abroad. As a result of news-fuelled awareness of outsourcing in Britain and the USA, *One Night @ the Call Centre* (2005) did, and it was co-published by Transworld Publishers (UK) and Ballantine Books (USA) in 2007. Large Internet vendors outside India, such as Amazon USA and Amazon UK, have consistently shown modest sales rankings for both.

Bhagat's novels largely tended to escape scholarly attention. Even in Tabish Khair's 2008 overview of 'Indian pulp fiction in English', Bhagat failed to make an appearance; he was mentioned in a footnote in Rajeswari Sunder Rajan's 2011 survey of post-*Midnight's Children* novels, and Rashmi Sadana's entry on 'Writing in English' in *The Cambridge Companion to Modern Indian Culture* (2012) ended with a few words on Bhagat. Those few words in the last are fairly indicative of academic attitudes. Here, Sadana compared Bhagat's *Five Point Someone* to the earlier *English, August* (1988) by Upamanyu Chatterjee, but on the understanding that '*English, August* is [...] a serious literary achievement, and became a cult classic as compared to the easy-reading, plot pulsating, *Five Point Someone*' (Sadana 2012b, p. 140). Consequently, the substantive content of Chatterjee's novel was bestowed with some critical attention, whereas Bhagat's work in general (the novel in question is disregarded after being mentioned) became the occasion for a brief comment on changing attitudes to English in India. Naturally, Bhagat's work received prolific mass media attention and numerous reviews in Indian broadsheets and magazines. These have been unanimous in doubting Bhagat's 'literary' achievement: 'with the release of his third book [...] Chetan Bhagat has made one thing quite clear. He really isn't a great writer. This shouldn't come as news to the Indian literary establishment' (Menon 2008, p. 71). Equally, such reports have been continuously struck by the fact that his novels sell quite as many copies as reported. Bhagat's work has received some mass media attention outside India, the tone of which speaks for itself. He was introduced thus to readers of *The Guardian*: 'He is the biggest-selling writer in English you've never heard of' (Ramesh 2008); and with the following to *Observer* readers: 'For [Indian] people [of the 'outsourcing generation'], there is only one author: Chetan Bhagat. Who?' (McCrum 2010). Whether in India or elsewhere, the tone says that it doesn't really matter to *us* what Bhagat writes, *we* won't get much from reading his texts; what matters is that *they* read him prolifically—those Bhagat readers in India. These *other* readers are somehow symptomatized in Bhagat's success, and *their* reading of Bhagat symptomatizes something. *They* are characterized in literary features as a new kind of readership. According to a *New York Times*' article: 'Mr. Bhagat might not be another Vikram Seth or Arundhati Roy, but he has authentic claims to being one of the voices of a generation of middle-class Indian youth facing the choices and frustrations that come with the prospect of growing wealth' (Greenlees 2008). All who have written about Bhagat, in India or elsewhere, agree on this: the Chetan Bhagat 'phenomenon', in brief, had something to do with middle-class youth in India and India's growing affluence and presence in a globalized world and consequently strengthened sense of national/local identity.

Bhagat is, as I have observed above, the tip of the iceberg of Indian commercial fiction in English. Much that can be said about the tip applies to the iceberg generally. Around the turn of the 2010s, numerous enthusiastic reports appeared about the continuing 'boom' in English-language fiction in India (see, for example, Kramatschek 2007; Dua 2009; Kumar 2009; Gulab 2010; Khan 2010; Tarafdar 2010; Ghosh 2011; Pathak 2011; Sarkar 2011). These registered a rapid proliferation of commercial fiction along the lines of 'genre' categories: detective fiction, science fiction and fantasies, chick lit, romances, campus novels, graphic novels and so on. Differentiations among producers and consumers were noted in these: for instance, the degree to which both international publishers (with India establishments) and independent publishers promote 'genre fiction' and which categories sell particularly well or are yet to reach their full potential. A growing divide between commercial fiction for Indian readers and literary fiction for Indian and international consumption was occasionally perceived, and sometimes it was suggested that interest in producing the latter is perhaps suffering (for example, see Ghosh 2011). The great majority were (and remain) sanguine about such a dip in literary fiction and celebratory about the growth and potential of commercial fiction. The celebratory tone was obviously about the economic prospects for the publishing industry in India, but it extended also to the changing socio-cultural environment evidenced thereby. The key points about the latter were summarized usefully by Claudia Kramatschek and coincided with media commentary on the popularity of Bhagat's novels:

> Many Indian authors – especially younger ones – will tell you that they experience a certain pressure, strengthened by internationally active publishers, to act as cultural ambassadors. In other words, either to turn out 'spice and curry' in the form of easily-digestible novels of the exotic variety, or else elucidations of 'Indianness' as such.
>
> But a younger generation of authors now appears to have emerged in the English-language literary sector whose common development manifests a kind of caesura. All are between 25 and 35 years of age – a fact which in and of itself represents a minor revolution in a country where the aura of the senior writer has always shaped the literary canon. All came of age in an India where access to the wider world was available via mouseclick, and all feel at home within the most divergent cultures – and they play with this intercultural network in their literary work as well. At the same time, nonetheless, they are rooted in India to an astonishing degree, and they write about this sense of connection in new and innovative – and at times surprising – ways. A marked turn toward localism is observable, meaning toward the microcosmos of one's own lived world, to the history of the individual towns where these authors lead their lives. In literary terms, this return is associated with an opening toward genre literature and toward what might be referred to as the small form. (Kramatschek 2007)

There we have it again: the condition of English-language commercial fiction in India has something to do with the English-speaking middle-class youth and with global awareness or globalization processes in relation to a changing sense of national awareness or local lives. These are obviously closely intertwined; arguably it is the youth in question who cultivate the local/global awareness, and equally the local/global awareness in question appeals to the youth.

Some attention to these two entwined factors in relation to English-language commercial fiction in India seems to be called for. Two sections consequently follow: on 'local/global' India and Indian 'middle-class youth' culture.

LOCAL/GLOBAL

There are two ways in which we can contemplate the global/local dimension in relation to Indian commercial fiction in English: first, in terms of processes of publication and circulation (the means of production); second, in terms of the broad characteristics and reception of such fiction (product and consumption).

The story of commercial fiction publishing is part of a larger story about the growth of the Indian publishing sector. In terms of absolute figures, this is an impressively large and diverse sector. According to Akshay Pathak (2011), 12,375 publishers were registered with the ISBN India agency at the end of 2007, with an estimated 90,000 titles being published each year, and with the industry showing an optimistic growth estimate of 30 %. A German Book Office publication (2012/2013, p. 19) reconfirmed these figures and estimated that the total number of publishers, including those unregistered, is around 19,000. The English-language element in this has superlative visibility because it is nationally and internationally accessible. International interest in the Indian publishing industry is evidenced in various ways. Most significantly, Indian subsidiaries of international publishing corporations enjoy a considerable media and commercial presence. The Association of Publishers in India (API), the representative body of such publishers, lists 27 members for 2010–2011. Beyond that, international interest is charted through various market reports commissioned abroad (such as Khullar Management 1999; Francis 2003/2008); particular attention at book fairs (India was special guest at the Frankfurt Book Fair, 4–8 October 2006 and featured prominently in the Paris Book Fair, 22–27 May 2007); and other initiatives (for example, in 2010 the British Council established the YCE Publishing Award for young publishers in India to network in the UK). The prospects for exporting Indian-English-language publications have been under occasional scrutiny (for example, Pathak 2011), and various economic and legal constraints discussed.

These might be regarded as signs of the globalization (and certainly of a growing global presence) of the Indian publishing industry, but that does not mean Indian commercial fiction in English (the product) has a global presence. That is an important distinction. As I have observed above, successful commercial fiction (such as Bhagat's) is produced mainly for circulation within India and travels indifferently elsewhere. The international publishers in India are there to generate profits by entering the Indian reading market, not by opening up Indian commercial fiction to an international market. The great bulk of commercial fiction produced by Penguin India, HarperCollins India, Hachette India, and so on, is only distributed within India. The international reports and initiatives mentioned above are employed more towards enabling international publishers to mould and exploit Indian products (commercial fiction) and consumers (the reading market), and very much less towards generating Indian products which can be used to exploit the international market. The idea is to set up an internal cycle of production and consumption which international publishers can tap into, rather than to make Indian products a global commodity. From the international corporation's perspective, Indian commercial fiction is a gigantic niche market enterprise. It is unclear to what extent the advent of international publishers might have affected independent publishing. Independent publishers in India, who may have stoked the flames of commercial fiction which international publishers have fanned since, may benefit from the large-scale moulding of production and consumption that international publishers undertake and may also be pushed more emphatically into ever-smaller niches within India. The general experience in Britain and the USA is that independent publishers tend to be consumed by international corporations (see Schiffrin 2000; Feather 2003); in India (I gathered from conversations with independent publishers) it is held that the market capacity is so large that international and independent publishers can both thrive in a symbiotic relationship. Sometimes independent Indian publishers are able to make useful co-publication deals with their counterparts abroad or with international publishers within.

For global players, an on-the-ground presence in India offers further advantages which are unavailable to independent publishers. It enables, for instance, exploitation of the uneven flow of commercial fiction. Not only are international publishers able to tap into the contained circuit of Indian commercial fiction, but they are also in a position to regulate the inflow of commercial fiction that they publish elsewhere—primarily British and American commercial fiction. The latter have a well-established place in the Indian market; however, until the 1990s, much of their distribution worked through the pirated book market (or, occasionally, through cheap legal reprints). Now, international corporations are able to regulate the situation to some extent. So, HarperCollins India, Random House India, Penguin India, and so on, are able to produce Indian commercial fiction in English and, at the same time, reprint their American and British commercial fiction lists for Indian readers, and set up their own distribution mechanisms for both. Further, it seems that the Indian market for commercial fiction by Indian emigrants in the UK or the USA coincides with the confined market for Indian commercial fiction in English—a presence in the Indian market is a useful position for international publishers to promote writings by Indian emigrants published first in other territories.

The globalization of the Indian publishing industry is easily charted through the presence of international publishers, but that is far from being the central feature of the process. More importantly, a global template of commercial fiction production and circulation has been imported and adapted for the Indian market. To begin with, this has to do with the structure of 'genre fiction', in terms of which production and circulation of Indian commercial fiction in English is now routinely mediated: the above-noted proliferation of science fiction, detective fiction, chick lit, fantasy, graphic novels, campus novels, and so on, replicates categorization and packaging and marketing practices which have been tried and tested over a considerable period in the UK, the USA and elsewhere. This entire *structure* has been imported wholesale into the Indian publishing industry and book market within a compressed period of a couple of decades. The precise ways in which this structure has been adapted (rather than simply mimicked) for Indian consumers are of considerable significance for research and analysis—a detailed exposition is beyond the scope of this chapter. It is possible that certain expectations and experiences associated with older traditions of commercial fiction production in Indian languages have been integrated within the global template. Some research has already been devoted to the predecessors of these 'genres' in Indian languages or earlier English-language productions, themselves often inspired by colonial commercial fiction from Britain: for example, Chandra (2008) for comics; Roy (2008) for Bengali detective fiction; Mathur (2006) and Orsini (2004) for detective fiction in the colonial period; Sengupta (2003) for Bengali science fiction; Daechsel (2003) for Urdu detective fiction; and Khair (2008) for a history of 'Indian-English pulp fiction' before

Shobhaa De. These are worth looking at closely in relation to the current production, marketing and circulation. Further, particular approaches to the English language, and social themes of specific moment in India, have played their part in the Indian adaptation of the global commercial fiction publishing template. These have enabled localization of the products fitted into the global template, without disturbing the structural coherence of the latter. Brief notes on such localization will soon follow. Beyond structuring in terms of 'genre' categories, the global publishing template also involves norms of material production—meeting 'global standards' in the physical appearance and shaping of the book (on this, see Ahuja 2004). The recently (post-1990) diversified channels of formal recognition through corporation-sponsored prizes, mass media-based 'bestseller' listings, creation of celebrity profiles, adaptations into films, and so on, also concretize the Indian importation of a global template. So do ongoing developments in retailing practices, from micro-matters, such as how bookshops should be arranged, to macro-matters such as establishing book-retailing chains and Internet vending.

While such globalization of the Indian book industry unfolds, the commercial fiction products (books) themselves are designed for and circulated within an emphatically contained national or local sphere. The discourse that articulates this circulatory matrix is addressed to Indian books by Indian authors being produced in India for Indian readers. In other words, this is a circuit of Indians talking to Indians in a closed space, a national space, albeit in the most international of languages. Localization of practice here is evidently in the service of globalization for the publishing industry; it is the local product and circuit instrumentalized for structural globalization and for the benefit of international corporations. Despite the oft-mooted antithetical positioning of globalization/commercial fiction/popular reception and postcolonialism/literary fiction/academic discernment (discussed above), there is arguably no significant opposition: no noteworthy flow *away* from postcolonial hangover *towards* globalized–localized ('glocalized') aspirations. The geopolitics of transfer and exploitation, the structuring of knowledge and know-how, present a convergent dynamics in accounts of globalization-localization and postcoloniality. Nevertheless, the burgeoning Indian commercial fiction in English is perceivably new and different from, and even resistant to, the established Indian-English literary fiction. It makes a claim of local rootedness, of national resurgence, which could be unpacked further—without, as I decided above, immediately undertaking textual analyses or surveys.

The localization that plays with the global template could be described variously. To begin with, the most global of languages is itself the site for localization in Indian commercial fiction in English. On the one hand, since the 1990s, cross-border commercial enterprise (strongly associated with Business Process Outsourcing) has resulted in an upward revaluation of 'standard' English as cultural capital. On the other hand, with increasing use in everyday life, the distinctiveness of Indian English has become more a repository of claims and anxieties about national identity than it was prior to the 1990s. Unsurprisingly, the use of a distinctively Indian idiom or of 'home-grown English' is regarded as key to the recent success of Indian commercial fiction in English: that is, 'the quick-fire campus English that young Indians use' (Ramesh 2008; McCrum 2010), 'English as unpretentious as a call-center cubicle' (Thottam 2008). A close analysis of such distinctive Indian English usage in fiction, with its regionally varied enunciations, syntax transferred from regional languages, code-switchings, idiomatic Indianisms and so on (see Sailaja 2009; Sedlatschek 2009; Sethi 2011) requires more space than this chapter has. In brief, however, the distinctiveness of Indian English usage in commercial fiction could be understood in terms of its *familiarized* relationship with the Indian context. This is a frequently traversed argument in the discussions cited above: Indian commercial fiction in English, the argument goes, is geared expressively for an internal Indian audience and therefore does not need to be explanatory and demonstrative in the way that literary fiction, with a potentially international readership, feels it should be. The latter is what Kramatschek (2007), quoted above, described as 'easily-digestible novels of the exotic variety, or else elucidations of "Indianness" as such'; or, in Chandrahas Choudhury's words:

> As the Indian novel in English, assisted by India's rising profile in global affairs, finds an audience wherever English is spoken, it often seems to sacrifice the particularities of Indian experience for a watered-down idiom that can speak to readers across the globe. (Choudhury 2009, p. 96)

These are descriptions of a defamiliarized relationship between the English language (for literature) and the Indian context. Underlying commercial fiction's claim of a familiarized relationship between language and context, we may detect insecurities related to some essentialist notion of Indian identity or nationalistic protectiveness about India's 'image' abroad— both, perhaps, ultimately anxieties about the status of English in India itself. Such anxieties are eloquently expressed in the form of the following questions in a 2010 news feature:

> If you write in what's called The Queen's English without the phrasing that may be grammatically incorrect in the UK but is how we usually speak English here, are you authentically Indian? On the other hand, if you write about villages or urban underbellies, are you not catering to a western readership with a taste for the exotic, rather than a homegrown Indian one? (Gulab 2010)

At any rate, it appears to be held that writing fiction about India in English has almost inevitably been an act of defamiliarization, and yet paradoxically English is an Indian language and should have the capacity of familiarized usage for fiction. It is averred that Indian commercial fiction in English, *à la* Bhagat and others, has now hit upon it: by eliding explanations and an exotic sensibility and by using English as if it is habitual within the locale that is described, as if English is 'native' to the Indian habitus.

The tacit drift towards enclosure and 'authentic' Indianness and the apprehensions about exoticization and exposure to 'foreigners' in such arguments seem wholly dubious to me (and possibly dangerous in the way that religious communalism is dangerous). Perhaps such arguments are after the fact—that such commercial fiction, designed to exploit the Indian reading market in English rather than internationalize Indian commercial literature in English, has a predetermined circulation *within* India—and such arguments may well be market-inspired. Possibly, these sentiments about Indian distinctiveness are offered in a spirit of the postfactum affirmation that industrial success is routinely greeted with. If we went along with Graham Huggan's analysis of homogenization and othering (exoticization) in practices of 'postcoloniality' that render India as a sort of brand, India as 'more available than ever for consumption' (Huggan 2001, p. 82), then this need not simply operate at the mismatched boundary of the 'Western' imperialist gaze and the diverse interior of India. It could just as well work within India. Arguably, the cultivated localization that operates through English in Indian commercial fiction, emphatically for internal circulation within a global publishing template, involves an internal branding of India for internal consumption. This could be a kind of internal branding in much the way that 'ethnic' clothing or 'Vedic lifestyle' commodities are brands for the nation within India.

By being unlinked to a regional place within India, English's localized and familiarized idiom in commercial fiction provides a useful medium for internally branding the nation. Reviewers of such fiction do not approach the texts as regional. They may be identified with urban locations, as 'Delhi-resident authors' and 'small town stories' and so on; mostly, they are simply expressions of India per se; their success symptomatizes India as a whole; their authors embody their Indian identities over their regional identities by dint of writing in English. Commercial fiction in Indian languages, even when translated into English (translations from Indian languages into English is also a much-referred 'boom' area), however, carry the weight of their regional identities with them. Satyajit Ray's 'Feluda' detective stories or Sharadindu Bandyopadhyay's 'Byomkesh Bakshi' detective stories (both available in several English-language editions) are strongly associated with their Bengali settings and authorship. In some cases, the regional identity of such commercial fiction works as a distancing device, so that the English translation is presented not so much as commercial fiction any longer but more as an object of ethnographic interest *for* the Indian reader. *The Blaft Anthology of Tamil Pulp Fiction* (Chakravarthy trans., 2008) is a case in point: to announce a collection as 'pulp fiction' is to take the contents out of the circuit of *being consumed* as pulp fiction and put them in the circuit of *being looked at* as pulp fiction—with the regional 'place' of this phenomenon foregrounded. Reviewers of the English translations of Hindi thriller writer Surender Mohan Pathak's novels (which started being published in 2009) obviously had to mediate across considerable internal distances to introduce them to Indian readers of English-language fiction. Some observations, for example, were: 'One reason why the books are catching on is that they represent a different world' (Swamy 2010); 'Long labelled lowbrow, these big sellers of small-town Hindustan have usually been printed on cheap paper ... and sold for a song' (Raaj 2009). The translator of Pathak's novels, Sudarshan Purohit, wrote a somewhat sad article on the low sales of the translations, wondering whether:

> We might be in this situation because we've imported the whole business of English books – writing, buying, marketing, even the genre names on the bookshelves, from the Western books ecosystem. This includes the reviewing and the top ten lists and the contacts with the press – everything that constitutes the hype that sells the books. Publishers in other languages are still waking up to the fact that the English publishing industry is dominating the literary supplements. (Purohit 2010)

The 'Western books ecosystem', which is more or less what I have called the global template for commercial fiction publishing, allows for a non-regionalized sort of localism to exist within the internal circuit of Indian commercial fiction in English. (For more on English translations of vernacular commercial fiction, see Gupta 2015, Chap. 3.)

These observations raise an obvious question: who will takes possession of this brand, substantiate the circulatory matrix of Indian commercial fiction in English and actualize the 'glocal' existence and national consolidation it reflects? In the newspaper and magazine articles I have cited above, the answer is pat and unanimous: it is the middle-class Indian youth.

Middle-Class Youth

Two surveys give some indication of the character and attitudes of this reading constituency: a CSDS-KAS (de Souza et al. 2009) survey of social attitudes among Indian youth and an NBT-NCAER (Shukla 2010) Indian youth readership survey. The CSDS-KAS 2009 survey used data collected from around 5000 respondents, aged between 14 and 34, more or less evenly distributed across the country, with some booster samples from areas with high population density (towns); and the NBT-NCAER 2010 survey covered 311,431 literate youth (13- to 35-year-olds), across 207 rural districts and 199 towns in India. The latter estimated the youth population of India to be 459 million (38 % of the total), of which 333 million are literate. Of the literate youth, this survey indicated, about 25 % read books for pleasure, relaxation and knowledge enhancement, and English was the preferred language for leisure reading of 5.3 % of them (Hindi was for 33.4 %, Marathi 13.2 %, Bengali 7.7 %). By these figures, the number of readers of an extraordinarily successful English-language commercial fiction book was unlikely to exceed 4.41 million. As a proportion of India's youth population, this is a miniscule figure, but as an absolute figure for commercial fiction publishers to aspire to, this is fairly respectable. The actual figure would have been considerably lower when we take into account that fiction was the preferred genre for 42 % of youth: if that breaks down proportionally for the languages, for English that would mean around 1.85 million readers (but maybe more English-language readers prefer fiction). Further, this was a very wide age group for the survey (13–35), and quite possibly a commercial fiction book targeting, for instance, any particular group of readers (women, professionals, university students, etc.) may not appeal to a considerable range here. Incidentally, according to this survey, the Internet was accessed by only 3.7 % of youth, of which a mere 4 % used it for reading books online and a tiny 1.2 % used it to search for book titles. We can assume that the great majority of those with access to the Internet have some level of proficiency in the English language.

The CSDS-KAS 2009 survey gave little indication of reading habits and focused more on TV and film viewing. It came up with the figure of 12 % of respondents claiming to use the Internet, as opposed to 3.7 % quoted above—but the latter had a much larger sample and is therefore statistically more reliable. The CSDS-KAS 2009 survey, however, usefully gestured towards an interesting mix of social and cultural attitudes among youth in general which may well have a bearing on reading habits. The level of interest in politics (46 % thought it very or somewhat important) was high; significant proportions were well-disposed towards other countries (except Pakistan); and more took democratic prerogatives and issues like gender equality and environmental sustainability, unemployment and poverty, seriously. However, 71 % declared that they haven't heard the word 'globalization'; 94 % were believers. Some strong conservative tendencies seemed to be indicated, especially in relation to marriage and sexual relations (67 % felt that marriages should take place within one's caste community; 63 % felt dating should be restricted, as against 32 % who didn't think so; 65 % felt the final decision of marriage should rest with parents, as against 32 % who felt it should be with those getting married), but also in other respects (for example, with regard to the top five friends, 52 % had none of the opposite sex, 54 % none from another religion, 34 % none from other castes, 66 % felt drinking alcohol is unacceptable). It is likely that these figures were quite different for the minority of English-language readers, and very probable that the great majority of these would have heard of 'globalization'.

What we have then is a complex picture of Indian youth culture in general and a sense of the scale of leisure readership among those proficient in English. It is evidently a small proportion of youth, middle class in a broad way (factoring in affluence, socio-cultural background and education in various combinations), which engages with Indian commercial fiction in English—and very likely a much smaller proportion that engages with literary fiction. The breadth of the readership of commercial fiction, relative to literary fiction, is apt to catch more of the complexity of attitudes among Indian youth in general. There appears to be some evidence that this complexity is evidenced in attitudes to the English language itself. Such attitudes are, it seems, pulled between the cultivation of social concerns and political awareness and the conservative tendencies that are evidenced above; similar contrary pulls are reflected, as I have noted in passing above, in cultivating the global cultural capital of English and making English a site for somewhat defiant localization. For instance, Vineeta Chand's observations on ideological approaches to English among Indian youth, based on a qualitative survey of English/Hindi bilinguals in Delhi, are indicative here—and may well apply more widely in India:

> These younger IE [Indian English] speakers [...] are English/Hindi bilinguals. Their entire education, through college, has been English-medium; they use English in intimate domains and with all technology (texting, e-mail, Internet, etc.); and their self-professed dominant language is English. And yet they are uncertain of how well their English meets external, global standards. This insecurity is a direct result of the disparate power relationship between inner-circle nations and third-world postcolonial outsourcing nations like India, where standard language ideologies directly affect individual and societal notions of fluency, competence, and nativeness.
>
> However, these youths also dialogically acknowledge that international normalized language practices, and their associated social authority, are not available for local uptake. They critically respond to local speakers who quickly acquire international language practices [...]. In India, discourse centers on 'fake accents,' which typically emerge in high-school and college-age IE speakers who unnaturally acquire an American accent through limited contact with AE [American English] speakers or travel to the United States. These youths all had personal favorite stories highlighting the ridiculousness of fake accents and their response to such 'wannabes' [...]. (Chand 2009, p. 411)

The success of Indian commercial fiction in English within India has possibly some connection to the anxiety and localized defiance that this quotation speaks of. Such fiction evades the perception of being fake and is regarded as domesticated and in a familiar local idiom; at the same time, such fiction appears to be structurally linked to global means of production in 'standard' English (following that global template). Moreover, commercial fiction generally has an oft-noted conservative character which can nevertheless be manipulated towards subversive ends apropos of the dominant establishment (on this, see Bloom 1996, particularly p. 16, and Gallagher 2006, particularly p. 15). Indian commercial fiction in English—disposed according to the global template amidst localization—offers a similar crossroad, which is perhaps accommodative of the complex contrary pulls in social attitudes that the above surveys show for contemporary Indian youth.

The small class-bound scale of this youth readership of commercial fiction may raise doubts about the class-character of such fiction and the class-contradictions that their consumption feed. Such doubts may well be analogous to those expressed feelingly but impressionistically by Arun Saldanha in a study of affluent Indian youth (in Bangalore) who cultivate a Western lifestyle (the focus here is on Western music): doubts about the 'interesting perverse form of exhibitionism/voyeurism' that such cultivation instantiates, and 'othering' of the poor working-class 'peepers' that is involved (Saldanha 2002, pp. 343–344). But the normative weight of such observations would, it seems to me, apply unevenly in relation to Indian commercial fiction in English. True, an increasing number of such productions revel in the blithe 'fun' of a middle-class lifestyle: Penguin India's 'Metroreads' series, for instance, seeks to appeal to readers looking for 'books which don't weigh you down with complicated stories, don't ask for much time' (http://www.metroreads.in/). However, in the midst of such a lightness of import we may find subversive as well as conservative strategies. And, it is certainly equally the case that Indian commercial fiction in English is also an arena for considering the unsavoury features of domestic hierarchies, sexual repression, class and gender inequalities, and caste oppression (various independent publishers of fiction particularly focus on these, such as Zubaan, Navayana or Queer Ink). Bhagat has increasingly been striving to become a spokesman for the social conscience of Indian youth (his efforts in this direction collected in the non-fictional *What Young India Wants*, 2012), and no doubt authors inspired by him have it in mind too. Before any normative pronouncements are offered, the texts in question need to be critically engaged, and these texts are a very mixed bag indeed.

WORKS CITED

Ahmad, A. (2005, July 17). Harry Potter: 1 lakh copies sold in India. *The Times of India* [Online]. Available from http://articles.timesofindia.indiatimes.com/2005-07-17/india/27850706_1_publishing-history-lakh-copies-penguin

Ahuja, V. (2004). Globalisation in Indian book production. In S. Das (Ed.), *The book industry in India: Context, challenge and strategy* (pp. 24–27). New Delhi: Federation of Publishers' and Booksellers' Association in India.

Bennett, T. (1990). *Popular fiction: Technology, ideology, production, reading*. London: Routledge.
Birch, M. J. (1987, Winter). The popular fiction industry: Market, formula, ideology. *Journal of Popular Culture*, 21(3), 79–102.
Bloom, C. (1996). *Cult fiction: Popular reading and pulp theory*. Basingstoke: Macmillan.
Chand, V. (2009). [v]hat is going on? Local and global ideologies about Indian English. *Language in Society*, 38(4), 393–419.
Chandra, N. (2008). *The classic popular Amar Chitra Katha 1967–2007*. New Delhi: Yoda.
Chaudhuri, A. (2008). 'Huge baggy monster': Mimetic theories of the India novel after Rushdie. In *Clearing a space: Reflections on India, literature, culture* (pp. 113–121). Witney: Peter Lang.
Choudhury, C. (2009, November/December). English spoken here. *Foreign Policy*, pp. 96–97.
Daechsel, M. (2003, April). Zalim Daku and the mystery of the rubber sea monster: Urdu detective fiction in 1930s Punjab and the experience of colonial modernity. *Journal of the Royal Asiatic Society*, 13(1), 21–43.
Dawson Varughese, E. (2013). *Reading new India: Post-millennial Indian fiction in English*. London: Bloomsbury.
de Souza, P. R., Kumar, S., Shastri, S. (Eds.). (2009). *Indian youth in a transforming world: Attitudes and perceptions*. New Delhi: Sage, with Centre for the Study of Developing Societies (CSDS) and Konrad Adenauer Stiftung (KAS).
Dua, A. (2009, November 29). The great Indian book bazaar. *The Telegraph* (Kolkata) [Online]. Available from http://www.telegraphindia.com/1091129/jsp/graphiti/story_11794227.jsp#
Feather, J. (2003). *Communicating knowledge: Publishing in the 21st century*. Munich: K.G. Saur.
Fernandes, J. R. (2010, October 30). Swapping pie charts for plots. *The Times of India: Crest Edition* [Online]. Available from http://www.timescrest.com/society/swapping-pie-charts-for-plots-3849
Francis, R. (2003, updated 2008). *Publishing market profile: India*. London: British Council/Publishers Association's Global Publishing Information.
Gallagher, M. (2006). *Action figures: Men, action films, and contemporary adventure narratives*. New York: Palgrave Macmillan.
German Book Office. (2012/2013). FAQ: BRIC markets. *Frankfurt Academy Quarterly* [Online]. Available from http://www.book-fair.com/img/ebooks/markets_trends.pdf
Ghai, S. K. (2008a). Glimpses of Indian publishing today in the words of publishing professionals. *Publishing Research Quarterly*, 24(3), 202–214.
Ghai, S. K. (Ed.). (2008b). *One to one: Glimpses of Indian publishing*. Delhi: Institute of Book Publishing.

Ghosh, A. (1988). *The shadow lines.* New Delhi: Ravi Dayal.
Ghosh, P. (2011, February 27). Write moves. *The Hindustan Times* [Online]. Available from http://www.hindustantimes.com/Write-moves/Article1-667329.aspx
Gopal, P. (2009). *The Indian English novel: Nation, history, and narration.* Oxford: Oxford University Press.
Greenlees, D. (2008, March 26). An investment banker finds fame off the books. *New York Times* [Online]. Available from http://www.nytimes.com/2008/03/26/books/26bhagat.html
Gulab, L. (2007, September 23). Desperately seeking writers. *Brunch (Hindustan Times Sunday Magazine)* [Online]. Available from http://www.open.ac.uk/Arts/ferguson-centre/indian-lit/documents/pub-doc-kushal-gulab-sept07.htm
Gulab, K. (2010, April 24). Novel adventures. *The Hindustan Times* [Online]. Available from http://www.hindustantimes.com/StoryPage/Print/534858.aspx
Gupta, S. (2009). *Globalization and literature.* Cambridge: Polity.
Gupta, S. (2015). *Consumable texts in contemporary India: Uncultured books and bibliographical sociology.* London: Palgrave Macmillan.
Huggan, G. (2001). *The postcolonial exotic: Marketing the margins.* London: Routledge.
Khair, T. (2008, September). Indian pulp fiction in English: A preliminary overview from Dutt to De. *The Journal of Commonwealth Literature, 43*(3), 59–74.
Khan, D. (2010, March 4). Boom time for English-language books in India. *The Hindu* [Online]. Available from http://www.thehindu.com/news/international/article148574.ece
Khullar Management and Financial Investment. (1999). *India: Book publishing.* Washington, DC: US Department of State.
Kramatschek, C. (2007, January 3). Farewell to spice and curry (I. Pepper, Trans.). *Sightandsound.com* [Online]. Available from http://www.signandsight.com/features/1117.html. [First published in German, 2006.]
Kumar, M. (2009, December 20). Stories for the young and restless. *The Times of India: Tech Talk,* p. 12.
Mahapatra, A. D. (2008, May 11). Priceless @ 95. *The Telegraph* (Kolkata) [Online]. Available from http://www.telegraphindia.com/1080511/jsp/7days/story_9254827.jsp
Mathur, S. (2006). Holmes's Indian reincarnation: A study in postcolonial transposition. In C. Matzke and S. Muehleisen (eds.) *Postcolonial Postmortems: Crime Fiction from a Transcultural Perspective* (pp. 87–108). Amsterdam: Rodopi.
McCrum, R. (2010, January 24). Chetan Bhagat: The paperback king of India. *The Observer* [Online]. Available from http://www.guardian.co.uk/books/2010/jan/24/chetan-bhagat-robert-mccrum

Mee, J. (2003). After midnight: The novel in the 1980s and 1990s. In A. K. Mehrotra (Ed.), *An illustrated history of Indian literature in English* (pp. 318–336). New Delhi: Permanent Black.
Menon, H. (2008, June 2). How the supermarket racks were won. *Outlook*, p. 71.
Naik, M. K., & Narayan, S. A. (2004). *Indian English literature 1980–2000*. New Delhi: Pencraft.
Nash, W. (1990). *Language in popular fiction*. London: Routledge.
Orsini, F. (2004). Detective novels: A commercial genre in nineteenth-century North India. In S. Blackburn and V. Dalmia (eds.) *India's literary history* (pp. 435–82). Delhi: Permanent Black.
Pathak, S. M. (2011). *The last goal*. Delhi: Diamond Books.
Purohit, S. (2010, March 21). Why Indian pulp fiction is not as popular. *DNA* [Online]. Available from http://www.dnaindia.com/lifestyle/report_why-indian-pulp-fiction-is-not-as-popular_1361444
Raaj, N. (2009, March 1). Found in translation: Hindi pulp gets English avatar. *The Times of India* [Online]. Available from http://timesofindia.indiatimes.com/home/sunday-toi/special-report/Found-in-translation-Hindi-pulp-gets-English-avatar/articleshow/4206344.cms
Raja, M. (2007, July 24). Harry Potter and India's curse. *Asia Times* [Online]. Available from http://www.atimes.com/atimes/South_Asia/IG24Df01.html
Rajan, R. S. (2011). After *Midnight's children*: Some notes on the new Indian novel in English. *Social Research*, 78(1, Spring), 203–230.
Ramesh, R. (2008, October 9). Author's mass-market success upsets Indian literati. *The Guardian* [Online]. Available from http://www.guardian.co.uk/world/2008/oct/09/india
Roy, P. (2008). *The Manichean investigators: A postcolonial and cultural rereading of the Sherlock Holmes and Byomkesh Bakshi stories*. New Delhi: Sarup and Sons.
Sadana, R. (2012a). *English heart, Hindi heartland: The political life of literature in India*. Ranikhet: Permanent Black.
Sadana, R. (2012b). Writing in English. In V. Dalmia & R. Sadana (Eds.), *The Cambridge companion to modern Indian culture* (pp. 124–141). Cambridge: Cambridge University Press.
Sailaja, P. (2009). *Indian English*. Edinburgh: Edinburgh University Press.
Saldanha, A. (2002). Music, space, identity: Geographies of youth culture in Bangalore. *Cultural Studies*, 16(3), 337–350.
Sarkar, C. (2009, August). Why Indian publishing is so much fun. *Seminar: Literary Landscapes* [Online]. Available from http://www.india-seminar.com/2009/600/600_chiki_sarkar.htm
Sarkar, C. (2011, May). Tracking the boom. *Himal South Asian* [Online]. Available from http://www.himalmag.com/component/content/article/4414-tracking-the-boom.html
Schiffrin, A. (2000). *The business of books*. London: Verso.

Sedlatschek, A. (2009). *Contemporary Indian English*. Amsterdam: John Benjamins.
Sengupta, D. (2003). Sadhanbabu's friends: Science fiction in Bengal from 1882–1961. In *Sarai reader: Shaping technologies* (Vol. 3, pp. 76–82). Delhi: Sarai.
Sethi, J. (2011). *Standard English and Indian usage: Vocabulary and grammar*. New Delhi: PHI.
Shukla, R. (2010). *Indian youth: Demographics and readership*. New Delhi: National Book Trust (NBT) and National Council of Applied Economic Research (NCAER).
Sinha, P. (2014). *Post-liberalization Indian genre-fiction in English*. Milton Keynes: Open University, unpublished Ph.D. dissertation.
Sudarshan, A. (2010, July 4). Indian publishing needs to get less fun. *The Hindu (Literary Review)* [Online]. Available from http://www.hindu.com/lr/2010/07/04/stories/2010070450040200.htm
Sutherland, J. (1981). *Bestsellers: Popular fiction of the 1970s*. London: Routledge and Kegan Paul.
Swamy, V. K. (2010, June 20). Move over Bond, Vimal is here. *The Telegraph* [Online]. Available from http://www.telegraphindia.com/1100620/jsp/7days/story_12585479.jsp
Tarafdar, S. (2010, May 30). Summer of pulp. *The Financial Express* [Online]. Available from http://www.financialexpress.com/news/summer-of-pulp/626787/#
Thottam, J. (2008, October 30). Techie lit: India's new breed of fiction. *Time* [Online]. Available from http://www.time.com/time/magazine/article/0,9171,1854931,00.html

Genre Fiction of New India: Post-millennial Configurations of Crick Lit, Chick Lit and Crime Writing

E. Dawson Varughese

The post-millennial publishing scene of Indian fiction in English within India has proved explosive with significant departures in Chick Lit, crime writing, detective fiction, narratives referred to as 'mythology'[1] as well as young, urban India storylines.[2] The identity of Indian fiction in English has changed significantly and also relatively quickly in the last 15 years. This change can be explained in part by a rise in commercial Indian fiction over Indian 'literary fiction'. The latter term—often 'regarded as coeval with "Indian English literature" per se' according to Suman Gupta (2012, p. 47)—has dominated the 'postcolonial' Indian literary scene in English for many years. Of the new Indian 'commercial fiction', Gupta explains that it is a domestic product, consumed primarily within India and that its narratives are of India, primarily for Indians. He describes it as 'the gossipy café of Indian writing in English at home' (2012, p. 47) underscoring its

---

[1] See Penguin India: http://www.penguinbooksindia.com/en/book-categories. I have elsewhere (Dawson Varughese 2013, 2014) categorized some of these texts as 'Bharati Fantasy'.
[2] For a critical survey of these genres see Dawson Varughese (2013).

E. Dawson Varughese
Faculty of Arts and Creative Technologies, Staffordshire University,
Stoke-on-Trent, UK

difference from the more 'literary' Indian writing in English which finds its home in the West. (See Gupta's chapter above.)

Arjun Appadurai and Carol A. Breckenridge, writing in the late 1990s, prophesied the change in literature consumerism which has taken place post-millennium in India when they wrote: 'Even at the most conservative estimates, there are at least a million Indians who already have disposable incomes that make them the economic support of new forms of cultural consumption' (1998, p. 7). The changes in literary tastes and the rise of the popular or 'commercial' novel in English within India echo the sociocultural changes of the last 20 or so years (see Dawson Varughese 2015a, b). The relaxation of economic regulations in the late 80s put India on a path of liberalization that is still evident today and since then, and demonstrably post the millennium, significant changes have taken place in Indian lifestyle, consumption and leisure activities. The consumption of sport as media entertainment, particularly cricket, is one of these developments. The powerful combination of television, satellite, the Indian Premier League (IPL) and a more liberalized economy has meant a surge in engagement with all things cricket (see Boria Majumdar 2008, p. 574). Amit Gupta (2010) writes about the impact of television on the sport, stating: 'The decision to expand television transmission was taken for political and educational reasons but it had the unintended impact of helping provide a national audience for competitive sports' (2010, p. 46). Young urban India especially has both disposable income and technological opportunity to consume Indian cricket through a variety of media. Although these media have been predominantly television, satellite, cell phone and Internet-driven, interest in cricket has also been manifest in other forms of cultural consumption such as film and popular fiction, the latter being our focus here.

Commercial fiction based on cricket, or 'Crick Lit', is a recent genre of popular fiction which foregrounds the world of cricket but refracts this world through other genres or narrative configurations.[3] Crick Lit is a term that I developed in *Reading New India* (2013) in response to a growing body of cricket narratives, and I continue to chart its course and developments.[4] On genre, Peter Stockwell (2002) writes: '[g]enres

---

[3] I am using the terms 'genre fiction' and 'popular fiction' interchangeably here. I use the term 'commercial fiction' following Suman Gupta (2012).

[4] This chapter does not mean to suggest that no fictional precursors to this body of fiction exist, although it must be acknowledged that sports journalism has been particularly more

can be defined socially, historically, functionally, authorially, politically, stylistically, arbitrarily, idiosyncratically, or by a combination of any of these' (2002, p. 28); as the discussion below illustrates, the term Crick Lit is a genre term I use to describe a novel which is first and foremost about cricket (be it socially or politically) but which in addition employs a second established genre such as crime or romance, which is usually evidenced stylistically and/or formulaically. Since the turn of the millennium, Crick Lit has met with Chick Lit (Anuja Chauhan's *The Zoya Factor*, 2008), crime and detective narratives (Geeta Sundar's *The Premier Murder League*, 2010; Vikas Singh's *The Big Fix*, 2013), politics and corruption (Tuhin A. Sinha's *22 Yards*, 2008; the anonymously authored *The Gamechangers*, 2010; Rajiv Rajendra's *Doosra*), celebrity and the underworld (Sowmya Aji's *Delirium*, 2014) and the *Bildungsroman* genre (Chetan Bhagat's *The 3 Mistakes of My Life*, 2008). Chauhan's *The Zoya Factor* (2008) can be doubly-categorized under 'celebrity and underworld' and Singh's *The Big Fix* (2013) under 'politics and corruption'. Scott McCracken (1998) observes that 'the artful weaving of several popular genres into one narrative can allow a more complex exploration of self-identity, while still giving the reader familiar boundaries within which to project his or her fantasies' (1998, p. 13). In terms of markets, by producing fiction which can be categorized in two (or more) genres, the authors widen their appeal, attracting a greater potential readership. Integrating the subject of the 'national game' into popular and enticing genres such as crime, romance and political or 'underworld' narratives, the authors are mindful of the prospective markets (in particular the young Indian market) and the publishers in turn are able to maximize sales through cross-genre marketing activity. Later in this chapter, two of the novels of those listed above, Geeta Sundar's *The Premier Murder League* (2010) and Anuja Chauhan's *The Zoya Factor* (2008), are explored for their literary engagement with what Chris Rumford describes as the 'postwesternization of cricket' (2010, pp. 271, 275). The narrative plots of these two novels also articulate some of the debate around societal and cultural changes that New India is facing, such as issues of corruption and

---

productive in writing about cricket culture(s). Alex Tadié (2010), however, offers a broad survey of Indian cricket fictions in his article 'The Fictions of (English) Cricket: From Nation to Diaspora' and there are also the Bengali novels of Moti Nandy—his Kolkata-based novella *Striker* (1973), followed by *Stopper* (1974)—published some 40 years ago.

globalization. (I say more on the relationship between popular fiction and present-day society below.)

DE-CENTRING THE CRICKET WORLD THROUGH IPL CRICK LIT NARRATIVES

In 2008, the Twenty20 cricket league was launched through the Indian Premier League (IPL), a professional league for this form of cricket (see Shyam Balasubramaniam and Vijay Santhanam, 2011, for a historical account of these developments) and it was this inauguration which catapulted cricket into the popular domain. Chris Rumford and Stephen Wagg (2010) write that the IPL has brought about the realization that 'cricket is now a global sport' (2010, p. 3). Notably, the formation of the IPL was chosen over a league of the altogether slower game of Test cricket. Although Test cricket has traditionally anchored international cricket to London, this association is increasingly tenuous given the globalization of the game and the physical relocation of cricket's headquarters from Lord's, England to Dubai in 2005 (Malcolm 2014, p. 125). Rumford (2010) observes that cricket as a typically English game is increasingly a nostalgic idea. He goes on to state that:

> the relationship between cricket and globalization is best understood not simply in terms of the global spread of the game outwards from its metropolitan (imperial) centres but in terms of the postwesternization of the game, which reveals a very different dynamic. (2010, p. 271)

James Astill (2013) writes of how the eight Indian Premier League franchises 'were sold to a who's who of Indian tycoons for a total of $723.5 million, payable over a decade in annual instalments' (2013, p. 193). This was a huge investment of money, made even more remarkable by the fact that the tournament at that point (of the franchise sales) didn't yet exist. Astill suggests that 'Indian cricket seemed to encapsulate India's national fortunes. The economy was putting on a blistering growth spurt, having expanded by 9 % in each of the previous three years' (2013, p. 193). The launch of the IPL changed the cricket scene in India immensely and sent waves across the cricket world as other cricketing nations were astounded by the amount of domestic money available for such a venture. Mehta et al. (2009) write of this rise of Indian domestic cricket when they quote Mukul Keswan (Kesavan): 'The Indians are not coming. They are already here' (p. 700), and on Keswan's declaration they write: 'That one sentence brings within it the entire gamut of post-colonial politics and tensions that continue to define modern cricket' (2009, p. 700).

It is evident that the IPL pushed the organization and the playing of cricket into a different mode, what Rumford (2010) speaks of as 'post-western' (see above quote). The IPL, although influential through its media, celebrity and consumption potential, is just as powerful in its (increasing) directives on the game of cricket itself. Rumford illustrates how the rise of Indian cricket has highlighted the fact that there is no one single global modernity and that we have been alerted to 'the emergence of a new East capable of shaping global affairs, previously seen as the preserve of the West' (2010, p. 274). As I have argued elsewhere (Dawson Varughese 2012, 2013), post-millennial fiction in English from India has been involved in a similar shift, an emergence of new fiction, forging new literary directions, the control of which has previously been 'the preserve of the West'. In this vein, the emergence of post-millennial Indian fiction in English reinforces Rumford's argument set out in the quote below as this fiction is also involved in redesigning the way the market is negotiated and played. Rumford (2010) points out that:

> over the past two decades or so cricket has been postwesternized, not only in terms of the administration of the game (the ICC) shifting eastwards and the economic balance of power residing in the subcontinent but importantly in terms of the development of the on-field game and the way it is played. (p. 275)

Crick Lit echoes this sentiment through its particular narratives as well as through the Indian domestic publishing industry and its markets. This overall 'production' of the Crick Lit novel resonates with Franco Moretti's 'law of literary evolution' (2013, p. 50) whereby literary production from the 'periphery', as Moretti calls it, appears as novels which 'arise not as an autonomous development but as a compromise between a western formal influence (usually French or English) and local materials' (2013, p. 50). Moretti's 'law of literary evolution' is mostly applied to retrospective studies of literary production rather than to studies of current production; however, it remains a useful paradigm to think through both the narrative content and production of the Crick Lit novel in India. As I have articulated elsewhere (Dawson Varughese 2013, 2014; Dawson Varughese and Lau 2015), many Indian novels in English are published 'for sale in India only' and the West knows little of what India is writing and reading as it relies on the books that make it to its shores, which are far from representative of the Indian writing in English (IWE) scene as a whole. Endorsement of Indian fiction is increasingly made from within India with less reliance on Western backing and support. Most importantly, India does not *need* the Indian fiction industry to have its gatekeepers in the West, as India (and the wider region) is increasingly developing its own organizations, festivals, prizes and parameters of various literary activity which are independent of former colonial and postcolonial connections. To further draw on Rumford's sentiment, Indian fiction in English, like cricket, is directing the manner in which the game is played and, in turn, de-centering the cricket world in both game and related cultural productions.

RE-WRITING THE TAO OF CRICKET THROUGH CRICK LIT

As outlined at the beginning of this chapter, my term Crick Lit describes a genre which foregrounds the world of cricket but refracts it through other types of genre or narrative configurations. In order to explore these various demonstrations of Crick Lit, this chapter now discusses the following primary texts: a Crick Lit–crime fiction novel by Geeta Sundar, *The Premier Murder League* (2010), and a Crick Lit–Chick Lit novel by Anuja Chauhan, *The Zoya Factor* (2008).

Fate and Match-Fixing

Lalit Modi, the Chairman of the IPL in 2010, was suspended by the BCCI due to accusations of being involved in match-fixing or, as Malcolm writes, 'at least, of being ineffectual in monitoring or addressing corruption during the tournament' (2014, p. 155). More recently, in 2014 the President of the Board of Control for Cricket in India (BCCI), N. Srinivasan, stepped down from post as his son-in-law Gurunath Meiyappan was reported to be involved in a betting and spot-fixing scandal which proved to be the biggest reported one of its kind within India to date (Rajesh Rao 2014). This theme of fixing games is explored in many of the post-millennial Crick Lit narratives (see Singh's *The Big Fix*, 2013, as an example) and the desire to twist and mould fate to personal advantage is also the theme of Geeta Sundar's novel *The Premier Murder League* (2010). This narrative is set around a fictional IPL involving a criminal cricket board which 'disposes' of anyone who might get in the way of the board running as the boss dictates. The novel opens as S. N. Rao, Union Sports Minister and, more importantly, cricket board member, dies after eating two poisoned paans following his evening meal. His death is painful and slow, slow enough for him to write on the wall of his living room: 'cell phone taken, door locked' (Sundar 2010, p. 10). From the crime wing of the police, Ravi Sharma, deputy commissioner of police, and Rahul Singh, assistant to the deputy commissioner, are in charge of the case. The two have worked together for some time when the death of Rao is set to be investigated and Sundar writes: 'Rahul and Ravi had become so close professionally that they seemed to operate on the same wavelength, often understanding each other without a word having been spoken' (p. 6). The death of Rao is followed by the death of the cricket board treasurer, Sunil Mane. Mane is also poisoned; the same poison used in Rao's paan is found in Mane's drink. With the deaths of two prominent members of the cricket board, Rahul is not surprised to discover that the dynamics between the members of the board were not always harmonious. The root of the discordant board, Rahul finds out, is the 'T20 League'. In their investigations into the dynamics of the cricket board, Ravi and Rahul decide to question Mrs Rao, the widow of the murdered S. N. Rao. She reports: 'I did get the feeling that there were serious issues between my husband and some members of the board, and that my husband was not acknowledging them … the problem was that he was probably privy to a number of secrets, and they could not let him leave easily' (p. 95).

The main motifs of Sundar's novel, secrecy and silence, conceal the illegal behaviour and the corruption practised by the cricket board. Sundar's narrative grossly undermines what Ashis Nandy claimed to be a leading principle of the game of cricket: 'fate'. Nandy, in his famous 1989 essay The Tao of Cricket, stated that 'fate is the first identifier of cricket' (2007, p. 21) and that the cricketer 'has to learn to maintain an inner balance by being simultaneously a firm believer in fate whiles all the while acting as if it did not exist' (p. 21). Many post-millennial Crick Lit narratives expose the culture of crime, corruption and the underworld of match-fixing which, in turn, refute any notion of 'fate'; rather, they foreground some of the more challenging aspects of post-millennial Indian society. Sundar's novel, alongside other Crick Lit novels of corruption and match-fixing, chime with the national debate on corruption which has emerged post the millennium, gathering momentum with the protests of Anna Hazare (the Lokpal Bill in 2011) and more latterly, the election of Narendra Modi as Prime Minister in 2014. Modi's drive to rid India of corrupt practices at all levels of civil society has recently seen the conviction of Tamil Nadu's Chief Minister, Jayalalithaa (following an 18 year-long court case), the first Chief Minister to be convicted under the Prevention of Corruption Act (Bhattacharya 2014b). Sundar's novel is not coincidentally timely; on the relationship between society and popular fiction, McCracken writes:

> Popular narratives play a vital role in mediating social change, informing their audience of new currents and allowing the reader to insert him- or herself into new scenarios in a way that can be related to her or his own experience. Its engagement in the present, in now-time, means that the political nature of popular fiction is never in doubt. (1998, p. 185)

Revealing Character: Celebrity and Media

The post-millennial Crick Lit novel often captures the intensity of the IPL season, an intensity of media hype, celebrity and popular culture. In her novel *The Premier Murder League* (2010), Sundar describes the cricket fans of young India caught up in the excitement of the season:

> Though cricket purists were horrified, to many youngsters in the country, Twenty20 cricket was thrilling, pulse-racing stuff that was about to catch the nation's imagination.... A youngster working for a BPO said, "Who wants to spend five days following a game that seems to run in slow motion? It 'tests' my patience." There was a roar of appreciative laughter from his friends at the intended pun. (Sundar 2010, p. 20)

The cricket advertising, the incessant television coverage of the matches, the 24-hour media reporting and celebrity hype that accompanies the various cricket teams are foregrounded throughout the novel. The closing ceremony of the ITL (a fictional IPL) and the 50,000-odd spectators attending it is described thus:

> For over a month, the nation, and half the world, had either watched the tournament 'live' or its highlights, and had been as involved in the league matches as the thirteen players on the ground or the nine sitting in the dugouts with the reserve players. As for the franchise owners, they too had given up their moneymaking ventures to be 'one with the boys'. Not that they didn't expect to make money out of these matches. In fact, many of them were physically present, but mentally plotting how to generate more wealth out of their latest acquisition! (p. 217)

Post-millennial Crick Lit novels often depict key aspects of IPL cricket culture such as media and celebrity hype, merchandise, mass cultural marketing and even mobile phone apps, all of which celebrate the modern, the secular and the immediacy of the contemporary moment. The cricket fans of these Crick Lit narratives who are enjoying the media and celebrity hype are an echo of the society in which they operate. Full of opportunity, entrepreneurship and ambition, these fans stand in complete divergence to those described by Nandy in his 1989 essay. Satadru Sen describes the pre-liberalization cricket fan when he writes: 'the memory of the older, pre-television, pre-liberalization cricket fan in India can be seen as a "failed" memory that coincides with a failed attempt to define the national community in liberal terms' (2008, p. 95). In remembering the older India as 'failed', the New India is further positioned as one of (liberal) success (to greater or lesser degrees), the latter an idea which is propagated throughout post-millennial genre fiction in general.

Internet-based news reporting, such as online newspapers with comprehensive sports sections, has had an impact on the growth and interest in IPL cricket in India; both satellite—in particular the English medium news channels—and online newspapers have meant that Indians abroad and Indians in the diaspora can follow news and sport more easily, that is, in terms of an Indian-produced media, and not a US, Australian or UK-mediated news channel (see Mihir Bose 2006, p. 259). Sundar's description of the media attention given to the Rao and Mane deaths captures something of the reporting styles seen in post-millennial news channels today:

> They carried mainly this news the whole day and speculations were rife as to the fate of the other members of the board. Anyone remotely connected to cricket or politics had become an 'expert' on the topic. There were innumerable talk shows, SMS polls, and panel discussions to do with the case—all good fodder for twenty-four-hour news channels. (Sundar 2010, p. 168)

The busy and feverish activity depicted in Sundar's novel (presented also in *The Big Fix*, 2013, and in Chauhan's *The Zoya Factor*, 2008, as other examples) stands in complete opposition to what Nandy (2007) identified as the 'slowness of cricket' for strategic and focused reflection. Rather, these post-liberalization Crick Lit narratives expose short-term and personal gain and such plots are strongly present in the fictional avatars of the IPL through the celebrity culture that surrounds the game.

In Chauhan's *The Zoya Factor* (2008), the hype is generated not by a celebrity figure (although she quickly becomes one) but by Zoya Singh Solanki, a 27-year-old, 'mid-level client-servicing executive in India's largest ad agency' (Chauhan 2008, p. 3). Her meeting with the Indian cricket team changes her life as she becomes the team's talisman. Zoya, Chauhan reveals, was born on the day that India won the World Cup, 25 June 1983, and this, alongside the fact that Zoya once had breakfast with the team in order to gain a No Objection Certificate for an advertising company— and this very 'breakfast with Zoya' resulted in India winning the day's match—transfigures into Zoya becoming the team's lucky charm. Nikhil Khoda, the captain of the team, sceptical of Zoya's 'gift', is mindful of the propensity India has for all things 'lucky'; Khoda states: 'Ours is a superstitious country and a precedent like this could lead to chaos in the future' (p. 114). As the breakfasts with Zoya continue and in turn, are all followed by winning games for the Indian team, the members of the team become increasingly convinced of Zoya's ability to guarantee their success. By combining the genres of Crick Lit and Chick Lit, *The Zoya Factor* reaches out to a wider audience than the supposed traditionally male readership of 'cricket fiction'. (Interestingly, Chauhan reproduced this strategy in her second novel, *Battle for Bittora*, 2010, where a female protagonist battles it out in politics against her [male] rival; see Dawson Varughese 2015b.) Not only does *The Zoya Factor* place a female character at the heart of the novel, it also moves social stereotypes of women's involvement in cricket beyond those of cheerleaders and Bollywood actresses (Tharoor 2010). (I say more on Zoya's gender with regard to cricket in the following section.) In terms of Zoya's personal journey in the novel, she rails against the pressure of post-millennial Indian media coverage, her 'supposed' identity as a young female Indian and society's views of her as the team's talisman. Her character invokes the experience of the young Indian, their questions of personal worth, friendships and disquietude set against a backdrop of post-millennial Indian life (see Subir Dhar's commentary on living in a 'contemporary postindustrial world scenario'; 2013, p. 161). The reader is left in no doubt that this is 'New India'.

Sports'man'ship and the Hyped, Mediatized Game

The world of Twenty20 has been conceived from the outset as a 'consumable sport', as Rumford and Wagg write: 'Twenty20 is a highly lucrative and TV-friendly form of the game (matches are played to completion within 3 ½ hours, with ample opportunity for commercial breaks)' (2010, pp. 3–4). The success of Twenty20 over the last 5 years has paved the way for other 'consumable sports' to move into the Indian market. An Indian football league—the Indian Super League—entered the Indian sport world in late 2014, heralded by famous European marquee players. Nilesh Bhattacharya (2014a) quotes Luis Garcia as the marquee player of 'Atletico de Kolkata' saying that he refuses to believe that 'the success of ISL depends on the performance of some retired or semi-retired "marquee" players. For him [Garcia], the league needs Indian heroes to survive.' As the IPL promoted itself as an Indian sports venture from the outset, the Indian Super League is following in the same vein. Based on the model of the Indian Premier League, 2014 also saw the first Pro Kabaddi League tournament. Bollywood actor Abhishek Bachchan, owner of 'Jaipur Pink Panthers' (as well as an ISL football team) has been quoted by the *The Times of India* as saying: 'I was in Rome recently and met old [*sic*] friend English Footballer Ashley Coles [*sic*]. He surprised me by calling me Kabaddi-Kabaddi. He too was aware that Pro Kabaddi has arrived on [*sic*] international sports scene' (Press Trust of India 2014a). Both the inauguration of the ISL and the success of the Pro Kabaddi tournament document Rumford's 'post-westernization' of sport as Indian money finances and develops its own 'commercial sports' scene in cricket, football and kabaddi for a growing Indian—domestic and diasporic—market.

Echoing these developments in commercial sports, Sundar's novel, *The Premier Murder League* (2010), centres its plot on the potential for personal, financial gain. As part of the formation of the ITL board, the character of 'the boss' elects Manik Jindal as president and Jindal's rousing speech at the inaugural meeting in Mumbai communicates the cricket board's mission: 'Our aim should be to become *the* richest sporting body in the world. And we can easily reach a figure of two billion dollars next year if we launch the ITL' (Sundar 2010, pp. 28–9). The focus on the financial opportunity in commercial sports contests earlier notions of 'sportsmanship'. The manifestation of 'sportsmanship' as an exercise in public relations is a recurring motif in post-millennial Crick Lit and in Chauhan's novel *The Zoya Factor*, it is the protagonist Zoya who becomes the face of the team's public relations. Zoya attains an almost celebrity-like status through her 'ability' to influence the game to India's advantage. Zoya becomes aware as the story unfolds that she might *actually* be responsible for the Indian team's success and is quickly accepted as the Indian cricket team's lucky charm. At first, Zoya's presence at the breakfast table is something that she agrees to go along with and her evident lack of general knowledge of cricket and, more strikingly, the Indian cricket team, reinforces the idea that Zoya is being pulled along with little control over the events. As the narrative progresses, more games are won after breakfast with Zoya and, on the occasions she doesn't meet the team before their match they lose their game. The idea of Zoya 'having breakfast' is replete with sexual suggestion and, in turn, contests traditional views about sportsmanship, performance and celibacy or chastity. Joseph S. Alter writes at length on this topic in *Moral Materialism: Sex and Masculinity in Modern India* (2011); he talks in some detail about the connections between sexual (im)potency, chastity (*urdhvaretas*) and ithyphallicism (worship of the erect penis) and of this trio as a complex nexus which bears cultural significance found across many Indian cultures. Masculinity in terms of power (*shakti*) and health are found in chastity and ithyphallicism and therefore, the release of semen reduces one's *shakti*. The topic of sportsmanship and chastity in the cricket world was alluded to recently through an article in *The Times of India* entitled 'Team India Manager Questions Anushka Sharma's Stay with Virat Kohli' (Press Trust of India 2014b). The couple were attacked for their decision to travel and stay together during Kohli's tour. The blame for Kohli's poor cricket performance was then ascribed to Sharma's attendance of the tour: 'Many fans and some quarters of BCCI have blamed Anushka Sharma's presence behind the vice-captain's poor form with the bat in a series, which India lost 1–3.' The article goes on to state that a girlfriend accompanying their partner on tour is 'against the culture of the country' (Press Trust of India 2014b). Given these particular cultural perceptions of women in relation to cricket players, Chauhan's novel pushes the boundaries of traditional moral thinking by placing Zoya not only as the main character of the cricket novel but also as a female mediator of the team's fortunes. Zoya's own *shakti* is found in her 'femaleness' as much as in her talismanic aptitude. Her female *shakti* is further embodied in her relationship *to* and, by the close of the novel, *with* Nikhil Khoda, the team's captain.

Zoya's *shakti* as a 'divine' power is emphasized during a visit from Swami Lingnath Baba. It is the arrival of the Swami at her bedside when she is struck down by a fever which jolts Zoya into a realization of not only her celebrity status but her God-like status. Chauhan writes: 'Clad in three delicious shades of saffron, tinkling gently with various charms and amulets, his hairy halo aglow, Swami Lingnath Baba stood in the doorway, smiling benignly' (Chauhan 2008, p. 360). Zoya knows that the Swami should be in his ashram in Uttar Pradesh, India, and not at her hotel door in Australia and his appearance leads her to a realization that she is now a major figure in this game of 'cricket luck'. This shift in celebrity status into divine being yet again contradicts Nandy's (2007) idea of the game where all involved are of equal importance and to become self-orientated is to undermine that bond. As the Swami takes his leave, he addresses Zoya: 'stay vigilant in your post as the celestial guardian who will lead our team to victory'. And he adds: 'Pressure is building. I see much conflict ahead. Stand strong, Devi!' (pp. 361, 362). The Swami's words evoke images of the defiant Hindu Goddess Durga whose immense feminine *shakti* sees victory over evil. Durga is a form of Devi and, as the Swami's entreaty to Zoya suggests, Durga is celestial in her patience, compassion and fearlessness. Zoya, up until this point in the narrative, has dismissed the superstition and urban myth-making about her cricket luck, but the presence of the godman challenges this conviction and she asks the Swami if it is indeed true that giving all her luck to the team will mean that she will be left with only bad luck in her personal life. As the relationship, albeit a tumultuous one, between Zoya and Khoda has recently developed, Zoya is keen to know if her personal life is set to suffer. The Swami's answer is grounded in the Hindu philosophy and belief that is befitting of 'Zoya Devi': 'Balance is what keeps the cosmos in motion, Devi' (p. 362). The doubt in Zoya's mind that her involvement with the cricket team will render her unlucky in her own life further foregrounds Nandy's expression of concern around the 'consumable game'. Here Zoya embodies the shift from 'play' to what Nandy calls 'organized professional sport' which he likens to 'institutionalized work, [which] is too structured, too dependent on techniques and technology, too much under the influence of market forces to serve the basic function of play' (2007, p. 118). Furthermore, Zoya's position within the team curiously echoes the balance that Alter (2011) speaks of in terms of masculinity and chastity. As Zoya unremittingly makes available her female *shakti*, manifest in good fortune for the team and her 'female' presence (as opposed to 'male' presence) at the breakfast table, her own power becomes depleted. Like sportsmen sacrificing for their game, so too does Zoya risk (her happiness in) her personal life for the greater success of the sport (and team).

Concluding Remarks

The post-millennial production of Crick Lit has grown out of the confluence of particular economic and sociocultural contexts: the rise of television and satellite, a liberalized economy, the birth of the Indian Premier

League and a growing (young) middle class of Indians with increased disposable income for leisure activities. The change in the consumption as well as the manner in which the game of cricket is organized and played has been described by Rumford as 'postwestern' (2010, pp. 271, 275) and Crick Lit echoes this notion in both its narrative content and domestic distribution. As we read above, while the narrative plots of Crick Lit chime with national debate around the societal and cultural changes that New India is facing, the narrative content also meditates on some of the political and economic changes of the post-millennial years, in particular the call for cessation of corruption in various areas of governance and private business activity. Crick Lit as popular fiction engages with these matters of social injustice and conflict as, following McCracken (1998), it 'can supply us with the narratives we need to resituate our*selves* in relation to the world. The reader of popular fiction is actively engaged in the remaking of him or herself and this act of remaking has a utopian potential' (1998, p. 17; original emphasis). The distribution of Crick Lit alongside other post-millennial genre fictions also parallels these sociocultural and economic changes, manifested through its India-focused, domestic publishing activity and markets (see Dawson Varughese 2014; Dawson Varughese and Lau 2015).

The novels discussed in this chapter demonstrate that Crick Lit is a genre of popular fiction which foregrounds the world of cricket but refracts this world through a secondary or further genre (crime, romance as examples). In the case of *The Premier Murder League* (2010), the novel brings together the genres of Crick Lit and crime fiction and in the case of *The Zoya Factor* (2008), the novel brings together the genres of Crick Lit and Chick Lit. Just as *The Premier Murder League* (2010) raises issues of corruption and match-fixing, both contemporary societal concerns of the post-millennial years to date, *The Zoya Factor* (2008) raises issues of female identity in New India, challenging (already) established perceptions of women and/in cricket. Chauhan's novel also contests traditional notions of sports'man'ship through the reversal of roles, foregrounding the female protagonist as the one who sacrifices her *shakti* for the greater success of the sport and team, although this is not without its problems as Zoya is simultaneously portrayed as a vehicle for the male team members' accomplishments.

As Crick Lit novels continue to be published and consumed with interest, domestically at least, the storying of cricket through its various genre configurations acts as a cultural barometer, charting the changes that India continues to undergo and, in turn, critiquing the wider social and cultural worlds associated with the game and its related cultural productions of fiction, film and television.

WORKS CITED

Alter, J. (2011). *Moral materialism: Sex and masculinity in modern India*. New Delhi: Penguin India.
Appadurai, A., & Breckenridge, C. A. (1998). Public modernity in India. In C. A. Breckenridge (Ed.), *Consuming modernity: Public culture in a South Asian world* (pp. 1–20). Minneapolis/London: University of Minnesota Press.
Astill, J. (2013). *The great tamasha*. London: Wisden Sports Writing, Bloomsbury Publishing Plc.
Balasubramaniam, S., & Santhanam, V. (2011). *The business of cricket: The story of sports marketing in India*. Noida: HarperCollins Publishers India.
Bhattacharya, N. (2014a, September 29). ISL needs an Indian idol: Luis Garcia. *Times of India* [Online]. Accessed 30 Sept 2014. Available from http://timesofindia.indiatimes.com/sports/football/indian-super-league/top-stories/ISL-needs-an-Indian-idol-Luis-Garcia/articleshow/43788096.cms
Bhattacharya, S. (2014b, September 27). The conviction of a chief minister. *The Hindu Centre for Politics and Public Policy* [Online]. Accessed 30 Sept 2014. Available from http://www.thehinducentre.com/the-arena/article6452901.ece
Bose, M. (2006). *The magic of Indian cricket: Cricket and society in India*. London: Routledge.
Chauhan, A. (2008). *The Zoya factor*. New Delhi: HarperCollins.
Dawson Varughese, E. (2012). *Beyond the postcolonial: World Englishes literature*. Palgrave: Basingstoke.
Dawson Varughese, E. (2013). *Reading new India: Post-millennial Indian fiction in English*. London/New Delhi: Bloomsbury.
Dawson Varughese, E. (2014). Celebrate at home: Post-millennial Indian fiction in English and the reception of 'Bharati fantasy' in global and domestic literary markets. *Contemporary South Asia, 22*(4), 350–361.
Dawson Varughese, E. (2015a). 'New India/n woman': Agency and identity in post-millennial chick lit. In U. Anjaria (Ed.), *The Cambridge history of the Indian novel in English*. Cambridge: Cambridge University Press.
Dawson Varughese, E. (2015b). Style in world literature in English(es): *Battle for Bittora* by Anuja Chauhan. In V. Sotirova (Ed.), *Companion to stylistics*. London/New York: Continuum/Bloomsbury [Forthcoming].
Dawson Varughese, E., & Lau, L. (2015). *Indian writing in English and issues of visual representation: Judging more than a book by its cover*. Basingstoke: Palgrave Macmillan.

Dhar, S. (2013). Inspiring India. In S. Krishna & R. Roy (Eds.), *Writing India anew: Indian English fiction 2000–2010* (p. 161). Amsterdam: Amsterdam University Press.
Gupta, A. (2010). India: The epicentre of global cricket? In C. Rumford & S. Wagg (Eds.), *Cricket and globalization* (pp. 41–59). Newcastle Upon Tyne: Cambridge Scholars Publishing.
Gupta, S. (2012). Indian 'commercial' fiction in English, the publishing industry, and youth culture. *Economic and Political Weekly, 46*(5), 46–53.
Majumdar, B. (2008). 'Soaps, serials and the Cpi(M), cricket beat them all: Cricket and television in contemporary India. *Sport in Society: Cultures, Commerce, Media, Politics, 11*(5), 570–582.
Malcolm, D. (2014). *Globalizing cricket: Englishness, empire and identity*. London: Bloomsbury.
McCracken, S. (1998). *Pulp: Reading popular fiction*. Manchester: Manchester University Press.
Mehta, N., Gemmell, J., & Malcolm, D. (2009). 'Bombay sport exchange': Cricket, globalization and the future. *Sport in Society: Cultures, Commerce, Media, Politics, 12*(4–5), 694–707.
Moretti, F. (2013). *Distant reading*. London/New York: Verso.
Nandy, A. (2007). *A very popular exile*. New Delhi: Oxford University Press.
Press Trust of India. (2014a, September 7). Pro kabaddi has made a huge impact: Abhishek Bachchan. *Times of India* [Online]. Accessed 30 Sept 2014. Available from http://timesofindia.indiatimes.com/sports/tournaments/pro-kabaddi-league/Pro-Kabaddi-has-made-a-huge-impact-Abhishek-Bachchan/articleshow/41961430.cms
Press Trust of India. (2014b, August 22). Team India manager questions Anushka Sharma's stay with Virat Kohli. *India Today* [Online]. Accessed 29 Sept 2014. Available from http://indiatoday.intoday.in/story/team-india-manager-questions-anushka-sharma-stay-with-virat-kohli/1/378522.html
Rao, R. (2014, March 27). N Srinivasan asked to step down: Pune speaks up. *DNA India* [Online]. Accessed 29 Sept 2014. Available from http://www.dnaindia.com/speak-up/report-n-srinivasan-asked-to-step-down-pune-speaks-up-1972593
Rumford, C. (2010). Cricketing controversies: Reverse swing, the doosra, and the postwestern dimensions of cricket's globality. In C. Rumford & S. Wagg (Eds.), *Cricket and globalization* (pp. 270–286). Newcastle Upon Tyne: Cambridge Scholars Publishing.
Rumford, C., & Wagg, S. (2010). Introduction: Cricket and globalization. In C. Rumford & S. Wagg (Eds.), *Cricket and globalization* (pp. 1–19). Newcastle Upon Tyne: Cambridge Scholars Publishing.
Sen, S. (2008). History without a past: Memory and forgetting in Indian cricket. In S. Wagg (Ed.), *Cricket and national identity in the postcolonial age: Following on* (pp. 94–109). London: Routledge.

Singh, V. (2013). *The big fix*. Chennai: Westland Ltd.
Stockwell, P. (2002). *Cognitive poetics: An introduction*. London/New York: Routledge.
Sundar, G. (2010). *The premier murder league*. New Delhi: Penguin India.
Tadié, A. (2010). The fictions of (English) cricket: From nation to diaspora. *International Journal of the History of Sport, 27*(4), 690–711.
Tharoor, K. (2010, March 27). Cheerleaders shame Indian cricket. *The Guardian* [Online]. Accessed 29 Sept 2014. Available from http://www.theguardian.com/commentisfree/2010/mar/27/cheerleaders-india-cricket-women

Vignettes of Change: A Discussion of Two Indian Graphic Novels

Pooja Sinha

The graphic novel, as a recent addition to Indian publishing, offers authors and artists a new medium of creative expression. Karin Kukkonen puts forth a succinct definition of the graphic novel as 'a publication format of the comics medium, which is a self-contained, non-serialised comics narrative' (2013, p. 172).[1] It is generally agreed that the publication of Indian graphic novelist Sarnath Banerjee's *Corridor: A Graphic Novel* (2004) introduced the term into Indian publishing (see Sarkar 2008, para. 2; Sareen 2010, para. 1; Chatterjee 2013, p. 209).[2] In this chapter I discuss two influential graphic novels by Banerjee and, through a close reading of the interplay between text and image in *Corridor* (2004) and *The Harappa Files* (2011), examine how both works explore social shifts in India after the 1990s while also reflecting and commenting on the contemporary urban landscape.

---

[1] 'Comics' is used in the singular to refer to the medium (for example, comics studies, comics medium, comics creator).

[2] While Orijit Sen's *River of Stories* (1994) employed the graphic medium, critics suggest that as a distinct publishing category, the anglophone Indian graphic novel appeared much later with the publication of Banerjee's *Corridor* (2004). Emma Dawson Varughese (2013), for instance, examines *River of Stories* as 'the first recognized Indian graphic novel' (p. 138), but clarifies that 2004 marks the expansion of 'the market of and for graphic novels' (p. 139).

P. Sinha
Open University, Milton Keynes, UK

© The Editor(s) (if applicable) and The Author(s) 2016
A. Tickell (ed.), *South-Asian Fiction in English*,
DOI 10.1057/978-1-137-40354-4_10

Comics creators such as Will Eisner (1985, 1996) and Scott McCloud (1993, 2006) have made important analytical observations about the comics medium and the verbal–visual interaction in graphic narratives, and how they influence readers' interpretations. As a form of artistic expression, the comics medium encompasses a variety of 'genres' and 'themes' (McCloud 1993, p. 6). Moreover, comics studies critics suggest that comics and graphic novels are not mutually exclusive categories that can readily be distinguished from each other; rather, their different circulation in the book market is a question both of form and of content (see Harvey 1996, pp. 116–17; Lefèvre 2000, p. 101). The graphic novel is generally thought to have broadened the scope of traditional comics by its consideration of topics and ideas that set it apart for adult consumption; however, definitions based on format or subject matter can be readily challenged. Discussing 'adult comics', Roger Sabin (1993) considers the manner in which they circulate in the market: both the format of the work as 'expensively produced (often in book form)' and its pitching in the market so that a title is likely to be 'reviewed in the quality press', Sabin suggests, appear to confer upon it market classifications such as 'adult comics' (1993, p. 1); yet these distinctions remain fluid (1993, p. 3). For example, while browsing books offered by the Indian e-retailer Flipkart, the category of 'Comics and Graphic Novels' is further divided into labels such as 'Romance' and 'Superheroes' (indicative of genre), 'Manga' (indicative of style) and 'Indian Graphic Novels' (indicative of region). Interestingly, within the subcategory of 'Indian Graphic Novels', not only can one buy the graphic novels of Sarnath Banerjee, but also 'double digest' and 'gift pack' editions of the long-running children's comics Chacha Chaudhary (available at http://www.flipkart.com/chacha-chaudhary-gift-pack/p/itmdffft3sjmqsj4?pid=RBKDFFFHFYWK9ASZ&ref=L%3A-1784975248343479558&srno=b_19). This is not a fault in Flipkart's categorization; instances such as this foreground how comics and graphic novels tend to be described not so much as distinct categories of writing, but rather as market categories that have accrued different associations. As already noted, the graphic novel represents a new entity in Indian publishing. This novelty has been commented upon in academic overviews of Indian comics publishing, and also highlighted in popular media articles, with readers being made aware of the new category of fiction and its Anglo-American tradition. Accounts of comics publishing in India have charted their history from the latter half of the twentieth century to current developments (see Chandra 2008; Sreenivas 2010; Khanduri 2010; Mehta 2010; Chatterjee 2013) and offered critiques of new works by Indian authors and creators (see Oza 2011; Dawson Varughese 2013, pp. 137–44). Dipavali Debroy, for example, notes that 'graphic narration in a general sense has a long and rich tradition in India' (2011, p. 33). However, she distances examples drawn from painting, sculpture and folk art traditions from 'the present graphic novel' (Debroy 2011, p. 33). Debroy's opening remarks point to the wealth of indigenous art forms, visual styles and storytelling traditions that Indian authors and artists can draw upon; however, her essay is most valuable for its listing of comics publishers in India and the various characters they introduced into the local market (2011, pp. 34–7). Bharat Murthy offers yet another perspective on Indian comics, commenting on the long history of cartooning in India (2009, pp. 3–4), a link also highlighted by Chatterjee (2013, pp. 206–7). A detailed examination of the literature on Indian comics publishing is beyond the scope of this chapter; particularly noteworthy, however, is how such scholarship is placing Indian comics within a historical perspective and providing the momentum for further critical engagement.

The Indian media has also registered the arrival of the graphic novel and reviewers frequently engage in list-making, thereby acquainting an Indian reader new to the medium with previous works in the Anglo-American tradition (see Sebastian 2006; Padmanabhan 2010; Sayeed 2011).[3] Such list-making also prepares a context of reception by attempting to define the new medium and emphasizing its suitability for exploring a number of themes. Banerjee himself has discussed the comics medium as 'a combined language of words and pictures' (Indrasimhan 2007, para. 2), and in an interview with Samit Basu he emphasizes, as particularly important, the image–text pairing that 'together create units of meaning' (Basu 2006, para. 5). It is this image–text pairing in Banerjee's graphic novels that I consider in the following sections.

A New Visual Lexicon: Reflecting on the Urban Landscape

In *Corridor* and *The Harappa Files*, Banerjee uses a visual lexicon specific to contemporary India, incorporating images from different media such as advertising and film. Such use of the familiar images of everyday life, and

---

[3] These lists usually include the works of Will Eisner, Frank Miller, Alan Moore, Art Spiegelman and Marjane Satrapi (see Sebastian 2006; Sayeed 2011). Readers familiar with Anglo-American graphic novels can appreciate how these lists could be used to highlight the potential of the graphic novel to address serious issues (Padamanbhan 2010, para. 3).

the new uses to which they are put in the graphic narrative, offer insights into how contemporary Indian graphic novels engage a local Indian readership, while also articulating sociocultural shifts. In analysing Banerjee's work, I will draw on McCloud's (2006) critical overview of the comics medium, engaging with his reading of compositional aspects such as the use of panels and the verbal–visual interaction within panels.[4]

Banerjee employs a visual style that is remarkable for both its economy and its vividness. *Corridor* opens with Brighu, a recurring character in Banerjee's work, hunting for a copy of James Watson's *Double Helix* in New Delhi's colonial-era shopping centre, Connaught Place. The mood is set with three panels on the opening page. The first shows a perspiring Brighu, tongue hanging out, braving the June heat: 'You need the soul of Chengiz Khan to survive a June afternoon in Delhi' (Banerjee 2004, p. 3). The second panel uses the double helix image, establishing Brighu's preoccupation on the one hand, and gently mocking the DNA encoding of, as Banerjee calls them, the 'urban warriors' out and about in the oppressive heat (2004, p. 3); word and image act in what McCloud calls an 'interdependent' (2006, p. 130) pairing in this panel, reinforcing the sense of an encoded resistance to heat while using the symbol that would be uppermost in Brighu's mind as he searches for Watson's book. The third panel, showing a figure lounging carelessly against the colonnade, undercuts Brighu's assertion that 'life seems to depend' on the successful purchase of the book (Banerjee 2004, p. 3); here, word and image interact in what McCloud calls a 'parallel' pairing (2006, p. 130), where the image undercuts the narrative voice and mocks the false urgency of Brighu's mission. The use of such pairings is very common in Banerjee's work, indicating a reflective awareness of how he uses the interplay between word and image, thus offering the reader rich interpretative possibilities. Snapshots from the lives of those who visit a pavement bookshop in Connaught Place form the vignettes of *Corridor*. The particularities and peculiarities of these lives are told with a gentle humour, and Banerjee creates his characters, visually and verbally, with the same quick strokes that he uses

---

[4] McCloud identifies some relationships in which word and image combine, such as 'word specific' and 'picture specific' pairings where image and word 'accentuate' the other, respectively. The two blend in 'intersecting' and 'interdependent' ways, as they convey information and do it so as to construct new meanings out of the interaction. Word and image can also appear in 'parallel' and 'montage' combinations, so that in the first combination they 'follow seemingly different paths without intersecting', and in the second are 'combined pictorially' (McCloud 2006, p. 130).

to recreate the city. This aspect of Banerjee's aesthetic lends itself readily to the vignette style of the two graphic novels discussed here, taking everyday life as its subject matter to reflect on contemporary India.

Banerjee creates a sense of place and atmosphere as he evokes pace or quietness, the bustle of a shopping area or languid mornings. Everyday details are brought to prominence through the choice of images; early in the book, for example, the morning stirrings of the city are illustrated against the fixed backdrop of a Mother Dairy outlet as shoppers arrive to buy milk, children walk past on the way to school and morning walkers appear (Banerjee 2004, p. 13). All of this is framed from within an autorickshaw, interrupted as the driver is awakened by an eager Brighu, ready to embark on yet another trip to Connaught Place. Banerjee employs differing panel lengths and compositions to illustrate specific moments, in this instance using a fixed camera angle for a series of panels on a page to offer a sense of duration. These morning scenes are drawn in short panels placed within a large one, and work together to give a sense of the gentle, unhurried passage of time: 'the city never jumpstarts the day; it slowly stretches itself awake' (Banerjee 2004, p. 13).[5] As Hemant Sareen comments, Banerjee's project appears to be one of 'an ethnographer and a chronicler of urbanity' (2010, para. 2). In employing a mix of media to render these vignettes of daily life, Banerjee references a visual lexicon peculiar to India, one that would be immediately recognizable to an Indian readership.

The story of the newlywed Shintu's sexual awakening in *Corridor*, as he seeks to enhance his prowess with advice from the quack Hakim Gulabkhus Peshawari, offers an example of how the images and materials of everyday life can be put to fresh use in a graphic narrative. Shintu's interactions with Peshawari are set in old Delhi, recreated in all its singularity and colourfulness with posters of deities, Bollywood stars and Arnold Schwarzenegger (Banerjee 2004, p. 49). Banerjee often frames his characters against a background of such collages, the black ink drawings sometimes contrasted with colour photographs, thus projecting his characters into snapshots of the urban landscape. In this particular instance, however, the character of Peshawari peeps out of a comical collection of

---

[5] Harvey explains how 'manipulating' elements of the graphic medium, such as panel compositions, 'creates pace, suspense, mood and the like'. 'Successive panels', for instance, offer a sense of 'duration' while the manner in which they are arranged 'control time' (1996, p. 108), speeding up an action or slowing it down (1996, p. 109).

'Ideal Boy' charts (Banerjee 2004, p. 65). These charts illustrate 'Good Habits', with a schoolboy around the age of ten shown practising these virtues under captions such as 'gets up early in the morning' or 'helps others'. The jarring contrast between the childlike simplicity of the good habits recommended for the 'Ideal Boy' and the reasons for Shintu's visit to Peshawari makes the quack's advice seem outdated and ludicrous. Sareen comments on the interplay between word and image in this instance, and argues that Shintu's story

> illustrates the intuitive equilibrium of language and image Banerjee can achieve to communicate ideas and evoke characters and milieus. In this case, the quack's archaic notions about sex and Shintu's kitschy sexual fantasies are suggested in collages of images culled from film posters, film stills, advertising bills and the didactic 'Ideal Boy' posters that dot the walls of schools across India bearing pious instruction on morality and personal hygiene for young men. (Sareen 2010, para. 3)

In satirizing cultural stereotypes of the preceding decades, Banerjee also moves away from the moralism of the 'Ideal Boy' charts. As Indian cartoonist Vishwajyoti Ghosh muses: 'When I think of little boys in the 1970s, I always think of these picture charts as a visual idiom of the age' (Ryan Holmberg 2013, para 50). Banerjee references this 'visual idiom' in his work, but does it in such a way as to distance himself from an association with the 1960s and 1970s in favour of a new sensibility. He does not appear to be demystifying for his reader the photo collages, watercolour drawings, film posters and book covers that he uses to recreate old Delhi; the audience is constructed as a knowing one, able to spot the cultural reference and appreciate the datedness of the 'Ideal Boy' charts.

The humour in such instances works upon the reader's recognition of stereotypes and the Indian peculiarities they evoke. In *Corridor*, Digital Dutta (another of Banerjee's recurring characters) gets into a fight (Banerjee 2004, pp. 37–8). As the hooligans shout a curse word containing 'mother' at him, Digital Dutta sees red. The desecration is made the more traumatic in his imagination through poignant film stills of the actor Nargis in Mehboob Khan's *Mother India* (1957) and Nirupa Roy, the latter typecast as a mother figure and helpless martyr (Bageshree 2004, para. 7). The humour of the encounter derives from the juxtaposition of Bollywood stereotypes with the narrative of the fight, which offers the opportunity for satire. Digital Dutta is inserted in a supposed still from a movie with Nirupa Roy putting a ceremonial mark (*tilak*) on his head, thus parodying the Bollywood convention of the mother sending her son to a confrontation with maternal blessing and divine help. With an ironically religious backdrop, Digital Dutta receives the *tilak* for victory in battle, which he begins with the cry of 'hit me fascists!' (Banerjee 2004, p. 38). As Bollywood clichés clash with the clichés of Digital Dutta's professed Marxist sympathies (Bageshree 2004, para. 7), the juxtaposition of these images creates not a realist but a satirized landscape. In *Corridor*, the 'Ideal Boy' charts and Bollywood references are used as popular currency, but are also taken out of their original context. That these images are presented ironically suggests a cultural shift wherein the emotions and attitudes associated with certain images have lost their original import for Banerjee's Indian readers. (For an insightful discussion of shifts in middle-class sensibilities perceived through an analysis of how children read traditional Amar Chitra Katha comics in post-liberalization India in the 1990s, see Deepa Sreenivas 2010, pp. 62–4.) The *Mother India* film still is not used in the context of the years immediately following India's independence, but is rather deployed in a comical way as a stock image for someone weighed down by the vicissitudes of life. With the distance of several decades, the use of these images serves to intensify the sense of their datedness. This can be interpreted as hinting at the new responses to India's pre-liberalization past, such as a self-aware distancing from overtly pious images and the associations they carry. This, however, raises the question of who Banerjee's readers might be.

Rimi B. Chatterjee notes that 'Banerjee has been hugely influential in introducing the new middle class to the possibilities of comics' (2013, pp. 209–10). Sareen similarly finds in Banerjee's work a 'rootedness in the urban Indian middle-class ethos' (2010, para. 7). The association of a visual lexicon with a certain demographic seems a curious one, yet it is worth exploring. The question to ask, perhaps, is not so much what this 'middle-class ethos' might be, but how it is being constructed and represented in works such as Banerjee's. It is therefore useful to examine not only the images that have currency in the popular media in India, but also the tone with which they are engaged. With the self-aware humour of the Shintu and Digital Dutta vignettes, what is reaffirmed is the playful stance that the new middle class adopts towards Indian peculiarities (such as Bollywood stereotypes). Contemporary Indian graphic novels thus need to be studied within the specific context of post-liberalization socio-economic and cultural shifts. Recent sociological analyses focusing on contemporary India, which I draw upon in the next section, examine the emergent middle class in terms of India's economic liberalization (Fernandes 2006; Brosius 2010). In his more recent graphic novel *The Harappa Files* (2011), Banerjee offers vignettes highlighting social change and mobility after India's economic liberalization as well as the concerns associated with these developments.

VIGNETTES OF SOCIAL CHANGE

In *The Harappa Files*, Banerjee discards the panel layout in favour of full page watercolour illustrations and the double page spread. While the book has been marketed and reviewed as a graphic novel, Banerjee identifies a distinct shift in his style, describing *The Harappa Files* as 'loosely bound graphic commentaries' (2011, p. 3). This shift is interesting as the double page format reinforces the vignette-like function of these 'graphic commentaries', and draws attention to how each of them engages with contemporary urban Indian middle-class culture. The premise for collecting these vignettes is the fictional 'Greater Harappa Rehabilitation, Reclamation and Redevelopment Commission', which has decided to 'conduct a gigantic survey of the current ethnography and urban mythologies of a country on the brink of great hormonal changes. Changes of such enormity, that they are barely comprehensible to its civil society' (p. 11). This mock-serious introduction, associating socio-economic shifts with 'hormonal changes', sets the tone for the book, as Banerjee illustrates these developments for the supposedly mystified urban Indian reader. The audience is constructed as one who might be more responsive to certain ways of presenting the committee's findings; the 'focus groups' and 'marketing agency' (p. 11) suggest that 'to tell new stories one needs new languages' (p. 12), and it is agreed that the Harappa committee's project of illustrating social shifts be attempted through the comics medium.

Not unlike *Corridor*, *The Harappa Files* draws on the images and material that are part of the everyday experiences of the middle class, and Banerjee describes its project as 'an examination of the near past and attempt to resurrect, examine and catalogue cultural, human and material relics' (2011, p. 15). The name Harappa (with its evocation of the ancient Indus Valley civilization, dating from the third millennium B.C.), as Dawson Varughese's reading suggests, conjures up 'a generational and cultural museum' (2013, p. 140). It also accentuates the sense that even the 'near past', as Banerjee calls it (2011, p. 15), is fast becoming old and outdated. Its 'relics' hint at the speed with which economic and social changes have swept over India (Dawson Varughese 2013, p. 140). Indian society, *The Harappa Files* suggests, has changed fast and needs to step back and review the ways in which it has changed. As Dawson Varughese explains, 'this act of remembering an India of "then" helps to interrogate an India of "now"', especially in 'the framing of these memories with New India and new ideas of middle-classness' (2013, p. 140). This emphasis on the 'new' and the recent, with the sense of an ongoing process of consolidating a middle-class identity in India after economic liberalization in the 1990s, is of special relevance to the following discussion. The need to 'catalogue' (Banerjee 2011, p. 15) everything, from soaps and toothpastes to cars, can then be interpreted as an attempt to keep these recent social shifts in view, and to historicize and understand these changes.

The 'files' themselves are presented in a mock-serious tone, appearing to be painstakingly numbered as File #0491/11c/NANO or File #1131/12C/IIT. The themes of these vignettes are ones that commonly crop up in commentaries on contemporary middle-class Indian society, such as education, infrastructure and access to goods and services. In many ways *The Harappa Files* appears to be an illustrated counterpart of the collected short essays format used for commentaries on India such as those by Shashi Tharoor (2007) and Santosh Desai (2010), which similarly discuss how the post-1990s sociocultural shifts can be located in everyday situations, and where the vignette style is commonly used to offer brief considerations of these developments. Of particular interest to the emergent middle class is educational achievement and its promise of upward mobility. In *The Harappa Files*, social aspiration is illustrated in the file on the IITs (Indian Institutes of Technology), with their promise of good jobs and social status (discussed in Chap. 2 of this collection in relation to Chetan Bhagat's novels). This vignette is illustrated with a double page spread showing two families staring warily at each other:

> Every year, during the month of May, IITs open their doors to prospective students of engineering and technology. And every Indian student worth his mother's milk must sit for the entrance exam.
> The elimination is often 10,000 to 1 […] A sense of dread descends upon the nation. (Banerjee 2011, pp. 70–1)

Banerjee thus touches upon a very common concern in Indian society, that of intense competition within the education system. The use of the word 'nation' is interesting here, suggesting a pan-Indian scenario of aspiration so that the country as a whole seems to share the suspense and apprehension associated with the results. This sense of grooming oneself in pursuit of social mobility starts when children are still young, as in File #2548/21D/ EXTRA-CURRICULAR where a mother marches her sons to a martial arts class, since 'being good in studies isn't enough' (Banerjee 2011, pp. 72–3). Nita Kumar's engaging discussion of the grooming of middle-class children in order to improve their chances of upward mobility through educational, 'economic, social and, particularly, cultural capital' (2011, p. 220), the last acquired through 'extra-scholastic activities' (p. 221), is especially pertinent here.

The IIT and Extra-Curricular vignettes in *The Harappa Files* present a notable contrast to the Digital Dutta and Shintu vignettes in *Corridor* that I discussed in the preceding section. The vignettes in *Corridor* appear to offer a commentary on the morality of the past decades, or the collective values associated with pre-liberalization India from which Banerjee's readers could distance themselves. In the IIT and Extra-Curricular vignettes, however, new forms of shared aspiration are suggested, in which the present middle class is participating. The visual style Banerjee uses in these two cases is of interest here. The distancing effect from values associated with the 1960s and 1970s in the *Corridor* vignettes was achieved through the use of film stills and collages. In the Extra-Curricular vignette, however, the packed lunchbox and the children dressed in Karate Gi are images that form part of the contemporary visual landscape, which reinforces the immediacy and familiarity of the scenario. The mother then represents a new conceptualization of the determined and aspirational Indian mother; one that, as future readers reconsider post-liberalization India, might perhaps appear as outdated as the Nirupa Roy and *Mother India* figures in *Corridor*. It is worth noting that this illustration of the mother resolutely marching her children to yet another 'extra-curricular' class features as the cover illustration of *The Harappa Files*, chosen perhaps for its typicality and its hint at middle-class preoccupations.

From education the focus shifts—for an Indian reader, with a great deal of familiarity—to File #5984/32G/BOROLINE, a locally produced antiseptic cream. Added to the 'Khushbudar [Fragrant] Antiseptic Cream, Boroline!' tagline is Banerjee's own wry humour, suggesting that intense competition carries its own heartbreaks: 'And for any cuts or bruises on the path to success' (2011, pp. 74–5). Interpretative possibilities are thus opened up between the verbal–visual interplay on the page and the cultural sensibility brought to bear on it. In a graphic narrative, the word–image pairing is all that is available to the reader for recreating sound (Harvey 1996, p. 176), as in the case of an advertisement jingle. Banerjee uses the most familiar and identifiable of images, which render an excess of text unnecessary; the entire two page spread in this example has two texts—a short comment and an advertising jingle. If the jingle is heard at all, bearing in mind that the word 'khushbudar' (fragrant) is a transliteration from Urdu, it is in the minds of the readers who have grown up hearing it on television and radio sets; the jingle remains a visual text unless the reader recognizes both the tune and its contexts. In a vital discussion of the verbal–visual interplay and interpretative possibilities in Banerjee's graphic novels, Esterino Adami takes the Boroline vignette as an example to comment on the use of 'iconic advertising' (2009, section 4.2.5), and suggests that the use of such images helps in 'scrutinising the tensions and anxieties of India today' (2009, section 3). In his reading, the manufacturing of Boroline in India also adds an additional dimension to the vignette, that of 'ironically hinting at discourses of national economic self-sufficiency in the twentieth century' (section 4.2.5).

My two concluding examples of *The Harappa Files*'s engagement with post-liberalization shifts are Banerjee's file on Tata's mini-car Nano and the file illustrating the gated residential communities in Delhi. As Amita Baviskar notes, the Nano was launched in India in 2009 at a reasonable Rs. 100,000 (2011, p. 413), or approximately £1000. On the one hand, a worrying aspect of the Nano vignette is that developments in technology are not matched by parallel developments in infrastructure, as traffic 'inches' along on streets crowded with Nanos at a pace that allows passengers to jump out and grab a snack (Banerjee 2011, p. 29). On the other hand, access to the Nano creates new equalities, as Banerjee comments on the upward social mobility offered by ownership of one: 'the last two spaces where democracy will be exercised in India are the roads and the airports' (p. 29). Commentators have variously highlighted the post-liberalization democratization of goods and services in India, as private companies offer competitive prices in the open market. A frequently cited example that is relevant to the understanding of the Nano vignette is the launch of 'budget airlines' (Nilekani 2009, p. 233), such as Air Deccan in 2003, SpiceJet in 2005 and IndiGo in 2006, which meant that the experience of flying was now not restricted to the rich but available at affordable prices to the middle class. The Nano made it possible for this constituency, that of the 'common' people, to own a car. In her study of Indian cartoonist R.K. Laxman's 'Common Man' character, Ritu Gairola

Khanduri examines how Laxman's social commentary takes as its subject 'the realm of everyday life in India' (2012, p. 305). It is the 'commonness' of this character, his ordinariness, which also makes him a powerful symbol: 'in his cartoons Laxman mediates a national response to politics in India' (p. 309). Interestingly, Khanduri argues that in Laxman's work, 'air travel is a persistent theme framing the discourse of development' (p. 311), noting that the budget airline Air Deccan featured Laxman's 'Common Man' as its 'brand ambassador' (pp. 315–16). This, as Khanduri also points out, contrasts with 'Air India's mascot, the little Maharajah, [that] encapsulated the exclusive context of flying' (p. 313). The accessibility of goods and services, therefore, is frequently commented upon when examining the effects of economic liberalization in India, and comparing it with the pre-liberalization past. Fernandes, for instance, offers the example of the Maruti car in the 1980s, 'which for the first time gave domestic customers an alternative to the Ambassador car, the long standing symbol of restrictions on choice for Indian consumers' (2006, p. 36). In these examples, emphasis is placed on equal access to consumer goods as a result of economic liberalization. The idea of this 'common man', however, changed considerably in the 1990s, and Banerjee's own treatment of the issue brings to attention certain conflicts within Indian society.

Intriguingly, in his review of *The Harappa Files*, Sareen claims that 'the book's sequences follow the travails of the common man in an ambiguously dated place somewhere between postcolonial and the postliberalization India of the 1990s' (2011, para. 2). This is a telling insight, not least because the 'common man' of post-independence and post-liberalization India are not the same. Fernandes comments on the 'mainstream national political discourses that increasingly portray urban middle class consumers as the representative citizens of liberalizing India' (2006, p. xv) that have taken hold in the country, and argues that 'the middle class consumer-citizen is in effect the new "common man"' (p. 187). The tensions that emerge in the 'Nano' and 'City of Gates' vignettes derive from these shifting ideas of representativeness. In *The Harappa Files*, those decrying traffic congestion are given unsympathetic treatment as the privileged few who meet at exclusive clubs and 'continue banging on about carbon footprints' (2011, p. 31), their concern not so much for the ecosystem but a result of their disinclination to share space and resources. While the file on the 'Nano' points to the tensions between the upper and the upwardly mobile middle classes, the file on the 'City of Gates' suggests far more worrying rifts between the middle class and the destitute working classes in India.

'City of Gates' is one of the longest vignettes in *The Harappa Files* (Banerjee 2011, pp. 106–21), and its complex narrative of interweaving stories is very different from the double page spreads that I have analysed above. Over 15 pages long, it deserves a more detailed and sustained critique than can be offered within this section, and I will therefore limit this discussion to just one recurring image in the vignette. Gates—tall, imposing, locked and barricaded with police stop signs, are the motifs of this vignette: 'The greater the wealth of the neighbourhood, the taller the gates', Banerjee comments (p. 108). As the towering gates in Banerjee's vignette declare all too emphatically, while the middle classes are thus fortifying themselves in gated communities, the poor and the homeless continue to die in the streets. The gated communities, critics have suggested, represent a politics of exclusivity (and also exclusion) practised by the new middle class (Fernandes 2006, p. 139; Brosius 2010, pp. 40–1): 'The internal uncertainties and instability of the new middle class are, in effect, managed through the reproduction of sociospatial distance from the urban poor and working classes' (Fernandes 2006, p. 139). Baviskar describes these tensions as pertaining to 'debates about regulating this public sphere, [so that] claims to the street bring to the fore a fundamental question: who constitutes an urban or civic public?' (Baviskar 2011, p. 391). In her insightful reading of history in Indian graphic novels by Sarnath Banerjee and Vishwajyoti Ghosh, Mridula Chari also comments upon the preoccupation with 'very middle-class English-speaking Indian concerns of space and ownership, of who belongs to a city' (2012, para 12). Belonging to the middle class, or being part of the collective of the 'common man', presents a complex picture of a new demographic negotiating its identity within the contemporary urban landscape.

The 'City of Gates' vignette closes with resigned acceptance of government callousness towards the plight of the poor, which is 'Based on three fundamental principles: (a) Public memory is short, (b) The nation is shining, poised, glowing or whatever, (c) History is written by garment exporters' (Banerjee 2011, p. 121). Banerjee's referencing of the term 'India Shining' is of interest here.[6] 'India Shining' was meant to

---

[6] Fernandes (2006, pp. 190–3) and Brosius (2010, pp. 1–7) have both discussed the term in some detail. They chart its history from its birth during the 2004 national election in India, when it was part of a 'massive media campaign' (Brosius 2010, p. 1). However, both Fernandes and Brosius distance the term from pat associations with party politics (Fernandes 2006, pp. 192–3; Brosius 2010, p. 2), and offer a more nuanced reading of how 'India Shining' continues to circulate within popular discourse.

highlight 'India's strong economic growth associated with liberalization' (Fernandes 2006, p. 190), and similar terms such as the 'feel good factor' were also popularized (Brosius 2010, p. 6). Banerjee satirizes the term, coming as it does towards the end of a long vignette on social inequality. He also ridicules terms related to 'India Shining', with the derisory 'whatever' at the end of the second point. What is thus emphasized is the need to remember not just the nation's past but also the plight of those suffering social injustice. Otherwise, with a partisan history written by those who have benefited from liberalization, one faces the prospect of losing the nuanced awareness of social and cultural shifts that Banerjee's works foreground.

Conclusion

In discussing Banerjee's graphic novels as exemplary texts, I have considered how this new form lends itself both to new creative expressions, and to a critique of the contemporary Indian sociocultural milieu. I have noted in the opening section of this chapter the emerging scholarship that examines the field of comics publishing in India, and explores the diversity of content and visual styles in Indian graphic novels. This chapter is a contribution to this ongoing dialogue, as it demonstrates the usefulness of close reading in appreciating distinctive visual styles, the recognition of the uses to which the image–text pairing is put (such as in visual or narrative irony), and the identification of the audience thus addressed. Through these initial explorations, one can begin to arrive at an understanding of the deep resonance the graphic novel might have for an Indian readership. As Banerjee claims, 'contemporary societal concerns could be best addressed by using the medium of comics' (2011, p. 14), and his works exemplify the ways in which the particular combination of image and text lends itself to thinking critically about contemporary Indian society. Banerjee's self-reflexive use of verbal–visual interaction shows how the graphic novel offers ways of rethinking history and commenting on current social developments, such as the politics of social aspiration in contemporary India highlighted in *The Harappa Files*. The graphic novel, and the comics medium more generally, offer exciting opportunities to explore history, politics and everyday lives in India. Not only has the comics medium introduced the Indian readership to a new form, it has also provided Indian graphic novel creators with the material needed for a new way of looking at Indian society.

Works Cited

Adami, E. (2009). *The signs of post-colonial identity: Ballooned words and drawn texts in Sarnath Banerjee's graphic novels* [Online]. University of Turin, Italy. Available at http://aperto.unito.it/bitstream/2318/120423/1/Signs%20of %20postcolonial_postprint.pdf. Accessed 7 May 2015.

Bageshree, S. (2004, April 19). The tango between panels. *The Hindu* [Online]. Available from http://www.thehindu.com/thehindu/mp/2004/04/19/stories/2004041901630300.htm. Accessed 5 Nov 2014

Banerjee, S. (2004). *Corridor: A graphic novel*. New Delhi: Penguin Books India.

Banerjee, S. (2011). *The Harappa files*. New Delhi: Harper Collins India.

Basu, S. (2006, July 3). Sarnath Banerjee interview. *Duck of destiny* [Online]. Available from http://samitbasu.blogspot.co.uk/2006/07/sarnath-banerjee-interview.html. Accessed 3 Sept 2014

Baviskar, A. (2011). Cows, cars and cycle-rickshaws: Bourgeois environmentalists and the battle for Delhi's streets. In A. Baviskar & R. Ray (Eds.), *Elite and everyman: The cultural politics of the Indian middle classes* (pp. 391–418). New Delhi: Routledge.

Brosius, C. (2010). *India's middle class: New forms of urban leisure, consumption and prosperity*. Delhi: Routledge.

Chandra, N. (2008). *The classic popular Amar Chitra Katha, 1967–2007*. New Delhi: Yoda Press.

Chari, M. (2012). *Humour and the contested city in Indian graphic novels* [Online]. Tata Institute of Social Sciences, India. Available from http://www.inter-disciplinary.net/at-the-interface/wp-content/uploads/2012/10/mchari_websitepaper.pdf. Accessed 7 May 2015.

Chatterjee, R. B. (2013). Frame/works: How India tells stories in comics and graphic novels. In K. Sen & R. Roy (Eds.), *Writing India anew: Indian English fiction 2000–2010* (pp. 205–227). Amsterdam: Amsterdam University Press.

Dawson Varughese, E. (2013). *Reading new India: Postmillennial Indian fiction in English*. London/New York: Bloomsbury Academic.

Debroy, D. (2011). The graphic novel in India: East transforms west. *Bookbird: A Journal of International Children's Literature, 49*(4), 32–39.

Desai, S. (2010). *Mother pious lady: Making sense of everyday India*. New Delhi: HarperCollins India.

Eisner, W. (1985). *Comics and sequential art*. London/New York: W.W. Norton and Company.

Eisner, W. (1996). *Graphic storytelling and visual narrative*. New York/London: W.W. Norton and Company.

Fernandes, L. (2006). *India's new middle class: Democratic politics in an era of economic reform*. Minneapolis/London: University of Minnesota Press.

Harvey, R. C. (1996). *The art of the comic book: An aesthetic history.* Jackson: University Press of Mississippi.
Holmberg, R. (2013, October 23). Inverted calm: An interview with Vishwajyoti Ghosh. *The Comics Journal* [Online]. Available from http://www.tcj.com/inverted-calm-an-interview-with-vishwajyoti-ghosh/. Accessed 5 Nov 2014.
Indrasimhan, L. (2007, February 4). Visual vocabularies. *Hindu Literary Review* [Online]. Available from http://www.hindu.com/lr/2007/02/04/stories/2007020400200500.htm. Accessed 25 Apr 2013.
Khanduri, R. G. (2010). Comicology: Comic books as culture in India. *Journal of Graphic Novels and Comics* [Online], *1*(2), 171–191. Available from http://www.tandfonline.com/doi/full/10.1080/21504857.2010.528641. Accessed 24 Mar 2014.
Khanduri, R. G. (2012). Picturing India: Nation, development and the common man. *Visual Anthropology, 25*, 303–323.
Kukkonen, K. (2013). *Studying comics and graphic novels.* Chichester: Wiley Blackwell.
Kumar, N. (2011). The middle-class child: Ruminations on failure. In A. Baviskar & R. Ray (Eds.), *Elite and everyman: The cultural politics of the Indian middle classes* (pp. 220–245). London/New York/New Delhi: Routledge.
Lefevre, P. (2000). The importance of being 'published'. In A. Magnussen & H. Christianson (Eds.), *Comics and culture: Analytical and theoretical approaches to comics* (pp. 91–107). Copenhagen: Museum Tusculanum Press.
Mehta, S. (2010). Wondrous capers: The graphic novel in India. In F. L. Aldama (Ed.), *Multicultural comics: From zap to blue beetle* (pp. 173–188). Austin: University of Texas Press.
McCloud, S. (1993). *Understanding comics: The invisible art.* Northampton: Kitchen Sink Press.
McCloud, S. (2006). *Making comics: Storytelling secrets of comics, manga and graphic novels.* New York/London: Harper.
Mother India (1957). [Film]. Directed by Mehboob Khan, Nargis Dutt and Sunil Dutt. London: Eros International.
Murthy, B. (2009). An art without a tradition: A survey of Indian comics. *Marg: A Magazine of the Arts* [Online], *61*(2), 1–38. Available from http://www.scribd.com/doc/26674355/An-Art-Without-a-Tradition-A-Survey-of-Indian-Comics-2008#scribd. Accessed 2 Jan 2015]
Nilekani, N. (2009). *Imagining India: The idea of a renewed nation.* New York: The Penguin Press.
Oza, V. (2011). Questions of reading and readership of pictorial texts: The case of Bhimayana, a pictorial biography of Dr. Ambedkar. *Journal of Writing in Creative Practice, 4*(3), 351–365.
Padmanabhan, M. (2010, July 17). Reading pictures. *Business Standard* [Online]. Available from http://www.business-standard.com/article/beyond-business/reading-pictures-110071700032_1.html. Accessed 2 Jan 2015.
Sabin, R. (1993). *Adult comics: An introduction.* London/New York: Routledge.

Sareen, H. (2010, July–August). Wondrous capers. *ArtAsiaPacific* [Online]. Available from http://artasiapacific.com/Magazine/69/WondrousCapers SarnathBanerje. Accessed 26 Apr 2013.

Sareen, H. (2011, April 12). Flipping through the Harappa files. *ArtAsiaPacific* [Online]. Available from http://artasiapacific.com/Blog/FlippingThrough TheHarappaFiles. Accessed 5 Nov 2014.

Sarkar, P. (2008, October 19). The novel in a speech balloon. *Times of India* [Online]. Available from http://timesofindia.indiatimes.com/home/stoi/The-novel-in-a-speech-balloon/articleshow/3613671.cms. Accessed 5 Nov 2014.

Sayeed, V. A. (2011, February 12–25). In graphic detail. *Frontline*. [Online]. 28(4). Available from http://www.flonnet.com/fl2804/stories/20110225280408100.htm. Accessed 26 Apr 2013.

Sebastian, P. (2006, August 6). Comic strip revolution. *Hindu Literary Review* [Online]. Available from http://www.hindu.com/lr/2006/08/06/stories/2006080600320600.htm. Accessed 26 Apr 2013.

Sen, O., & Baviskar, A. (1994). *River of stories*. New Delhi: Kalpavriksh.

Sreenivas, D. (2010). *Sculpting a middle class: History, masculinity and the Amar Chitra Katha in India*. London/New York/New Delhi: Routledge.

Tharoor, S. (2007). *The elephant, the tiger, and the cell phone: Reflections on India, the emerging 21st-century power*. New York: Arcade Publishing.

The New Pastoral: Environmentalism and Conflict in Contemporary Writing from Kashmir

Ananya Jahanara Kabir

On 16 June 2013, a new Facebook group, The Kashmir Bicycle Movement (KBM), appeared. Its aims were 'to reclaim streets of Kashmir for people, displace cars and restore pride in riding bicycles' (Kashmir Bicycle Movement 2013). Through photographs, commentary, and organization and reportage of mass cycling events, KBM combined ecocritical consciousness with a concern specific to Jammu and Kashmir: the long-term effects of political conflict as reflected through an alienation of Kashmiri people from their natural environment. The movement promised resistance not just to modernity's accelerated temporalities, but also to the conflict's impact on a Kashmiri's relationship to Kashmir. Unsurprisingly for this volatile region, KBM's freshness of purpose was from the start compromised by vulnerability to political violence. A month later (19 July 2013), a post announced the cancellation of a mass bicycle ride through downtown Srinagar, which was to have reclaimed an urban space marked by heritage monuments, indigenous protests as well military and state-sponsored demonstrations (Kabir 2013). This was to be KBM's last effective post.

KBM's brief virtual life materialized a fragile but potent nexus between the vernacular, the micro-urban and the landscape around Srinagar. Its mass

---

A.J. Kabir
King's College London, UK

cycling 'zalgur events' (*zalgur* is the Koshur [Kashmiri] word for bicycle) devised routes that combined vistas of lakes and mountains, precolonial heritage sites, downtown Srinagar and the appreciation of local economic initiatives related to trade in cycles and other non-spectacular aspects of Kashmiri heritage. This rhizomatic micro-political initiative transmitted a mode of surviving brutalization in a long-term conflict zone and the Indian occupation of both Kashmiri mind and territory. Its photographs of Kashmiri cyclists caught in the headlights of army vehicles did double work: they signalled the signs of the modern (the vehicular) and the timeless (the cyclist's Kashmiri *pheran*, or woollen tunic) and pine trees lining the road, heavy with snow. The consequent assemblage asserted the contiguity of a vernacular modern habitus with the natural world, in order to draw attention to the contrastive and disharmonious presence of the Indian army's traces.

This semiotic chain is enabled by its participation within a pre-existing *pastoral* discourse on the Kashmir Valley. Celebrated in precolonial, colonial and postcolonial periods for its natural beauty, and, for urban plains-dwellers from Mughal emperors and British imperial administrators to domestic tourists in independent India, as a place to refresh and re-imagine the self, the Valley has functioned as a colonial and postcolonial 'territory of desire' (Kabir 2009). Because the pastoral mode of representing Kashmir is intimately connected to the genesis and prolongation of political conflict in the region, Kashmiri attempts to reclaim Kashmiri landscape must be seen as a manifestation of the struggle for *azadi* (sovereignty, freedom). A conflict that has been born out of desire for a space defined as possessing unique natural beauty is *a priori* enmeshed in discourses about the appreciation, depreciation, management, enjoyment of as well as responsibility towards nature. It is only recently, however, that cultural production from the Valley has started overtly mobilizing environmentalist discourses and practices. This mobilization is what I now call 'the new pastoral'. This chapter uses the 'new pastoral' as an analytical lens for how Kashmiri cultural producers are staking claims to a much praised, much-fought-over space. I first examine social media and cyber-initiatives, and then move on to the new pastoral's evocation within the novel *The Collaborator* by Mirza Waheed, and the work of graphic artist Malik Sajad.

Beyond Green Postcolonialism

'An poshi teli yeli wan poshi' (as long as there are forests there will be food): this is a Koshur proverb attributed to the fourteenth-century Sufi saint of Kashmir, Nund Rishi/Sheikh Nooruddin. In healthy circulation within common speech in Kashmir, the proverb is currently undergoing a renaissance within internet-based discourse on Kashmiri environmentalism. It is prominent on the homepage of the online initiative KEWA (Kashmir Environmental Watch Association). Taking refuge in the anonymity offered by this medium, it provides no personal or postal information on its website. But its manifesto is very clear on the link between the conflict in Kashmir and environmental degradation:

> Kashmir is one of the most beautiful and isolated regions of the Himalaya. Unfortunately, Kashmir has been entangled in a conflict between India and Pakistan since 1947. The failure to resolve this issue over the last 50 years has fueled tensions and violent conflict. As a result, the inhabitants of Kashmir have suffered greatly. Beyond the human tragedy, the conflict has also had an impact on the environment. Environmental protection is generally weak. Deforestation is a major issue in both Pakistan-administered Kashmir and India-administered Kashmir. Kashmir's delicate environment has steadily deteriorated. Observing the continuing destruction of the environment of Jammu & Kashmir and believing that it is impossible to separate the environment from human condition, K.E.W.A. came into being as a voluntary effort to create online awareness and in hopes of starting a trend towards serious and concerted efforts to protect Jammu & Kashmir's environmental treasures. (KEWA n.d.)

This relationship between environmental degradation and political conflict that KEWA asserts is triangulated with an awareness of what its homepage calls 'a deep sense of nostalgia for Kashmir, "paradise on earth"'. KEWA's site links to an online collection of paintings of Kashmir by contemporary artists as well as 'a 100 year-old collection of paintings which portray Kashmir as it once was': Major A. Molyneux's watercolours of Kashmiri landscapes that illustrated Francis Younghusband's book on Kashmir (1909). Portraying 'the snow capped peaks, lakes, forests, flowers, and meadows of Kashmir' as well as 'the tranquil scenes of life in the villages and towns', these paintings are accompanied on the website by recordings of Kashmiri folk music. KEWA thereby attempts a multi-dimensional sensory recall of 'the pristine natural beauty of Kashmir and the harmonious ways in which the Kashmiri people lived within this environment' (KEWA n.d.).

KEWA turns to an imperial artist's paintings of Kashmir to generate 'appreciation for the need to safeguard the heavenly environment of Kashmir for our generations to come'. This association of nostalgia with the representation of Kashmir as what I have termed 'territory of desire' is, I have argued (Kabir 2009, pp. 80–106), an infinitely regressive affective complex that is a by-product of imperial modernity. Indeed, Molyneux's paintings were themselves an attempt to de-modernize the images of Kashmir already captured by the then cutting-edge technology of high altitude photography (Kabir 2009, pp. 54–79). And in turn, those early photographic views had been distilled out of a particular nostalgia for the vistas of England, the home the imperial adventurer-photographers had left behind. In our post-postmodern age characterized by viral circulation, the mechanically reproduced image of nostalgia, caught up in what Michael Taussig has called the sticky webs of copy and contact (Taussig 1993, p. 21), enters another portal to render further service to a much-represented, much-fought-over space. The new direction taken by this long trajectory of the visual image of Kashmir as 'paradise on earth' is its explicit alignment with an environmentalist approach to this conflict zone. There is a concomitant mobilization of what we may identify as 'positive' or even 'critical nostalgia' for its natural beauty—and here I use 'critical nostalgia' after Ranjana Khanna's concept of 'critical melancholia' as an enabling rather than debilitating psychological state (Khanna 2003).

The KEWA website must be placed in the context of a widespread, if somewhat counter-intuitive, trend within Kashmiri cultural production which consciously responds to the long-term consequences of political conflict: a return to that same tradition of praising the natural beauty which, since the late nineteenth century, has trapped the Valley of Kashmir in a spiralling libidinal economy of other people's desires. Kashmiri creative writers, irrespective of their language of expression, visual artists and even political ideologues regularly turn to their relationship to the landscape to assert the primacy and authenticity of their claims as 'indigenes' who have been erased from representations of Kashmir. 'Strategic essentialism' (Spivak 1987) in Kashmir, rendered even more urgent by decades of conflict, is characterized by assent rather than dissent regarding Kashmir's natural beauty, which is the prime motor of its emotional valence within South Asia. What distinguishes a Kashmiri from a non-Kashmiri turn to this natural beauty is the difference in motivation: participation in hegemonic discourse in one case, creating resistance in the other. The discourse of resistance returns the Kashmiri body to the Kashmiri landscape in a manner we can call 'proto-environmentalist': aligned to wider movements to reclaim nature from colonial or neo-colonial forces. Building on this implicit engagement with environmentalist discourse are recent interventions within the spectacle of Kashmir in the Indian nation space through an assortment of explicitly environmentalist claims, such as the KBM and the KEWA website.

To understand this trend we must go beyond ecocriticism's intersection with Postcolonial Studies in the avatar of 'green postcolonialism' (Huggan and Tiffin 2009). Pablo Mukherjee's pioneering essay on this topic omits Kashmir from his roll call of environmentally fragile conflict zones (Mukherjee 2006, p. 144), but recent scholarship on Kashmir is demonstrating the entanglement of conflict and environmental degradation, as well as its motivated mobilization within a spectrum of political positions. Unlike 'movements such as Narmada Bachao [in Western India] and Chiapas (in Mexico)', which Mukherjee urges 'practitioners of postcolonial and ecocritical studies' (2006, p. 147) to institute solidarity with, the Kashmir conflict presents no definitive movement as such. Mukherjee privileges the conflict between Northern and Southern actors as illuminating the shared burden of postcolonial and ecocritical studies, but what happens to inequalities within the postcolony itself, which have not claimed the attention of the world and the national public sphere through spectacular image-assemblages and icons—for example, the Save the Tiger campaign, the Bhopal disaster and its aftermath, the Chipko movement or the Narmada Bachao Andolan? As 'the continuing vulnerability of marginalised people is no longer simply a question of the colonised throwing off the shackles of colonisation, [...] how particular groups can find themselves targeted by their own government' should be the focus of critical enquiry (Huggan and Tiffin 2007, p. 4). But we also need to ask: what can a conflict, not associated in the public imagination with environmental hazards, gain when its subjects make their case in environmentalist terms?

The Pastoral in Kashmir

It is here that the concept of 'pastoral' reveals its utility and appropriateness. The 'pastoral' is a literary critical term signalling the penchant of city-dwellers to present the countryside as an idyllic space—of escape, rediscovery of the self and, eventually, transformation (Empson 1974). It is a narrative or a visual representation of the dialectical relationship between the urban and the rural (Williams 1973). The rural is marked not by labour and alienation, but by the romance of a carefree bond between human beings and nature, which, experienced temporally by the city-dweller, can help him or her resolve the specific complication that has set into motion the narrative plot—be it manifested in drama, fiction, or narrative poetry. Inasmuch as the pastoral originated in the Western classical world, it has participated in modern European self-fashioning, playing a heightened role within nineteenth-century romanticism as a reaction to the Industrial Revolution (Williams 1973; Gifford 1999, p. 37). Romanticism was also an aesthetic and ideological perspective through which the colonies were viewed, appreciated and consumed; certainly, the early photographers in Kashmir brought a vision both romantic and pastoral to their pioneering framing of Kashmir through the camera's lens. There is a direct link between the 'pastoral' as it functions within the Western imaginary, and its circulation as a mode of nostalgia and escape in the colonial context. Kashmir's political and geographical liminality heightened the allure of its pastoralist capture, which, as I have argued (Kabir 2009), was inherited by postcolonial India.

An important conduit for the movement of this imperial pastoralism to a postcolonial one was the writings of Jawaharlal Nehru, particularly his *The Discovery of India* (2004 [1946]). This foundation of an anticolonial imagining of India rests on strategic appropriations of Kashmir's natural beauty, which must remain untouched by capitalism, urbanism and other forms of modernity to furnish a fitting other to the emergent national self (Nehru 2004, pp. 56, 619). Nehru, India's first Prime Minister, had ancestral roots in Kashmir, and also wrote about his treks through the state as a salve for a political life caught up in the whirl of anticolonial nationalism (Nehru 2004, pp. 633–4). Kashmir as a spiritual reservoir for the formation of Indian-ness, where spirituality drew equally on pantheistic appreciation of its beauty, pre-eminence as a centre for Sanskrit learning (Kabir 2009, pp. 80–106) and a space where one could trek, fish and relax—these two approaches defined the Valley for the immediate postcolonial generation. A pastoral Kashmir, inflected by spirituality, antiquity and pre-capitalism alike, seeped into popular culture, defining an entire genre of 'Kashmir films' churned out by the Bombay film industry throughout the 1960s (Kabir 2005). These wildly popular films, the first to bring Technicolor to Indian cinema, showed world-weary young men and women travelling from Indian cities such as Bombay to the Valley for rest and recuperation, falling in love, generating endless complications, and then returning home to enact 'happily ever after' endings.

Until the 1990s, when the Kashmiri separatist movement gained visibility, the Kashmir Valley provided for postcolonial India a non-urban imagined space where the complications of becoming modern could be narratively enacted and resolved. Thus the term 'pastoral' is not merely genealogically appropriate given the history of Kashmir's landscape fetishization and the creation of desire; indeed, this genealogy provides us the key to appreciate the 'new pastoral' emerging from contemporary Kashmiri cultural production through the strategic use of environmentalist tropes. Kashmiri novelist Waheed's depiction of a nomadic shepherd community and cartoonist Sajad's iconographic use of the endangered Hangul deer contribute to a counter-discourse on Kashmir that reworks Nehruvian myths of the Valley as a pastoral paradise, a space of escape and the remaking of the collective modern self. Their appropriation of the pastoral mode speaks back to the classic 'Kashmir films' of the 1960s as well as Kashmir's continuing pastoralization within Nehruvian thought. Doubling back on that representational history of Kashmir, these texts participate in a movement that asserts both the constructed nature of Kashmir's desirability and the need to reclaim it as part of a collective healing of the Kashmiri self. Their articulations of 'the new pastoral' also play with the current mainstream spectacle of Kashmir as an eruptive and dangerous place that threatens the pastoral fantasy—a change initiated by the film *Roja* (dir. Mani Ratnam) 20 years ago (Kabir 2009, pp. 31–53).

Given these changing modes of representing the space in the national imaginary, we must ask why contemporary Kashmiri cultural producers present Kashmir to the local, national, global and cyber-publics as 'a new pastoral', and how this environmentalist turn relates to the new resistance movements emerging from Indian Kashmir since 2010. The etymological derivation of 'pastoral' from the Latin 'pastor', or shepherd, offers a clue. It is indeed striking how frequently the pastoral depiction of Kashmir has devolved on images of sheep and shepherding. In the box office hit, *Jab Jab Phool Khile* (dir. Suraj Prakash) from 1965, in many ways the peak of the Bollywood Kashmir films, the hero, a guileless Kashmiri lad Raja, is a houseboat owner. But in the first song introducing him, he is depicted repeatedly as racing up and down mountain pasture in the company of sheep he presumably herds. Images of sheep grazing in pasture continue to be prominent within presentations of Kashmir as 'paradise on earth', as for instance Indian handicrafts entrepreneur Jaya Jaitly's handsome coffee-table-style book on Kashmiri arts and crafts, which presents, in several consecutive frontispieces, images of craft, craftsmen, landscape and sheep (Jaitly 1999). While the image of Kashmir in the public sphere certainly involves lakes, mountains, flower-laden *shikaras* (small boats) and handicrafts, a literal connection of the pastoral with the pasture and its sheep is also part of this composite picture.

The pastoral in this case works to consolidate an impression of the Kashmir Valley as a place outside of capitalism and industrialized modernity.

There are other emphases that predicate this reception of the Valley in the popular Indian imagination—most importantly, the Kashmiri artisan, who labours to produce beautiful, small and fragile objects by hand and who, in the immediate postcolonial period, became exemplary of the confusions of an elite who wished to both protect the Indian craftsman from capitalism and gently lever him or her into the market. Through this desire to keep the craftsperson as an emblem of India's timelessly archaic spirituality, Kashmir became further straitjacketed as a state of exception, the realm of an unchanging pastoralism that the modern nation needs to define its capitalist progress against. I have shown elsewhere how this process fed into the political conflict (Kabir 2009, pp. 107–34); here, I wish simply to point out that there is a discursive equivalence between the artisan and the nomadic *gujjar* or shepherd. *Gujjar* communities, together with their flocks of sheep, have long traversed the routes between the hills and valleys of Jammu and Kashmir, engaged in seasonal migration and thus not rooted to land that must be owned, rented, ploughed and tilled. The *gujjar* who seems to stand outside of capitalist circuits of possession and control, as well as the containment of geopolitical boundaries, thus strengthens by metonymic association the understanding of the Kashmir Valley as a pastoral space.

Marvellous Shepherds and Domesticated Kitchen Gardens

It is this connection that Waheed exploits in his novel *The Collaborator* (2012a), which is set in a *gujjar* village in Indian Kashmir. These settled *gujjars* have adapted to a sedentary lifestyle while maintaining close links with nomadic culture and individuals who still practise it. These continuing affiliations are enabled by the village's proximity to traditional *gujjar* pathways of seasonal migration, which, however, are now also proximate to the Line of Control (LOC) dividing the region of Kashmir into Indian and Pakistani controlled sections. Waheed has conceded that his choice of setting and community was a deliberate act of deflecting emotional pressure from more autobiographical possibilities centred on Srinagar and the Kashmir Valley (Waheed 2012b); but placing the *gujjar* village in this contested and confused borderland, traversed by the dual lines of the official Indo-Pak border and the de facto LOC (Kabir 2011), also highlights the novel's primary preoccupation as situating the political conflict over Kashmir within a meditation on the relationship between the Kashmiri subject and the landscape. While the macabre relationship between the protagonist, the Collaborator, and the corpses of 'disappeared Kashmiris' functions as the novel's most literal example of returning the body to the landscape, it is the *gujjar* community, emplaced in the novel's unnamed but cartographically freighted valley, which offers a more philosophical response to the conflict and its emotional consequences for the Kashmiri.

Opening the novel with a description of the 'Valley of yellow flowers', Waheed is able to use the Valley's closeness to the LOC to drive home the contrast between this unnatural cartography—rendered even more peculiar by the lack of consensus over its geopolitical status—and the topography of the area. 'These undulating rows of peaks, some shining, some white, some brown, like layers of piled-up fabrics, are to the west and hide in their folds the secret tracks into Azad Kashmir, into Pakistan. [...] Valleys are beautiful' (p. 4). The 'secret tracks' counter the army's panopticon and encourage alternative collaboration with the mountains. Paths of resistance to the map's authority open up. The setting, a palimpsest of topography and cartography, allows Waheed to juxtapose, to searing effect, vignettes of the protagonist's past innocence and the horror-stricken reality of the present. While the past is defined through the Collaborator's play in the Valley—cricket, swimming in its stream, running through its meadows, lying on the grass to observe its flowers—the present is defined through the 'wretched human remains [that] lie on the [same] green grass like cracked toys' (p. 4). These are the dead Kashmiri bodies that the Collaborator must comb for ID cards and other incriminatory evidence on behalf of the Indian Army. These ID cards insert the Kashmiri into the bureaucratic apparatus of the state. But the communion with the Valley signals an autochthonous mode of self-fashioning which relocates the conflict from the map to the land.

This Kashmiri mode of self-fashioning gains an explicitly environmental register when the novel describes the desecration of the forests through encounters between two armies hiding on either side of the mountains:

> The Pakistanis were pounding a mountain pass some distance away, the Indians were replying in kind. There would be blood, and sulphur, on the trees. Dark plumes of smoke would emerge from the green canopies. Pines, those majestic umbrella pines, would be broken, their spectacular dark green spreads turning to umbrellas of crumbling flame, smoke and ash [...]. Bodies

would be dragged, bayonets would come down, eyes would be gouged, faces would be stamped on, mauled, amidst exultant cries of *Har Har Mahadev*. (pp. 115–16)

The philosophical ramifications of this environmentalist emphasis are brought out by Waheed's choice of a settled *gujjar* community, with live connections to nomadism, as the narrative vehicle for this tale of the Kashmiri autochthon versus military brutality. The novel's two emotional centres emerge as the Collaborator's mother's kitchen garden, a manifestation of sedentary domestication, and his boyhood encounter with the legendary *gujjar* Azad Range Wah-Wah ('the one who is free and [a figurative manifestation] of marvellous colours'), a manifestation of continuing nomadic pastoralism. These emotional centres illustrate the two poles of *gujjar* identity that circumscribe the protagonist's affective universe. Waheed thereby presents a nuanced view of the contradictions as well as the possibilities inherent within the *gujjar* as a symbol of the new pastoralist reclamation of Kashmir (see also Morey 2015).

The Collaborator's mother lavishes extraordinary care on her kitchen garden, which brings forth vegetables and herbs with fecundity almost unnatural for its miniature size:

> Square partitions separate the produce in Ma's garden, Green chillies, tomatoes, aubergines, cucumbers, potatoes, wild mint—she grows them all with motherly attention [...] miniature canals irrigate the garden [...] the borders of the garden are fence, feebly, with wilted conifer shoots and stout stumps of axed fir wood. Baba worked hard on them. The cucumber plants cling dearly to the fence and stick out stunted cucumbers here and there. Mother insists on growing cucumbers, even though she knows it's a little too high for them to prosper. Nonetheless, the plants look handsome. (p. 50)

Lulled by the domesticating rhythms, the reader is caught unawares by the inexplicable rage the garden incites in the young man:

> Her tomatoes are like any other[s ...] and she's got too many of them. Sometimes I want to crush them and mangle them with my feet and hands; break the tiny, hairy stems into garbled trash; smash the unripe ones into raw pulp and smear the ground with it! The tomato plants, I don't know why. It's a fleeting feeling, though, and I haven't reached a point of no return yet. (p. 50)

The image of the mother, who 'tills, digs, packs, repairs, irrigates, ever so silently, except for the jingle of her large gold earrings' (pp. 50–51), survives the onslaught, but her reined-in passion signifies the cathexis of a severed relationship to the environment which is the trade-off for the security of a settled existence.

The opposite is connoted by the marvellous shepherd Azad Range Wah-Wah, who tends his multicoloured flock wearing an outfit of fabulously variegated green and plays melodies of unbearable sweetness on his flute amidst the pine trees. A beautiful passage describes the Collaborator as a boy, walking with his friend through the forest 'heavy with a thousand unknown events' until they encounter him, standing among the trees, embellished by a 'big transistor around his neck, a thin bent stick in one hand, and a heavily stuffed bag, hanging, bouncing, by his waist as if it were an animal tied to his body', radiating a 'verdant glory' (pp. 84–5). Range Wah-Wah, who is so un-possessive that he does not even worry about the whereabouts of his sheep ('I set them free, like I myself am, and see them only when *they* want to see me', p. 85), induces in the protagonist a mystical communion with the forest. However, fear of his father brings him back to the village before he has had a chance to glimpse Wah-Wah's mythically colourful sheep. But Hussain, his friend who later becomes the first young man to disappear through the 'secret tracks' to Pakistan-occupied Kashmir, stays behind, oblivious to the family's demands for obedience. Through these opposed pathways of the *gujjar*'s relationship to nature, then, Waheed encodes a lament for his divided self, a Kashmiri who would be free like Azad Range Wah-Wah in his one-ness with the forest, but who loves his mother, and her miniaturized kitchen garden, too much to let go.

Endangered Species and Secret Tracks

These compromises include the circulation of the book and the author within the literary festival circuit in India, which has offered Kashmiri authors a new visibility and a new platform from which to launch their battles. Yet the irony of incorporation into a parallel regime of conformity within the supposedly democratic space of the postcolony is never lost on the Kashmiri cultural producer, who has to constantly tread the fine line between resistance and co-optation as he or she plays to the gallery of the Indian liberal intelligentsia. This irony itself becomes the subject of the Kashmiri cartoonist Sajad's auto-referential graphic novella *Terrorism of Peace* (Sajad 2011). A young cartoonist for a Kashmiri newspaper (just like Sajad himself) is picked up by the police at a Delhi internet café as he tries to email his daily cartoon to his employers. The police, and a gathering mob, treat him as brutally as they do the average Kashmiri Muslim youth. Ironically, our protagonist is in Delhi to exhibit his artwork on 2010's stone-throwing revolution in Kashmir. The shaken cartoonist manages to return to the exhibition site, but decides to smash the art installation with an act of stone-throwing. This keen awareness of the multiple ironies around the Kashmiri cultural producer in liberal India's 'exhibitionary complex' (for the phrase, see Bennett 1988) frames Sajad's invocation of the Hangul deer within his other graphic novella, *Endangered Species*, which also enables us to return to the issue I began with: Kashmiri environmentalism's reclaiming of vernacular modernity.

The threat of extinction that hangs over the Hangul deer, a species confined to the region of Jammu and Kashmir, is a trope frequently encountered in conversation with Kashmiris about their political and cultural fate. I have elsewhere discussed in detail the evolution and deployment of this trope within poetry, prose and photography from Kashmir (Kabir 2009, pp. 140–50). Indeed, it was actually a news report of Sajad's use of the Hangul deer in his illustrations that first drew my attention to his work. In *Endangered Species*, which recounts the stories and motivations of some of Kashmir's stone-throwers, Sajad chooses to depict all his Kashmiri characters as human beings with the antlered heads of the Hangul. The Hangul head is clearly a privileged icon for him, for he even chooses a more stylized version of it as his personal logo on his website. A precedent for this use of a composite animal–human figure may be found in Art Spiegelman's famous graphic novel of Holocaust survivors and their descendants, *Maus*, in which all the characters are depicted with heads of mice (Spiegelman 1986). As a graphic novelist, Sajad would have surely come across the guru of all graphic novels, and particularly one whose concerns with trauma and its retelling (Hirsch 1997) resonate so closely with his agenda of preserving and disseminating knowledge of Kashmir's heritage in resistance to conflict. Like Spiegelman's half-human, half-mouse characters, Sajad's Hangul-humans shock the viewer out of complacency, generating a dissonance through which to calibrate the effects of trauma on the reporting subject.

Just as Spiegelman's choice of a mouse was dictated by specific discursive inheritance (the vilification of Jews as vermin by the Nazis) so too is Sajad's choice of the Hangul, an endangered species native to Kashmir, of discursive significance within the context of the Kashmir conflict, especially given my observations on its ubiquity as a trope. However, the surreal logic of Sajad's illustrations releases the Hangul from Kashmir's forests into the urban space of Srinagar. Sajad thereby transplants the pastoral's concern with the natural beauty of Kashmir, which eulogizes the lake complex of Srinagar but not its downtown areas, precisely to those areas out of bounds for the landscape-seeking tourist. The implosion of the Hangul's forested habitat into the urban habitat of bored Kashmiri teenagers seeking an outlet through stone-pelting is Sajad's 'new pastoral'. Furthermore, his interest lies, as his website *Kashmir in Black and White* reveals (Sajad 2011), in reclaiming the Kashmiri landscape in conjunction with the Kashmiri vernacular architectural heritage. His illustrations play with the importance of wood for this heritage, which is part of a rich crafts tradition: themselves reminiscent of woodcuts, they repeatedly depict the typical wooden latticed windows of older buildings in downtown Srinagar. His personal space of expression and self-representation thus takes the environmental discourse of saving an endangered species from extinction to update an internal conversation amongst Kashmiris. The de-territorialized technology of the web, which addresses the Indian public sphere and goes beyond it, brings that conversation into a wider arena.

But, as the citation from Kashmiri poet Zareef Ahmad Zareef on the homepage of Sajad's website confirms (Sajad 2011), the Hangul deer is not a mere metaphor; rather, it functions metonymically within a larger whole. 'Who stole the fragrance from my rose?' Zareef's poem asks, 'was it a conspiracy of autumn and spring? Whom should I ask?' The residual romance of these images is pressed out by the subsequent confession that involves bodily labour but also bitterness: 'I sowed seed on the mounds and left my paddy crop desolated. Now nettle has grown out of my crop. Whom should I ask?' The overall effect, heightened through repetition ('whom should I ask?'), is of a dislocation of inherited knowledge on how to best use the land and its resources, leaving nettles and desolation in its wake. Yet in placing these questions alongside the Hangul-head, Sajad offers a composite effort to articulate for the Kashmiri, for India, and for the world a mode of indigenous belonging that goes beyond the fetish of the pastoral. His 'endangered species', let loose in downtown Srinagar, signals a deep disorder in the moral universe which must be set right in order to fulfil the promise of an immanent new Kashmir. In another panel on his website, a hand whose digits morph into mass graves, mountains and Kashmiri women, is framed on one side, Guernica-like, by a marching row of Hangul heads, and on the other, by a Hangul-headed youth confronting an army vehicle.

This coexistence of the surreal, the disrupted, and the rooted is the continuum on which the ordinary Kashmiri leads his or her life. Yet the satirical and dark narrative content of his images are balanced by their fairy-tale, naïve visual quality that takes us back to the more innocent worlds of childhood, the 'secret tracks' of the Collaborator's world when he was a boy. Indeed, a visual equivalent of these tracks appears in one of Sajad's illustrations that show a panoramic view of undulating hills and valleys, studded by not-to-scale villages announced by name on the illustration's surface, and connected by black lines signifying roads or pathways. This infantilized map subverts cartography and roadways, both key tools of postcolonial control, to re-insert 'Kashmir' within a home-grown vernacular world crystallized in the place names of Kashmiri villages and small towns. The association of this world with childhood is the defence mechanism of the adult who came of age during the 1990s and 2000s, through the mundane brutalization of life in a conflict zone. Kashmiri cultural producers of successive age groups, such as Waheed, an adolescent in the 1990s, and Sajad, an infant at that period, use different technologies and media of creative expression, but they share an interest in reclaiming the lost innocence of childhood through a combined turn to their environment and their vernacular cultural heritage to mount new forms of resistance and resilience. The rhizomatic cycle tracks across the Valley, which the KBM traversed through its 'zalgur events', enact the body's reclaiming of space, time and history.

Between 2003 and 2006, I travelled to Srinagar several times a year to conduct research for a book that was eventually published in 2009. Although not that long ago, the time of this travel already feels like a distant memory of a time apart, and it was probably so in more ways than one. In retrospect, the 'noughties' were a decade suspended between the overt violence of the 1990s and the resurgence of resistance in 2010; an interregnum between the Kalashnikovs and the *kani jung* (stone-pelting war). Looking back, it was also the period when liberalization and globalization were slowly penetrating the Valley in below-the-radar ways, and the coming generation of stone-pelters were preparing for their new assault on the Indian state. At that time, it did not seem so at all. In the mid- to late-2000s, the Valley seemed a place quite apart from all the social, cultural and economic transformations taking place across most of India. Srinagar was the city where you had to relinquish the use of your mobile phone, the place where you could not rely on walking into a cybercafé to check your email on a daily basis (forget about Wi-Fi hotspots and the like). Its urban geography was marked by the traces of conflict as well as the psychology of resistance. Everywhere, there were bunkers on the one hand, half-finished buildings on the other: 'the rooms that were never finished', in the words of poet Agha Shahid Ali (2003).

In the summer of 2010, two decades on from the emergence of armed militancy in the Valley, India witnessed a resurgence of protest here. The weapons were no longer the Kalashnikovs that were so obviously an outside import. Now, young people picked up the stones from the Kashmiri ground and hurled them at those they considered to be standing between themselves and the freedom to be themselves. This was done without coercion or humiliation. Simultaneously, there sprung up a prolific stream of commentary about these events on social media sites, most prominently Facebook. From those commentators, many Kashmiri in origin, we learnt that stone-pelting, or *kani jung*, was an ancient and indigenous form of protest in the Valley. One must see in that most unsophisticated tool of protest, indigenous both in its origin and deployment, a forceful return of the repressed ordinary, which adheres to the material object of and from Kashmir in order to launch its projectile course into the spectacle of 'shining India'. This interruptive and unpredictable trajectory from Kashmir is now in the hands of a new generation of cultural producers that includes Sajad, Kashmiri rappers and Kashmiri cyclists, all of whom use Facebook, YouTube and Myspace to carve a niche in cyber-territory. Their efforts are consolidated by members of the 'older guard' such as Waheed, who personally experienced the militarization of the 1990s, and who have matured into users of more conventional print media and publishing networks. Both generations of cultural producers share the desire and ability to 'scramble the codes' (Deleuze and Guattari 1983, p. xxi) of public culture in contemporary India in order to make their experiences of Kashmir accessible to the wider world. The environmentalist language and sentiments that they use for their interventions are both a continuation of pre-existing Kashmiri modes of asserting indigenous claims to a territory much desired by others, as well as a new response to one of South Asia's oldest conflicts.[1]

Note

1. Many of the themes in Malik Sajad's internet-based graphic work analysed in this chapter are developed in his recent graphic novel *Munnu: A boy from Kashmir* (2015), which appeared too late to be discussed here.

Works Cited

Ali, A. S. (2003). *Rooms are never finished*. New York: Norton.
Bennett, T. (1988). The exhibitionary complex. *New Formations, 4*, 73–102.
Deleuze, G., & Guattari, F. (1983). *Anti-Oedipus: Capitalism and schizophrenia* (R. Huxley et al., Trans.). Minneapolis: University of Minnesota Press.
Empson, W. (1974). *Some versions of pastoral*. New York: New Directions Publishing.
Gifford, T. (1999). *Pastoral*. London: Routledge.
Hirsch, M. (1997). *Family frames: Photography, narrative, and postmemory*. Cambridge, MA: Harvard University Press.
Huggan, G., & Tiffin, H. (2007). Green postcolonialism. *Interventions, 9*(1), 1–11.
Huggan, G., & Tiffin, H. (2009). *Postcolonial ecocriticism: Literature, animals, environment*. London: Routledge.
Jaitly, J. (Ed.). (1999). *Crafts of Jammu, Kashmir and Ladakh*. Ahmedabad: Mapin and Co.
Kabir, A. J. (2005). Nipped in the bud: Pleasure and politics in the 1960s Kashmir films. *SAPC, 1*(2), 141–160.
Kabir, A. J. (2009). *Territory of desire: Representing the valley of Kashmir*. Minneapolis: University of Minnesota Press.
Kabir, A. J. (2011). Cartographic irresolution and the line of control. *Social Text, 27*(4), 45–66.
Kabir, A. J.(2013, Summer). 'You can only appreciate Kashmir through the cycle pace': Reclaiming Kasheer through Zalgur. *Kashmir Lit: An Online Journal of Kashmiri and Diasporic Writing* [Online]. Available from http://www.kashmirlit.org/category/archive/2013-summer/. Accessed 9 Aug 2013.
Kashmir Bicycle Movement. (2013). [Online]. Available from https://www.facebook.com/KashmirBicycleMovement?fref=ts. Accessed 8 Aug 2013.
KEWA (Kashmir Environmental Watch Association). (n.d.). [Online]. Available from http://www.kewa.org. Accessed 8 Aug 2013.
Khanna, R. (2003). *Dark continents: Psychoanalysis and colonialism*. Durham: Duke University Press.
Morey, P. (2015). Hamlet in paradise: The politics of procrastination in Mirza Waheed's *The collaborator*. In C. Chambers & C. Herbert (Eds.), *Imagining Muslims in South Asia and the diaspora: Secularism, religion, representations* (pp. 97–112). Abingdon/New York: Routledge.
Mukherjee, P. (2006). Surfing the second waves: Amitav Ghosh's tide country. *New Formations, 15*, 144–157.
Nehru, J. (2004). *The discovery of India*. Delhi: Penguin India.
Sajad, M. (2011). *Kashmir in black and white* [Online]. Available from http://kashmirblackandwhite.com. [Site currently under construction]. Accessed Sept 2012.

Sajad, M. (2015). *Munnu: A boy from Kashmir*. London: Harper Collins.
Spiegelman, A. (1986). *Maus I: A survivor's tale: My father bleeds history*. New York: Pantheon.
Spivak, G. C. (1987). *In other worlds: Essays in cultural politics*. London: Taylor and Francis.
Taussig, M. (1993). *Mimesis and alterity: A particular history of the senses*. New York: Routledge.
Waheed, M. (2012a). *The collaborator*. Delhi: Penguin India.
Waheed, M. (2012b). Public reading of *The collaborator* at Leeds Metropolitan University.
Williams, R. (1973). *The country and the city*. Oxford: Oxford University Press.
Younghusband, F. (1909). *Kashmir*. London: Adam and Charles Black.

Solidarity, Suffering and 'Divine Violence': Fictions of the Naxalite Insurgency

Pavan Kumar Malreddy

A bonded labourer who is ill-treated by his landlord feels that the latter has no heart. So, when the peasants attack the landlord's house, the labourer says that he would like to kill his master himself and check whether he has a heart underneath his ribcage. (Pandita 2011, p. 134)

VIOLENCE AND COUNTER-VIOLENCE

After the killing of the high-ranked police officer K.S. Vyas in Hyderabad in January 1993, the People's War squad member Mohammed Nayeemuddin alias Nayeem was offered a deal by the Andhra Pradesh police department, allegedly under the orders of the then Home Minister A. Madhava Reddy: to buy his freedom he was to organize the murders of top Maoist leaders with the help of a criminal gang run by his brothers. Even before his release, Nayeem's gang would mastermind a spate of killings under police protection, but the most shocking of them was the brutal murder of a Maoist sympathizer and a revolutionary singer called Belli Lalitha in 1999, whose body was cut into 17 pieces and thrown into wells and lakes around the Bhonagir district (Sridhar 2012). Buoyed by the ruthlessness

---

P. K. Malreddy
Institute of English and American Studies,
Goethe-University Frankfurt am Main, Germany

of Nayeem's gang, during the 1990s the state of Andhra Pradesh would go on to fund and sponsor a number of anti-Maoist groups with names like Fear Vikas, Green Tigers, Narsa Cobras and Nallamalla Nallatrachu, among others, which would inspire the Salwa Judum ('Purification Hunt')—a private army of anti-Maoists—in Chhattisgarh a decade later. When the Maoists finally captured the Salwa Judum's founder, Mahendra Karma, a local legislator, in October 2013 in an ambush near the town of Dharba, they 'fired 30 to 40 bullets' into his body and 'smashed his head with the butt of their guns *after* killing him' (Singh 2013, para. 5; italics added).

Could the brutality of these killings by both Maoists and government-sponsored militias be merely a matter of personal revenge, political retribution or 'redemptive' justice? How do we make sense of this seemingly excessive violence? Should we see it as a response to the excessive violence of state power or a form of 'divine violence'—a term which Slavoj Žižek borrows from Walter Benjamin (Žižek 2008, p. 199, 2009, p. 483)? This chapter responds to the theoretical implications of these questions about the violence carried out by non-state actors such as the Naxalites in India. While uncovering the discursive limits of narrating violence in popular media, journalism and other fictional and non-fictional works, the chapter attends to alternative representations of the Naxalite insurgency in three recent novels: Diti Sen's *Red Skies and Falling Stars* (2012), Jhumpa Lahiri's *The Lowland* (2013) and Diptendra Raychaudhuri's *Seeing Through the Stones* (2007).

In the post-9/11 context, as 'most international actors were not keen to distinguish between "insurgencies" and "terrorist outfits"' (Fair 2005, p. 12), armed rebellions in the postcolonial world fell prey to the global 'war on terror' discourse led by the USA and its allies. In India, 2 weeks after the 9/11 attacks, the then Foreign Minister Jaswant Singh labelled the Maoists terrorists, a tag the succeeding Congress government endorsed by proclaiming the insurgency as '"the Gravest Internal Security Threat" to India ' (Roy 2010, section 8). According to critics, the pro-American stand of the Indian state helped consolidate its counter-terrorism strategy by framing all insurgency-related activity arising from both within and outside of the national borders as 'terrorist' acts (Roy 2010; Myrdal 2012, pp. 83–5). By challenging this uneasy conflation of insurgency violence with terrorism, this chapter draws upon Emmanuel Levinas's notion of 'useless suffering' and Slavoj Žižek's distinction between subjective and objective violence. The chapter benefits from Frank Schulze-

Engler's critique of the 'enchanted solidarity' of intellectuals and writers in endorsing anti-colonial or anti-oppressive resistance movements, which helps situate Žižek's and Levinas's theses on political violence in the postcolonial context.

According to Levinas (1998, p. 96), 'useless suffering' refers to the rationalization of the suffering of 'the neighbors' or 'others' in the guise of theodicy—'a vindication of divine justice in the face of evil' (Martin 2011, p. 162). In the post-9/11 context, as Joseph Pugliese (2013, pp. 5–11) observes, such theodicy has assumed secular forms, while rendering certain forms of suffering as socially acceptable (for example, the terrorists') and inducing 'a meaning and order in a suffering that is essentially gratuitous, absurd, and apparently arbitrary' (Levinas 1998, p. 96). Against this, Levinas calls for an ethical suffering through 'the suffering of suffering' (p. 94), or what critics have dubbed as 'non-useless' or 'useful' suffering (Pugliese 2013), by which the suffering *in the Other* can be made useful and meaningful by acknowledging the 'suffering in me for the unjustifiable suffering of the other' (Levinas 1998, p. 94). Slavoj Žižek's notion of subjective violence, too, resonates with Levinas's critique of the norms that construct socially acceptable violence through which the suffering of the Other can be justified. Žižek argues that subjective violence is generally presented in the media and popular discourses as a 'brutal exposition of violence', such as terrorist violence, which is carried out by an identifiable subject. Such violence, however, conceals what Žižek calls objective violence: 'the more subtle forms of coercion that sustain relations of domination and exploitation' (2008, p. 9). On the basis of this distinction, Žižek reformulates Walter Benjamin's notion of divine violence as a response to objective violence, one that is distinguished from ideologically motivated violence, be it terrorist, state or revolutionary violence:

> When those outside the structured social field strike 'blindly,' demanding and enacting immediate justice/vengeance, this is divine violence. Recall, a decade or so ago, the panic in Rio de Janeiro when crowds descended from the favelas into the rich part of the city and started looting and burning supermarkets. This was indeed divine violence. (2008, p. 202)

Both Levinas's and Žižek's observations on the violence of the oppressed and the ethics of suffering have special relevance to the politics of representation in postcolonial literature. In the context of anti-colonial liberation struggles, for instance, Frank Schulze-Engler identifies 'enchanted solidarity' as the unconditional support extended by academic, intellectual and artistic communities to a group of people on the basis of the collective, systemic injustices brought forth by oppressive regimes. For Schulze-Engler (2015), such unconditional solidarity fails to anticipate, or even account for, the internal disunity of what he calls the 'disenchanted solidarity' of the anti-colonial liberation movements at large, as evinced in the unfulfilled promises of anti-colonial nationalism (of Fanon, Cabral or Hồ Chí Minh).

These conceptual injections into post-9/11 discourses on terrorist violence, I shall contend, create space for new avenues of theoretical inquiry into the organized violence of non-state actors. In particular, challenging the normative discourses on armed insurgencies since the 1970s, which have been absorbed into sub-nationalist discourses in the postcolonial world (Burke III 1998), and those that have been recast under the umbrella term 'terrorism' in the post-9/11 context, this chapter contends that insurgency violence cannot be understood as a mere response, or in relation, to the state violence 'from above'. Since 9/11, the Naxalite insurgency in India has come to be portrayed as just that: a redemptive, derivative yet alternative ideology to the state's systemic violence, an extremist organization driven by the sovereign ambitions of sub-regional, secular and even tribal nationalism. Such views, often reinforced by the enchanted solidarity for the oppressed, fail to register the ideological and organizational fractures that undermine the liberationist tendencies of the non-state violence 'from below'.

Parallel Sovereignty and Enchanted Solidarity

Inspired by the Maoist doctrine of 'proletarian revolution', the Naxalite movement began in May 1967 as an uprising against landlords in the eponymous village of Naxalbari in the Darjeeling district of West Bengal. Made up of landless villagers and lower-caste labourers, the Naxalites also had a strong *adivasi* tribal base and included Santals, Mariyas, Gonds of Orissa and Girijans of Andhra Pradesh from the start in the fight against 'the annihilation of class enemies' (see Malreddy 2014, p. 596). In the mid-1970s, the Naxalite movement expanded its base into the cities, and the neighbouring regions of Bihar and Telangana as a result of a massive crackdown by the West Bengal state (Chakravarti 2007, p. 97). Between the 1980s and 1990s, the movement broke into several factions such as CPI (ML) People's War, Party Unity, and Janashakti. In October 2004, the two largest factions, CPI (ML) People's War and the Maoist Communist Center (Bihar), merged to form the CPI (Maoist).

For decades, the Indian state saw Maoism as an internal security problem, although it was only in the wake of 9/11 attacks, and particularly after signing a series of agreements for the excavation of mineral resources with transnational corporations such as Tata, ESSAR and Vedanta in the insurgency-affected areas in 2006 (which was met with opposition by some 45 tribal organizations across Chhattisgarh, West Bengal, and Orissa), that Maoists were represented as a 'terrorist' threat (Roy 2010). Despite the fact that clashes between the Indian state, state-sponsored private armies and the Maoists have taken a deadly turn in the past decade and a half, the 'official' accounts of the conflict—custodial killings, 'encounter' killings, outright executions—remain highly unreliable, due to their propagandist nature. As Sudeep Chakravarti notes, '[t]he central Ministry of Home Affairs prefers not to release much of the data on Maoist activity and planning that its own intelligence agencies, in collaboration with the police apparatus of the affected states, have gathered' (2007, p. 103).

It is thus not surprising to note that academic literature on the Naxalite insurgency suffers from the same limitations as popular media, and to a lesser extent journalism: it is often hampered by limited access to first-hand sources, lack of adequate ethnographic or independent empirical studies and, in most cases, the problem of how to contend with the propaganda literature emanating from state and revolutionary sources (Chakrabarty and Kujur 2012; Paul 2013). Accordingly, much of the secondary literature on the Naxalite insurgency tends to simply reiterate and rehistoricize the causes, conditions and 'failures' of the state as well as of the extreme Left in India, resulting in the Manichean reading of the conflict as a '"state versus the revolutionaries" battle' (Chakravarti 2007, p. 97), or what Achille Mbembe would in a different context call the axis of 'vertical sovereignty' (2003, p. 29).

Such a perspective, far from registering the shifting political alliances that cut across caste, ethnic and tribal identities among the insurgents, ideologues and other stakeholders, ascribes a certain sovereign character to the Naxalite insurgency, often reinforcing the latter's self-appointed rhetoric of an 'armed struggle for a new democratic revolution' waged against the failed Indian democracy. It is only recently that the 'literary turn', ushered in by Arundhati Roy's well-known travelogue *Walking with the Comrades* (2010), bore witness to a new wave of writings on the Naxalite insurgency: testimonies, travelogues, reportage narratives, memoirs and journalistic accounts. Shifting the focus from state violence to the organization of insurgency violence—the mobilization of armed squads, ground level operations and the 'parallel governments' administered by the Maoists in the so-called 'liberated zones'—this set of works portrays violence of the insurgency as 'mythic violence' (Žižek n.d.), one that is inspired by sovereign aspirations of establishing a new state and a new rule of law. In Roy's aforementioned *Walking with the Comrades*, for instance, the Naxalite insurgency is legitimized as a sovereign struggle for authentic nationalism by depicting the existing sovereignty as morally illegitimate:

> Almost from the moment India became a sovereign nation, it turned into a colonial power, annexing territory, waging war. It has never hesitated to use military interventions to address political problems—Kashmir, Hyderabad, Goa, Nagaland, Manipur, Telangana, Assam, Punjab, the Naxalite uprising in West Bengal, Bihar, Andhra Pradesh and now across the tribal areas of Central India. (Roy 2010, section 14)

It is against this very hyperbolic formulation that Roy's narrative takes on a literary dimension by constructing protagonists and antagonists, through emotionally charged characters such as Mahendra Karma and Chidambaram (as villains) and Comrade Venu and Chandu (as heroes).

Satnam's *Jangalnama: Travels in a Maoist Guerrilla Zone* (2010), a reportage work translated from Punjabi, documents the 'everyday' struggles of the *adivasis* in the Bastar region of Chhattisgarh. Based on his travels in the Maoist 'liberated zones' in 2001, Satnam's narrative builds on the views of anonymous and fictionalized tribal insurgents, covering the history of their association with Naxalites from the 1980s, following their failed resistance against Bailadilla (iron ore) mines owned by Japanese companies in the 1970s, to the 'white terror' campaign of the Indian state led by the aforementioned Salwa Judum in 2006. Like Roy's travelogue, Satnam's enchanted solidarity for the insurgency moves through an excessive dramatization, if not romanticization, of the jungle life, or 'life as lived in a pastoral society' (2010, p. 96) against the 'lust profiteers' (p. 132) of the Indian mainstream. Lumping the *adivasis* of the Bastar region and the Indian Maoists together, Satnam claims that their ultimate objective is marching to Delhi to establish a 'permanent tribal right over jal, jungle aur zameen' (p. 94). By positioning himself as the narrator of *Jangalnama*, Satnam employs an unusual blend of literary journalism and fictionalized historical and collective memory, as evinced in his inconsistent, haphazard, at times contradictory portrayal of *adivasis* as progressive revolutionaries on the one hand (pp. 98–9, 127) and naive, jungle-bound, neglected and oppressed indigenous communities on the other (pp. 144–5).

Gautam Navlakha's 'Days and Nights in the Heartland of Rebellion' (2010), another reportage work set in the Bastar region, builds on the metaphor of the 'people's war' waged against the state: 'They want an alternative democratic model, which only Maoists are today in a position to demonstrate because they alone hold base areas i.e. something distinct and outside the pale of the system' (2010, 'What Do I Believe?', para. 23). Navlakha goes to great lengths to narrate this alternative model known as the Revolutionary People's Committee; its origins, structure, administration and execution of public policy in their liberated zones—from revenue collection and health care to agrarian development—all mimic the sovereignty of the (absent) state. In this way, the semi-fictional and non-fictional works build on an enchanted solidarity for the causes of the insurgency, while depicting its postrevolutionary idealism as a viable, if not a competing, alternative to the state's failed sovereignty.

(DIS)ENCHANTED SOLIDARITY AND USELESS SUFFERING

Unlike the non-fictional and semi-fictional accounts detailed above, fictional works on the Naxalite movement reveal an internal shift from enchanted to 'disenchanted' solidarity. This is particularly the case with two recent novels, Diti Sen's *Red Skies and Falling Stars* and Jhumpa Lahiri's *The Lowland*, which feature urban middle-class protagonists who join the Naxalite movement by empathizing with the objective violence of oppressed, unidentifiable subjects, against the subjective violence of identifiable agents—police, paramilitary forces, insurgents, fighters or their victims.[1] In Sen's novel, which spans four decades of Naxalite insurgency, the youngest of the three sisters, Rumi, narrates the spread of the Naxalite uprising into the affluent neighbourhood of Moghal Serai in Calcutta. Like the entire student generation of the 1960s, Amu, Rumi's older sister, begins to challenge her bourgeois privileges, 'questioning why we had everything while the others we saw around us had nothing'

---

[1] See Neel Mukherjee's novel *The Lives of Others* (2014) for a more situated historical account of the urban response to the Naxalite movement in 1960s Calcutta.

(Sen 2012, p. 31). For sisters Rumi and Shiela, their subjective response to the Naxalites as seasoned '*goondas* [...] having a field day' (p. 27) effectively undermines the objective conditions that led to the insurgency. As in Rumi's confession, whenever Amu spoke of the 'man-made suffering all around us [...] Shiela and I would gape at her, wondering who she was referring to, wondering who were these "others" she spoke of. We couldn't see anyone suffering all that much in our lives' (p. 31).

However, it is only after Amu's mysterious disappearance from the family that Rumi's perspective shifts from that of 'denial of oppression' to 'disenchanted solidarity' for the oppressed. Amu's unwarranted decision to join the Naxalites not only disrupts the stability of Rumi's bourgeois upbringing but in doing so, it enables her to understand the objective violence that led to her sister's path. Retracing Amu's journey into the insurgency areas through her narrative eye, Rumi begins to empathize with the plight of the *adivasis*: 'the original inhabitants of the country [...] had been driven increasingly farther from their original habitats [...] [and] were terrorized and threatened, resulting in abject poverty' (p. 72). Yet, Rumi's increasing solidarity for the *adivasis* remains firmly 'disenchanted' insofar as she refuses to sacrifice her bourgeois privileges for the welfare of the former. Years after Amu's disappearance, for instance, Rumi resents the improvements made in *adivasi* lives due to the Naxalite presence near her family's second home in Ghatshila, rural Bihar, and when the *adivasi* housekeeper Koda's son Mangaldas shows no signs of servitude or submissiveness like his father, she finds him irreverent and arrogant (p. 129).

Amu's stint with the Naxalites ends with the death of her nameless husband in combat and, following her capture and release from prison, she moves to Provence in France. Upon her return following her father's death, she reflects on her decision to leave the insurgency:

> Yes, I did believe in it but once we were in the countryside and I saw the killing, the brutality, the terror that was being unleashed in the name of civil justice, it was very difficult, I couldn't reconcile the two, the ideals and the method used. (p. 154)

Evidently, Amu's endorsement of the insurgency, too, grows into 'disenchanted solidarity', as she invokes subjective violence as the source of her disenchantment, as opposed to the objective violence that drew her to Naxalism in the first place. Yet, in an attempt to offset the middle-class guilt of the two estranged sisters, having survived the threat of Naxalism in their own life trajectories, Sen introduces an external, sacrificial character named Ishaan, a distant cousin of the sisters from Canada, who arrives in India to do research on Naxalism. Curiously, Ishaan's character enters as Amu disappears from the narrative; in Chapter 18, Sen interjects an experimental move, in which Ishaan assumes the narrator's role (p. 177). Consequently, Ishaan's narrative eye provides a first-hand account of the suffering of *adivasi* characters such as Parboti and Kanai, whom he encounters during his research in the Naxalite-controlled areas of Birbhum. Yet, Ishaan finds it irresistible to compare Amu's enchanted solidarity with Parboti's objective violence:

> From my Mashi to Parboti. The ever widening gap yawned in my face. Yet they were bound by the common cause. The beautiful, fragile, orchid-like, upper-class Amu and the hardbitten, unlettered, underprivileged, driven Parboti. Revolutionaries? Anti-socials? Criminals? Or simply, women, humans, fighting a continued battle to balance the order of things, to even out the distribution of justice? (p. 224)

As Ishaan's narrative eye helps justify Amu's enchanted solidarity for the Naxalites, Sen goes on to reinstate Rumi as the homodiegetic narrator in the final chapter to reflect upon Ishaan's death in a 'police encounter':

> Could his death be the start of a public quest to reinstate those forgotten people, could it become an episode which shone the spotlight on how innocents were being slaughtered in the crossfire between the elected and the rebels? Could his death have a significance that went far beyond its immediate mundane reality, to become a symbol of all that was going so wrong in our society, of all that needed to be put right? (p. 236)

In portraying Ishaan as the ultimate martyr of the Naxalite insurgency, Rumi's judgement fails to capture the divine violence of the dispossessed *self* that Žižek ('Robespierre' n.d.) defines as

> a decision (to kill, to risk or lose one's own life) made in the absolute solitude, with no cover in the big Other. [...] The motto of divine violence is fiat iustitia, pereat mundus: it is JUSTICE, the point of non-distinction between justice and vengeance, in which 'people' (the anonymous part of no-part) imposes its terror and makes other parts pay the price—the Judgment Day for the long history of oppression, exploitation, suffering. ('Robespierre' n.d., para 6)

In Sen's narrative, neither Rumi nor Amu nor Ishaan represents the 'absolute solitude' forged by the *recipients* of objective violence as they tendentiously invoke 'the big Other' in the name of enchanted, disenchanted and even guilt-ridden solidarity. It is only the likes of Kanai—the tribal woman who dies in combat, but remains conspicuously absent from Rumi's reflections on the martyrdom of 'forgotten people'—who represent the 'absolute solitude [...] demanding AND enacting immediate justice/vengeance' (Žižek, 'Robespierre' n.d., paras. 5–6).

Here, Žižek is careful to distinguish divine violence from the violence in the name of 'any other Leftist dream of a "pure" event' in which violence is relegated to a revolutionary organization or a sovereign authority with its mythical function of law or 'state founding' ('cover of the big Other'). Žižek further asserts that divine violence is essentially foregrounded by objective violence, one that breeds the very dispossession (as in 'solitude') of the violating subject. By virtue of this, any form of external solidarity arising from enchanted or disenchanted subject positions is essentially a partial, if not a mythic, response to subjective violence, as in the case of middle-class characters who represent the Naxalites in Sen's novel.

Featuring yet another urban middle-class family affected by Naxalite violence, Jhumpa Lahiri's *The Lowland*, too, fails to resolve such representational impasses of the agency as well as the agents of divine violence. Udayan, younger brother of Subhash—both sons of a railway clerk living in Calcutta—makes no secret of his enchanted solidarity for the Naxalbari: 'Of course it was worth it. They rose up. They risked everything. People with nothing. People those in power do nothing to protect' (Lahiri 2013, p. 21). He goes as far as to challenge Subhash to imagine: 'If you were born into that life, what would you do?' (p. 21).

A year after the Naxalbari uprising in 1967, Udayan joins the insurgency, leaving his wife Gauri with his parents. Subhash, who moves to Rhode Island to do a PhD in Chemistry, returns to Calcutta after Udayan's execution in a police encounter, marries a pregnant Gauri and takes her along to Rhode Island to save her from his conservative parents and harassment by the police about her possible involvement with the Naxalites. Soon after Gauri's move to Rhode Island, where she gives birth to Bela, the narrative focus shifts from Naxalism to the effects of Udayan's death on the three generations of their family. As the narrator recounts:

> Udayan had given his life to a movement that had been misguided, that had caused only damage, that had already been dismantled. The only thing he'd altered was what their family had been. (p. 115)

Unable to reconcile herself with Udayan's death, and unwilling to consummate her marriage, Gauri leaves her daughter Bela with Subhash to pursue her academic ambitions in California. As Bela enters her teens, she, too, withdraws from her stepfather and leaves him to work on a farm, leading a life without fixed address or insurance—a mark of Udayan's renegade character.

Given that Udayan's death becomes the source of the instability, suffering and loss for three generations of his family, I concur with Jennifer Marquardt's (2014) reading that, in *The Lowland*,

> [t]his understanding of personal historical trajectories is also applied to political historical events. While Gauri indulges in constructing a version of her life that contains Udayan, the novel poses the same question of the impossibly idealistic and violent Naxalite movement. (2014, p. 2)

Sure enough, throughout *The Lowland*, the failure of Naxalism in its idealistic pursuit of equality and justice provides the 'dramatic buffer' necessary for the agony of familial failures in maintaining stability, unity and harmony. Marquardt draws attention to the connection between these parallel narratives—familial and political:

> While it is possible to understand the Naxalite movement and Udayan himself as idealized entities and their subsequent failures and deaths as historical events, Gauri can only comprehend each as the moment when history shifted in the wrong direction, away from the intended trajectory of what should have been her life: marital bliss, an equalized India that she might never have left. (2014, p. 2)

Nina Martyris (2014) takes this view of failed idealism a step further by arguing that 'Udayan's family is shattered not just by his death but by what he has done for the revolution. If three generations of a family can be crippled by a single act of violence, asks *The Lowland*, what sort of utopia will be built out of blood?' (2014, p. 42). In my view, although these readings accurately capture the superimposition of political emotions over familial ones, they fail to register the novel's complicity with pedagogic nationalist aspirations for stability, unity and continuity. The disunity of Udayan's family in *The Lowland*, for instance, can be read as an allegorical representation of the threat posed by Naxalism to the desired homogeneity of India. Yet, given that the narrative constantly strives to reunite a broken family, Udayan's refusal to concede the internal ruptures of the family can be compared to pedagogic discourses of nationalism that fail to register the deferred nationalism of the Naxalites. As a result, not only is Udayan's death in *The Lowland* rendered as a failed case of divine violence, but it makes a compelling case for Levinas's 'useless suffering'. For instance, the moments before his surrender and execution, a dejected Udayan reckons:

> in this case it had fixed nothing, helped no one. In this case there was to be no revolution. He knew this now. If he was worth nothing, then why was he so desperate to save himself? Why, in the end, did the body not obey the brain? (Lahiri 2013, p. 334)

Like Amu's and Ishaan's fate in Sen's novel, it is his enchanted solidarity for Naxalism that becomes Udayan's undoing. With no inkling or insight into the objective violence of the peasants, tribals and insurgents who rebelled, except for the theoretical knowledge that '[t]hey risked everything' (p. 21), *The Lowland* portrays Udayan as the sole representative of the Naxalites through the lens of subjective violence. As the novel invests heavily in the idiom of Udayan's death as the ultimate outcome of Naxalism, and constructs a drama of middle-class familial pathos on that basis, it leaves no room for the subjects of objective violence to represent *their* pathos, *their* deaths and *their* suffering which is expiatory, divine and non-transcendental.

For Emmanuel Levinas, the secular theodicy of modern societies to justify the Other's suffering as 'useless', such as the suffering of the tribals who 'risked everything', can only be challenged by an ethical suffering of the Self that is inflected by the Other's suffering, a suffering that is 'useful' and is no longer 'for nothing' (Levinas 1998, p. 100). In *The Lowland*, however, Udayan's death fails to register such inter-human perspective forged by an engagement with radical alterity on a number of accounts. For Gauri, it is the futility of Udayan's death that determines her own suffering, which only results in her unforgiving choices that make the latter's death even more meaningless: 'After his death began the internal knowledge that came from remembering him, still trying to make sense of him. [...] Without that there would be nothing to haunt her. No grief' (Lahiri 2013, pp. 230–1). For the narrator, however, Udayan himself fails to 'suffer the unjustifiable suffering' of the peasants, *adivasis* or his fellow Naxalites, whom he invokes as the ultimate benefactors of his revolutionary path, but whose existence he barely acknowledges.

Divine Violence and Useful Suffering

Unlike the urban middle-class protagonists of Sen's and Lahiri's narratives, Diptendra Raychaudhuri's *Seeing Through the Stones*—a lesser-known, locally published and circulated work of fiction—provides enabling perspectives on the divine violence and ethical suffering of the lower castes, untouchables and tribals who are drawn to the Naxalite insurgency. *Seeing Through the Stones* traces the journey of Mahendra Chamar, an untouchable from rural Bihar, who grows increasingly disillusioned by the senselessness of the violence he witnesses as a member of various Naxalite splinter groups between the 1970s and 1990s. While situating his characters in the political vacuum that allows both the Maoists and the state functionaries to negotiate their respective claims and entitlements in the insurgency-affected areas, Raychaudhuri's dense, yet carefully crafted narrative debunks the 'parallel sovereignty' model of much semi-fictional and non-fictional works. When a fellow Maoist questions why they should move their bases because a road is being built, Chamar, instead of halting the state's encroachment, responds:

> Our interest should always be subservient to the greater interest of the people. [...] We are not here to serve the interest of an organisation that itself is an end. [...] we know that a government only serves the rich... but still, if they do something that helps the people, we shall not stall that. (Raychaudhuri 2007, pp. 45–6)

Not only does such intermediary positioning between the state and the people diffuse the anti-state character that is commonly attributed to the Maoists, but in doing so, it gestures towards the internal disunity of the revolutionary organization or ideology among the various splinter groups within the insurgency. When asked by a member of a rival Maoist group why he thinks of revolution 'in terms of castes only' (p. 127), excluding the upper-caste proletarians, Chamar answers:

> A poor Brahmin has his pride, his education and caste-culture. Even if he has not gone the school... he would surely inherit these from the family. [...] He can perform *puja* and earn something. He is acceptable to all. He lives in a world so far away from the world of the Untouchables! (p. 127)

These views, however, are not endorsed by the very ideology of the Emancipation Group, which would later reprimand Chamar for killing the landlords in support of his caste-war theory (pp. 78–9). Although other splinter groups of the Maoist insurgency such as MCO (Maoist Communist Organization) of Bihar operated along caste lines, Chamar would join another rival group called Party Unity (Bengal and Bihar), which worked towards building a 'mass base' along class lines, while distancing itself from the earlier Naxalite group, CPI (ML)'s theory of 'annihilation of the class enemy'.

The various internal fissures within the Naxalite–Maoist organizational nexus, which closely resonate with real-life events, and their ideological orientations to caste, class, mass lines and armed economism, as Chamar concedes, are evidently the greatest weakness of the insurgency: 'in my life time, [if] I see the Maoists have united… I will die with a hope' (p. 187). Curiously, Chamar arrives at this conclusion after flirting with every Maoist doctrine in postindependence India: the Communist Party of India (CPI), CPI (ML), Emancipation Group, Red Salute Group, Party Unity and the MCO. As Chamar moves from one organization to the other, he grows increasingly dissatisfied with their ideologies which undermine the conditions of objective violence that inspired him to turn to a revolutionary path in the first place: he leaves the CPI because the party dissuades him from protesting the killing of a food rioter; he abandons the Emancipation Group as they fail to respond to the caste violence that affects his untouchable *tola*; he launches his own faction called Red Salute merely to respond to the violence that affects his immediate family, the rape and murder of his sister-in-law, Munni, by upper-caste men. Indeed, the defining moment of Chamar's redemptive violence, as in his innocent query addressed to his mentor, serves no 'big Other' than himself, and leaves no trace of sacrifice or idolatry other than himself: 'Do the Communists want to demolish all the *havelis* where the landlords live?' (p. 155). Here, Chamar's violence is 'divine' not only because it demands 'immediate vengeance' (Žižek, 'Robespierre' n.d., para. 6) but also because it 'redeems' the 'unity' and the 'dignity' (Fanon 2004, pp. 37, 40) of the oppressed subject, as in the words of Chamar's admirer who goes on to quote Fanon: 'violence is a cleansing force. It frees the native from his inferiority complex and from his despair and inaction; it makes him fearless and restores his self-respect' (Fanon, cited in Raychaudhuri 2007, p. 126).

In *Seeing Through the Stones*, it is not merely the Naxalite insurgency but also the state itself that is represented as a diversified, diffused and non-sovereign entity. In dealing with the Naxalites, state functionaries in the police force, such as Pascal and Ashok Sharma, hold an entirely different view from that of the state: 'the Naxalite problem should be handled with care' though the 'Special Task Force believes the Naxalites are bandits, and should be killed' (Raychaudhuri 2007, p. 203). Ashok Sharma grows progressively sympathetic to the Naxalite cause, particularly after a tribal policeman, whom he believes had every reason to join the Naxalites instead of the police force, risks his life to save Sharma's. Following this incident, Sharma encourages his wife Rani to open a medical clinic in the Naxal controlled areas, and goes so far as to challenge the views of his superiors on the root cause of Naxalism:

> I have seen young girls, dressed like fairies, throwing biscuits at the footpath and enjoying the fight over the crumbs. No empathy, no consideration. Given a chance why shouldn't those footpath-dwellers turn into Naxalites? (p. 275)

Unlike enchanted solidarity, which merely responds to subjective violence, such empathetic reception of the Other's suffering through one's own suffering is premised on the objective violence that precedes both insurgency and counter-insurgency. In Chamar's case, too, 'the suffering of suffering' is reciprocated as he foils the Naxalite plot to kill Sharma, and repents for the suffering caused by his actions: 'I killed my first wife by indifference. [...] I killed Damni by making wrong moves. And I have sacrificed my son' (p. 309). Yet, the usefulness of Chamar's suffering lies not in the apologetic gesture to the Other's suffering, but in its divine, redemptive force, which responds to the immediacy of objective violence:

> Whatever I did was correct. I had no other option. [...] They will address me as *tu*. They address each other as *aap*. They address their children as *tum* [...] because we are not human beings. Even young upper caste boys addressed my grandfather, who was a doddery old man, as *tu*. They will address me as *tu* now, because I do not possess arms. (p. 310)

It is this unhinging nexus between objective violence and ethical, non-useless suffering that provides new perspectives on the divine violence of the Maoists such as the brutal killing of Mahendra Karma, beyond the partial response evoked by the subjective violence in contemporary discourses on terrorism. As this chapter has highlighted, in the semi-fictional and non-fictional works that advocate enchanted solidarity, there is a marked tendency to respond to the subjective violence of the Naxalites in a way that fails to account for the fractures, fault lines and inherent disunity of the insurgency. Although the novels of Diti Sen and Jhumpa Lahiri reveal an internal shift from enchanted to disenchanted solidarity, their middle-class protagonists fail to translate their 'disenchantment' into ethical, non-useless suffering due to their privileged, inaccessible relationship to the domain of objective violence.

NOTE

I would like to thank Ashok Kumbamu for discussing Belli Lalitha's case and for verifying a number of historical facts related to the Naxalite movement.

WORKS CITED

Burke, E., III. (1998). Orientalism and world history: Representing middle eastern nationalism and Islamism in the twentieth century. *Theory and Society*, 27(4), 489–507.
Chakrabarty, B., & Kujur, R. K. (Eds.). (2012). *Maoism in India: Reincarnation of ultra-left wing extremism in the twenty-first century*. London: Routledge.
Chakravarti, S. (2007). *Red sun: Travels in the Naxalite country*. New Delhi: Penguin.
Fair, C. C. (2005). *Urban battlefields of South Asia: Lessons learned from Sri Lanka, India, and Pakistan*. Santa Monica: Rand Corporation.
Fanon, F. (2004). *The wretched of the earth* (R. Philcox, Trans.). New York: Grove Press. (Original work published 1961.)
Lahiri, J. (2013). *The lowland*. London: Bloomsbury.
Levinas, E. (1998). *Entre Nous: Essays on thinking-of-the-other* (M. B. Smith & B. Harshav, Trans.). New York: Columbia University Press.
Malreddy, P. K. (2014). Domesticating the 'new terrorism': The case of the Maoist insurgency in India. *The European Legacy*, 19(5), 590–605.
Marquardt, J. A. (2014). Jhumpa Lahiri *The lowlands* [sic]. *Transnational Literature*, 6(2), 1–2.
Martin, E., & Sachs, N. (2011). *The poetics of silence and the limits of representation*. Berlin and Boston: Walter de Gruyter.
Martyris, N. (2014). The Naxal novel. *Dissent*, 61(4), 38–44.
Mbembe, A. (2003). Necropolitics. *Public Culture*, 15(1), 11–40.
Mukherjee, N. (2014). *The lives of others*. London: Chatto & Windus.
Myrdal, J. (2012). *Red star over India*. Kolkata: Imprinta.
Navlakha, G. (2010, April 1). Days and nights in the heartland of rebellion. *Sanhati* [Online]. Available from http://sanhati.com/articles/2250/. Accessed 9 May 2013.

Pandita, R. (2011). *Hello, Bastar – The untold story of India's Maoist movement*. Chennai: Tranquebar Press.
Paul, S. (Ed.). (2013). *Maoist movement in India: Perspectives and counterperspectives*. London: Routledge.
Pugliese, J. (2013). *State violence and the execution of law: Biopolitical caesurae of torture, black sites, drones*. London: Routledge.
Raychaudhuri, D. (2007). *Seeing through the stones: A tale from the Maoist land*. New Delhi: Vitasta Publishing.
Roy, A. (2010, March 29). Walking with the comrades. *Outlook* [Online]. Available from http://www.outlookindia.com/printarticle.aspx?264738. Accessed 9 May 2012.
Satnam. (2010). *Jangalnama: Travels in a Maoist guerrilla zone* (V. Bharti, Trans.). Delhi: Penguin.
Schulze-Engler, F. (2015). Once were internationalists? Postcolonialism, disenchanted solidarity and the right to belong in a world of globalized modernity. In P. K. Malreddy, B. Heidemann, O. B. Laursen, & J. Wilson (Eds.), *Reworking postcolonialism: Globalization, labour and rights* (pp. 19–35). Basingstoke: Palgrave Macmillan.
Sen, D. (2012). *Red skies and falling stars*. Mumbai: Jaico Publishing House.
Singh, H. (2013, May 27). Indian politician suffered brutal treatment in Maoist attack. *CNN Online* [Online]. Available from http://edition.cnn.com/2013/05/27/world/asia/india-maoist-attack/. Accessed 30 Oct 2014.
Sridhar, A. (2012). Belli Lalitha. *Reporter Sridhar* [Online]. Available from http://journalistsridhar.blogspot.de/2012/01/hi.html. Accessed 31 Oct 2014.
Žižek, S. (2008). *Violence: Six sideways reflections*. New York: Picador.
Žižek, S. (2009). *In defense of lost causes*. New York: Verso.
Žižek, S. (n.d.). Robespierre or the 'divine violence' of terror. *lacan.com* [Online]. Available from http://www.lacan.com/zizrobes.htm. Accessed 31 Oct 2014.

Writing South-Asian Diasporic Identity Anew

Maya Parmar

> On the one hand, 'diaspora' is deeply conservative and imbricated in historical narratives concerning a timeless exile from an autochthonous 'homeland'. On the other, 'diaspora' is also commonly understood as a state of creatively disruptive impurity which imagines emergent transnational and postethnic identities and cultures. (Cheyette 2013, p. xiii)
>
> [T]his woman's neighbour wonders why her children refer to Bangladesh as 'abroad' because Bangladesh isn't abroad, *England* is abroad; Bangladesh is *home*. (Aslam 2004, p. 46)

Embedded so often within the conceptual term 'diaspora' is a sense of fragmented and splintered belonging, a longing for home, and a forfeiture of a well-defined cultural identity: it is this that a scattering of an imagined community of people engenders. Yet, as my first epigraph contends, the diaspora can also be a space of creativity, of innovation, and the productive rupturing of boundaries and prescribed limits. Lingering primarily upon the pain of resettlement, the eloquent prose of Nadeem Aslam's *Maps for Lost Lovers* portrays an isolated and unnamed Pakistani community somewhere in contemporary Britain.[1] My second epigraph, taken from that novel,

---

[1] Hereafter Aslam's novel is referred to as *Maps*.

M. Parmar
The Open University, English Department, Milton Keynes, UK

gestures towards this dispossession, but it too reveals emerging distinctions of perceived belonging amongst different generations of the same diaspora. It is these reorientations of the term 'diaspora' within 'new South-Asian diaspora writing' that this chapter will explore, via Aslam's *Maps*, Gautam Malkani's *Londonstani* and M.G. Vassanji's *The Assassin's Song*. Initially drawing together the two novels *Maps* and *Londonstani*—in many ways an unequal levelling, as I shall later comment—I explore the dual trajectories Bryan Cheyette describes in my first epigraph, as well as the ways in which we can productively nuance our approach to new South-Asian diaspora writing.

Following this brief introduction, where I have begun to delineate critical and imaginative responses to the term 'diaspora', I offer an exploration of popular and relevant research within the field. This chapter then moves on to explore how diasporic identity is represented in recent fictional imaginings of South-Asian life in Britain. To examine how diasporic identity can differ generationally, I first read Malkani's *Londonstani*. Then, taking account of how *Maps* inspires an understanding of the difference amongst South-Asian immigrant communities in Britain, I recommend ways in which we should begin to read South-Asian identity in new diaspora fiction. In closing, I turn to M.G. Vassanji who portrays his diasporic characters on a global stage, often across three continents, yet the author regularly refuses neat classifications of identity. Through these readings, I attempt to define certain shifts in diasporic writing, in turn recalibrating our understanding of the diasporic condition as represented in the contemporary novel.

Mapping South-Asian Diasporic Literature and Criticism

The conceptual term 'diaspora', within the academy, has prospered over the last few decades, stimulating scholarship in a number of fields, particularly in literary postcolonial and cultural studies. Indeed, diaspora studies is recognized as a discipline in itself, whilst diaspora literature too has formed its own niche canon of writing. Acknowledging here earlier conceptualizations of the term, which refer to Jewish diasporas and often exile and victimhood, this chapter's discussion narrows its focus, as the title of this collection would suggest, to representations of the South-Asian diaspora. There are, in addition to the many lesser known as well as emerging writers,[2] well-known and successfully established diaspora authors, including Attia Hosain, V.S. Naipaul, Salman Rushdie, Hanif Kureishi, Amitav Ghosh and Meera Syal.[3] It is contemporary literary works from 1990s onwards, and how they map and remap South-Asian British and global diasporic identity, that shall be of interest here. Before we delve into these novels, let us first take stock of where 'diaspora' has been positioned within scholarship.

Early theoretical works on the term 'diaspora' have included Sudesh Mishra's *Diaspora Criticism* (2006) and Rajagopalan Radhakrishnan's *Diasporic Mediations: Between Home and Location* (1996). Mishra's key work is an overview of diaspora critical trends, which seizes upon a far-reaching range of major theoretical works and thinkers, from Homi Bhabha to Avtar Brah, from Stuart Hall to Arjun Appadurai. Mishra's complex review is undertaken by dividing diaspora criticism into three 'scenes of exemplification', resulting in a focus upon these criticisms rather than on 'diasporas' themselves. Radhakrishnan's earlier work overlaps the frameworks of poststructuralism and postcoloniality to map out identity politics. This account is often self-reflexive in its readings and for Radhakrishnan, both intellectually and subjectively, 'the diasporic location is the space of the hyphen that tries to coordinate, within an evolving relationship, the identity politics of one's place of origin with that of one's present home' (1996, p. xiii). More recently Kim Knott's collection of essays *Diasporas: Concepts, Intersections, Identities* (2010) offers an updated, comprehensive, interdisciplinary overview of major diaspora concepts, themes and theories. This has been followed by Joya Chatterji and David Washbrook's edited volume, *Routledge Handbook of the South Asian Diaspora* (2013), in which Ananya Kabir's chapter entitled 'Literature of the South Asian Diaspora' is included.

Kabir offers to her readers an introduction 'to the richness of diasporic literature produced by authors of movement and resettlement'

---

[2] Noteworthy here is the literary magazine *Wasafiri* for the platform it provides in showcasing a range of emerging diasporic writers.

[3] There have been various studies into these authors: for instance, see Sara Upstone who, in *British Asian Fiction: Twenty-first-century Voices* (Manchester: Manchester University Press, 2010), reflects upon many of these writers in her author-specific chapters; Dave Gunning, *Race and Antiracism in Black British and British Asian Literature* (Liverpool: Liverpool University Press, 2010); Susheila Nasta, *Home Truths: Fictions of the South Asian Diaspora in Britain* (Basingstoke: Palgrave, 2001).

and a delineation of the 'different literary critical models for the analysis and appreciation of this body of imaginative expression' (2013, p. 397). Rather than providing a literary or critical delineation of diasporic literature or diasporic studies, the current chapter aims to read a select few contemporary diasporic works. These fictional writings, often as reflections of diasporic life itself, help us to re-evaluate diasporas as well as how they are imagined today. Within the literary works I consider here, diasporic issues of belonging, memory, and cultural and political identity are re-envisaged. I suggest that for those settled in the diaspora there are distinct shifting relationships with the 'homeland'. Imagined connections to the subcontinent not only differ amongst generations of the same diaspora, but also forms of self and collective identification amongst that group are beginning to fragment the umbrella conceptual category of the 'South-Asian' diaspora.

Within this chapter, I therefore return to a framework where 'diaspora' is a space of interpretation, one that is fluid and open, rather than predetermined and closed. Whilst a space of critical pluralism, it is also one of cultural self-fashioning, 'a constructing space to negotiate many identifications', as one critic comments (Shukla 2003, p. 14).[4] Of the two trajectories of 'diaspora', Cheyette tells us that '[o]ne definition moves in the direction of historicism, the other in the direction of the imagination'. He concludes that the word remains 'unstable and elusive' (2013, p. xiii). In this ongoing elusiveness, and instability, the way in which we critically and creatively engage with the designation of 'diaspora' is shifting, mimicking those transitions the people of the diaspora themselves are experiencing. It is in this very moment of evolution that this chapter intervenes.

Refusing Hyphens, Claiming 'Bling Bling' Culture

South-Asian literature can now be demarcated from the homogenous, catch-all category of black writing. Referring specifically to a settled South-Asian diaspora in Britain, Sara Upstone asserts that we can 'mark the establishment of a definitive genre of British Asian writing deserving recognition in its own right' (2010, p. 1). This distillation of South-Asian writing from the broad category of black writing is also a disentanglement from the coalition of resistance once formed between minorities who shared experiences of prejudice and racism. Furthermore, this disengagement from

---

[4] In her introduction, Shukla discusses the term 'Indian diaspora' in depth.

a homogenous black-British identity also bears witness to emerging forms of cultural identity amongst second generation South Asians in Britain, or those who were born and brought up in Britain.

In his novel, Malkani demonstrates this reconception of diasporic being in the city, showcasing a generation that is loudly, and often aggressively, self-assured and at home in their 'Londonstan'. The novel alludes to this evolution of belonging, making reference to the dynamics of an earlier minority alliance, as well as the shift in identity politics amongst the 'black' diasporas of Britain. Describing the crowd at an organized fight, Malkani's protagonist, Jas, tells us in his hybridized, vernacular English that both 'desis an black kids' were 'kickin round together again, just like it was back when goras still shouted the word Paki an black kids told them to watch it when they did' (2007, p. 99). Jas's observations of the mixed heritage of the spectators harks back to a time when minority groups stuck together, the more established, tougher factions defending the vulnerable, unseasoned ones. The evolution of these dynamics, with South Asians carving out their own territory and reputation is made clear at the beginning of the novel:

> These days, lager louts had got more to fear from us lot [South-Asian diasporic youths] than us lot had to fear from them. I in't lyin to you, in pinds like Hounslow an Southall, they feared us even more than they feared black kids. Round some parts, *even black kids feared people like us.* (p. 5; emphasis added)

No longer do discriminated-against minorities stick together in Malkani's London; the South-Asian youth generation have instead marked themselves out from the black-British diaspora. Although they aspire to and emulate certain aspects of American black gang culture, and borrow freely from it, they have learnt to stand on their own two feet, and distinguish themselves from any former coalition of resistance. In keeping with this collapsing of a collective minority diasporic identity, the reader is told that it is the 'Oriental kids" turn now—their coming of age, so to speak: 'Those guys are coming the way a black kids an desis. I in't lyin to you. In't nobody messes with em no more, an not just cos they kick ass at Nintendo' (p. 100).

Londonstani imagines a diasporic space where the identity politics of South-Asian Britons is no longer just about an incessant struggle to fit in. The daily grind of attempting to quietly escape taunts of 'Paki' and 'go back home' on the bus, at work or school, experiences that are all too familiar in Aslam's novel *Maps*, is replaced by an aggressive self-confidence that even results in one-time black comrades being afraid of their South-Asian counterparts. The characters of *Londonstani* have shed any ambition of assimilating into a collective of marginalized peoples, or even within a humdrum mainstream society; instead, via the novel, we see a shift in how the diaspora conceives itself. These transformations are unique to the youth generation of South Asians, who were born and bred in Britain. This group establish a particular brand of 'desi', urban, youth culture, one that is intimately interwoven with a preoccupation with a culture of conspicuous consumption. Unlike their parents who favour material culture broadly, the quartet Jas, Hardjit, Amit and Ravi formulate diasporic cultural identity around the acquisition and exhibitionist showcasing of flash cars, designer clothes and the latest mobile phones.

Sanjay, Jas's mentor-turned-sinister-business-partner, offers the reader a slick, but warped, lesson in the financial theory and philosophy behind the growth of this urban youth culture: a run down on what he 'like[s] to call Bling-Bling Economics' (p. 169). Although Sanjay's economics lecture aims to encourage the boys to subscribe to an unsustainable and unaffordable lifestyle, and therefore to his highly profitable illegal mobile phone scam involving VAT carousel fraud, the model is one that the characters are already invested in. Ultimately, Sanjay suggests that there are those 'who drive hatchbacks and are happy being average' (p. 170) and there are those:

> who actually want to be someone, their basket of typical goods and services would include a pair of D&G jeans, some bling jewellery, some covers for China White, a pair of new Nikes. (p. 171)

He goes on to tell us that '[t]his isn't about society becoming more affluent, this is about subculture that worships affluence becoming mainstream culture' (p. 171). It is within this economic, social and cultural subculture that the quartet of self-styled rude boys locate themselves. They do not aspire to be part of mainstream society; on the contrary, they are fashioning the mainstream itself.

Whilst Sanjay does not link his 'Bling-Bling Economics' to race, ethnicity or the diaspora, there are connotations of this connection throughout the novel. In one episode, the boys are driving their metallic grey-lilac BMW when they pull up beside a diasporic South-Asian peer who drives a Peugeot 305. They proceed to abuse the owner of the Peugeot because of the 'poncey novel an newspaper on his dashboard an Coldplay album playin in his car', all of which indicate he is 'a muthafuckin coconut' (p. 21).

The insults, which up until this point encircle cultural identity and accuse the Peugeot driver of being metaphorically a coconut (brown on the outside and white on the inside), culminate rather oddly: 'Your car. Ain't u noticed? It's crap. Your car's a piece a crapped-up shit, innit' (p. 22). The Peugeot driver attempts to defend his vehicle, and himself, to then be immediately probed by Hardjit whether he is 'embarrass'd to b a desi? Embarrass'd a your own culture, huh?' (p. 22). Hardjit's abuse suggests that somehow the car you drive is linked to your cultural identity. It distinguishes whether you are an imitation 'gora' (a white person), a coconut, or are faithful to your culture as a bona fide South Asian who consumes luxury goods. According to Hardjit, by choosing a Peugeot, the recipient of this abuse is deserving of it as he is rejecting 'desi' culture. This formulation of 'desi' culture is followed by a further accusation of not being able to speak 'yo mother tongue' (p. 22). The equation between the inability to speak a 'mother tongue', and the replacement of this linguistic knowledge with only English, is a far more familiar way of characterizing those who have 'lost their culture'. The boys in this instance, however, draw alongside linguistic capability the conspicuous consumption of luxury goods as a measure of 'desiness'. Amit reinforces this formulation of cultural identity, and reiterates Hardjit's accusations, when he adds to the exchange: '[a]in't your own culture good enuf for you, you fuckin gora lover', ... '[l]ook at us. We's b havin a nice car, nice tunes, nuff nice designer gear, nuff bling mobile' (p. 22).

This form of urban youth culture, partly outlined by Sanjay, hinges upon materialism. As the novel evidences, such materialism, just as much as the languages you can speak, is a legitimate indicator of a collective membership of a particular brand of diasporic South-Asian, or 'desi', identity. Whilst some of the characters subscribe to this brand of 'desi' diasporic identity, it is worth remembering that others, like the Peugeot driver, do not. And, of course, this brand of culture, which places an emphasis on the conspicuous consumption of luxury goods, should be contextualized by the ubiquitous late capitalist urban environment that the boys inhabit. Perhaps the novel presents us with a form of social assimilation to widespread capitalist culture, rather than the glimpses of a revisioned, albeit vulgar, diasporic identity? It would follow then that Malkani's Londonstan is a place of dispossession, of loss, rather than one of belonging. The novel's conclusion, which sees things end rather messily for Jas, abandoned by his peers and his mentor, could be read as a condemnation of the boys' bling bling economics; however, whilst there might be a rejection of the materialism that permeates the entire novel, Malkani denies us any reading of how this then impacts upon diasporic identity in the wider community. Instead, the end leaves us with something else entirely: a white male protagonist with a double-barrelled surname.

Drawn as the nerdy South-Asian teenager who is just trying to get along throughout the novel, the big reveal of Jason Bartholomew-Clivedon's ethnicity in the last pages of the plot arguably unbalances what has come before. If this closing revelation is unconvincing, it does however make a point about Jason's desire to belong. It is Jason who is seeking a sense of community, and his ambition to find this is fulfilled, in the short term at least, by refashioning himself as the Indian Jas. Malkani deliberately subverts stereotypical models of diasporic belonging and dispossession. Where usually we find in these novels brown characters searching for a unified selfhood, or investment in a meaningful collective, within the ubiquitous, alienating white mainstream, here it is a white character who is doing the searching, and indeed finds this in the minority South-Asian community.

Perhaps Jason is belatedly subscribing to a more general form of 'Asian kool', a phenomenon that saw bhangra music and dance, and in turn 'Asianness', become trendy during the 1990s.[5] However, the context of any allusion to Asian kool cannot be easily placed, given that, as Dave Gunning underlines, whilst *Londonstani* is set in the 'contemporary period of its composition' (the early twentieth-first century), 'the desi culture portrayed is closer to that which Malkani's undergraduate research unearthed in the 1990s' (2010, p. 119). Nevertheless, the end of the novel, in conjunction with the representation of the boys' cultural claims, suggests that a form of 'desi' identity is being forged. This is an identity that others of different ethnicities, such as Jason, wish to share in. Rather than South-Asian identities of imposture or impersonation (Mitchell 2008), the reader is presented with a crude, consumer-driven brand of 'desi' culture. In *Londonstani* we by no means have a utopian model for cultural identity in the diaspora; instead, we have a diasporic belonging within the wider community that moves beyond the middleman identity politics of Bhabha's 'liminal', 'in-between' spaces (1994, p. 2), as well as Radhakrishnan's hyphenated selfhood (1996, p. xiii). In literal terms, Malkani's novel title bears no hyphen. If 'diaspora' is often construed as a byword for dislocation, we see in the fiction discussed here how such

---

[5] See Haq (1996) for a reading of the phenomena of 'Asian kool', as well as Roy (2010), p. 17.

boundaries can be more comfortably traversed. These are slight shifts—tremors in the landscape of diasporic literature—in how and where that hyphen is now being claimed, or indeed rejected, by the South-Asian diaspora.

Splintering the 'South-Asian' Diaspora

Thus far I have argued that there is a divergence in the experiences of different diasporic generations when we reflect upon modes of self-representation and identity formation. In reading *Londonstani* I have referred fleetingly to Aslam's novel *Maps for Lost Lovers*. *Maps*' protagonists represent a different generation, one that was not born and brought up in the UK, and one that suffers a profound sense of alienation in their diasporic lives. Whilst the marginalized first generation of *Maps* ceaselessly articulates their sense of being outsiders, alongside their never-ending attempt to negotiate the centre—and indeed the margin itself—Hardjit and his peers do not share these daily difficulties. *Maps* centres on the middle-aged, Muslim, married Shamas and Kaukab, and whilst we have glimpses of their three children's lives, the reader's purview is firmly focused on how the couple experience their diasporic life. In the moments Charag, Mah-Jabin and Ujala appear within the narratorial frame of Dasht-e-Tanhaii, The Wilderness of Solitude or The Desert of Loneliness, we are reminded of the all too familiar hyphenated identities of dispossession and contestation.[6] How these children of the first generation exist outside of this suffocating hermetic isolation, how they experience the diaspora beyond, is not clear. Whilst the novel gestures towards the lives beyond the vacuum of Dasht-e-Tanhaii, and most fully opens up Charag's place in the world to the reader, these are but glimpses of how the second generation find a home in Aslam's Britain.

Whilst these moments in the novel are relegated in favour of presenting how the first generation negotiates life in contemporary Britain, my second epigraph intimates the divergence in generational diasporic experience. This extract from *Maps*, albeit from a first-generation parent's perspective, identifies the woman's homeland as somewhere else, a home that is there and not here. In this familiar formulation of the diasporic

---

[6] For a reading of the isolation, alienation and struggle between an orthodox formulation of Islam and modernity in *Maps*, see Butt (2008).

condition, we are reminded of Rushdie's widely-cited reflections on an 'imaginary homeland', where 'invisible' villages and cities are reclaimed in the place of those lost to the migrant (1991, p. 10). It is India that Rushdie refers to here; however, this fictive, imagined reconstruction is relevant to the homes and homelands in the minds of Aslam's characters. Whilst this articulation of belonging, or longing, is expressed by one generation, it is juxtaposed with the next generation's sentiments on home, a reconception that presents confusion. It would suggest that there is a burgeoning, but fledgling, re-envisaging of the diasporic condition amongst the second generation of Aslam's diaspora.

Given this shift, and taking into account Malkani's urban youth vernacular culture, I contend that the way in which we imagine diasporas, and consequently deploy the term, requires reshaping. If we are to continue to utilize the designation 'diaspora', a category that has been encircled by the experience of loss, dislocation and return, we should revisit and readjust the limits within which the term has been set. Of the circumstances and characters in *Maps,* Nadia Butt suggests that 'dislocation or displacement is an inevitable dimension of the present age of mass migration' (2008, p. 156), yet I would argue that this does not always mean a dispossession of selfhood or collectivity.

Though I have embarked upon a reading of *Maps* in conjunction with *Londonstani*, putting aside generational shifts, there are key disparities within this comparison that should be explored. Alongside the varying geographies against which these narratives are created, there is a difference in the religious affiliations of each set of characters. Aslam's novel is set in the north of England, amongst an underprivileged, Muslim Pakistani community. In contrast, Malkani's Hindu and Sikh characters play out their 'bling bling' economics within the relatively affluent setting of Hounslow, London. In consequence, whilst Malkani's Hindu and Sikh characters might be getting along with some success and affluence, this is not to say that this achievement is shared by their Muslim Pakistani counterparts in the north of the country.[7] The difference in geography and religion must be accounted for in our critical understanding of new diaspora writing. If South-Asian writing has been demarcated from the umbrella category of black writing, we

---

[7] Indeed, as Ali's novel *Brick Lane* (2003) suggests, it is worth noting that the prosperity of Malkani's Hounslow characters is also not shared by the Bangladeshi diaspora in the East End of London.

must now carve out a critical terrain for the differentiation between religious groups previously homogenously designated as South-Asian, as well as class positionings within different sectors of this splintered category.

In his critical reading of contemporary fiction, Anshuman Mondal makes a similar point when he explains that '[f]iction published in Britain prior to the Rushdie controversy saw young Muslims appear in its pages largely as Asians, for example, or Indians, Pakistani, Africans, Arabs, and so on, but very rarely as Muslims' (2015, p. 31).[8] It is only recently that, within literature and within critical literary commentary, we are beginning to reflect upon religious difference and its implications. In making this argument, I should pause a moment to consider the terminology deployed throughout this chapter. In my readings and critical appraisal of new diaspora writing, I have consistently made reference to 'South Asians'. In doing so, I signal towards a group of people from a number of parts of India and Pakistan, who share a long, entangled history and heritage dating back to before the cartographical fragmentation of the 1947 partition. Whilst I argue that it is now critically appropriate to fragment this placeholder term along lines of generation, religion and class, and further, as I discuss shortly, here the homogenous expression of 'South-Asian' is a useful one. It enables a group of people to be marked out, so as to reveal a terrain of study that allows for critical analysis of the practices of belonging and homemaking. Like 'diaspora', as Mondal indicates above, the marker 'South-Asian' requires further explication, otherwise we risk overwriting the nuances of cultural and religious identity.

If an imperative to fracture South-Asian identity exists, this splintering of a homogenous identity should be extended in the study of new diaspora writing. An understanding of how ethnic specificity is manifested, beyond the broad category of being Indian, Pakistani, Bengali and so forth, is necessary. Regional homeland affiliations that define the cultural identities

---

[8] Via Kureishi's *My Son the Fanatic*, Mondal also offers a reading of generational difference amongst the diaspora, with a focus on how religious identity is claimed amongst varying age groups. Within the growing body of research on 'Muslim writing', in addition to the edited collection in which Mondal's chapter appears (Chambers and Herbert 2015), notable works include: Ahmed et al.'s *Culture, Diaspora, and Modernity in Muslim Writing* (2012), Nash's *Writing Muslim Identity* (2012) and Santesso *Disorientation: Muslim Identity in Contemporary Anglophone Literature* (2012).

of 'Punjabiness' and 'Gujaratiness' are relevant to the diasporic condition.[9] In addition, there are further nuances of localized identity affiliation that pinpoint specific belonging to villages and towns 'back home'. *Maps* makes reference to how these relationships of belonging characterize everyday life in the diaspora. Speaking of a headscarf to the town matchmaker, Kaukab tells the reader it is '[f]rom the shop way over there on Ustad Allah Bux Street'. She continues: 'I don't go there often—white people's houses start soon after that street, and even the Pakistanis there are not from our part of Pakistan'(p. 42). In familiarizing the streets of the British landscape via a strategy of renaming that geography, Kaukab simultaneously expresses an anxiety of not only the white communities that live beyond her comfort zone, but also the unknown Pakistanis. These people are from a different Pakistani village, a different town, and might therefore subscribe to dissimilar cultural and religious practices. Despite being Pakistani, they are still an unknown to Kaukab and, like the white people of the same area, are imagined as the 'other'. Consequently, Kaukab's movements are determined by this changing demographic of the surrounding streets. Just as coexisting Pakistani village spaces would have defined everyday social life back in the homeland, so they do in the diaspora.

Thus, whilst it is important to splinter black writing to acknowledge South-Asian writing, and a fragmentation of this category should involve the recognition of religious diversity, a further cognizance of regional and localized identity affiliation offers a valuable lens through which new diaspora writing can be analysed. If *Londonstani* represents and problematizes some form of homogenous 'Asian kool', then *Maps* marks this critical shift by taking account of difference. As Upstone suggests, Aslam's *Maps* 'is a profound intervention that more than any other

[9] There is little study of the regional identity affiliations. With the exploration of the diasporic popularity of the dance and music form bhangra, there is some excavation of 'Punjabiness'; however, scant attention has been paid to other forms of regional identity. The specificity of 'Gujaratiness', and the way in which it manifests itself in the diaspora, fracturing Indian nationalism, is discussed in my doctoral thesis 'Reading the Double Diaspora: Cultural Representations of Gujarati East Africans in Britain'(unpublished thesis: University of Leeds, Parmar 2013a). Jessica Marie Falcone (2013) also engages with a sense of Gujaratiness as manifested during *garba* dance. Tommaso Bobbio (2012) provides some study on the notion of what he describes as a 'subnational' identity. He offers a political understanding of Gujarati identity within India itself, an identity that is framed by economic development and Hindu extremism. In light of the current political climate in India, this is a useful article that speaks to India's Bharatiya Janata Party's proposition of Gujaratiness, and to my later reading of M.G. Vassanji's *The Assassin's Song*.

[of his novels] marks the shift from the "Asian cool" of the 1990s to post-9/11 concerns with British Muslim alienation' (2010, p. 101). Though religious difference is emphasized here, as I have suggested, other differentiations are central to the diasporic world Aslam creates. In addition to these, there are further categories of differentiation that are relevant in a critical fragmentation of the catch-all 'South-Asian diaspora': they include the identification of linguistic difference and caste membership. These variances are now slowly being acknowledged within literary representations, and within critical cultural and literary studies too. As a result, the way in which we implement the conceptual term 'diaspora' can also be updated, taking account of these differentiating specificities.

Conclusion

To bring this chapter to a close, let us briefly move beyond the remit of British South-Asian diasporic fiction to the writings of M.G. Vassanji, which span several continents. Vassanji, a Canadian author who has won the Giller Prize twice, has not always received the critical attention his fictions merit. Weaving together layers of marginalized, competing historical narrative, themes of citizenship, religious and cultural identity, and gender, his fictions often centre on the lives of the South Asians of East Africa. This 'double diaspora', a community of migrants who have moved from undivided India to Kenya, Uganda and Tanzania, have often moved on yet again (see Parmar 2013a, b). Their non-linear, multiple migratory trajectory deviates from the more familiar narrative of peoples and communities moving directly from the subcontinent to Europe or North America. Vassanji, in his writings, thus offers us yet another lens through which to examine South-Asian diasporic cultural identity: that of being South-Asian and not merely hailing from the subcontinent, but from Africa too.[10] In considering the trade, migration and slave networks of the Indian Ocean seascape we are once again able to splinter the opaque, homogenous designation of 'diaspora'. Vassanji interlaces these stories that traverse the Indian Ocean, ones of multiplicity, particularly in his popular novels *The Gunny Sack* (1989), *The Book of Secrets* (1996), and *The In-Between World of Vikram Lall* (2003).

---

[10] It is worth noting the experience and skill set of these double migrants is different from migrants directly settled in the UK from India.

Vassanji is known for his refusal of labels though: a previous biography on his website warns that 'attempts to pigeonhole him along communal or other lines' are considered by the author 'narrow-minded, malicious and oppressive'. This aversion to categorization is reflected in the author's fictional prose: his characters rarely exhibit singular, flat identities; instead they offer the reader complex, multidimensional, contested forms of belonging and being. In establishing how we might move forward with the term 'diaspora', I have suggested that we productively rupture the homogeneity of the designation. As a consequence of this fragmentation, the nuances of the South-Asian diaspora are revealed, and become available to critical studies; however, in doing this we risk insisting upon further labels. In turning to Vassanji in this conclusion, and his insistent rejection of pigeonholing, I explore how identification categories can be confounded within fiction.

As indicated by his self-identification as 'African-Asian-Canadian' (Barber 2012) Vassanji's heritage easily traverses three continents. His writings generally take into account this wide-ranging experience, but often set against a central backdrop of East Africa. His recent novel *The Assassin's Song*, however, is the first to be set in India, and specifically the state of Gujarat. The regional nature of Gujarat, within the larger geography of a non-unified India, is very prominent in the novel. Taking us back to the pre-colonial thirteenth century, Vassanji depicts a medieval, autonomous Gujarat, which existed alongside the other regional states of India. This is a geography determined not by contemporary notions of the national, but by the regional state. Consequently, cultural and political identities within the novel are shaped accordingly, along regional parameters. The contemporary political landscape of modern Gujarat via the 2002 Gujarat riots and Hindu nationalist ideologies connected with the operations of the Bharatiya Janata Party headed by Narendra Modi, are woven into the narrative alongside the representations of the thirteenth-century mythical figure Nur Fazal. Through the juxtaposition of these two periods of Gujarat, the religious and cultural fragmentation of contemporary, unified India is exposed. Medieval Gujarat is depicted as a largely syncretic and harmonious space, where religious factions and cultural difference are present, but coexist as well as interweave. Within the medieval Gujarati royal court, there is strong promotion of intellectual debate, and receptivity to new ideas and peoples. Consequently, a strand of Sufism flourishes, and a mystical and spiritual mediation of both Hinduism and Islam is the result.

The narratorial reversions to the protagonist's childhood memories demonstrate how this syncretic existence is gradually eroded, replaced by divisions between religious groups. As the reader steps back through Karsan's memories to revisit moments from his youth, when he grew up as the 'gaadi-varas' or successor to the shrine in Pirbaag, we witness the corrosion of Gujarat's syncretic harmony. These moments of decay occur repeatedly throughout the narrative, and include a local Muslim man, Salim Buckle, being mutilated to death by Hindus (p. 82), the emergence of the National Patriotic Youth Party (NAPYP), led by the Hindu fundamentalist Pradhan Shastri, and the Indo-China war. These tensions continue in Karsan's adult life, and even after he rejects his destined position of Lord and Keeper of Nur Fazal's shrine, he can no longer hide from the reality of modern India. Not only must he face up to the 2002 pogroms of Gujarat, and the knowledge that these were likely to have been state-sponsored, but he is confronted by a younger brother, grown into a Muslim fundamentalist (p. 266).

The ultimate desecration of the syncretic Sufi ideals, where spirituality and pluralism take precedence over Hindu or Islamic doctrine, is revealed towards the end of the novel. From the very beginning of the novel, we are aware that Karsan's father is no more, but it is only at the very end that the reader, along with Karsan himself, learns of the demigod's ultimate demise. During some disturbances, he is cut down by a 'long sword' which 'went straight through him'. The '[d]etails don't matter': the reader knows that this violence, and that which ensues within the shrine itself, is enough to 'curdle the blood' (p. 307). The brutal murder, by religious fundamentalists, is in contradiction to Karsan's father's lifetime teachings of harmony and syncretism. Throughout the novel, the patriarch opposes religious ideology that divides, and instead favours those teachings that unite. His passing is a sad culmination of everything he had petitioned against in life. The death, given Karsan's refusal of his birthright as heir to the shrine, also marks the collapse of the legend and tradition of Nur Fazal. The shrine and its followers are left doubly bereft, and throughout the novel, the protagonist wonders whether his refusal of his destiny as avatar led to the demise of the syncretic harmony it symbolizes.

Vassanji's *The Assassin's Song*, like his other novels, reminds us that diasporic identities can take many guises, and are indeed often composite in nature. Whilst this chapter has argued for the consciousness of multiple difference—class, ethnic, linguistic, generational—in the diaspora these can sometimes be, returning to Cheyette and my first epigraph, elusive. In insisting upon a cognizance of communal difference amongst diasporic South Asians, there is a risk of not only formulating further labels, as I have suggested earlier, but of occluding the composite identities Vassanji represents. Through such a fragmentary approach, syncretic diasporic culture can quickly be rendered invisible. Any critical treatment of 'diaspora' must be suitably alert to these oscillations. It remains timely and appropriate, however, that we recalibrate our understanding of 'diaspora' and diasporas. As the title of this collection suggests, I have done this through the analysis of fictional works; however, representations of mosaic identities are manifesting themselves continually in other forms of cultural production.

Along with its portrayal in fiction, cultural identity is being embodied innovatively on digital networks, within culinary practices and within dance and music.[11] The manifold ways in which diasporic identity is being manifested underlines its unstable, challenging, yet fascinating nature. This is, of course, reflected in the literary form of the novel, as explored here. In *Londonstani* we are confronted with a hybrid dialect, synthesized from Punjabi, urban gang culture, English and slang. This vernacular, experimental language, the subject of much debate, is an innovative representation in writing of the spoken language of the street. *Maps* offers a less controversial style of writing, but is distinctive for its delicately crafted, poetic prose. Thus, whether manifested in imaginative writings or elsewhere, South-Asian global diasporas are creative, playful and slippery in their contemporary conceptions of cultural identity. And, indeed, so often now are no longer confined to the outdated territory of the simple hyphen.

WORKS CITED

Ahmed, R., Morey, P., & Yaqin, A. (Eds.). (2012). *Culture, diaspora, and modernity in Muslim writing*. Abingdon: Routledge.
Ali, M. (2003). *Brick lane*. London: Doubleday.
Aslam, N. (2004). *Maps for lost lovers*. London: Faber & Faber.
Barber, J. (2012. October 16). M.G. Vassanji: Seeking identity while dodging pigeonholes. *Globe and Mail* [Online]. Available from http://www.theglobeandmail.com/arts/books-and-media/mg-vassanji-seeking-identity-while-dodging-pigeonholes/article4686245/. Accessed 2 Nov 2014.
Bhabha, H. K. (1994). *The location of culture*. London: Routledge.
Bobbio, T. (2012). Making Gujarat vibrant: Hindutva, development and the rise of subnationalism in India. *Third World Quarterly, 33*(4), 657–672.
Butt, N. (2008). Between orthodoxy and modernity: Mapping the transcultural predicaments of Pakistani immigrants in multi-ethnic Britain in Nadeem

[11] Parmar 2013b, 2014.

Aslam's *Maps for lost lovers* (2004). In L. Eckstein, B. Korte, E. U. Pirker, & C. Reinfandt (Eds.), *Multi-ethnic Britain 2000+: New perspectives in literature, film and the arts* (pp. 153–169). Amsterdam: Rodopi.
Chambers, C., & Herbert, C. (Eds.). (2015). *Imagining Muslims in South Asia and the diaspora: Secularism, religion, representations*. Abingdon: Routledge.
Cheyette, B. (2013). *Diasporas of the mind: Jewish and postcolonial writing and the nightmare of history*. London: Yale University Press.
Falcone, J. M. (2013, February). 'Garba with attitude': Creative nostalgia in competitive collegiate Gujarati American folk dancing. *Journal of Asian American Studies, 16*(1), 57–89.
Gunning, D. (2010). *Race and antiracism in black British and British Asian literature*. Liverpool: Liverpool University Press.
Haq, R. (1996). Asian kool? Bhangra and beyond. In S. Sharma, J. Hutnyk, & A. Sharma (Eds.), *Disorienting rhythms: The politics of the new Asian dance music* (pp. 61–79). London: Zed.
Kabir, A. J. (2013). Literature of the South Asian diaspora. In J. Chatterji & D. Washbrook (Eds.), *Routledge handbook of the South Asian diaspora* (pp. 388–399). Oxon: Routledge.
Knott, K., & McLoughlin, S. (2010). *Diasporas: Concepts, intersections, identities*. London: Zed Books.
Malkani, G. (2007). *Londonstani*. London: Harper Perennial.
Mishra, S. (2006). *Diaspora criticism*. Edinburgh: Edinburgh University Press.
Mitchell, M. (2008). Escaping the matrix: Illusions and disillusions of identity in Gautam Malkani's *Londonstani* (2006). In L. Eckstein, B. Korte, E. U. Pirker, & C. Reinfandt (Eds.), *Multi-ethnic Britain 2000+: New perspectives in literature, film and the arts* (pp. 329–340). Amsterdam: Rodopi.
Mondal, A. A. (2015). Representations of young Muslims in contemporary British South Asian fiction. In C. Chambers & C. Herbert (Eds.), *Imagining Muslims in South Asia and the diaspora: Secularism, religion, representations* (pp. 30–41). Abingdon: Routledge.
Nash, G. (2012). *Writing Muslim identity*. London: Continuum.
Nasta, S. (2001). *Home truths: Fictions of the South Asian diaspora in Britain*. Basingstoke: Palgrave.
Parmar, M. (2013a). Reading the double diaspora: Cultural representations of Gujarati East Africans in Britain. Unpublished thesis, University of Leeds.
Parmar, M. (2013b, June). Reading the double diaspora: Representing Gujarati East African cultural identity in Britain. *Atlantis, 35*(1), 137–156.
Parmar, M. (2014). Memorialising 40 years since Idi Amin's expulsion: Digital 'memory mania' to the 'right to be forgotten'. *South Asian Popular Culture, 12*(1), 1–14.
Radhakrishnan, R. (1996). *Diasporic mediations: Between home and location*. London: University of Minnesota Press.

Roy, A. G. (2010). *Bhangra moves: From Ludhiana to London and beyond.* Farnham: Ashgate.
Rushdie, S. (1991). *Imaginary homelands: Essays and criticism, 1981–1991.* London: Granta Books in association with Penguin.
Santesso, E. (2013). *Disorientation: Muslim identity in contemporary anglophone literature.* Basingstoke: Palgrave.
Shukla, S. (2003). *India abroad: Diasporic cultures of postwar America and England.* Princeton: Princeton University Press.
Upstone, S. (2010). *British Asian fiction: Twenty-first-century voices.* Manchester: Manchester University Press.
Vassanji, M. G. (1989). *The gunny sack.* Oxford: Heinemann.
Vassanji, M. G. (1996). *The book of secrets.* London: Macmillan.
Vassanji, M. G. (2003). *The in-between world of Vikram Lall.* Edinburgh: Canongate.
Vassanji, M. G. (2008). *The assassin's song.* London: Canongate.

Minor Literature and the South-Asian Short Story

Neelam Srivastava

In what ways does the short story inform or disrupt our understanding of South-Asian literary history? In this chapter, I examine the South-Asian short story as a form of 'minority literature', in Deleuze and Guattari's celebrated formulation, a genre that effects a de-territorialization of the terrain of prose fiction, which has been traditionally dominated by the novel (Deleuze and Guattari 1986).

The hegemony of the novel is particularly true for postcolonial South-Asian literature in English. Over the last 40-odd years, the Indian novel in English has become *the* defining genre of the subcontinent for audiences abroad, thanks to the global success of a string of Booker Prize winners, beginning with Salman Rushdie's *Midnight's Children* in 1981 and culminating with Aravind Adiga's *The White Tiger* in 2008, reinforcing the sense that the 'Great Indian Novel' was India's foremost contribution to 'world literature'. And yet, as Amitav Ghosh remarks, not only have stories and story cycles been the staple of Indian literature for centuries, but the 'modern' form of the short story 'for the first few decades after 1947 [...] was consistently in the vanguard of Indian writing' (Ghosh 1994, p. 48). A case in point was the prominence of the Hindi short story in the 1950s and 1960s, which came to dominate the production of Hindi

N. Srivastava
Newcastle University,
Newcastle upon Tyne, UK

literature in those years, thanks to acclaimed writers like Nirmal Verma and Kamleshwar.

It is clear that any account of the South-Asian short story will have several different possible trajectories, mainly because of the ways in which the South-Asian literary field is marked by its multilingual production. Thus an account of the Indian short story in English will be different from that of the Hindi, Urdu, Bengali or Tamil short story. The topic of this chapter is the South-Asian short story in English and in English translation, which I argue can be seen to form part of an anglophone South-Asian canon, with a focus on production from 1990 onwards. While the novel has often been touted (or vilified) as the quintessential Indian English genre, the short story is, in fact, quite successful and influential in the panorama of contemporary South-Asian literary writing, including work by Salman Rushdie, Rohinton Mistry, Vikram Chandra, Mahasweta Devi, Aravind Adiga, Daniyal, Jhumpa Lahiri and Bharati Mukherjee.[1] In what follows, I look at some iconic short stories by contemporary South-Asian authors, with an eye to thematic continuity but also to artistic innovations: Mahasweta Devi (India), Daniyal Mueenuddin (Pakistan) and the diasporic short stories of Jhumpa Lahiri (US). Central to my analysis will be two formats in which the short story appears, namely the anthology and the short story cycle.

The short story cycle is worthy of particular critical attention because of its importance in defining a sense of place in South-Asian fiction. R.K. Narayan's south Indian town Malgudi occupies a central space in 'literary' India for anglophone readers, through his humorous, understated narratives of the town's inhabitants. (Unsurprisingly, perhaps, Narayan has not enjoyed the same critical status as other major Indian-English practitioners of his generation, such as Raja Rao and Mulk Raj Anand, who

[1] Recent critical work has focused on the postcolonial short story, a relatively neglected genre within postcolonial studies; see, for example, Maggie Awadalla and Paul March-Russell's recent collection, *The Postcolonial Short Story: Contemporary Essays* (Palgrave, 2012). Shital Pravinchandra in particular explores the role of this form as a way of reflecting on the 'place of non-Anglophone literatures in the field of postcolonial studies' (Pravinchandra 2014, p. 425). She identifies the presence of a 'master text' in Ghosh's *The Calcutta Chromosome* (1995), namely vernacular short fiction by Rabindranath Tagore and Phanishwarnath Renu. Her work opens up a productive space for thinking about the dialogue between the South-Asian short story in the vernacular and Indian Anglophone literature. In critical terms, this dialogue can yield a more 'comparative' and 'inter-lingual' intertextual reading than one based on the usual model of 'writing back' to the colonial literary canon.

are more well-known for their 'nation-forming' novels engaging with the Indian nationalist movement.) Like Narayan, Adiga, in his recent short story cycle, *Between the Assassinations* (2008), locates its recurring characters in a single small town, Kittur, situated on the south-western coast of India; the locality binds the stories together while also lending itself to the specific form of 'episodic' or 'composite' novel, as the short story cycle can be defined. The short story cycle, as we shall see with Mueenuddin and Lahiri, allows for a detailed exploration of place and theme from a multiplicity of narrative perspectives; it uses a different narrative strategy to novels, as it is 'composed of independent narrative episodes that are ultimately unified through structure, movement and thematic development' (Trussler 2002, p. 601).

The short story in South Asia is a popular genre because it has roots in orality and perhaps also relies on reading practices that tend to privilege the magazine format over the novel format; short stories in magazines are read quickly, consumed quickly and are often passed around among different readers in the same household. The prominence of the short story as an early post-independence genre 'undoubtedly had to do with the peculiar mechanics of publishing in India: the part that magazines play in supporting writers and the calendrical rhythms they follow' (Ghosh 1994, p. 48). Different ways of publishing the text and presenting it to the reader also produce different levels of canonicity and 'literariness', as I discuss below.

While its placement within a collection of explicitly inter-linked stories makes the short form more akin to the novel, its inclusion within an anthology performs a different type of contextualizing work. The South-Asian literary system highlights in particular the relationship between the short story and the process of anthologization, namely what happens to the visibility and canonicity of the short story once it leaves the ephemeral context of its first appearance—the magazine, the literary periodical—and becomes part of a larger textual assemblage such as the anthology—which places together texts *by different authors*—that is used for establishing a literary canon of sorts.[2] It is interesting to see what happens when this minor genre, the short story, is re-inscribed within a type of text such as the anthology that *foregrounds* canonicity, with the aspiration to produce, in Deleuze and Guattari's formulation (1986, p. 27), a sort of 'state language' of literature.

---

[2] As Ana Miller notes, 'anthologies have a potentially valuable role to play in expanding the circulation and awareness of regional literatures that struggle to travel' (Miller 2015, p. 117).

The Short Story and Anthologization

Literary anthologies tend to be seen as a 'pedagogical' genre, with especially close links to canon formation in the university context. In what follows, I consider a short story by Mahasweta Devi, 'Shishu' ('Children'), and examine what happens to the reading experience when it is placed within an influential anthology that presents it as part of a narrative about a 'national' literature, a 'major' literature. As James Procter remarks about the short story in Trinidad, 'Short stories (like poems) are especially susceptible to decontextualisation as they are republished and recollected within different settings, sequences and contexts' (2011, p. 163). Despite the risk of decontextualization, it is undoubtedly true that anthologies enable otherwise little-known texts to circulate among a wider audience.

Contemporary South-Asian literary production is profoundly marked by the power dynamics obtaining between English and the other Indian languages, which produce sharply divided readerships on the basis of class and geographical location. The anthology of Indian literature in English translation makes accessible a wide variety of writing for a national audience, who may not read Hindi, Bengali, Marathi, Urdu, as well as for an international audience, which is even less familiar with the cultures that are associated with these languages. The role played by translation in constructing a canon of South-Asian literature for national and transnational audiences is key. English tends to be the language in which anthologies of South-Asian writing are published for the West, but also for 'national' readerships; significantly, translations from the *bhashas* (Indian indigenous languages) into English are called vertical translations, whereas those between *bhashas* are called horizontal translations.

In addition to the process of translation and availability, the anthologization of the short story produces a second consequence: that of drastically altering the original effect it has on the reader when it first appears in a magazine. In this sense, the literary anthology plays a cultural role in determining canons, especially in the university context, as anthologies destined for pedagogical use 'tend to cultivate an ideal reader trained in specialized reading skills', as opposed to the more 'casual' reader of short fiction (March-Russell 2009, p. 56).

Short stories have traditionally suffered from poor critical reception in inverse proportion to their popularity with readers, and rarely do publishers view short story collections with favour; thus 'in the late twentieth century the short story form [was] still tied to the magazine outlet and to a potentially disabling publishing context' (Hanson 1989, p. 2). As a form that circulates easily within economically accessible formats, namely the magazine or the periodical, and maintains close links to genre literature such as the detective story or the romance tale, it has often been dismissed as popular, and therefore inferior. Its placement within an anthology helps to 'elevate' it into the canon of prose literature, in which the novel predominates.

The popular appeal of the short story is intimately linked to the effect it has on its readers. Edgar Allan Poe, in a famous early reflection on the short story (1842), argued that what made it the highest form of artistic expression after the poem was its 'unity of effect or impression'; and

> without unity of impression, the deepest effects cannot be brought about. [...] In the brief tale [...] the author is enabled to carry out the fullness of his intention, be it what it may. During the hour of perusal the soul of the reader is at the writer's control. There are no external or extrinsic influences—resulting from weariness or interruption. (Poe 1842, p. 47)

Poe was attempting to bestow a form of canonicity on the 'tale of effect'; for him the great advantage of the short prose narrative over the rhythmic poem was that it could also convey 'terror, passion, or horror', and truth, not just beauty. Poe thus elevates genre writing, and specifically the 'sensational tale', to the status of art. His comments demonstrate that a debate about canonicity has always been at the heart of discussions around the short story as a literary form with its own specific formal characteristics, rather than as merely the little sister of the novel.

In this sense, then, we can think of the short story's relationship to the novel as analogous to that between minor and major literature in Deleuze and Guattari: a genre that strikes a discordant note, that sends a revolutionary message, an intensive use of language that 'will make it take flight on a line of escape' (Deleuze and Guattari 1986, p. 26). Like minor literature, the short story resolutely defends a 'becoming-minor', namely a refusal to enter the official literary canon, or at the very least a will to defend its position on its margins. Its status as a minor form allows the short story a flexibility and a capability to speak for the 'oppressed minority'—and for oppressed languages—in a way that other literary forms don't.

Adrian Hunter observes that 'the short story is particularly suited to the representation of liminal or problematized identities', and that in cultures with small or non-existent publishing infrastructures, the low-capital, low-circulation literary magazine tends to be the main outlet for new writing. (Hunter 2007, p. 138)

Deleuze and Guattari's notion of a writing 'which a minority constructs within a major language', is particularly apt for a reading of the short story, especially one that focuses on conditions of marginalization and exclusion, such as the condition of subaltern citizenship in South Asia.[3] Thus the short story as a minor form becomes its very source of resistance, as is evident in Mahasweta Devi's 'Shishu', which was translated for Susie Tharu and K. Lalita's ground-breaking two-volume anthology *Women Writing in India* (1993).

As always, the textual history of this story is important; 'Shishu' was first published in a Bengali magazine, *Sharodiya Paromash*, in 1978, then in a collection of Mahasweta Devi's short stories, *Nairete Megh* (1979), subsequently translated for *Women Writing in India*, and finally re-translated in a 1998 collection entitled *Bitter Soil*. Tharu and Lalita discuss this story in their introduction to the anthology. Their re-assessment of the Nehruvian era and its aftermath includes a trenchant critique of the 'normalizing' tendencies of postcolonial nationalist historiography and state policy; they argue that the '50s and early '60s in India defused the radical energies and ambitions of the anti-colonial movement, and tended to place the state at the centre of any project involving the development of Indian subjecthood. The state became the custodian of people's welfare, and as Mahasweta's story all too aptly demonstrates, a statist approach to historically marginalized groups such as the Indian tribal populations inevitably replicated colonialist mindsets in the postcolonial context. The story is told from the perspective of a Hindu relief officer who is posted in a locality called Lohri, a deprived area of West

---

[3] Here I draw on Gyanendra Pandey's discussions of the subaltern citizen as a disenfranchised member of a national population who seeks political and historical agency. 'Citizen' acts as a qualifier of the subaltern, indicating the 'political quality of all subalternity' (Pandey 2008, p. 277). This is an obvious shift from the idea of the subaltern as a 'Third World peasant' at the centre of the *Subaltern Studies* project, to the idea of a minority citizen (lower-caste, tribal, immigrant) who is nevertheless part of what Partha Chatterjee calls 'political society', a wider and more inclusive group than 'civil society' (which he mainly conceives of in bourgeois terms). This citizen is barely a rights-bearing subject, and yet works to brings about his/her own political agency (Chatterjee 2004).

Bengal. The opening of the story sets the parameters of the conflicting worldviews that jostle for dominance:

> On the official records it belonged to Ranchi district, but the place was a vast stretch scorched and burnt beyond reclaim, as if the earth underneath were a furnace. (Pinaki Bhattacharya's translation; Devi 1993, p. 236)

The official discourse of development is fiercely critiqued through a form of linguistic irony that sets the English words apart from the Bengali: all the words to do with development, government and governance are in English. A subsequent translation to the one in *Women Writing in India* renders this linguistic dissonance very clearly, by leaving the words that are originally in English in the text in italics:

> *Officially* it's in Ranchi. But the entire area is a burnt-out desert. As if the earth here bears a fire of unbearable heat in her womb. (Ipsita Chanda's translation; Devi 1998, p. 1)

This translation by Ipsita Chanda feminizes and embodies the land, the imagery wresting it from the state's control, expressed through the governmental language of English, and which seeks to shape it according to its own developmental planning. The story takes on the overtones of an eerie, almost supernatural tale, flirting with the generic boundaries of the ghost story; in Lohri, there are mysterious beings who look like small children. At night they make off with sacks of food destined for the relief programme in the villages. The relief officer's colleague explains that the local tribe, the Aagariyas, had rebelled against the geologists and officers who had come to look for iron ore in their hills a few years before. Traditionally, the Aagariyas' profession was that of iron miners, and they had a myth in which this hill was made sacred.

> Two Punjabi officers, a Madrasi *geologist*—why would they believe in these *junglee* tales of asur *deotas*? They *blasted* the hillock flat. (Devi 1998, p. 5)

In retaliation, the Aagariyas killed the officers and scientists. The previous sentence is revealing for the different layers of discourse embedded in its multilingualism—a multilingualism that is absent from the more uniform and pedestrian translation in *Women Writing in India,* where none of the English words are italicized, and thus are not marked as different or dissonant from the Bengali original. The target language in Ipsita Chanda's translation, on the other hand, bears the marks of the violence of representation: who is being allowed to represent the point of view, the subjecthood of the tribals in this story? The development officer dismisses the legends of the Aagariyas as '*junglee*', a generic Hindi term to mean 'wild, uncultured'; the translation by Pinaki Bhattacharya translates this as 'barbarian', which in the upper-caste Hindu imaginary of the relief officer is one and the same thing. *Junglee* is barbarian, since the Aagariyas are deemed to be thus, and for this reason need to be governed and understood according to a binary logic of civilization versus wilderness, which the Indian state had directly inherited from the colonial administration. Multilingualism signals the conflict of ideologies and worldviews in contemporary India, in which English functions as a 'semiotic system of modernity' (Dhareshwar 1993, pp. 117–18), as does Hindi, albeit on a national rather than international scale. As Tharu and Lalita note,

> In his 'rational' daylight mode, the well-intentioned administrator-reformer in Mahasweta Devi's 'Shishu' draws on anthropology, a discipline founded by colonialism, and development theory to understand the tribals. (1993, p. 59)

But at night, Singh is overcome by fear and 'irrational' superstition towards the Aagariyas, who are not seen as Hindus and thus not 'proper', civilized citizens. The story ends in a dramatic dénouement. After much effort to establish a functioning network of relief in the villages, one night Singh is confronted by the mysterious beings who steal the sacks of food. When he gets closer, he realizes with horror that they are not children; they are stunted adults. These are the Aagariyas who had killed the geologists who had '*blasted* their hillock flat', and who are now in hiding; their stunted growth is due to the fact that they do not have enough to eat.

The story ends with Singh being surrounded by the stunted Aagariyas, who touch him with their genitals in a way that they know will render him 'impure' and 'unclean'. In a startling juxtaposition, we are made privy to Singh's thought that his body, and that of the Aagariyas, are seen as a 'crime' by the World Health Organization: a human body without enough calories is considered a 'crime against humanity'. The bitter irony directed at development rhetoric is clearer than ever in this last paragraph. When will the tribals finally be allowed a voice of their own? Significantly, since even their legends are hijacked and reduced to the level of *junglee* tales, their only resource is their bodies, which they rub against the mainstream body of the nation, represented by the 'normal' Indian, Singh.

Tharu and Lalita include this story in their anthology because they consider it emblematic of the oppositional energies that built up among activist and political groups in India during the 1970s; this is a post-Emergency narrative and, as such, it is a fierce critique of the failure of Indian democracy, a stab at the failed promises of independence. The sheer drama of the last scene introduces a theatricality to the narrative which is enabled by the finitude of the short story form; the point of the story, its teleology, is enabled by its ending.

Let us now turn to the short story cycle, which presents us with some striking examples of South-Asian short fiction today.

The South-Asian Short Story Cycle

Obviously, the South-Asian short story cycle did not spring forth fully formed in the last decades of the twentieth century; the genre's development owes much to R. K. Narayan, whose short stories set in the fictional South Indian town of Malgudi established the 'small town' as a privileged locus of Indian English fiction, and resonated with the story cycles of classical Indian literature.

The closing years of the twentieth century were an interesting moment for Indian English literature more generally. The success of short story collections such as Vikram Chandra's *Love and Longing in Bombay* (1994), Rohinton Mistry's *Tales of Firozsha Baag* (1991), Salman Rushdie's *East, West* (1994) and Jhumpa Lahiri's *Interpreter of Maladies* (2000) was partly due to the boom of Indian English fiction in those years, which had consolidated the canonical status (and thus marketability) of certain Indian authors writing in English. The authors mentioned above were part of a globalized Indian literary canon that was marketed and produced by Anglo-American publishing houses such as Random House, HarperCollins and Faber. In some cases, the appearance of a short story collection rode on the wave of the immense success of a first novel (Rushdie, Chandra). But the inverse was also true: for example, Mistry's first published book was *Tales from Firozsha Baag*, with Faber, and his success as a novelist came afterwards.

It remains a fact, however, that publishing short prose goes against the trend of such a canon. The role of magazines in the production of an 'alternative' Indian English canon based on *the short form* has been significant, if neglected. *Civil Lines*, a literary periodical published irregularly between 1994 and 2011, set out its remit in the first issue, namely to present 'fine unpublished writing connected with India [...] with a casual disregard of strict taxonomies' (Advani et al. 1994, p. 1). With its striking photographic covers and unorthodox editorial choices, the journal clearly set out to make its own unique impact. Firstly, it aimed to present a variety of Indian English writing that differed from the 'Great Indian Novel' trajectory: there was an emphasis on memoir, non-fiction, understatement, the narrative fragment, and a conspicuous lack of focus on 'nation as narration' characteristic of the Indian Booker Prize winners of recent years.

Secondly, in Rukun Advani's retrospective appraisal, it was conceived as a 'specifically Indian literary journal' (2009, p. xxiv): unlike many of its contemporary novelistic counterparts, the magazine was not marketed outside of India, which may explain why the references to nationhood were less marked than for Indian fiction marketed abroad. The type of prose writing favoured by the editors was for a sophisticated, knowing audience, an Indian English written and read by an intellectual class based in the Civil Lines area of Delhi, once home to diplomats, professors and civil servants, and of course steeped in a British colonial legacy. This middle class had now largely vanished, replaced by media-savvy and *nouveau riche* professionals who produced 'slangy, colloquial' Indian English far removed from the 'superior, literary English' published in *Civil Lines* (Advani 2009, xxiv). This 'civilized' Indian English may seem now like a quintessentially Brahminical enterprise, both caste-bound and class-bound, and yet the selections attest to the fact that is far from being mere 'Babu English'; indeed, its editors viewed with some disdain the wars of position around Indian English and its 'authenticity' (or lack thereof), and strove to create a space for Indian writing that was not wholly subsumed by the global publishing conglomerates and Anglo-American literary trends, dominated by the creative writing workshop and by obsession with the novel.

Recent short story collections by South-Asian writers further add to the emergence of an alternative 'short' canon in English, while maintaining some generic links to the longer novel form. Mueenuddin's and Lahiri's collections present us with worlds that emerge out of the various perspectives and narratives contained in each individual short story. If the short story is characterized, as a genre, by a deliberately partial, unfinished view of its subject, then a collection of 'linked stories', also known as a short story cycle or sequence, perhaps vies with the novel form for a more rounded view of the imaginary universe it constructs.

Interconnected short narratives may even enhance the dialogism inherent in the novel form, according to Mikhail Bakhtin (1984). But they are also indicative of new trends in South-Asian fiction, which is witnessing a shift in focus from the postcolonial nation to the postcolonial state: this gets articulated through a critique of the developmental state, the neo-colonial state, and the oppressions of caste and class as they operate *within* national boundaries. The short stories by Mahasweta and Mueenuddin, while centrally concerned with the politics of South-Asian nationalism, focus on the fraught conditions of subaltern citizenship in India and Pakistan: those who are citizens, but only tenuously so, and thus not full members of 'civil society', though they are definitely within the domain of governmental control and developmental planning (Chatterjee 2004, p. 38).

Neil Lazarus has also recently argued for the need to refocus critical attention on the 'specific agency of the postcolonial *state*', as opposed to the representations of nation and nationalism, in postcolonial writing (2011, p. 70). Post-independence South-Asian fiction in particular deals with issues of class, caste and state violence or oppression, in a continuing debate with the institutions that are supposed to protect and legislate in favour of its postcolonial citizens.

Daniyal Mueenuddin's short fiction is a case in point. His first (and only) full-length published work was a collection of short stories, *In Other Rooms, Other Wonders* (2009). This marked a distinct departure from prevailing trends within contemporary South-Asian fiction. Firstly, the stories helped showcase Mueenuddin as a rising star in the exciting new work being produced by young Pakistani authors; until recently, the panorama of South-Asian fiction in English had been dominated by Indian authors, but at the turn of this century, Mohsin Hamid, Kamila Shamsie, Nadeem Aslam and Mueenuddin emerged as major new literary players. Second, some of Mueenuddin's tales were interwoven, almost episodic narratives of a singular world that was little-known to English-language readers: that of rich Pakistani feudal landlords or *zamindars*, their servants, labourers and dependants. Certain characters recurred in different stories (such as the *zamindar* K.K. Harouni), suggesting a continuity between them, and enabling the reader to learn about multiple aspects of the same character from different narrative perspectives.

In contrast to the dominant diasporic strain of South-Asian fiction popular among anglophone audiences and critics, Mueenuddin's short fiction is profoundly located and has a strong sense of place, namely Lahore and its surrounding countryside.[4] Part of his aim in using a single setting was to create a unified fictional universe akin to William Faulkner's Yoknapatawpha Country (Jahangir 2010). The short story cycle can intensify what Trussler calls 'duplicative time', a narrative technique that provides 'multiple representations of an event', something which is similar, but not identical to, synchronicity (Trussler 2002, p. 605). The narratives explore the effects of feudalism's distinctive social hierarchies on the relationships between the characters, as well as on their economic livelihoods. In addition to an established sense of location, Mueenuddin also firmly dates his fictions, which are mainly set in Pakistan in the early 1970s, a time that coincided with major land reforms aimed at abolishing feudal land-holdings, and with a shift in previous power structures that had upheld Pakistani society.

In the story 'Saleema', the world of the Pakistani feudal landlord K. K. Harouni is built around social relations that are all but forgotten in the developed world: those between a master and his live-in servants, which create an astounding intimacy between widely diverging social classes without any accompanying equality. Servants are both carers and subordinates: when K. K. Harouni dies, his servant Rafik, who has worked for him for 50 years, has lost his cardinal point, as 'K. K. Harouni had been his life, his morning and night, his charge, his wealth' (p. 48). The death of K. K. Harouni also symbolizes the passing of the feudal era in Pakistan in those years: the family house is located

> in the heart of Old British Lahore, where the great houses were gradually being demolished, to make way for ugly flats and townhouses [...]. Gone, and they the servants would never find another berth like this one, the gravity of the house, the gentleness of the master, the vast damp rooms, the slow lugubrious pace, the order within disorder. (Mueenuddin 2009, p. 47)

The supposed 'progress' of modern Pakistan is seen through the eyes of the servants as a negative development, as it symbolizes their total disenfranchisement within the new social order; at least in the older dispensation, they knew their place.

---

[4] Asked about his lack of interest in the diasporic theme, Mueenuddin replied that 'I am not really an immigrant. My mother is American and father is Pakistani. I have traveled between the cultures, but I have never been an immigrant' (Jahangir 2010).

Saleema, the protagonist of the short story, is in a relationship of dependency due to her social class and her gender; as a servant in K.K. Harouni's establishment, she knows she can only survive if she can become the mistress of one of the men working in the household. Patriarchal feudalism, in which women are on the lowest rung of the social ladder, maps gender relations onto those between the lord and his vassal. The story showcases the varying degrees of subalternity that are completely invisible to the *zamindar* who controls their destiny: 'The old man did not merely lack interest in the affairs of the servants—he was not conscious they had lives outside his purview' (Mueenuddin 2009, p. 33). Throughout the stories, the reader inhabits the consciousness of the servants, not of the landowner. There are three striking aspects about Mueenuddin's resolutely realist depiction of this world. First, its precise location within a mixed economy: Pakistan's emerging financial elites are still dependent on the status of feudal landowners, thus questioning any 'teleological' stagist view of Pakistan as 'transitioning' from feudalism to modernity; in fact, the pre-modern and the modern economies are seen as coeval. Saleema's story is cyclical, ending where it began, as she dies penniless and her son 'begged in the streets, one of the sparrows of Lahore' (p. 49). She is denied any possibility of social mobility and betterment once she is cast out of feudalism's ambiguous, patronizing embrace (and the state here is wholly absent). Secondly, Mueenuddin's stories, while utterly riveting, are devoid of explicit political critique, and are indeed almost fatalistic. Thirdly, his depictions of rural Pakistan, though intensely evocative of a world unknown to its readers, decidedly eschew the pastoral mode:

> She arrived at her village at dusk, taking a rickshaw from the bus station. The open field next to the village had become a collecting pool for the sewage from the city, the water black. (p. 39)

In Pakistan, the villages have become as polluted as the cities. Just as there is no clear juxtaposition between the pre-modern and the modern economy, there is no clear distinction between the urban and the rural:

> During Saleema's childhood twenty years later the village was gradually being absorbed into the slums cast off by an adjacent provincial town called Kotla Sardar. (p. 17)

This lack of nostalgic idealization of the nation's rural past also raises a larger point about 'new Pakistan's' impact on landscapes and the environment, one that is to the detriment of its subaltern citizens. But ultimately, Mueenuddin's precise, empathetic and moving prose delivers a stunningly effective realism without social critique.

Jhumpa Lahiri's work examines the ways in which the repressed realities of South-Asian political violence return in the form of vicarious trauma in her short story 'When Mr Pirzada Came to Dine', part of her debut collection *Interpreter of Maladies* (2000). As Susan Koshy notes, Lahiri's stories are about the emergence of a *diasporic citizenship*, which is presented as

> not an identity but a condition that affects the long-settled and the migrant in multiple locations. Through this figure, Lahiri pushes us to imagine an impossible hospitality from the position of the other who cannot feel at home. (2011, p. 594)

Thus being a migrant is a condition, rather than an identity. Lahiri's fiction constructs a diasporic everyday and a diasporic subject/citizen, through the narration of lived experiences that bring together Indian (specifically Bengali) modes of being in the world, and the negotiation with new cultural and social settings, that come with their own bewildering array of interactions and rituals. The narrator and protagonist of 'When Mr Pirzada Came to Dine' is the 10-year-old Lilia. Lilia is born in the US, unlike her parents, who are from Calcutta; thus she is educated into both cultures simultaneously, and the story delineates the divide between her public life as an American schoolgirl and her domestic life as a Bengali child. The story tracks her deepening understanding about South Asia, the land of her familial origins. The opening of the story, which acts as a sort of historical introduction to the political events framing the narrative, is not first-hand knowledge on the part of the narrator; it is reconstructed from research. We gradually learn that the experiences of the 10-year-old Lilia are mediated through her adult memories of her childhood; the representation of her young life as a second-generation Bengali American, caught between the demands of cultural adjustment and the powerful pull of events happening back 'home', is juxtaposed with the knowledge of the 1971 Bangladesh War of Independence she has gained as an adult.

The story also follows Lilia's gradual embrace of the legacy bestowed on her through her parents, the South-Asian 'home'. For her, Indianness is not a known identity, it is at best an acquired one. When her father informs her that Mr Pirzada is no longer Indian, not since the country was partitioned in 1947, Lilia is confused and disoriented, since to all intents and purposes, 'Mr Pirzada and my parents spoke the same language, laughed at the same jokes, looked more or less the same' (Lahiri 2000, p. 25). But her father shows her a map of South Asia and explains to her that, although Mr Pirzada is a Bengali like they are, he is Muslim from East Pakistan; as Lilia gazes at the map of India, she attempts to make sense of South-Asian geographies in terms of US geography, which is the normative understanding of the national space as she learns it in class. Her father perceives that she has no knowledge of Partition, and asks her what exactly they teach her at school. Her mother intervenes, constructing a 'new American' identity for Lilia that has the power to erase the dangers of the country that has been left behind:

> In her estimation, I knew, I was assured a safe life, an easy life, a fine education, every opportunity. I would never have to eat rationed food, or obey curfews, or watch riots from my roof-top, or hide neighbors in water-tanks to prevent them from being shot, as she and my father had. 'Imagine having to place her in a decent school. Imagine her having to read during power failures by the light of kerosene lamps. Imagine the pressures, the tutors, the constant exams.' [...] 'How can you possibly expect her to know about Partition? [...]'. (p. 27)

A lack of knowledge, a *repression* of Partition is what her mother wants for her daughter, so Lilia, at school, learns only American geography. But in Lilia's memory, her childhood is sharply split into two domains: the public sphere of her American school and the domestic sphere, into which Lilia's parents invite Mr Pirzada, a hospitable gesture that is symbolically reminiscent of the millions of refugees taken in by India from East Pakistan when war broke out. The diasporic space of the home is constelled with Indian food and rituals, though American customs make periodic incursions, as is seen in Lilia's preparation for Halloween, when she carves the Jack O'lantern with her parents. Lilia is a quintessentially liminal figure, negotiating her way between Bengali and North American affective landscapes. Through the rituals of nationalist pedagogy, she learns how to become an American citizen by memorizing the dates of the American War of Independence. This imposition of an American historical narrative functions to erase the current war of independence being fought in East Pakistan, which her parents and Mr Pirzada are following so anxiously on the news. Lilia is caught between two systems of meaning, nationhood and citizenship. While in the library, supposedly writing a report about the

American Revolution, she picks up a book entitled *Pakistan: A Land and its People*. But she is called out by her teacher:

> 'Is this book a part of your report, Lilia?'
> 'No, Mrs Kenyon.'
> 'Then I see no reason to consult it,' she said, replacing it in the slim gap on the shelf. 'Do you?' (p. 33)

For Lilia, the facts of the war in East Pakistan 'remained, for the most part, a remote mystery with haphazard clues' (p. 40), since she sees the scenes of the war as disconnected, almost exotic images in the sporadic news coverage by American television (where it gradually fades from view). But she is also privy to the whispered conversations between her parents and Mr Pirzada about the advance of the war, the deaths, the refugees flowing across the border into India. Mr Pirzada is concerned about his family, his seven daughters; his concern for them is transferred vicariously to his anxiety for Lilia's well-being when she is about to embark on an evening of trick-or-treating.

> Mr Pirzada knit his brows together. 'Is there any danger?' [...] 'Perhaps I should accompany them?' Mr Pirzada suggested. He looked suddenly tired and small, standing there in his splayed, stockinged feet, and his eyes contained a panic I had never seen before. (Lahiri 2000, p. 38)

The story powerfully evokes the contrast between the security of the American suburban neighbourhood on Halloween—it is so safe even small children can roam around alone—and the civil war taking place on the streets of Dacca. Lilia hastens to reassure Mr Pirzada:

> 'Don't worry,' I said. It was the first time I had uttered those words to Mr Pirzada, two simple words I had tried but failed to tell him for weeks, had said only in my prayers. It shamed me now that I had said them for my own sake. (p. 38)

Lilia has the role of listener, almost of an outsider standing at the edges of a story that is not quite hers, and yet to which she feels irresistibly drawn. For her, the dangers of home are at one remove, and the trauma of Partition is lived vicariously, through the anxieties of the older generation whose sense of a shared cultural, psychic identity emerges most strongly at this moment, despite their national and religious differences:

Most of all I remember the three of them operating during that time as if they were a single person, sharing a single meal, a single body, and a single fear. (p. 41)

Cathy Caruth's theory of traumatic memory resonates meaningfully with the structure of South-Asian narratives about the Partition and its aftermath, of which the Bangladesh war was a part; an event that has yet to find a truly comprehensive, overarching historical interpretation presents itself as a psychic wound that ruptures the skein of forgetfulness necessary for moving on. While the repression of trauma may ensure its subject's survival, the event also imposes a form of isolation, as Caruth reminds us: and thus 'the history of a trauma, in its inherent belatedness, can only take place through the listening of another' (Caruth 2007, p. 204). Lilia acts as listener, but also as historian: 'All of these facts I know only now, for they are available to me in any history book, in any library' (Lahiri 2000, p. 40). Here history is divided along national lines, but amidst the traumas of history, fictional narrative opens up the possibilities for understanding the past in a more holistic, less fragmented sense. A sense of loss pervades the narrative of Lahiri's story; Lilia knows that her condition is marked by an inherent lack of plenitude, which characterizes the stereoscopic vision of the migrant, in lieu of 'whole sight' (Rushdie 1991, p. 19). As in many of Lahiri's stories, there is no sense of an attempt to impose meaning or closure on a contradictory experience, and the story ends with Lilia's first experience of diasporic loss:

It was only then ... that I knew what it meant to miss someone who was so many miles and hours away, just as he had missed his wife and daughters for so many months. (Lahiri 2000, p. 42)

Thus, the fragmentation of migrant experience is structurally connected to its narrative, the short story.

The difficulties of theorizing the South-Asian short story in the twenty-first century are also due to the fact that different canons circulate in the South-Asian literary field, and are constituted by groups of critics, readers and publishers that do not necessarily overlap. It might be apt to end with a remark by Adrian Hunter about the short story as a minor genre:

The interrogative story's 'unfinished' economy, its failure literally to express, to extend itself to definition, determination or disclosure, becomes, under the rubric of a theory of 'minor' literature, a positive aversion to the entailment of 'power and law' that defines the major literature. (Hunter 2007, p. 140)

Each of the tales I have examined are, in their own way, about minority—whether this is the buried voice of an Aagariya tribal, a servant woman attempting to gain a secure foothold in a feudal patriarchy, or a bi-cultural child grappling with conflicting notions of belonging. Any attempt at canonization and inclusion risks overlooking one of the short story's most important features: its singularity, its brevity and above all, the particular appeal deriving from its ability to capture most intensely the epiphanic moments of a particular life experience.

Works Cited

Advani, R. (2009). Introduction: Civility, civilization, and chivas regal. In R. Advani (Ed.), *Written for ever: The best of Civil Lines* (pp. xiii–xxv). New Delhi: Penguin/Viking.

Advani, R., Hutnik, I., Kesavan, M., & Kumar, D. (1994). Introduction. *Civil Lines: New Writing from India, 1*, 1–4.

Awadalla, M., & March-Russell, P. (2012). *The postcolonial short story: Contemporary essays*. London: Palgrave.

Bakhtin, M. M. (1981). *The dialogic imagination: Four essays* (M. Holquist, Ed., C. Emerson & M. Holquist, Trans.). Austin: University of Texas Press.

Caruth, C. (2007). From *trauma and experience*. In M. Rossington, & A. Whitehead (Eds.), *Theories of memory: A reader* (pp. 199–205). Edinburgh: Edinburgh University Press.

Chatterjee, P. (2004). *The politics of the governed: Reflections on popular politics in most of the world*. New York: Columbia University Press.

Deleuze, G., & Guattari, F. (1986). What is a minor literature? In G. Deleuze, & F. Guattari (Eds.), *Kafka: Toward a minor literature* (Dana Polan with a foreword by Réda Bensmaïa, Trans., pp. 16–27), Minneapolis: University of Minnesota Press.

Devi, M. (1993). Shishu ('Children') (P. Bhattacharya, Trans.). In S. Tharu & K. Lalita (Eds.), *Women writing in India: 600 BC to the present*. Vol. II: *The twentieth century* (pp. 236–251). Delhi: Oxford University Press.

Devi, M. (1998). Shishu ('Little ones'). In *Bitter soil* (I. Chanda, Trans., pp. 1–21). Calcutta: Seagull Books.

Dhareshwar, V. (1993). Caste and the secular self. *Journal of Arts and Ideas, 25–26*, 115–126.

Ghosh, A. (1994). The Indian story. *Civil Lines: New Writing from India, 1*, 35–50.

Hanson, C. (1989). Introduction. In C. Hanson (Ed.), *Re-reading the short story* (pp. 1–27). London: Macmillan.

Hunter, A. (2007). *The Cambridge introduction to the short story in English*. Cambridge: Cambridge University Press.

Jahangir, J. (2010, February 23). Interview with Daniyal Mueenuddin. *Beyond the margins* [Online]. Available from http://beyondthemargins.com/2010/02/interview-with-daniyal-mueenuddin/. Accessed 15 Feb 2015.

Koshy, S. (2011). Minority cosmopolitanism. *PMLA*, 126(3), 592–609.

Lahiri, J. (2000). *Interpreter of maladies: Stories*. London: Flamingo.

Lazarus, N. (2011). *The postcolonial unconscious*. Cambridge: Cambridge University Press.

March-Russell, P. (2009). *The short story: An introduction*. Edinburgh: Edinburgh University Press.

Miller, A. (2015). Circulating the peripheries: Small publishers, short story collections and *Madinah: City stories from the Middle East*. *Journal of Commonwealth Literature*, 50(2), 115–132.

Mistry, R. (1991). *Tales from Firozsha Baag*. London: Faber.

Mueenuddin, D. (2009). *In other rooms, other wonders*. London: Bloomsbury.

Pandey, G. (2008). Introduction: Subaltern citizens and their histories. *Interventions: International Journal of Postcolonial Studies*, 10(3), 271–284.

Poe, E. A. (1842/1976). Review of *Twice-told tales*. In C. E. May (Ed.), *Short story theories* (pp. 45–51). Athens: Ohio University Press.

Pravinchandra, S. (2014). Not just prose: *The Calcutta chromosome*, the South Asian short story and the limitations of postcolonial studies. *Interventions: International Journal of Postcolonial Studies*, 16(3), 424–444.

Procter, J. (2011). 'To see oursels as others see us!': Seepersad Naipaul, modernity and the rise of the Trinidadian short story. In L. Evans, M. McWatt, & E. Smith (Eds.), *The Caribbean short story* (pp. 163–176). Leeds: Peepal Tree Press.

Rushdie, S. (1991). *Imaginary homelands*. London: Granta.

Rushdie, S. (1994). *East, west*. London: Vintage.

Tharu, S., & Lalita, K. (1993). The twentieth century: Women writing the nation. In S. Tharu, & K. Lalita (Eds.), *Women writing in India: 600 BC to the present*. Vol. II: *The twentieth century* (pp. 43–116). Delhi: Oxford University Press.

Trussler, M. (2002). On the short story and the short-story cycle. *Contemporary Literature*, 43(3, Autumn), 598–605.

INDEX

A
Adami, Esterino, 191
Adiga, Aravind, 47–8, 49, 51, 117, 119–36, 253, 255
adivasis, 46, 220, 222–5. *See also* tribal groups
Afghanistan, 21–8, 32
Ahmed, K. Anis, 67–9, 71, 75–6
Alam, Fakrul, 61–3, 65n., 74–5
Alter, Joseph S., 174, 175
Amritsar, 103–8
Anam, Tahmima, 59, 66, 71–4
Anand, Mulk Raj, 104, 254–5
anthologies, 37, 153, 255–61. *See also* canon formation
anti-colonial resistance, 84, 204, 219–20, 258
Appadurai, Arjun, 46, 164, 237
Arasanayagam, Jean, 90–1
Aslam, Nadeem, 21, 23–8, 35–6, 235–6, 239, 243–4, 246–7, 250, 263

authenticity
  anglophone fiction, 4–5, 47, 80, 119–36, 156, 262
  and linguistic choice, 121, 151–2
  non-fiction, 120–4

B
Bajwa, Rupa, 103–4, 105–8, 141
Banerjee, Sarnath, 181–94
Bangladesh
  anglophone literature, 4, 59–76
  diaspora communities, 235, 244n.
  language policy, 62–3, 75
  nationalism 62–4, 71–5
  1971 Liberation War, 65–74, 266–9
  relationship with Pakistan, 62, 70
  relationship with US, 68–9
  socio-economic change, 3–4
Bengal Lights, 59, 62
Bhagat, Chetan, 50–5, 143–6, 157, 165, 189

Note: All names have been indexed under their final element.

Bhopal, 104, 108–13, 203
black-British culture, 238–40, 246
Bombay. *See* Mumbai
Boo, Katherine, 120, 122–4, 129, 132, 135
Bourdieu, Pierre, 40, 50
British empire, 26, 61, 200, 260, 262. *See also* colonialism; imperialism

C
canon formation, 5, 141, 254–7, 261–2, 270. *See also* anthologies
capitalism, 27–35, 44, 46, 128, 204–6. *See also* globalization; liberalization; neo-colonialism; neoliberalism
Caruth, Cathy, 269
caste
  contemporary attitudes, 155
  identity, 247
  literary representations, 45–6, 104–5, 115
  oppression, 45–6, 83, 97n., 122n., 263
  role in Maoist insurgency, 46, 240, 229
  violence, 46, 229–30
  See also class; *dalits*; India: socio-economic change
Chakrabarty, Dipesh, 3
Chandra, Vikram, 121, 141, 254, 261
Chatterjee, Upamanyu, 40n., 51n., 144
Chauhan, Anuja, 165, 171–6
Cheyette, Bryan, 235–6, 238, 249
chick lit, 7, 44–5, 145, 149, 165, 171–6. *See also* commercial fiction; genre fiction
cinema
  American, 23, 29, 104
  Indian, 51, 52, 119, 186–7, 204–5
  'Kashmir films', 204–5

literary adaptations, 23, 50, 123, 150
cities, 103–18, 127–8, 136, 193. *See also* Amritsar; Bhopal; Delhi; Karachi; Lahore; London; Mumbai; Srinagar; urban geography
citizenship, 42, 81, 258 & n., 263, 266, 267
Civil Lines, 261–2
class
  inequality in post-liberalization India, 46, 48, 128–32
  and language, 52–3, 81, 98
  literary representations of lower classes, 104–5, 117, 120–3
  new middle-class in India, 42–4, 47–8, 52, 187–93
  novel as middle-class form, 39–46, 104–5, 117, 154–7
  See also caste; *dalits*; India: socio-economic change
colonialism, 49–50, 83–4, 122, 204, 258. *See also* anti-colonial resistance; British empire; imperialism; neo-colonialism
comics, 149, 181–4, 187, 194. *See also* graphic novels
commercial fiction, 41–2, 50–5, 139–57, 163–4. *See also* genre fiction
communism, 22, 25–8, 131. *See also* Maoism; Naxalite movement
Conrad, Joseph, 26, 47, 122
corruption, 3, 38, 68–9, 94, 124–6, 168–70. *See also* Jan Lokpal Bill
cricket, 80, 93–4, 164–77

D
dalits, 46, 104–5, 115, 229–30. *See also* caste
Dasgupta, Rana, 39, 120n., 130–1, 141

Deleuze, Gilles, 213, 253, 255, 257–8
Delhi, 9, 47–8, 52–4, 60, 107n., 120n., 184–6, 191, 262
Deraniyagala, Sonali, 94–5
Desai, Anita, 1–2, 105, 141
Devi, Mahasweta, 258–61, 263
diaspora
  authors and authenticity, 4–5, 121–2
  communities, 4, 42, 54, 88, 171, 235, 239–50, 266–9
  criticism, 236–8, 245–7
  fiction, 40, 66n., 80–2, 238–50, 266–9.

E
education
  campus novels, 51–3, 145
  English language, 43, 61–3, 151, 156
  language policy, 61–3
  politics, 34, 52, 88
  social mobility, 43, 51–3, 189–90
  university curricula in the global North, 5, 256
English
  and authenticity, 121, 151–2, 241, 262
  education, 61, 62–3, 156
  elite language in South Asia, 4, 40, 52–3, 81, 84, 105–6, 256, 259
  exclusion from education system, 62–3
  global language, 81, 146, 156
  nationalist opposition, 62–3
  regional versions, 86, 151–3, 156, 250, 262
  as signifier of modernity, 260
  status in Bangladesh, 59–60, 62–5
  See also language politics

environmentalism, 199–213

F
Farrukhi, Asif, 65–6, 70–1
Fernandes, Leela, 43–4, 192–4

G
Ganeshananthan, V. V., 82, 88–9
genre fiction, 7, 145, 149, 163–77, 257. *See also* chick lit; commercial fiction
Ghosh, Amitav, 40n., 139, 141, 237, 253, 254n.
Ghosh, Vishwajyoti, 186, 193
Ghuznavi, Farah, 60, 62–3
globalization, 39, 42, 48–50, 132–6, 147–54, 166, 212. *See also* capitalism; India: socio-economic change; liberalization; neo-colonialism; neoliberalism
graphic novels, 7, 145, 181–94, 205, 209–12. *See also* comics
Guattari, Félix, 213, 253, 255, 257–8
Gujarat, 246n., 248–9
Gunawardena, Edward, 87
Gunesekera, Romesh, 16, 80, 82n., 96–7

H
Hall, Stuart, 42, 52, 237
Hamid, Mohsin, 1–2, 21, 23, 29–36, 104, 113–16, 263
Hanif, Mohammed, 21, 23, 104, 114–17
Haq, Kaiser, 59–60, 62
Harvey, David, 54, 127–8, 130, 133
Hunter, Adrian, 257–8, 269
Hussein, Ameena, 86n., 96n., 97–8

I

imperialism, 6, 28, 30, 33–4, 49, 152. *See also* British empire; neo-colonialism; UK: foreign policy; US: foreign policy; 'war on terror'
Imtiaz, Saba, 114
India
  anglophone literature, 39–55, 103–13, 117, 119–36, 139–57, 163–77, 181–94, 221–6, 229–32, 254–63
  Hindi literature, 153–4, 253–4
  nationalism, 35, 37–8, 204, 255, 258
  relationship with Pakistan, 33, 201
  relationship with Sri Lanka, 80
  relationship with US, 218
  socio-economic change, 38, 42–55, 125–36, 164, 175–6, 187–94
  translated literature, 139, 153–4, 254, 256, 258–60
insurgency, 46, 92–3, 217–32
internet, 4, 144, 150, 155, 156, 164, 171, 199, 201, 213
Islam
  literary representations, 24–5
  representation in the global North, 24, 30
Islam, Khademul, 59, 60, 62, 66
Islamism, 22, 25–8, 35, 97–8

J

Jameson, Fredric, 26, 29
Jan Lokpal Bill, 12, 169. *See also* corruption
Jeganathan, Pradeep, 85n., 87–8
journalism, 7, 46, 126, 134–5, 164n., 171. *See also* reportage

K

Kabir, Ananya, 237–8
Kapur, Manju, 41, 48–50
Karachi, 9, 103–4, 114–15
Karunatilaka, Shehan, 80, 86, 93–4
Kashmir, 12–14, 199–213
Kaushal, Swati, 44–5, 53
Khan, Adib, 60, 66
Khanduri, Ritu Gairola, 191–2
Khanna, Ranjana, 202
Kodithuwakku, Isankya, 95–6
Krishna, Sankaran, 132–3, 136
Kumar, Amitava, 119–22, 125–7, 135

L

Lahiri, Jhumpa, 223, 226–8, 254, 255, 261, 262, 266–70
Lahore, 1–2, 32, 34, 104n., 114, 263–5
Lalita, K., 258, 260–1
Lalitha, Belli, 217
language politics, 62–5, 75, 84. *See also* English; translation
Laxman, R.K., 191–2
Levinas, Emmanuel, 218–9, 228
liberalization, 38–41, 42–55, 164, 187–94. *See also* capitalism; globalization; India: socio-economic change; neoliberalism
literacy, 4
literary festivals, 4, 59, 140, 168, 209
literary journals, 4, 59, 80, 255, 261–2
literary prizes, 4, 21n., 45, 80–1, 140, 150, 168, 253
literary traditions
  Anglo-American, 22, 29, 53, 119, 167
  European, 39–40, 75, 167
  South-Asian, 34, 60, 62, 71, 74–5, 255, 261
London, 239–44

M

McCloud, Scott, 182, 184
McCracken, Scott, 165, 170, 176

magical realism, 46, 117
Mahasweta. *See under* Devi,
  Mahasweta
Malkani, Gautam, 239–44, 246, 250
Maoism, 46, 217–8, 220–3, 229–31.
  See also communism; Naxalite
  movement
media, 134–5, 142–7, 164, 170–7,
  213, 219. *See also* internet;
  journalism
Mehta, Suketu, 120, 125–6, 129n.
melodrama, 119, 122
memoir, 7, 82, 94–5, 262
memory, 66, 70, 81–2, 95, 96–7, 269
Mirza Waheed. *See under* Waheed,
  Mirza
Mistry, Rohinton, 141, 254, 261
Modi, Narendra, 169–70, 248
Moretti, Franco, 40, 167
Mueenuddin, Daniyal, 21, 254, 255,
  262–6
Mukherjee, Meenakshi, 121
Mukherjee, Pablo, 125, 135, 203
Muller, Carl, 85–6
Mumbai, 9, 117, 120, 123–36

N

Nandy, Ashis, 3, 169, 171, 175
Narayan, R.K., 16, 254–5, 261
nationalism, 220, 227–8, 263
  American, 32–3, 267
  Bangladeshi and Bengali, 62–4,
    71–5
  Hindu, 248
  Indian, 35, 37–8, 204, 255, 258
  Pakistani, 33, 62
  Sinhala, 82–8, 93, 96–8
  Tamil, 82–8
Navlakha, Gautam, 223
Naxalite movement, 46, 48, 217–32.
  See also communism

Nayeemuddin, Mohammed, *alias*
  Nayeem, 217–18
Nehru, Jawaharlal, 37–9, 130–1,
  204–5, 258
neo-colonialism, 6–7, 54, 125, 202,
  263. *See also* globalization;
  imperialism; UK: foreign policy;
  US: foreign policy; 'war on terror'
neoliberalism, 38–9, 42–55, 124–36.
  See also capitalism; globalization;
  liberalization
9/11, 7, 21–36, 218–21, 247
non-fiction. *See* journalism; memoir;
  reportage
nostalgia, 31–4, 39, 66, 95, 131,
  201–2, 204

O

Ondaatje, Michael, 80, 82, 92–3

P

Pakistan
  anglophone literature, 1–2, 21–36,
    65–6, 263–6
  nationalism, 33, 62
  political change, 1–3
  relationship with Bangladesh/East
    Pakistan, 62, 70
  relationship with India, 33, 201
  relationship with US, 22–3, 33–4,
    68
  representation in the global North,
    23, 30
  socio-economic change, 1–2, 264–5
  See also Bangladesh: 1971
    Liberation War
Pal, Deepanjana, 124, 132
partition, 63, 245, 266–9
pastoral, 200, 203–6, 208, 211, 265
Poe, Edgar Allan, 257

popular fiction. *See* commercial fiction; genre fiction
publishing industry
  in Bangladesh, 59, 65
  differentiation between literary and commercial, 40–2, 50–1, 139–47
  differentiation between domestic and international markets, 41, 79–80, 145–54, 167–8, 256
  in India, 4, 139–57, 163–4, 167–8, 181–3, 255
  role in canon formation, 261
  in Sri Lanka, 79–80
  See also media; readerships

R
Radhakrishnan, Rajagopalan, 237, 242
Rahman, Mahmud, 75
Rajan, Rajeswari Sunder, 141, 144
Rao, P. V. Narasimha, 38, 45
Rao, Raja, 254–5
Raychaudhuri, Diptendra, 229–32
readerships
  commercial fiction, 41–2, 50–1, 54–5, 139–47
  domestic, 4, 50–5, 80–1, 133–4, 139–41, 144–6, 150, 163–4, 183–8
  international, 22, 40, 80, 123–4, 151–2, 256
  literary fiction, 40
  surveys, 154–5
  youth, 50, 145, 154–7
realism, 39–41, 46–8, 119–20, 265–6.
  See also magical realism
reportage, 120–4, 221–3. *See also* journalism; memoirs
Roy, Arundhati, 5, 41, 45–7, 141, 221–2
Rumford, Chris, 165–8, 172–3, 176

Rushdie, Salman, 37, 46, 61, 105, 117, 141, 237, 244, 253, 254, 261

S
St Stephen's College, Delhi, 40, 46, 48, 51n., 52–3
Sajad, Malik, 205, 209–12
Sardar, Ziauddin, 35
Sareen, Hemant, 185, 186, 187, 192
Satnam, 222–3
Schendel, Willem van, 61, 62n., 63–5, 72
Schulze-Engler, Frank, 218–20
Selvadurai, Shyam, 79 & n., 80, 82–3, 85n., 87, 96, 97 & n.
Sen, Diti, 223–6, 232
Sen, Satadru, 171
Seth, Vikram, 39, 44–5, 141
Shah, Bina, 21–2
Silva, Nihal De, 91–2
Singh, Manmohan, 38–9, 44
Singh, Vikas, 165, 168, 171
Sinha, Indra, 104, 108–13
Sivanandan, A., 81–5, 89, 91, 95
slums. *See* urban geography
socialism, 43–4, 92n., 130–1
Spiegelman, Art, 183n., 210
Spivak, Gayatri, 120, 124, 202
Sri Lanka
  anglophone literature, 16, 79–98
  civil war, 3, 16, 81–2, 86–94
  language policy, 84
  nationalisms, 82–8, 93, 96–8
  political change, 80, 96–7
  publishing, 79–80
  relationship with India, 80
  relationship with UK, 80
  Sinhala literature, 81
  Tamil literature, 81
Srinagar, 199–200, 211–12

Sundar, Geeta, 165, 168–71, 173
Swarup, Vikas, 123

T
Tagore, Rabindranath, 5–6, 254n.
Tharoor, Shashi, 40n., 141, 189
Tharu, Susie, 258, 260–1
Thwaites, Jean, 90
translation, 81, 98, 139, 153–4, 256, 258–60
tribal groups, 46, 220–5, 228–9, 258–60
tsunami (2004), 3, 94–6

U
UK
 foreign policy, 28
 literature, 22, 53, 119
 relationship with Sri Lanka, 80
 South-Asian communities, 235, 239–50
untouchables. *See dalits*
Upstone, Sara, 237n., 238, 246–7
urban geography, 103–4, 107–8, 125–36, 193. *See also* cities
US
 foreign policy, 22–3, 28, 68–9, 218
 literary representations, 29–35, 266–8
 literature, 22, 29, 124n., 182–3, 262
 prosperity, 30–1
 publishing, 148–9, 261–2
 relationship with Bangladesh, 68–9
 relationship with India, 218
 relationship with Pakistan, 22–3, 33–4, 68
 representative of capitalism, 27, 35
 See also 9/11; 'war on terror'

V
Vassanji, M.G., 236, 247–50

W
Wagg, Stephen, 166, 172–3
Waheed, Mirza, 205, 206–9, 212, 213
'war on terror', 3, 21–2, 23, 218
Wijesinghe, Manuka, 87

Y
youth culture, 50–2, 145–7, 154–7, 164, 239–43

Z
Zaman, Niaz, 65–6, 67, 69–71
Zareef, Zareef Ahmad, 211
Žižek, Slavoj, 218–19, 225–6